SO-ARK-996

KAREN HABER and JONATHAN STRAHAN

SCIENCE FICTION
THE BEST OF 2003

KAREN HABER is the acclaimed editor of the Hugo Award-nominated *Meditations on Middle Earth*, a collection of essays by some of fantasy's best-known writers. Most recently, she edited *Exploring the Matrix*, an examination of the popular film series by some of science fiction's top writers. She also created the bestselling *The Mutant Season* series of novels, of which she co-authored the first volume with her husband, Robert Silverberg. She is a respected journalist and an accomplished fiction writer. Her short fiction has appeared in *Asimov's The Magazine of Fantasy and Science Fiction*, *Science Fiction Age*, and *Full Spectrum*.

JONATHAN STRAHAN is the award-winning editor of *The Year's Best Australian Science Fiction and Fantasy* anthology series, co-founder and editor of *Eidolon: The Journal of Australian Science Fiction and Fantasy*, and publisher of *The Coode Street Press*. He has won the Australian National Science Fiction Achievement Award on several occasions and is the recipient of the William Atheling Jr Award for Criticism and Review. He is the Reviews Editor for *Locus: The Magazine of the Science Fiction and Fantasy Field*, and is co-editor of *The Locus Awards: 30 Years of the Best in Science Fiction and Fantasy*.

FANTASY AND SCIENCE FICTION
published by ibooks, inc.:

Science Fiction: The Best of 2001
Fantasy: The Best of 2001
Science Fiction: The Best of 2002
Fantasy: The Best of 2002
Robert Silverberg & Karen Haber, Editors

The Ultimate Cyberpunk
Pat Cadigan, Editor

The Ultimate Halloween
Marvin Kaye, Editor

SCIENCE FICTION
THE BEST OF 2003

KAREN HABER
and JONATHAN
STRAHAN
Editors

ibooks
new york
www.ibooks.net

DISTRIBUTED BY SIMON & SCHUSTER, INC.

ACKNOWLEDGMENTS

Robert Silverberg, Marianne Jablon, Charles N. Brown, John Joseph Adams, Brian Bienkowski, Simon Brown, Jack Dann, Ellen Datlow, Cory Doctorow, Neil Gaiman, Nick Gevers, Gavin J. Grant, John Helfers, Rich Horton, Jay Lake, Deborah Layne, Robin Pen, Tim Pratt, Larry Segriff, Charles Stross, Gordon Van Gelder, and Sean Williams.

CONTENTS

INTRODUCTION

Traditionally, the home of short form science fiction has been the nationally distributed specialist magazine—major professional publications like *Analog*, *Asimov's*, *F&SF*, and *Interzone*. But the last decade or so has been hard on them, with *Science Fiction Age* closing and *Analog*, *Asimov's* and *Interzone* all recently announcing cutbacks. In fact, 2002 was the first time since *Weird Tales* was launched in 1923 that there has been no major monthly science fiction magazine published in the English language anywhere in the world.

All of this has led to a seismic shift in placement as short stories explode out of time-honored markets into new and unexpected places. Over the past decade online publication has grown in importance, and websites like *SciFiction* now have the same prominence and significance as any of the print magazines as sources of original—and archival—fiction. Mainstream magazines like *The New Yorker* and *Esquire* are embracing stories that contain fantastic elements, while presses large and small are homes for some of the most interesting and intriguing writing being produced in the field.

One of the changes that has followed on from the pressures placed on the magazines, is the flourishing of the original anthology market. Anthologies designed around a central theme and ones that are sufficiently offbeat that they defy categorization are playing an increasingly important part in bringing the best short fiction of the year into print. This year we were particularly impressed by Lou Anders *Live Without A Net*, Kelly Link's *Trampoline*, Claude Lalumiere and Marty Halpern's *Witpunk*, Michael Chabon's *McSweeny's Mammoth Treasure of Thrilling Tales*, Mike Resnick's *New Voices in Science Fiction*, Julie Czerneda's *Space Inc.*, Janis Ian and Mike Resnick's *Stars*, and Claude Lalumiere's *Island Dreams*. And those are just the science fiction anthologies.

The traditional specialist magazines are, of course, still with us: *Asimov's Science Fiction Magazine*, *The Magazine of Fantasy & Science Fiction*, *Analog*, and *Interzone* continue to publish fine fiction, providing us with the compelling chorus of voices we've come to expect. Each is vitally important to the field, and each deserves your support.

To put it bluntly, science fiction is everywhere, and we've gone after it, casting wide our net over publications and websites, small press jewels and blockbuster anthologies. From *Absolute Magnitude*, *The 3rd Alternative*, *On Spec* and *Lady Churchill's Rosebud Wristlet* to *Esquire*, *The New Yorker* and Salon.com; in anthologies like *Shadows Over Baker Street*, *The*

INTRODUCTION

Silver Gryphon and *The Thackery T. Lambshead Guide to Eccentric and Discredited Diseases*; and in collections like *Changing Planes*, *Bibliomancy* and *Things That Never Happen*, we've tried to read beyond the obvious, looking for the unusual, the special, the unexpected and unique. One look at our contents page will show the happy results of our quest.

The publication of *Science Fiction, The Best of 2003*, the third in an annual series, marks a change in editorial team makeup and perspective as editor Robert Silverberg steps down after having launched the series. Joining me at the helm of this year's—and future—anthologies is well-known Australian-based editor Jonathan Strahan.

Jonathan brings to this demanding job a deep grounding in and appreciation of the literature. Founder and publisher of *Eidolon: The Journal of Australian Science Fiction and Fantasy*, Jonathan was also co-publisher of Eidolon Books, and has worked for *LOCUS: The Newspaper of the Science Fiction Field* in a variety of categories including reviewing and copyediting. He is currently Reviews Editor for the magazine. In 2003 he won the Australian National Science Fiction Achievement "Ditmar" Award for best Australian Professional Achievement and the William J. Atheling Jr. Award for Criticism or Review. As a freelance editor, he co-edited two volumes of *The Year's Best Australian Science Fiction and Fantasy* with Jeremy G. Byrne for HarperCollins Australia, and is currently co-editing several anthologies for publication in Australia and the United States.

With Jonathan's advent we'll be casting our editorial net ever wider each year, looking for the best short science fiction in unexpected places, large and small, on and off the net, and around the world. As science fiction moves, we'll stay on its trail.

—Karen Haber
Oakland, California
December 2003

The Fluted Girl
Paolo Bacigalupi

The fluted girl huddled in the darkness clutching Stephen's final gift in her small pale hands. Madame Belari would be looking for her. The servants would be sniffing through the castle like feral dogs, looking under beds, in closets, behind the wine racks, all their senses hungry for a whiff of her. Belari never knew the fluted girl's hiding places. It was the servants who always found her. Belari simply wandered the halls and let the servants search her out. The servants thought they knew all her hiding places.

The fluted girl shifted her body. Her awkward position already strained her fragile skeleton. She stretched as much as the cramped space allowed, then folded herself back into compactness, imagining herself as a rabbit, like the ones Belari kept in cages in the kitchen: small and soft with wet warm eyes, they could sit and wait for hours. The fluted girl summoned patience and ignored the sore protest of her folded body.

Soon she had to show herself, or Madame Belari would get impatient and send for Burson, her head of security. Then Burson would bring his jackals and they would hunt again, crisscrossing every room, spraying pheromone additives across the floors and following her neon tracks to her hidey-hole. She had to leave before Burson came. Madame Belari punished her if the staff wasted time scrubbing out pheromones.

The fluted girl shifted her position again. Her legs were beginning to ache. She wondered if they could snap from the strain. Sometimes she was surprised at what broke her. A gentle bump against a table and she was shattered again, with Belari angry at the careless treatment of her investment.

The fluted girl sighed. In truth, it was already time to leave her hidey-hole, but still she craved the silence, the moment alone. Her sister Nia never understood. Stephen though…he had understood. When the fluted girl told him of her hidey-hole, she thought he forgave because he was kind. Now she knew better. Stephen had bigger secrets than the silly fluted girl. He had secrets bigger than anyone had guessed. The fluted girl turned his tiny vial in her hands, feeling its smooth glass shape, knowing the amber drops it held within. Already, she missed him.

Beyond her hidey-hole, footsteps echoed. Metal scraped heavily across stone. The fluted girl peered out through a crack in her makeshift fortress. Below her, the castle's pantry lay jumbled with dry goods. Mirriam was looking for her again, poking behind the refrigerated crates of champagne for Belari's party tonight. They hissed and leaked mist as Mirriam struggled to shove them aside and look deeper into the dark recesses behind. The fluted girl had known Mirriam when they were both children in the town. Now, they were as different as life and death.

Mirriam had grown, her breasts burgeoning, her hips widening, her rosy face smiling and laughing at her fortune. When they both came to Belari, the fluted girl and Mirriam had been the same height. Now, Mirriam was a grown woman, a full two feet taller than the fluted girl, and filled out to please a man. And she was loyal. She was a good servant for Belari. Smiling, happy to serve. They'd all been that way when they came up from the town to the castle: Mirriam, the fluted girl, and her sister Nia. Then Belari decided to make them into fluted girls. Mirriam got to grow, but the fluted girls were going to be stars.

Mirriam spied a stack of cheeses and hams piled carelessly in one corner. She stalked it while the fluted girl watched and smiled at the plump girl's suspicions. Mirriam hefted a great wheel of Danish cheese and peered into the gap behind. "Lidia? Are you there?"

The fluted girl shook her head. No, she thought. But you guessed well. A year ago, I would have been. I could have moved the cheeses, with effort. The champagne would have been too much, though. I would never have been behind the champagne.

Mirriam stood up. Sweat sheened her face from the effort of moving the bulky goods that fed Belari's household. Her face looked like a bright shiny apple. She wiped her brow with a sleeve. "Lidia, Madame Belari is getting angry. You're being a selfish girl. Nia is already waiting for you in the practice room."

Lidia nodded silently. Yes, Nia would be in the practice room. She was the good sister. Lidia was the bad one. The one they had to search for. Lidia was the reason both fluted girls were punished. Belari had given up on discipline for Lidia directly. She contented herself with punishing both sisters and letting guilt enforce compliance. Sometimes it worked. But not now. Not with Stephen gone. Lidia needed quiet now. A place where no one watched her. A place alone. Her secret place which she showed to Stephen and which he had examined with such surprised sad eyes. Stephen's eyes had been brown. When he looked at her, she thought that his eyes were almost as soft as

Belari's rabbits. They were safe eyes. You could fall into those safe brown eyes and never worry about breaking a bone.

Mirriam sat heavily on a sack of potatoes and scowled around her, acting for her potential audience. "You're being a selfish girl. A vicious selfish girl to make us all search this way."

The fluted girl nodded. Yes, I am a selfish girl, she thought. I am a selfish girl, and you are a woman, and yet we are the same age, and I am smarter than you. You are clever but you don't know that hidey-holes are best when they are in places no one looks. You look for me under and behind and between, but you don't look up. I am above you, and I am watching you, just as Stephen watched us all.

Mirriam grimaced and got up. "No matter. Burson will find you." She brushed the dust from her skirts. "You hear me? Burson will find you." She left the pantry.

Lidia waited for Mirriam to go away. It galled her that Mirriam was right. Burson would find her. He found her every time, if she waited too long. Silent time could only be stolen for so many minutes. It lasted as long as it took Belari to lose patience and call the jackals. Then another hidey-hole was lost.

Lidia turned Stephen's tiny blown-glass bottle in her delicate fingers a final time. A parting gift, she understood, now that he was gone, now that he would no longer comfort her when Belari's depredations became too much. She forced back tears. No more time to cry. Burson would be looking for her.

She pressed the vial into a secure crack, tight against the stone and roughhewn wood of the shelving where she hid, then worked a vacuum jar of red lentils back until she had an opening. She squeezed out from behind the legume wall that lined the pantry's top shelves.

It had taken weeks for her to clear out the back jars and make a place for herself, but the jars made a good hidey-hole. A place others neglected to search. She had a fortress of jars, full of flat innocent beans, and behind that barrier, if she was patient and bore the strain, she could crouch for hours. She climbed down.

Carefully, carefully, she thought. We don't want to break a bone. We have to be careful of the bones. She hung from the shelves as she gently worked the fat jar of red lentils back into place then slipped down the last shelves to the pantry floor.

Barefoot on cold stone flagging, Lidia studied her hidey-hole. Yes, it looked good still. Stephen's final gift was safe up there. No one looked able to fit in that few feet of space, not even a delicate fluted girl. No one would suspect she folded herself so perfectly into such a place. She was slight as a mouse, and sometimes fit into surprising places. For that, she could thank Belari. She turned and hurried from the pantry, determined to let the servants catch her far away from her last surviving hidey-hole.

By the time Lidia reached the dining hall, she believed she might gain the practice rooms without discovery. There might be no punishments. Belari was kind to those she loved, but uncompromising when they disappointed her. Though Lidia was too delicate to strike, there were other punishments. Lidia thought of Stephen. A small part of her was happy that he was beyond Belari's tortures.

Lidia slipped along the dining hall's edge, shielded by ferns and blooming orchids. Between the lush leaves and flowers, she caught glimpses of the dining table's long ebony expanse, polished mirror-bright each day by the servants and perpetually set with gleaming silver. She studied the room for observers. It was empty.

The rich warm smell of greenery reminded her of summer, despite the winter season that slashed the mountains around the castle. When she and Nia had been younger, before their surgeries, they had run in the mountains, amongst the pines. Lidia slipped through the orchids: one from Singapore; another from Chennai; another, striped like a tiger, engineered by Belari. She touched the delicate tiger blossom, admiring its lurid color.

We are beautiful prisoners, she thought. Just like you.

The ferns shuddered. A man exploded from the greenery, springing on her like a wolf. His hands wrenched her shoulders. His fingers plunged into her pale flesh and Lidia gasped as they stabbed her nerves into paralysis. She collapsed to the slate flagstones, a butterfly folding as Burson pressed her down.

She whimpered against the stone, her heart hammering inside her chest at the shock of Burson's ambush. She moaned, trembling under his weight, her face hard against the castle's smooth gray slate. On the stone beside her, a pink and white orchid lay beheaded by Burson's attack.

Slowly, when he was sure of her compliance, Burson allowed her to move. His great weight lessened, lifting away from her like a tank rolling off a crushed hovel. Lidia forced herself to sit up. Finally she stood, an unsteady pale fairy dwarfed by the looming monster that was Belari's head of security.

Burson's mountainous body was a cragged landscape of muscle and scars, all juts of strength and angry puckered furrows of combat. Mirriam gossiped that he had previously been a gladiator, but she was romantic and Lidia suspected his scars came from training handlers, much as her own punishments came from Belari.

Burson held her wrist, penning it in a rock-like grasp. For all its unyielding strength, his grip was gentle. After an initial disastrous breakage, he had learned what strain her skeleton could bear before it shattered.

Lidia struggled, testing his hold on her wrist, then accepted her capture. Burson knelt, bringing his height to match hers. Red-rimmed eyes studied her. Augmented irises bloodshot with enhancements scanned her skin's infrared pulse.

Burson's slashed face slowly lost the green blush of camouflage, abandoning stone and foliage colors now that he stood in open air. Where his hand touched her though, his skin paled, as though powdered by flour, matching the white of her own flesh.

"Where have you been hiding?" he rumbled.

"Nowhere."

Burson's red eyes narrowed, his brows furrowing over deep pits of interrogation. He sniffed at her clothing, hunting for clues. He brought his nose close to her face, her hair, snuffled at her hands. "The kitchens," he murmured.

Lidia flinched. His red eyes studied her closely, hunting for more details, watching the unintentional reactions of her skin, the blush of discovery she could not hide from his prying eyes. Burson smiled. He hunted with the wild fierce joy of his bloodhound genetics. It was difficult to tell where the jackal, dog, and human blended in the man. His joys were hunting, capture, and slaughter.

Burson straightened, smiling. He took a steel bracelet from a pouch. "I have something for you,

Lidia." He slapped the jewelry onto Lidia's wrist. It writhed around her thin arm, snakelike, chiming as it locked. "No more hiding for you."

A current charged up Lidia's arm and she cried out, shivering as electricity rooted through her body. Burson supported her as the current cut off. He said, "I'm tired of searching for Belari's property."

He smiled, tight-lipped, and pushed her toward the practice rooms. Lidia allowed herself to be herded.

Belari was in the performance hall when Burson brought Lidia before her. Servants bustled around her, arranging tables, setting up the round stage, installing the lighting. The walls were hung in pale muslin shot through with electric charges, a billowing sheath of charged air that crackled and sparked whenever a servant walked near.

Belari seemed unaware of the fanciful world building around her as she tossed orders at her events coordinator. Her black body armor was open at the collar, in deference to the warmth of human activity. She spared Burson and Lidia a quick glance, then turned her attention back to her servant, still furiously scribbling on a digital pad. "I want everything to be perfect tonight, Tania. Nothing out of place. Nothing amiss. Perfect."

"Yes, Madame."

Belari smiled. Her face was mathematically sculpted into beauty, structured by focus-groups and cosmetic traditions that stretched back generations. Cocktails of disease prophylaxis, cell-scouring cancer inhibitors, and Revitia kept Belari's physical appearance at twenty-eight, much as Lidia's own Revitia treatments kept her frozen in the first throes of adolescence. "And I want Vernon taken care of."

"Will he want a companion?"

Belari shook her head. "No. He'll confine himself

8

to harassing me, I'm sure." She shivered. "Disgusting man."

Tania tittered. Belari's chill gaze quieted her. Belari surveyed the performance hall. "I want everything in here. The food, the champagne, everything. I want them packed together so that they feel each other when the girls perform. I want it very tight. Very intimate."

Tania nodded and scribbled more notes on her pad. She tapped the screen authoritatively, sending orders to the staff. Already, servants would be receiving messages in their earbuds, reacting to their mistress's demands.

Belari said, "I want Tingle available. With the champagne. It will whet their appetites."

"You'll have an orgy if you do."

Belari laughed. "That's fine. I want them to remember tonight. I want them to remember our fluted girls. Vernon particularly." Her laughter quieted, replaced by a hard-edged smile, brittle with emotion. "He'll be angry when he finds out about them. But he'll want them, anyway. And he'll bid like the rest."

Lidia watched Belari's face. She wondered if the woman knew how clearly she broadcast her feelings about the Pendant Entertainment executive. Lidia had seen him once, from behind a curtain. She and Stephen had watched Vernon Weir touch Belari, and watched Belari first shy from his touch and then give in, summoning the reserves of her acting skill to play the part of a seduced woman.

Vernon Weir had made Belari famous. He'd paid the expense of her body sculpting and made her a star, much as Belari now invested in Lidia and her sister. But Master Weir extracted a price for his aid, Faustian devil that he was. Stephen and Lidia had watched as Weir took his pleasure from Belari, and

9

Stephen had whispered to her that when Weir was
gone, Belari would summon Stephen and reenact the
scene, but with Stephen as the victim, and then he
would pretend, as she did, that he was happy to
submit.

Lidia's thoughts broke off. Belari had turned to her.
The angry welt from Stephen's attack was still visible
on her throat, despite the cell-knitters she popped like
candy. Lidia thought it must gall her to have a scar
out of place. She was careful of her image. Belari
seemed to catch the focus of Lidia's gaze. Her lips
pursed and she pulled the collar of her body armor
close, hiding the damage. Her green eyes narrowed.
"We've been looking for you."

Lidia ducked her head. "I'm sorry, Mistress."

Belari ran a finger under the fluted girl's jaw, lifting
her downcast face until they were eye to eye. "I should
punish you for wasting my time."

"Yes, Mistress. I'm sorry." The fluted girl lowered
her eyes. Belari wouldn't hit her. She was too expensive to fix. She wondered if Belari would use electricity,
or isolation, or some other humiliation cleverly devised.

Instead, Belari pointed to the steel bracelet. "What's
this?"

Burson didn't flinch at her question. He had no
fear. He was the only servant who had no fear. Lidia
admired him for that, if nothing else. "To track her.
And shock her." He smiled, pleased with himself. "It
causes no physical destruction."

Belari shook her head. "I need her without jewelry
tonight. Take it off."

"She will hide."

"No. She wants to be star. She'll be good now,
won't you, Lidia?"

Lidia nodded.

Burson shrugged and removed the bracelet, unperturbed. He leaned his great scarred face close to Lidia's ear. "Don't hide in the kitchens the next time. I will find you." He stood away, smiling his satisfaction. Lidia narrowed her eyes at Burson and told herself she had won a victory that Burson didn't know her hidey-hole yet. But then Burson smiled at her and she wondered if he did know already, if he was playing with her the way a cat played with a maimed mouse.

Belari said, "Thank you, Burson," then paused, eyeing the great creature who looked so man-like yet moved with the feral quickness of the wilds. "Have you tightened our security?"

Burson nodded. "Your fief is safe. We are checking the rest of the staff, for background irregularities."

"Have you found anything?"

Burson shook his head. "Your staff love you."

Belari's voice sharpened. "That's what we thought about Stephen. And now I wear body armor in my own fief. I can't afford the appearance of lost popularity. It affects my share price too much."

"I've been thorough."

"If my stock falls, Vernon will have me wired for TouchSense. I won't have it."

"I understand. There will be no more failures."

Belari frowned at the monster looming over her. "Good. Well, come on then." She motioned for Lidia to join her. "Your sister has been waiting for you." She took the fluted girl by the hand and led her out of the performance hall.

Lidia spared a glance back. Burson was gone. The servants bustled, placing orchid cuttings on tables, but Burson had disappeared, either blended into the walls or sped away on his errands of security.

Belari tugged Lidia's hand. "You led us on a merry

search. I thought we would have to spray the pheromones again."

"I'm sorry."

"No harm. This time." Belari smiled down at her. "Are you nervous about tonight?"

Lidia shook her head. "No."

"No?"

Lidia shrugged. "Will Master Weir purchase our stock?"

"If he pays enough."

"Will he?"

Belari smiled. "I think he will, yes. You are unique. Like me. Vernon likes to collect rare beauty."

"What is he like?"

Belari's smile stiffened. She looked up, concentrating on their path through the castle. "When I was a girl, very young, much younger than you, long before I became famous, I used to go to a playground. A man came to watch me on the swings. He wanted to be my friend. I didn't like him, but being near him made me dizzy. Whatever he said made perfect sense. He smelled bad, but I couldn't pull away from him." Belari shook her head. "Someone's mother chased him away." She looked down at Lidia. "He had a chemical cologne, you understand?"

"Contraband?"

"Yes. From Asia. Not legal here. Vernon is like that. Your skin crawls but he draws you to him."

"He touches you."

Belari looked down at Lidia sadly. "He likes my old crone experience in my young girl body. But he hardly discriminates. He touches everyone." She smiled slightly. "But not you, perhaps. You are too valuable to touch."

"Too delicate."

"Don't sound so bitter. You're unique. We're going

12

to make you a star." Belari looked down at her protégé hungrily. "Your stock will rise, and you will be a star."

Lidia watched from her windows as Belari's guests began to arrive. Aircars snaked in under security escort, sliding low over the pines, green and red running lights blinking in the darkness.

Nia came to stand behind Lidia. "They're here."

"Yes."

Snow clotted thickly on the trees, like heavy cream. The occasional blue sweeps of search beams highlighted the snow and the dark silhouettes of the forest; Burson's ski patrols, hoping to spy out the telltale red exhalations of intruders crouched amongst pine shadows. Their beams swept over the ancient hulk of a ski lift that climbed up from the town. It was rusting, silent except when the wind caught its chairs and sent its cables swaying. The empty seats swung lethargically in the freezing air, another victim of Belari's influence. Belari hated competition. Now, she was the only patron of the town that sparkled in the deep of the valley far below.

"You should get dressed," Nia said.

Lidia turned to study her twin. Black eyes like pits watched her from between elfin lids. Her skin was pale, stripped of pigment, and she was thin, accenting the delicacy of her bone structure. That was one true thing about her, about both of them: their bones were theirs. It was what had attracted Belari to them in the first place, when they were just eleven. Just old enough for Belari to strip them from their parents.

Lidia's gaze returned to the view. Deep in the tight crease of the mountain valley, the town shimmered with amber lights.

"Do you miss it?" she asked.

Nia slipped closer. "Miss what?"

13

Lidia nodded down at the shimmering jewel. "The town."

Their parents had been glassblowers, practicing the old arts abandoned in the face of efficient manufacturing, breathing delicate works into existence, sand running liquid under their supervision. They had moved to Belari's fief for patronage, like all the town's artisans: the potters, the blacksmiths, the painters. Sometimes Belari's peers noticed an artist and his influence grew. Niels Kinkaid had made his fortune from Belari's favor, turning iron to her will, outfitting her fortress with its great hand-wrought gates and her gardens with crouching sculptural surprises: foxes and children peering from amongst lupine and monkshood in the summers and deep drifted snow in the winters. Now he was almost famous enough to float his own stock.

Lidia's parents had come for patronage, but Belari's evaluating eye had not fallen on their artistry. Instead, she selected the biological accident of their twin daughters: delicate and blond with cornflower eyes that watched the world blinkless as they absorbed the fief's mountain wonders. Their trade flourished now thanks to the donation of their children.

Nia jostled Lidia gently, her ghostly face serious. "Hurry and dress. You mustn't be late."

Lidia turned away from her black-eyed sister. Of their original features, little remained. Belari had watched them grow in the castle for two years and then the pills began. Revitia treatments at thirteen froze their features in the matrix of youth. Then had come the eyes, drawn from twins in some far foreign land. Lidia sometimes wondered if in India, two dusky girl children looked out at the world from cornflower eyes, or if they walked the mud streets of their village guided only by the sound of echoes on cow-dung walls and the scrape of their canes on the dirt before them.

Lidia studied the night beyond the windows with her stolen black eyes. More aircars dropped guests on the landing pads then spread gossamer wings and let the mountain winds bear them away.

More treatments had followed: pigment drugs drained color from their skins, leaving them Kabuki pale, ethereal shadows of their former mountain sun-blushed selves, and then the surgeries began. She remembered waking after each successive surgery, crippled, unable to move for weeks despite the wide-bore needles full of cell-knitters and nutrient fluids the doctor flushed through her slight body. The doctor would hold her hand after the surgeries, wipe the sweat from her pale brow and whisper, "Poor girl. Poor poor girl." Then Belari would come and smile at the progress and say that Lidia and Nia would soon be stars.

Gusts of wind tore snow from the pines and sent it swirling in great tornado clouds around the arriving aristocracy. The guests hurried through the driving snow while the blue search beams of Burson's ski patrols carved across the forests. Lidia sighed and turned from the windows, obedient finally to Nia's anxious hope that she would dress.

Stephen and Lidia went on picnics together when Belari was away from the fief. They would leave the great gray construct of Belari's castle and walk carefully across the mountain meadows, Stephen always helping her, guiding her fragile steps through fields of daisies, columbine, and lupine until they peered down over sheer granite cliffs to the town far below. All about them glacier-sculpted peaks ringed the valley like giants squatting in council, their faces adorned with snow even in summer, like beards of wisdom.

15

At the edge of the precipice, they ate a picnic lunch and Stephen told stories of the world before the fiefs, before Revitia made stars immortal.

He said the country had been democratic. That people once voted for their lieges. That they had been free to travel between any fief they liked. Everyone, he said, not just stars. Lidia knew there were places on the coasts where this occurred. She had heard of them. But it seemed difficult to credit. She was a child of a fief.

"It's true," Stephen said. "On the coasts, the people choose their own leader. It's only here, in the mountains, that it's different." He grinned at her. His soft brown eyes crinkled slightly, showing his humor, showing that he already saw the skepticism on her face.

Lidia laughed. "But who would pay for everything? Without Belari who would pay to fix the roads and make the schools?" She picked an aster and twirled it between her fingers, watching the purple spokes blur around the yellow center of the flower.

"The people do."

Lidia laughed again. "They can't afford to do that. They hardly have enough to feed themselves. And how would they know what to do? Without Belari, no one would even know what needs fixing, or improving." She tossed the flower away, aiming to send it over the cliff. Instead, the wind caught it, and it fell near her.

Stephen picked up the flower and flicked it over the edge easily. "It's true. They don't have to be rich, they just work together. You think Belari knows everything? She hires advisors. People can do that as well as she."

Lidia shook her head. "People like Mirriam? Ruling

16

a fief? It sounds like madness. No one would respect her."

Stephen scowled. "It's true," he said stubbornly, and because Lidia liked him and didn't want him to be unhappy, she agreed that it might be true, but in her heart, she thought that Stephen was a dreamer. It made him sweet, even if he didn't understand the true ways of the world.

"Do you like Belari?" Stephen asked suddenly.

"What do you mean?"

"Do you like her?"

Lidia gave him a puzzled look. Stephen's brown eyes studied her intensely. She shrugged. "She's a good liege. Everyone is fed and cared for. It's not like Master Weir's fief."

Stephen made a face of disgust. "Nothing is like Weir's fief. He's barbaric. He put one of his servants on a spit." He paused. "But still, look at what Belari has done to you."

Lidia frowned. "What about me?"

"You're not natural. Look at your eyes, your skin and…," he turned his eyes away, his voice lowering, "your bones. Look what she did to your bones."

"What's wrong with my bones?"

"You can barely walk!" he cried suddenly. "You should be able to walk!"

Lidia glanced around nervously. Stephen was talking critically. Someone might be listening. They seemed alone, but people were always around: security on the hillsides, others out for walks. Burson might be there, blended with the scenery, a stony man hidden amongst the rocks. Stephen had a hard time understanding about Burson. "I can walk," she whispered fiercely.

"How many times have you broken a leg or an arm or a rib?"

"Not in a year." She was proud of it. She had learned to be careful.

Stephen laughed incredulously. "Do you know how many bones I've broken in my life?" He didn't wait for an answer. "None. Not a single bone. Never. Do you even remember what it's like to walk without worrying that you'll trip, or bump into someone? You're like glass."

Lidia shook her head and looked away. "I'm going to be star. Belari will float us on the markets."

"But you can't walk," Stephen said. His eyes had a pitying quality that made Lidia angry.

"I can too. And it's enough."

"But—"

"No!" Lidia shook her head. "Who are you to say what I do? Look what Belari does to you, but still you are loyal! I may have had surgeries, but at least I'm not her toy."

It was the only time Stephen became angry. For a moment the rage in his face made Lidia think he would strike her and break her bones. A part of her hoped he would, that he would release the terrible frustration brewing between them, two servants each calling the other slave.

Instead, Stephen mastered himself and gave up the argument. He apologized and held her hand and they were quiet as the Sun set, but it was already too late and their quiet time was ruined. Lidia's mind had gone back to the days before the surgeries, when she ran without care, and though she would not admit it to Stephen, it felt as though he had ripped away a scab and revealed an aching bitter wound.

The performance hall trembled with anticipation, a room full of people high on Tingle and champagne. The muslin on the walls flickered like lightning as Belari's guests, swathed in brilliant silks and sparkling gold, swirled through the room in colorful clouds of revelry, clumping together with conversation, then breaking apart with laughter as they made their social rounds.

Lidia slipped carefully amongst the guests, her pale skin and diaphanous shift a spot of simplicity amongst the gaudy colors and wealth. Some of the guests eyed her curiously, the strange girl threading through their pleasure. They quickly dismissed her. She was merely another creature of Belari's, intriguing to look at, perhaps, but of no account. Their attention always returned to the more important patterns of gossip and association swirling around them. Lidia smiled. Soon, she thought, you will recognize me. She slipped up against a wall, near a table piled high with finger sandwiches, small cuts of meat and plates of plump strawberries.

Lidia scanned the crowds. Her sister was there, across the room, dressed in an identical diaphanous shift. Belari stood surrounded by mediascape names and fief lieges, her green gown matching her eyes, smiling, apparently at ease, even without her new-found habit of body armor.

Vernon Weir slipped up behind Belari, stroking her shoulder. Lidia saw Belari shiver and steel herself against Weir's touch. She wondered how he could not notice. Perhaps he was one of those who took pleasure in the repulsion he inflicted. Belari smiled at him, her emotions under control once again.

Lidia took a small plate of meats from the table. The meat was drizzled with raspberry reduction and was sweet. Belari liked sweet things, like the strawberries she was eating now with the Pendant Entertainment executive at the far end of the table. The sweet addiction was another side effect of the Tingle.

Belari caught sight of Lidia and led Vernon Weir

19

toward her. "Do you like the meat?" she asked, smiling slightly.

Lidia nodded, finishing carefully.

Belari's smile sharpened. "I'm not surprised. You have a taste for good ingredients." Her face was flushed with Tingle. Lidia was glad they were in public. When Belari took too much Tingle she hungered and became erratic. Once, Belari had crushed strawberries against her skin, making her pale flesh blush with the juice, and then, high with the erotic charge of overdose, she had forced Lidia's tongue to Nia's juice-stained flesh and Nia's tongue to hers, while Belari watched, pleased with the decadent performance.

Belari selected a strawberry and offered it to Lidia. "Here. Have one, but don't stain yourself. I want you perfect." Her eyes glistened with excitement. Lidia steeled herself against memory and accepted the berry.

Vernon studied Lidia. "She's yours?"

Belari smiled fondly. "One of my fluted girls."

Vernon knelt and studied Lidia more closely. "What unusual eyes you have."

Lidia ducked her head shyly.

Belari said, "I had them replaced."

"Replaced?" Vernon glanced up at her. "Not altered?"

Belari smiled. "We both know nothing that beautiful comes artificially." She reached down and stroked Lidia's pale blond hair, smiling with satisfaction at her creation. "When I got her, she had the most beautiful blue eyes. The color of the flowers you find here in the mountains in the summer." She shook her head. "I had them replaced. They were beautiful, but not the look I wished for."

Vernon stood up again. "She is striking. But not as beautiful as you."

Belari smiled cynically at Vernon. "Is that why you want me wired for TouchSense?"

Vernon shrugged. "It's a new market, Belari. With your response, you could be a star."

"I'm already a star."

Vernon smiled. "But Revitia is expensive."

"We always come back to that, don't we, Vernon?"

Vernon gave her a hard look. "I don't want to be at odds with you, Belari. You've been wonderful for us. Worth every penny of your reconstruction. I've never seen a finer actress. But this is Pendant, after all. You could have bought your stock a long time ago if you weren't so attached to immortality." He eyed Belari coldly. "If you want to be immortal, you will wire TouchSense. Already we're seeing massive acceptance in the marketplace. It's the future of entertainment."

"I'm an actress, not a marionette. I don't crave people inside my skin."

Vernon shrugged. "We all pay a price for our celebrity. Where the markets move, we must follow. None of us is truly free." He looked at Belari meaningfully. "Certainly not if we want to live forever."

Belari smiled slyly. "Perhaps." She nodded at Lidia. "Run along. It's almost time." She turned back to Vernon. "There's something I'd like you to see."

Stephen gave her the vial the day before he died. Lidia had asked what it was, a few amber drops in a vial no larger than her pinky. She had smiled at the gift, feeling playful, but Stephen had been serious.

"It's freedom," he said.

She shook her head, uncomprehending.

"If you ever choose, you control your life. You don't have to be Belari's pet."

"I'm not her pet."

21

He shook his head. "If you ever want escape," he held up the vial, "it's here." He handed it to her and closed her pale hand around the tiny bottle. It was handblown. Briefly, she wondered if it came from her parents' workshop. Stephen said, "We're small people here. Only people like Belari have control. In other places, other parts of the world, it's different. Little people still matter. But here," he smiled sadly, "all we have is our lives."

Comprehension dawned. She tried to pull away but Stephen held her firmly. "I'm not saying you want it now, but someday, perhaps you will. Perhaps you'll decide you don't want to cooperate with Belari anymore. No matter how many gifts she showers on you." He squeezed her hand gently. "It's quick. Almost painless." He looked into her eyes with the soft brown kindness that had always been there.

It was a gift of love, however misguided, and because she knew it would make him happy, she nodded and agreed to keep the vial and put it in her hidey-hole, just in case. She couldn't have known that he had already chosen his own death, that he would hunt Belari with a knife, and almost succeed.

No one noticed when the fluted girls took their places on the center dais. They were merely oddities, pale angels, entwined. Lidia put her mouth to her sister's throat, feeling her pulse threading rapidly under her white, white skin. It throbbed against her tongue as she sought out the tiny bore hole in her sister's body. She felt the wet touch of Nia's tongue on her own throat, nestling into her flesh like a small mouse seeking comfort.

Lidia stilled herself, waiting for the attention of the people, patient and focused on her performance. She felt Nia breathe, her lungs expanding inside the frail cage of her chest. Lidia took her own breath. They began to play, first her own notes, running out through unstopped keys in her flesh, and then Nia's notes beginning as well. The open sound, haunting moments of breath, pressed through their bodies.

The melancholy tones trailed off. Lidia moved her head, breathing in, mirroring Nia as she pressed her lips again to her sister's flesh. This time, Lidia kissed her sister's hand. Nia's mouth sought the delicate hollow of her clavicle. Music, mournful, as hollow as they were, breathed out from their bodies. Nia breathed into Lidia and the exhalation of her lungs slipped out through Lidia's bones, tinged with emotion, as though the warm air of her sister came to life within her body.

Around the girls, the guests fell quiet. The silence spread, like ripples from a stone thrown into a placid pool, speeding outward from their epicenter to lap at the farthest edges of the room. All eyes turned to the pale girls on stage. Lidia could feel their eyes, hungry, yearning, almost physical as their gazes pressed against her. She moved her hands beneath her sister's shift, clasping her close. Her sister's hands touched her hips, closing stops in her fluted body. At their new embrace a sigh of yearning came from the crowd, a whisper of their own hungers made musical.

Lidia's hands found the keys to her sister, her tongue touching Nia's throat once more. Her fingers ran along the knuckles of Nia's spine, finding the clarinet within her, stroking keys. She pressed the warm breath of herself into her sister and she felt Nia breathing into her. Nia's sound was dark and melancholy, her own tones, brighter, higher, ran in counterpoint, a slowly developing story of forbidden touch.

They stood embraced. Their body music built, notes intertwining seductively as their hands stroked one another's bodies, bringing forth a complex rising tide

23

of sound. Suddenly, Nia wrenched at Lidia's shift and Lidia's fingers tore away Nia's own. They stood revealed, pale elfin creatures of music. The guests around them gasped as the notes poured out brighter now, unmuffled by clinging clothes. The girls' musical graftings shone: cobalt boreholes in their spines, glinting stops and keys made of brass and ivory that ran along their fluted frames and contained a hundred possible instruments within the structure of their bodies.

Nia's mouth crept up Lidia's arm. Notes spilled out of Lidia as bright as water jewels. Laments of desire and sin flowed from Nia's pores. Their embraces became more frenzied, a choreography of lust. The spectators pressed closer, incited by the spectacle of naked youth and music intertwined.

Around her, Lidia was vaguely aware of their watching eyes and flushed expressions. The Tingle and the performance were doing their work on the guests. She could feel the heat rising in the room. She and Nia sank slowly to the floor, their embraces becoming more erotic and elaborate, the sexual tension of their musical conflict increasing as they entwined. Years of training had come to this moment, this carefully constructed weave of harmonizing flesh.

We perform pornography, Lidia thought. Pornography for the profit of Belari. She caught a glimpse of her patron's gleaming pleasure, Vernon Weir dumbstruck beside her. Yes, she thought, look at us, Master Weir, look and see what pornography we perform, and then it was her turn to play upon her sister, and her tongue and hands stroked Nia's keys.

It was a dance of seduction and acquiescence. They had other dances, solos and duets, some chaste, others obscene, but for their debut, Belari had chosen this one. The energy of their music increased, violent, climactic, until at last she and Nia lay upon the floor, expended, sheathed in sweat, bare twins tangled in musical lasciviousness. Their body music fell silent.

Around them, no one moved. Lidia tasted salt on her sister's skin as they held their pose. The lights dimmed, signaling completion.

Applause exploded around them. The lights brightened. Nia drew herself upright. Her lips quirked in a smile of satisfaction as she helped Lidia to her feet. You see? Nia's eyes seemed to say. We will be stars. Lidia found herself smiling with her sister. Despite the loss of Stephen, despite Belari's depredations, she was smiling. The audience's adoration washed over her, a balm of pleasure.

They curtsied to Belari as they had been trained, making obeisance first to their patron, the mother goddess who had created them. Belari smiled at the gesture, however scripted it was, and joined the applause of her guests. The people's applause increased again at the girls' good grace, then Nia and Lidia were curtseying to the corners of the compass, gathering their shifts and leaving the stage, guided by Burson's hulking presence to their patron.

The applause continued as they crossed the distance to Belari. Finally, at Belari's wave, the clapping gave way to respectful silence. She smiled at her assembled guests, placing her arms around the slight shoulders of the girls and said, "My lords and ladies, our Fluted Girls," and applause burst over them again, one final explosion of adulation before the guests fell to talking, fanning themselves, and feeling the flush of their own skins which the girls had inspired.

Belari held the fluted girls closely and whispered in their ears, "You did well." She hugged them carefully.

Vernon Weir's eyes roved over Lidia and Nia's exposed bodies. "You outdo yourself, Belari," he said.

Belari inclined her head slightly at the compliment. Her grip on Lidia's shoulder became proprietary. Belari's voice didn't betray her tension. She kept it light, comfortably satisfied with her position, but her fingers dug into Lidia's skin. "They are my finest."

"Such an extraordinary crafting."

"It's expensive when they break a bone. They're terribly fragile." Belari smiled down at the girls affectionately. "They hardly remember what it's like to walk without care."

"All the most beautiful things are fragile." Vernon touched Lidia's cheek. She forced herself not to flinch. "It must have been complex to build them."

Belari nodded. "They are intricate." She traced a finger along the boreholes in Nia's arm. "Each note isn't simply affected by the placement of fingers on keys; but also by how they press against one another, or the floor; if an arm is bent or if it is straightened. We froze their hormone levels so that they wouldn't grow, and then we began designing their instruments. It takes an enormous amount of skill for them to play and to dance."

"How long have you been training them?"

"Five years. Seven if you count the surgeries that began the process."

Vernon shook his head. "And we never heard of them."

"You would have ruined them. I'm going to make them stars."

"We made you a star."

"And you'll unmake me as well, if I falter."

"So you'll float them on the markets?"

Belari smiled at him. "Of course. I'll retain a controlling interest, but the rest, I will sell."

"You'll be rich."

Belari smiled, "More than that, I'll be independent."

Vernon mimed elaborate disappointment. "I suppose this means we won't be wiring you for Touch-Sense."

"I suppose not."

The tension between them was palpable. Vernon, calculating, looking for an opening while Belari gripped her property and faced him. Vernon's eyes narrowed.

As though sensing his thoughts, Belari said, "I've insured them."

Vernon shook his head ruefully. "Belari, you do me a disservice." He sighed. "I suppose I should congratulate you. To have such loyal subjects, and such wealth, you've achieved more than I would have thought possible when we first met."

"My servants are loyal because I treat them well. They are happy to serve."

"Would your Stephen agree?" Vernon waved at the sweetmeats in the center of the refreshment table, drizzled with raspberry and garnished with bright green leaves of mint.

Belari smiled. "Oh yes, even him. Do you know that just as Michael and Renee were preparing to cook him, he looked at me and said 'Thank you'?" She shrugged. "He tried to kill me, but he did have the most eager urge to please, even so. At the very end, he told me he was sorry, and that the best years of his life had been in service to me." She wiped at a theatrical tear. "I don't know how it is, that he could love me so, and still so desire to have me dead." She looked away from Vernon, watching the other guests. "For that, though, I thought I would serve him, rather than simply stake him out as a warning. We loved each other, even if he was a traitor."

Vernon shrugged sympathetically. "So many people dislike the fief structure. You try to tell them that you provide far more security than what existed before, and yet still they protest, and," he glanced meaningfully at Belari, "sometimes more."

Belari shrugged. "Well, my subjects don't protest. At least not until Stephen. They love me."

Vernon smiled. "As we all do. In any case, serving him chilled this way." He lifted a plate from the table. "Your taste is impeccable."

Lidia's face stiffened as she followed the conversation. She looked at the array of finely sliced meats and then at Vernon as he forked a bite into his mouth. Her stomach turned. Only her training let her remain still. Vernon and Belari's conversation continued, but all Lidia could think was that she had consumed her friend, the one who had been kind to her.

Anger trickled through her, filling her porous body with rebellion. She longed to attack her smug patron, but her rage was impotent. She was too weak to hurt Belari. Her bones were too fragile, her physique too delicate. Belari was strong in all things as she was weak. Lidia stood trembling with frustration, and then Stephen's voice whispered comforting wisdom inside her head. She could defeat Belari. Her pale skin flushed with pleasure at the thought.

As though sensing her, Belari looked down. "Lidia, go put on clothes and come back. I'll want to introduce you and your sister to everyone before we take you public."

Lidia crept toward her hidey-hole. The vial was still there, if Burson had not found it. Her heart hammered at the thought: that the vial might be missing, that Stephen's final gift had been destroyed by the monster. She slipped through dimly lit servant's tunnels to the kitchen, anxiety pulsing at every step.

The kitchen was busy, full of staff preparing new platters for the guests. Lidia's stomach turned. She wondered if more trays bore Stephen's remains. The stoves flared and the ovens roared as Lidia slipped through the confusion, a ghostly waif sliding along the walls. No one paid her attention. They were too busy laboring for Belari, doing her bidding without thought or conscience: slaves, truly. Obedience was all Belari cared for.

Lidia smiled grimly to herself. If obedience was what Belari loved, she was happy to provide a true betrayal. She would collapse on the floor, amongst her mistress's guests, destroying Belari's perfect moment, shaming her and foiling her hopes of independence.

The pantry was silent when Lidia slipped through its archway. Everyone was busy serving, running like dogs to feed Belari's brood. Lidia wandered amongst the stores, past casks of oil and sacks of onions, past the great humming freezers that held whole sides of beef within their steel bowels. She reached the broad tall shelves at the pantry's end and climbed past preserved peaches, tomatoes, and olives to the high-stored legumes. She pushed aside a vacuum jar of lentils and felt within.

For a moment, as she slid her hand around the cramped hiding place, she thought the vial was missing, but then her grasp closed on the tiny blown-glass bulb.

She climbed down, careful not to break any bones, laughing at herself as she did, thinking that it hardly mattered now, and hurried back through the kitchen, past the busy, obedient servants, and then down the servants' tunnels, intent on self-destruction.

As she sped through the darkened tunnels, she smiled, glad that she would never again steal through dim halls hidden from the view of aristocracy. Freedom was in her hands. For the first time in years she controlled her own fate.

Burson lunged from the shadows, his skin shifting from black to flesh as he materialized. He seized her and jerked her to a halt. Lidia's body strained at the abrupt capture. She gasped, her joints creaking. Burson gathered her wrists into a single massive fist. With his other hand, he turned her chin upward, subjecting her black eyes to the interrogation of his red-rimmed orbs. "Where are you going?"

His size could make you mistake him for stupid, she thought. His slow rumbling voice. His great animal-like gaze. But he was observant where Belari was not. Lidia trembled and cursed herself for foolishness. Burson studied her, his nostrils flaring at the scent of fear. His eyes watched the blush of her skin. "Where are you going?" he asked again. Warning laced his tone.

"Back to the party," Lidia whispered.

"Where have you been?"

Lidia tried to shrug. "Nowhere. Changing."

"Nia is already there. You are late. Belari wondered about you."

Lidia said nothing. There was nothing she could say to make Burson lose his suspicions. She was terrified that he would pry open her clenched hands and discover the glass vial. The servants said it was impossible to lie to Burson. He discovered everything.

Burson eyed her silently, letting her betray herself. Finally he said, "You went to your hidey-hole." He sniffed at her. "Not in the kitchen, though. The pantry." He smiled, revealing hard sharp teeth. "High up."

Lidia held her breath. Burson couldn't let go of a problem until it was solved. It was bred into him. His eyes swept over her skin. "You're nervous." He sniffed. "Sweating. Fear."

Lidia shook her head stubbornly. The tiny vial in her hands was slick, she was afraid she would drop it, or move her hands and call attention to it. Burson's great strength pulled her until they were nose to nose. His fist squeezed her wrists until she thought they would shatter. He studied her eyes. "So afraid."

"No." Lidia shook her head again.

Burson laughed, contempt and pity in the sound. "It must be terrifying to know you can be broken, at any time." His stone grip relaxed. Blood rushed back into her wrists. "Have your hidey-hole, then. Your secret is safe with me."

For a moment, Lidia wasn't sure what he meant. She stood before the giant security officer, frozen still, but then Burson waved his hand irritably and slipped back into the shadows, his skin darkening as he disappeared. "Go."

Lidia stumbled away, her legs wavering, threatening to give out. She forced herself to keep moving, imagining Burson's eyes burning into her pale back. She wondered if he still watched her or if he had already lost interest in the harmless spindly fluted girl, Belari's animal who hid in the closets and made the staff hunt high and low for the selfish mite.

Lidia shook her head in wonderment. Burson had not seen. Burson, for all his enhancements, was blind, so accustomed to inspiring terror that he could no longer distinguish fear from guilt.

A new gaggle of admirers swarmed around Belari, people who knew she was soon to be independent. Once the fluted girls floated on the market, Belari would be nearly as powerful as Vernon Weir, valuable not only for her own performances, but also for her stable of talent. Lidia moved to join her, the vial of liberation hidden in her fist.

Nia stood near Belari, talking to Claire Paranovis from SK Net. Nia nodded graciously at whatever the woman was saying, acting as Belari had trained them: always polite, never ruffled, always happy to talk, nothing to hide, but stories to tell. That was how you handled the media. If you kept them full, they never looked deeper. Nia looked comfortable in her role.

For a moment, Lidia felt a pang of regret at what she was about to do, then she was beside Belari, and Belari was smiling and introducing her to the men and women who surrounded her with fanatic affection. Mgumi Story. Kim Song Lee. Maria Blyst. Takashi Ghandi. More and more names, the global fraternity of media elites.

Lidia smiled and bowed while Belari fended off their proffered hands of congratulation, protecting her delicate investment. Lidia performed as she had been trained, but in her hand the vial lay sweaty, a small jewel of power and destiny. Stephen had been right. The small only controlled their own termination, sometimes not even that. Lidia watched the guests take slices of Stephen, commenting on his sweetness. Sometimes, not even that.

She turned from the crowd of admirers and drew a strawberry from the pyramids of fruit on the refreshment table. She dipped it in cream and rolled it in sugar, tasting the mingled flavors. She selected another strawberry, red and tender between her spidery fingers, a sweet medium for a bitter freedom earned.

With her thumb, she popped the tiny cork out of the vial and sprinkled amber jewels on the lush berry. She wondered if it would hurt, or if it would be quick. It hardly mattered, soon she would be free. She would cry out and fall to the floor and the guests would step back, stunned at Belari's loss. Belari would be humiliated, and more important, would lose the value of the fluted twins. Vernon Weir's lecherous hands would hold her once again.

Lidia gazed at the tainted strawberry. Sweet, Lidia thought. Death should be sweet. She saw Belari watching her, smiling fondly, no doubt happy to see another as addicted to sweets as she. Lidia smiled inwardly, pleased that Belari would see the moment of her rebellion. She raised the strawberry to her lips.

Suddenly a new inspiration whispered in her ear.

An inch from death, Lidia paused, then turned and held out the strawberry to her patron.

She offered the berry as obeisance, with the humility of a creature utterly owned. She bowed her head and proffered the strawberry in the palm of her pale hand, bringing forth all her skill, playing the loyal servant desperately eager to please. She held her breath, no longer aware of the room around her. The guests and conversations all had disappeared. Everything had gone silent.

There was only Belari and the strawberry and the frozen moment of delicious possibility.

A Study in Emerald
Neil Gaiman

I. The New Friend.

***Fresh* From Their Stupendous European
Tour**, where they performed before several
of the CROWNED HEADS OF EUROPE,
garnering their *plaudits* and *praise* with
magnificent dramatic performances, com-
bining both COMEDY and TRAGEDY, the
Strand Players wish to make it known that
they shall be appearing at the *Royal Court
Theatre, Drury Lane*, for a LIMITED
ENGAGEMENT in April, at which they will
present *"My Look-Alike Brother Tom!" "The
Littlest Violet-Seller"* and *"The Great Old
Ones Come,"* (this last an Historical Epic of
Pageantry and Delight); each an *entire play*
in one act! Tickets are available now from
the Box Office.

It is the immensity, I believe. The hugeness of things
below. The darkness of dreams.

But I am woolgathering. Forgive me. I am not a literary man.

I had been in need of lodgings. That was how I met him. I wanted someone to share the cost of rooms with me. We were introduced by a mutual acquaintance, in the chemical laboratories of St. Bart's. "You have been in Afghanistan, I perceive," that was what he said to me, and my mouth fell open and my eyes opened very wide.

"Astonishing," I said.

"Not really," said the stranger in the white lab-coat, who was to become my friend. "From the way you hold your arm, I see you have been wounded, and in a particular way. You have a deep tan. You also have a military bearing, and there are few enough places in the Empire that a military man can be both tanned and, given the nature of the injury to your shoulder and the traditions of the Afghan cave-folk, tortured."

Put like that, of course, it was absurdly simple. But then, it always was. I had been tanned nut-brown. And I had indeed, as he had observed, been tortured.

The gods and men of Afghanistan were savages, unwilling to be ruled from Whitehall or from Berlin or even from Moscow, and unprepared to see reason. I had been sent into those hills, attached to the _____th Regiment. As long as the fighting remained in the hills and mountains, we fought on an equal footing. When the skirmishes descended into the caves and the darkness then we found ourselves, as it were, out of our depth and in over our heads.

I shall not forget the mirrored surface of the underground lake, nor the thing that emerged from the lake, its eyes opening and closing, and the singing whispers that accompanied it as it rose, wreathing their way about it like the buzzing of flies bigger than worlds.

That I survived was a miracle, but survive I did,

and I returned to England with my nerves in shreds and tatters. The place that leech-like mouth had touched me was tattooed forever, frog-white, into the skin of my now-withered shoulder. I had once been a crack-shot. Now I had nothing, save a fear of the world-beneath-the-world akin to panic which meant that I would gladly pay sixpence of my army pension for a Hansom cab, rather than a penny to travel underground.

Still, the fogs and darknesses of London comforted me, took me in. I had lost my first lodgings because I screamed in the night. I had been in Afghanistan; I was there no longer.

"I scream in the night," I told him.

"I have been told that I snore," he said. "Also I keep irregular hours, and I often use the mantelpiece for target practice. I will need the sitting room to meet clients. I am selfish, private and easily bored. Will this be a problem?"

I smiled, and I shook my head, and extended my hand. We shook on it.

The rooms he had found for us, in Baker Street, were more than adequate for two bachelors. I bore in mind all my friend had said about his desire for privacy, and I forbore from asking what it was he did for a living. Still, there was much to pique my curiosity. Visitors would arrive at all hours, and when they did I would leave the sitting room and repair to my bedroom, pondering what they could have in common with my friend: the pale woman with one eye bone-white, the small man who looked like a commercial traveller, the portly dandy in his velvet jacket, and the rest. Some were frequent visitors, many others came only once, spoke to him, and left, looking troubled or looking satisfied.

He was a mystery to me.

We were partaking of one of our landlady's magnificent breakfasts one morning, when my friend rang the bell to summon that good lady. "There will be a gentleman joining us, in about four minutes," he said. "We will need another place at table."

"Very good," she said, "I'll put more sausages under the grill."

My friend returned to perusing his morning paper. I waited for an explanation with growing impatience. Finally, I could stand it no longer. "I don't understand. How could you know that in four minutes we would be receiving a visitor? There was no telegram, no message of any kind."

He smiled, thinly. "You did not hear the clatter of a brougham several minutes ago? It slowed as it passed us—obviously as the driver identified our door, then it sped up and went past, up into the Marylebone Road. There is a crush of carriages and taxicabs letting off passengers at the railway station and at the waxworks, and it is in that crush that anyone wishing to alight without being observed will go. The walk from there to here is but four minutes..."

He glanced at his pocket-watch, and as he did so I heard a tread on the stairs outside.

"Come in, Lestrade," he called. "The door is ajar, and your sausages are just coming out from under the grill."

A man I took to be Lestrade opened the door, then closed it carefully behind him. "I should not," he said, "But truth to tell, I have had not had a chance to break my fast this morning. And I could certainly do justice to a few of those sausages." He was the small man I had observed on several occasions previously, whose demeanour was that of a traveller in rubber novelties or patent nostrums.

My friend waited until our landlady had left the

room, before he said, "Obviously, I take it this is a matter of national importance."

"My stars," said Lestrade, and he paled. "Surely the word cannot be out already. Tell me it is not." He began to pile his plate high with sausages, kipper fillets, kedgeree and toast, but his hands shook, a little.

"Of course not," said my friend. "I know the squeak of your brougham wheels, though, after all this time: an oscillating G sharp above high C. And if Inspector Lestrade of Scotland Yard cannot publically be seen to come into the parlour of London's only consulting detective, yet comes anyway, and without having had his breakfast, then I know that this is not a routine case. Ergo, it involves those above us and is a matter of national importance."

Lestrade dabbed egg yolk from his chin with his napkin. I stared at him. He did not look like my idea of a police inspector, but then, my friend looked little enough like my idea of a consulting detective—whatever that might be.

"Perhaps we should discuss the matter privately," Lestrade said, glancing at me.

My friend began to smile, impishly, and his head moved on his shoulders as it did when he was enjoying a private joke. "Nonsense," he said. "Two heads are better than one. And what is said to one of us is said to us both."

"If I am intruding—" I said, gruffly, but he motioned me to silence.

Lestrade shrugged. "It's all the same to me," he said, after a moment. "If you solve the case then I have my job. If you don't, then I have no job. You use your methods, that's what I say. It can't make things any worse."

"If there's one thing that a study of history has

taught us, it is that things can always get worse," said my friend. "When do we go to Shoreditch?"

Lestrade dropped his fork. "This is too bad!" he exclaimed. "Here you were, making sport of me, when you know all about the matter! You should be ashamed—"

"No one has told me anything of the matter. When a police inspector walks into my room with fresh splashes of mud of that peculiar mustard yellow hue on his boots and trouser-legs, I can surely be forgiven for presuming that he has recently walked past the diggings at Hobbs Lane, in Shoreditch, which is the only place in London that particular mustard-coloured clay seems to be found."

Inspector Lestrade looked embarrassed. "Now you put it like that," he said, "It seems so obvious."

My friend pushed his plate away from him. "Of course it does," he said, slightly testily.

We rode to the East End in a cab. Inspector Lestrade had walked up to the Marylebone Road to find his brougham, and left us alone.

"So you are truly a consulting detective?" I said.

"The only one in London, or perhaps, the world," said my friend. "I do not take cases. Instead, I consult. Others bring me their insoluble problems, they describe them, and, sometimes, I solve them."

"Then those people who come to you…"

"Are, in the main, police officers, or are detectives themselves, yes."

It was a fine morning, but we were now jolting about the edges of the rookery of St Giles, that warren of thieves and cutthroats which sits on London like a cancer on the face of a pretty flower-seller, and the only light to enter the cab was dim and faint.

"Are you sure that you wish me along with you?"

In reply my friend stared at me without blinking.

"I have a feeling," he said. "I have a feeling that we were meant to be together. That we have fought the good fight, side by side, in the past or in the future, I do not know. I am a rational man, but I have learned the value of a good companion, and from the moment I clapped eyes on you, I knew I trusted you as well as I do myself. Yes. I want you with me."

I blushed, or said something meaningless. For the first time since Afghanistan, I felt that I had worth in the world.

2. The Room.

Victor's "*Vitae*"! An electrical fluid! Do your limbs and nether regions lack life? Do you look back on the days of your youth with envy? Are the pleasures of the flesh now buried and forgot? Victor's "*Vitae*" will bring life where life has long been lost: even the oldest warhorse can be a proud stallion once more! Bringing Life to the Dead: from an old family recipe and the best of modern science. To receive signed attestations of the efficacy of Victor's "*Vitae*" write to the V. von F. Company, 1b Cheap Street, London.

It was a cheap rooming house in Shoreditch. There was a policeman at the front door. Lestrade greeted him by name, and made to usher us in, and I was ready to enter, but my friend squatted on the doorstep, and pulled a magnifying glass from his coat pocket. He examined the mud on the wrought iron boot-scraper, prodding at it with his forefinger. Only when he was satisfied would he let us go inside.

We walked upstairs. The room in which the crime had been committed was obvious: it was flanked by two burly constables.

Lestrade nodded to the men, and they stood aside. We walked in.

I am not, as I said, a writer by profession, and I hesitate to describe that place, knowing that my words cannot do it justice. Still, I have begun this narrative, and I fear I must continue. A murder had been committed in that little bedsit. The body, what was left of it, was still there, on the floor. I saw it, but, at first, somehow, I did not see it. What I saw instead was what had sprayed and gushed from the throat and chest of the victim: in colour it ranged from bile-green to grass-green. It had soaked into the threadbare carpet and spattered the wallpaper. I imagined it for one moment the work of some hellish artist, who had decided to create a study in emerald.

After what seemed like a hundred years I looked down at the body, opened like a rabbit on a butcher's slab, and tried to make sense of what I saw. I removed my hat, and my friend did the same.

He knelt and inspected the body, inspecting the cuts and gashes. Then he pulled out his magnifying glass, and walked over to the wall, examining the gouts of drying ichor.

"We've already done that," said Inspector Lestrade.

"Indeed?" said my friend. "Then what did you make of this, then? I do believe it is a word."

Lestrade walked to the place my friend was standing, and looked up. There was a word, written in capitals, in green blood, on the faded yellow wallpaper, some little way above Lestrade's head. "*Rache...*?" said Lestrade, spelling it out. "Obviously he was going to write *Rachel*, but he was interrupted. So—we must look for a woman..."

My friend said nothing. He walked back to the corpse, and picked up its hands, one after the other. The fingertips were clean of ichor. "I think we have established that the word was not written by his Royal Highness—"

"What the Devil makes you say—?"

"My dear Lestrade. Please give me some credit for having a brain. The corpse is obviously not that of a man—the colour of his blood, the number of limbs, the eyes, the position of the face, all these things bespeak the blood royal. While I cannot say *which* royal line, I would hazard that he is an heir, perhaps…no, second to the throne,…in one of the German principalities."

"That is amazing." Lestrade hesitated, then he said, "This is Prince Franz Drago of Bohemia. He was here in Albion as a guest of Her Majesty Victoria. Here for a holiday and a change of air…"

"For the theatres, the whores and the gaming tables, you mean."

"If you say so." Lestrade looked put out. "Anyway, you've given us a fine lead with this Rachel woman. Although I don't doubt we would have found her on our own."

"Doubtless," said my friend.

He inspected the room further, commenting acidly several times that the police, with their boots had obscured footprints, and moved things that might have been of use to anyone attempting to reconstruct the events of the previous night.

Still, he seemed interested in a small patch of mud he found behind the door.

Beside the fireplace he found what appeared to be some ash or dirt.

"Did you see this?" he asked Lestrade.

"Her majesty's police," replied Lestrade, "tend not

to be excited by ash in a fireplace. It's where ash tends to be found." And he chuckled at that.

My friend took a pinch of the ash and rubbed between his fingers, then sniffed the remains. Finally, he scooped up what was left of the material and tipped it into a glass vial, which he stoppered and placed in an inner pocket of his coat.

He stood up. "And the body?"

Lestrade said, "The palace will send their own people."

My friend nodded at me, and together we walked to the door. My friend sighed. "Inspector. Your quest for Miss Rachel may prove fruitless. Among other things, *Rache* is a German word. It means *revenge*. Check your dictionary. There are other meanings."

We reached the bottom of the stair, and walked out onto the street. "You have never seen royalty before this morning, have you?" he asked. I shook my head. "Well, the sight can be unnerving, if you're unprepared. Why my good fellow—you are trembling!"

"Forgive me. I shall be fine in moments."

"Would it do you good to walk?" he asked, and I assented, certain that if I did not walk then I would begin to scream.

"West, then," said my friend, pointing to the dark tower of the Palace. And we commenced to walk.

"So," said my friend, after some time. "You have never had any personal encounters with any of the crowned heads of Europe?"

"No," I said.

"I believe I can confidently state that you shall," he told me. "And not with a corpse this time. Very soon."

"My dear fellow, whatever makes you believe—?"

In reply he pointed to a carriage, black-painted, that had pulled up fifty yards ahead of us. A man in a black top-hat and a greatcoat stood by the door, holding it open, waiting, silently. A coat of arms familiar to every child in Albion was painted in gold upon the carriage door.

"There are invitations one does not refuse," said my friend. He doffed his own hat to the footman, and I do believe that he was smiling as he climbed into the box-like space, and relaxed back into the soft leathery cushions.

When I attempted to speak with him during the journey to the Palace, he placed his finger over his lips. Then he closed his eyes and seemed sunk deep in thought. I, for my part, tried to remember what I knew of German royalty, but, apart from the Queen's consort, Prince Albert, being German, I knew little enough.

I put a hand in my pocket, pulled out a handful of coins—brown and silver, black and copper-green. I stared at the portrait stamped on each of them of our Queen, and felt both patriotic pride and stark dread. I told myself I had once been a military man, and a stranger to fear, and I could remember a time when this had been the plain truth. For a moment I remembered a time when I had been a crack-shot—even, I liked to think, something of a marksman—but my right hand shook as if it were palsied, and the coins jingled and chinked, and I felt only regret.

3. The Palace.

At Long Last **Doctor Henry Jekyll is proud to announce the general release of the world-renowned "Jekyll's Powders" for**

44

popular consumption. No longer the province of the privileged few. *Release the Inner You!* **For Inner and Outer Cleanliness! TOO MANY PEOPLE, both men and women, suffer from CONSTIPATION OF THE SOUL! Relief is immediate and cheap—with Jekyll's powders! (Available in Vanilla and Original Mentholatum Formulations.)**

The Queen's consort, Prince Albert, was a big man, with an impressive handlebar moustache and a receding hairline, and he was undeniably and entirely human. He met us in the corridor, nodded to my friend and to me, did not ask us for our names or offer to shake hands.

"The Queen is most upset," he said. He had an accent. He pronounced his S's as Z's: *Mozt. Upzet.* "Franz was one of her favourites. She has so many nephews. But he made her laugh so. You will find the ones who did this to him."

"I will do my best," said my friend.

"I have read your monographs," said Prince Albert. "It was I who told them that you should be consulted. I hope I did right."

"As do I," said my friend.

And then the great door was opened, and we were ushered into the darkness and the presence of the Queen.

She was called Victoria, because she had beaten us in battle, seven hundred years before, and she was called Gloriana, because she was glorious, and she was called the Queen, because the human mouth was not shaped to say her true name. She was huge, huger

45

than I had imagined possible, and she squatted in the shadows staring down at us, without moving.

Thizsz muzzst be zsolved. The words came from the shadows.

"Indeed, ma'am," said my friend.

A limb squirmed and pointed at me. *Zstepp forward.*

I wanted to walk. My legs would not move.

My friend came to my rescue then. He took me by the elbow and walked me toward her majesty.

Isz not to be afraid. Isz to be worthy. Isz to be a companion. That was what she said to me. Her voice was a very sweet contralto, with a distant buzz. Then the limb uncoiled and extended, and she touched my shoulder. There was a moment, but only a moment, of a pain deeper and more profound than anything I have ever experienced, and then it was replaced by a pervasive sense of well-being. I could feel the muscles in my shoulder relax, and, for the first time since Afghanistan, I was free from pain.

Then my friend walked forward. Victoria spoke to him, yet I could not hear her words; I wondered if they went, somehow, directly from her mind to his, if this was the Queen's Counsel I had read about in the histories. He replied aloud.

"Certainly, ma'am. I can tell you that there were two other men with your nephew in that room in Shoreditch, that night, the footprints were, although obscured, unmistakable." And then, "Yes. I understand.... I believe so.... Yes."

He was quiet when we left the palace, and said nothing to me as we rode back to Baker Street.

It was dark already. I wondered how long we had spent in the Palace.

Fingers of sooty fog twined across the road and the sky.

Upon our return to Baker Street, in the looking glass of my room, I observed that the frog-white skin across my shoulder had taken on a pinkish tinge. I hoped that I was not imagining it, that it was not merely the moonlight through the window.

4. The Performance.

LIVER COMPLAINTS?! BILIOUS ATTACKS?! NEURASTHENIC DISTURB-ANCES?! QUINSY?! ARTHRITIS?! These are just a handful of the *complaints* for which a professional exsanguination can be the *remedy*. In our offices we have sheaves of TESTIMONIALS which can be inspected by the public *at any time*. Do not put your health in the hands of *amateurs!!* We have been doing this for a very long time: V. TEPES–PROFESSIONAL EXSAN-GUINATOR. (Remember! It is pronounced *Tzsep-pesh!*) Romania, Paris, London, Whitby. *You've tried the rest–NOW TRY THE BEST!!*

That my friend was a master of disguise should have come as no surprise to me, yet surprise me it did. Over the next ten days a strange assortment of characters came in through our door in Baker Street—an elderly Chinese man, a young roué, a fat, red-haired woman of whose former profession there could be little doubt, and a venerable old buffer, his foot swollen and bandaged from gout. Each of them would walk into my friend's room, and, with a speed that would have done justice to a music-hall "quick change artist", my friend would walk out.

He would not talk about what he had been doing on these occasions, preferring to relax, staring off into space, occasionally making notations on any scrap of paper to hand, notations I found, frankly, incomprehensible. He seemed entirely preoccupied, so much so that I found myself worrying about his well-being. And then, late one afternoon, he came home dressed in his own clothes, with an easy grin upon his face, and he asked if I was interested in the theatre.

"As much as the next man," I told him.

"Then fetch your opera glasses," he told me. "We are off to Drury Lane."

I had expected a light opera, or something of the kind, but instead I found myself in what must have been the worst theatre in Drury Lane, for all that it had named itself after the royal court—and to be honest, it was barely in Drury Lane at all, being situated at the Shaftesbury Avenue end of the road, where the avenue approaches the Rookery of St. Giles. On my friend's advice I concealed my wallet, and, following his example, I carried a stout stick.

Once we were seated in the stalls (I had bought a threepenny orange from one of the lovely young women who sold them to the members of the audience, and I sucked it as we waited), my friend said, quietly, "You should only count yourself lucky that you did not need to accompany me to the gambling dens or the brothels. Or the madhouses–another place that Prince Franz delighted in visiting, as I have learned. But there was nowhere he went to more than once. Nowhere but–"

The orchestra struck up, and the curtain was raised. My friend was silent.

It was a fine enough show in its way: three one-act

plays were performed. Comic songs were sung between the acts. The leading man was tall, languid, and had a fine singing voice; the leading lady was elegant, and her voice carried through all the theatre; the comedian had a fine touch for patter songs.

The first play was a broad comedy of mistaken identities: the leading man played a pair of identical twins who had never met, but had managed, by a set of comical misadventures, each to find himself engaged to be married to the same young lady—who, amusingly, thought herself engaged to only one man. Doors swung open and closed as the actor changed from identity to identity.

The second play was a heartbreaking tale of an orphan girl who starved in the snow selling hothouse violets—her grandmother recognised her at the last, and swore that she was the babe stolen ten years back by bandits, but it was too late, and the frozen little angel breathed her last. I must confess I found myself wiping my eyes with my linen handkerchief more than once.

The performance finished with a rousing historical narrative: the entire company played the men and women of a village on the shore of the ocean, seven hundred years before our modern times. They saw shapes rising from the sea, in the distance. The hero joyously proclaimed to the villagers that these were the Old Ones whose coming was foretold, returning to us from R'lyeh, and from dim Carcosa, and from the plains of Leng, where they had slept, or waited, or passed out the time of their death. The comedian opined that the other villagers had all been eating too many pies and drinking too much ale, and they were imagining the shapes. A portly gentleman playing a priest of the Roman God tells the villagers that the shapes in the sea were monsters and demons, and must be destroyed.

At the climax, the hero beat the priest to death with his own crucifer, and prepared to welcome Them as They came. The heroine sang a haunting aria, whilst, in an astonishing display of magic-lantern trickery, it seemed as if we saw Their shadows cross the sky at the back of the stage: the Queen of Albion herself, and the Black One of Egypt (in shape almost like a man), followed by the Ancient Goat, Parent to a Thousand, Emperor of all China, and the Czar Unanswerable, and He Who Presides over the New World, and the White Lady of the Antarctic Fastness, and the others. And as each shadow crossed the stage, or appeared to, from out of every throat in the gallery came, unbidden, a mighty "Huzzah!" until the air itself seemed to vibrate. The moon rose in the painted sky, and then, at its height, in one final moment of theatrical magic, it turned from a pallid yellow, as it was in the old tales, to the comforting crimson of the moon that shines down upon us all today.

The members of the cast took their bows and their curtain calls to cheers and laughter, and the curtain fell for the last time, and the show was done."

There," said my friend. "What did you think?"

"Jolly, jolly good," I told him, my hands sore from applauding.

"Stout fellow," he said, with a smile. "Let us go backstage."

We walked outside and into an alley beside the theatre, to the stage door, where a thin woman with a wen on her cheek knitted busily. My friend showed her a visiting card, and she directed us into the building and up some steps to a small communal dressing room.

Oil lamps and candles guttered in front of smeared

looking-glasses, and men and women were taking off their make-up and costumes with no regard to the proprieties of gender. I averted my eyes. My friend seemed unperturbed. "Might I talk to Mr Vernet?" he asked, loudly.

A young woman who had played the heroine's best friend in the first play, and the saucy innkeeper's daughter in the last, pointed us to the end of the room. "Sherry! Sherry Vernet!" she called.

The young man who stood up in response was lean; less conventionally handsome than he had seemed from the other side of the footlights. He peered at us quizzically. "I do not believe I have had the pleasure...?"

"My name is Henry Camberley," said my friend, drawling his speech somewhat. "You may have heard of me."

"I must confess that I have not had that privilege," said Vernet.

My friend presented the actor with an engraved card.

The man looked at the card with unfeigned interest. "A theatrical promoter? From the New World? My, my. And this is...?" He looked at me.

"This is a friend of mine, Mister Sebastian. He is not of the profession."

I muttered something about having enjoyed the performance enormously, and shook hands with the actor.

My friend said, "Have you ever visited the New World?"

"I have not yet had that honour," admitted Vernet, "although it has always been my dearest wish."

"Well, my good man," said my friend, with the easy informality of a New Worlder. "Maybe you'll get your wish. That last play. I've never seen anything like it. Did you write it?"

"Alas, no. The playwright is a good friend of mine. Although I devised the mechanism of the magic lantern shadow show. You'll not see finer on the stage today."

"Would you give me the playwright's name? Perhaps I should speak to him directly, this friend of yours."

Vernet shook his head. "That will not be possible, I am afraid. He is a professional man, and does not wish his connection with the stage publically to be known."

"I see." My friend pulled a pipe from his pocket, and put it in his mouth. Then he patted his pockets. "I am sorry," he began. "I have forgotten to bring my tobacco pouch."

"I smoke a strong black shag," said the actor, "but if you have no objection—"

"None!" said my friend, heartily. "Why, I smoke a strong shag myself," and he filled his pipe with the actor's tobacco, and the two men puffed away, while my friend described a vision he had for a play that could tour the cities of the New World, from Manhattan Island all the way to the furthest tip of the continent in the distant south. The first act would be the last play we had seen. The rest of the play might perhaps tell of the dominion of the Old Ones over humanity and its gods, perhaps telling what might have happened if people had had no Royal Families to look up to—a world of barbarism and darkness—"But your mysterious professional man would be the play's author, and what occurs would be his alone to decide," interjected my friend. "Our drama would be his. But I can guarantee you audiences beyond your imaginings, and a significant share of the takings at the door. Let us say fifty per-cent!"

"This is most exciting," said Vernet. "I hope it will not turn out to have been a pipe-dream!"

"No sir, it shall not!" said my friend, puffing on his own pipe, chuckling at the man's joke. "Come to my rooms in Baker Street tomorrow morning, after breakfast-time, say at ten, in company with your author friend, and I shall have the contracts drawn up and waiting."

With that the actor clambered up onto his chair and clapped his hands for silence. "Ladies and Gentlemen of the company, I have an announcement to make," he said, his resonant voice filling the room. "This gentleman is Henry Camberley, the theatrical promoter, and he is proposing to take us across the Atlantic Ocean, and on to fame and fortune."

There were several cheers, and the comedian said, "Well, it'll make a change from herrings and pickled-cabbage," and the company laughed.

And it was to the smiles of all of them that we walked out of the theatre and out onto the fog-wreathed streets.

"My dear fellow," I said. "Whatever was—"

"Not another word," said my friend. "There are many ears in the city."

And not another word was spoken until we had hailed a cab, and clambered inside, and were rattling up the Charing Cross Road.

And even then, before he said anything, my friend took his pipe from his mouth, and emptied the half-smoked contents of the bowl into a small tin. He pressed the lid onto the tin, and placed it into his pocket.

"There," he said. "That's the Tall Man found, or I'm a Dutchman. Now, we just have to hope that the cupidity and the curiosity of the Limping Doctor proves enough to bring him to us tomorrow morning."

"The Limping Doctor?"

My friend snorted. "That is what I have been calling him. It was obvious, from footprints and much else besides, when we saw the Prince's body, that two men had been in that room that night: a tall man, who, unless I miss my guess, we have just encountered, and a smaller man with a limp, who eviscerated the prince with a professional skill that betrays the medical man."

"A doctor?"

"Indeed. I hate to say this, but it is my experience that when a Doctor goes to the bad, he is a fouler and darker creature than the worst cut-throat. There was Huston, the acid-bath man, and Campbell, who brought the procrustean bed to Ealing..." and he carried on in a similar vein for the rest of our journey.

The cab pulled up beside the kerb. "That'll be one and tenpence," said the cabbie. My friend tossed him a florin, which he caught, and tipped to his ragged tall hat. "Much obliged to you both," he called out, as the horse clopped out into the fog.

We walked to our front door. As I unlocked the door, my friend said, "Odd. Our cabbie just ignored that fellow on the corner."

"They do that at the end of a shift," I pointed out.

"Indeed they do," said my friend.

I dreamed of shadows that night, vast shadows that blotted out the sun, and I called out to them in my desperation, but they did not listen.

5. *The Skin and the Pit.*

Inspector Lestrade was the first to arrive.

"You have posted your men in the street?" asked my friend.

"I have," said Lestrade. "With strict orders to let anyone in who comes, but to arrest anyone trying to leave."

"And you have handcuffs with you?"

In reply, Lestrade put his hand in his pocket, and jangled two pairs of cuffs, grimly.

"Now sir," he said. "While we wait, why do you not tell me what we are waiting for?"

My friend pulled his pipe out of his pocket. He did not put it in his mouth, but placed it on the table in front of him. Then he took the tin from the night before, and a glass vial I recognised as the one he had had in the room in Shoreditch.

"There," he said. "The coffin-nail, as I trust it shall prove, for our Master Vernet." He paused. Then he took out his pocket watch, laid it carefully on the table. "We have several minutes before they arrive." He turned to me. "What do you know of the Restorationists?"

"Not a blessed thing," I told him.

Lestrade coughed. "If you're talking about what I

think you're talking about," he said, "perhaps we should leave it there. Enough's enough."

"Too late for that," said my friend. "For there are those who do not believe that the coming of the Old Ones was the fine thing we all know it to be. Anarchists to a man, they would see the old ways restored—mankind in control of its own destiny, if you will."

"I will not hear this sedition spoken," said Lestrade. "I must warn you—"

"I must warn you not to be such a fathead," said my friend." Because it was the Restorationists that killed Prince Franz Drago. They murder, they kill, in a vain effort to force our masters to leave us alone in the darkness. The Prince was killed by a *rache*—it's an old term for a hunting dog, Inspector, as you would know if you had looked in a dictionary. It also means *revenge*. And the hunter left his signature on the wallpaper in the murder-room, just as an artist might sign a canvas. But he was not the one who killed the Prince."

"The Limping Doctor!" I exclaimed.

"Very good. There was a tall man there that night—I could tell his height, for the word was written at eye level. He smoked a pipe—the ash and dottle sat unburnt in the fireplace, and he had tapped out his pipe with ease on the mantel, something a smaller man would not have done. The tobacco was an unusual blend of shag. The footprints in the room had, for the most part been almost obliterated by your men, but there were several clear prints behind the door and by the window. Someone had waited there: a smaller man from his stride, who put his weight on his right leg. On the path outside I had several clear prints, and the different colours of clay on the bootscraper outside gave me more information: a tall

56

man, who had accompanied the Prince into those rooms, and had, later, walked out. Waiting for them to arrive was the man who had sliced up the Prince so impressively..."

Lestrade made an uncomfortable noise that did not quite become a word.

"I have spent many days retracing the movements of his highness. I went from gambling hell to brothel to dining den to madhouse looking for our pipe-smoking man and his friend. I made no progress until I thought to check the newspapers of Bohemia, searching for a clue to the Prince's recent activities there, and in them I learned that an English Theatrical Troupe had been in Prague last month, and had performed before Prince Franz Drago..."

"Good lord," I said. "So that Sherry Vernet fellow..."

"Is a Restorationist. Exactly."

I was shaking my head in wonder at my friend's intelligence and skills of observation, when there was a knock on the door.

"This will be our quarry!" said my friend. "Careful now!"

Lestrade put his hand deep into his pocket, where I had no doubt he kept a pistol. He swallowed, nervously.

My friend called out, "Please, come in!"

The door opened.

It was not Vernet, nor was it a Limping Doctor. It was one of the young street Arabs who earn a crust running errands—"in the employ of Messrs. Street and Walker", as we used to say when I was young. "Please sirs," he said. "Is there a Mister Henry Camberley here? I was asked by a gentleman to deliver a note."

"I'm he," said my friend. "And for a sixpence, what

can you tell me about the gentleman who gave you the note?"

The young lad, who volunteered that his name was Wiggins, bit the sixpence before making it vanish, and then told us that the cheery cove who gave him the note was on the tall side, with dark hair, and, he added, he had been smoking a pipe.

I have the note here, and take the liberty of transcribing it.

My Dear Sir,

I do not address you as Henry Camberley, for it is a name to which you have no claim. I am surprised that you did not announce yourself under your own name, for it is a fine one, and one that does you credit. I have read a number of your papers, when I have been able to obtain them. Indeed, I corresponded with you quite profitably two years ago about certain theoretical anomalies in your paper on the Dynamics of an Asteroid.

I was amused to meet you, yesterday evening. A few tips which might save you bother in times to come, in the profession you currently follow. Firstly, a pipe-smoking man might possibly have a brand-new, unused pipe in his pocket, and no tobacco, but it is exceedingly unlikely—at least as unlikely as a theatrical promoter with no idea of the usual customs of recompense on a tour, who is accompanied by a taciturn ex-army officer (Afghanistan, unless I miss my guess). *Incidentally, while you are correct that the streets of London have ears, it might also behoove you in future not to take the first cab that comes along. Cab-drivers have ears too, if they choose to use them.*

You are certainly correct in one of your suppositions: it was indeed I who lured the half-blood creature back to the room in Shoreditch.

If it is any comfort to you, having learned a little of his recreational predilections, I had told him I had procured for him a girl, abducted from a convent in Cornwall where she had never seen a man, and that it would only take his touch, and the sight of his face, to tip her over into a perfect madness.

Had she existed, he would have feasted on her madness while he took her, like a man sucking the flesh from a ripe peach leaving nothing behind but the skin and the pit. I have seen them do this. I have seen them do far worse. And it is not the price we pay for peace and prosperity. It is too great a price for that.

The good doctor—who believes as I do, and who did indeed write our little performance, for he has some crowd-pleasing skills—was waiting for us, with his knives.

I send this note, not as a catch-me-if-you-can taunt, for we are gone, the estimable doctor and I, and you shall not find us, but to tell you that it was good to feel that, if only for a moment, I had a worthy adversary. Worthier by far than inhuman creatures from beyond the Pit.

I fear the Strand Players will need to find themselves a new leading man.

I will not sign myself Vernet, and until the hunt is done and the world restored, I beg you to think of me simply as,

Rache.

Inspector Lestrade ran from the room, calling to his men. They made young Wiggins take them to the place where the man had given him the note, for all the world as if Vernet the actor would be waiting there for them, a-smoking of his pipe. From the window we watched them run, my friend and I, and we shook our heads.

"They will stop and search all the trains leaving London, all the ships leaving Albion for Europe or the New World," said my friend, "Looking for a tall man, and his companion, a smaller, thickset medical man, with a slight limp. They will close the ports. Every way out of the country will be blocked."

"Do you think they will catch him, then?"

My friend shook his head. "I may be wrong," he said, "But I would wager that he and his friend are even now only a mile or so away, in the rookery of St. Giles, where the police will not go except by the dozen. And they will hide up there until the hue and cry have died away. And then they will be about their business."

"What makes you say that?"

"Because," said my friend, "If our positions were

reversed, it is what I would do. You should burn the note, by the way."

I frowned. "But surely it's evidence," I said.

"It's seditionary nonsense," said my friend.

And I should have burned it. Indeed, I told Lestrade I *had* burned it, when he returned, and he congratulated me on my good sense. Lestrade kept his job, and Prince Albert wrote a note to my friend congratulating him on his deductions, while regretting that the perpetrator was still at large.

They have not yet caught Sherry Vernet, or whatever his name really is, nor was any trace of his murderous accomplice, tentatively identified as a former military surgeon named John (or perhaps James) Watson. Curiously, it was revealed that he had also been in Afghanistan. I wonder if we ever met.

My shoulder, touched by the Queen, continues to improve, the flesh fills and it heals. Soon I shall be a dead-shot once more.

One night when we were alone, several months ago, I asked my friend if he remembered the correspondence referred to in the letter from the man who signed himself *Rache*. My friend said that he remembered it well, and that "Sigerson" (for so the actor had called himself then, claiming to be an Icelander) had been inspired by an equation of my friend's to suggest some wild theories furthering the relationship between mass, energy and the hypothetical speed of light. "Nonsense, of course," said my friend, without smiling. "But inspired and dangerous nonsense nonetheless."

The palace eventually sent word that the Queen was pleased with my friend's accomplishments in the case, and there the matter has rested.

I doubt my friend will leave it alone, though; it will not be over until one of them has killed the other.

I kept the note. I have said things in this retelling of events that are not to be said. If I were a sensible man I would burn all these pages, but then, as my friend taught me, even ashes can give up their secrets. Instead, I shall place these papers in a strongbox at my bank with instructions that the box may not be opened until long after anyone now living is dead. Although, in the light of the recent events in Russia, I fear that day may be closer than any of us would care to think.

S_____ M____ Major (Ret'd)
Baker Street,
London, New Albion, 1881.

Flowers from Alice
Cory Doctorow and Charles Stross

I don't know why I invited Al to my wedding. Nostalgia, maybe. Residual lust. She was the first girl I ever kissed, after all. You never forget your first. I couldn't help but turn my head when round-hipped, tall girls with pageboy hair walked by, hunched over their own breasts in terminal pubescent embarrassment, awkward and athletic at the same time. You don't get much of that these days outside of Amish country, no parent would choose to have a kid who was quite so visibly strange as Al had been as a teenager, but there were still examples of the genre to be had, if you looked hard enough, and they stirred something within me.

I couldn't forget Al, though it had been twenty years since that sweet and sloppy kiss on the beach, ten years since I'd run into her last, so severely post-that I hardly recognized her. Wasn't a week went by that she didn't wander through my imagination, evoking a lip-quirk that wasn't a smile by about three notches. My to-be recognized it; it drove her up the wall, and she let me know about it during post-coital self-criticism sessions.

It was a very wrong idea to invite Al to the wedding, but the wedding itself was a bad idea, to be perfectly frank. And I won't take all the blame for it, since Al decided to show up, after all, if "decided" can be applied to someone as post- as she (s/he?) (they?) [(s|t)/he(y)?] was by then. But one morning as we sat at our pre-nuptial breakfast table, my to-be and me, and spooned marmalade on our muffins and watched the hummingbirds visit the feeder outside our nook's window, one morning as we sat naked and sated and sticky with marmalade and other fluids, one morning I looked into my fiancee's eyes and I prodded at the phone tattooed on my wrist and dialed a directory server and began to recite the facts of Al's life into my hollow tooth in full earshot of my lovely lovely intended until the directory had enough information to identify Al from among all the billions of humans and trillions of multiplicitous post-humans that it knew about and the phone rang in my hollow tooth and I was talking to Al.

"Al," I said, "Alice? Is that you? It's Cyd!"

There was no sound on the end of the line because when you're as self-consciously post- as Al, you don't make unintentional sound, so there was no sharp intake of breath or other cue to her reaction to this voice from her past, but she answered finally and said, "Cyd, wonderful, it's been too long," and the voice was warm and nuanced and rich as any human voice but more so, tailored for the strengths and acoustics of my skull and mouth which she had no doubt induced from the characteristics of the other end of the conversation. "You're getting married, huh? She sounds wonderful. And you, you're doing well too. Well! I should say so. Cyd, it's good to hear from you. Of course one of me will come to your wedding. Can we help? Say we can! I, oh, the caterer, no, you don't want to use that caterer, she's booked for another wedding the day before and a wedding *and* a Bar

Mitzvah the day after, you know, so, please, let me help! I'm sending over a logistics plan now, I just evolved it for you, it's very optimal,

And my to-be shook her head and answered *her* phone and said, "Why hello, Alice! No, Cyd sprang this on me without warning – one of his little surprises. Yes, I can see you're talking to him, too. Of course, I'd love to see the plans, it was so good of you to come up with them. Yes, yes, of course. And you'll bring a date, won't you?"

Meanwhile, in my tooth, Al's still nattering on, "You don't mind, do you? I respawned and put in a call to your beautiful lady. I'm resynching with the copy every couple instants, so I can tell you we're getting along famously, Cyd, you always did have such great taste but you're *hopeless* with logistics. I see the job is going well, I knew you'd be an excellent polemicist, and it's such a vital function in your social mileu!"

I didn't get more than ten more words in, but the society of Al kept the conversation up for me. I never got bored, of course, because she had a trillion instances of me simulated somewhere in her being, and she tried a trillion different conversational gambits on all of them and chose the ones that evoked the optimal response, fine tuning as she monitored my breathing and vitals over the phone. She had access to every nuance of my life, of course, there's no privacy with the post-humans, so there was hardly any catching up to do.

I didn't expect her to show up on my door that afternoon.

My betrothed took it very well. She was working in her study on her latest morph porn, down on the ground floor, and I was upstairs with my neurofeedback machine, working up a suitable head of bile before writing my column. She beat me to the door.

"Who is it?" I called irritably, responding more to the draft around my ankles than to any conscious stimulus. No reply. I unplugged myself, swore quietly, then closed my eyes and began to ramp down the anger. I found people responded all wrong to me when I was mad. "Who?" I called again.

"Cyd! How cozy, what a great office!" A flock of silver lighter-than-air golf-balls caromed off the doorframe and ricocheted around me—one softly pinged me on the end of the nose with a warm, tingling shock. It smelled utterly unlike a machine: human and slightly flowery—

"Al?" I asked.

The ball inflated, stretching its endoskeleton into a transducer surface. The others homed in on it, merging almost instantly into an inflatabubble that suddenly flashed into a hologram of Al as I'd last seen her in the flesh—only slightly tuned, her back straight and proud, her breasts fetchingly exposed by a Cretan-style dress that had been in fashion around the time we split up. "Hiya, Cydonia!" That grin, those sturdy, well-engineered teeth, and a sudden flashback to a meeting in a mall all those years ago. "Don't worry I'm downstairs talking to your love wearing the real primary-me body, this is just a remote, *hey* I *love* the antique render farm but isn't it a bit out of tune? Please, let me to fix it!"

"Ung," I said, shivering with fright, guts turning to jelly, and hackles rising—exactly the wrong reaction and deeply embarrassing, but there's a *reason* I work behind a locked door most of the time. "Gimme five."

"How kawaii!" Al burst apart into half a dozen

beachball-sized balloons and bounced out onto the landing. "See you downstairs!"

I just stood there, muscles twitching in an adrenalin-induced haze as I wrestled to get my artificially induced anger under control. It took almost a minute, during which time I forced myself to listen as a series of loud thumping noises came from the hall downstairs and I heard the sound of voices, indistinct, through the open doors: my fiancee's low and calm, and Al as enthusiastic and full of laughter as a puppy in a mid-belly-rub. Al had left an after-scent behind, one that gave me dizzying flashbacks to teenage sexual experimentation—my first sex change, Al's first tongue job—and left me weak at the knees in an after-shock of memories. It's funny how after the fire's burned down all you can remember are the ashes of conflict, the arguments that drove you apart: until your ex shows up and reminds you what you've lost. Although knowing Al it might just as well be a joke as deliberate.

Presently I went downstairs, to find the door open and a couple of huge crates sitting in the front yard—too big to come through the door without telling the house to grow a service entrance. I followed the voices to the living room, where my fiancee was curled up in our kidney-shaped sofa, opposite Al, who had somehow draped herself across the valuable antique tube TV, and was reminiscing about nothing in particular at length. Her main incarnation looked alarmingly substantial, nothing like the soap-bubbles except for a slightly pearlescent lustre to her skin. "You're so lucky with Cyd! So to speak. He's such a stable, consistent, unassuming primal male pre-post-! I won't say I envy you but you really need to make more of your big day together, I promise you, you won't regret it. Remember when we spoofed out from under our teachers one day and we blew a month's allowance at the distraction center and he said, Al, if I ever get—"

"Hello there," I said, nodding to Al, civil enough now my autonomic nervous system wasn't convinced I was under attack. "Do you metabolize? If so, can I offer you anything? Coffee, perhaps? What have you been up to all this time?" I barely registered my fiancee's fixed, glassy-eyed stare, which was glued to Al's left nipple ring like a target designator, or the way she was twitching her left index finger as if it was balanced on the hi-hat of a sidearm controller. These were normally bad signs, but right then I was still reeling from the shocking smell of Al's skin. I know it was all part of her self-rep, but how could I possibly have forgotten it?

"Cyd!" She was off the television and across the room like the spirit of electricity, and grabbed me in a very physical bearhug. The nipple ring was hard, and even though her body wasn't made of CHON any more she felt startlingly real. She grinned at me with insane joy. "Whee! Three hundred and twenty seven million eight hundred and ninety six thousand one hundred and four, five, six, seconds, and you *still* feel good to grab!" Over her shoulder, "you're a *very lucky person* to be marrying him, you know. Have you made up your mind what to do about are you doing about the catering? Did you like my suggestion for the after-banquet orgy? What about the switch fetish session? You are going to be so *good* together!"

My affianced had a strained smile that I recognized as the mirror image of my own bared-teeth snarl when someone interrupted my work. As usual, her face was reflecting my own mood, and I stared at her tits until I had the rhythm of her breath down, then matched it with my own, slowing down, bringing her down to the calm that I was forcing on myself. "Hey, Al," I said, patting her shoulder awkwardly.

"Oh, I'm doing it again, aren't I? Hang on, let me underclock a little." She closed her eyes and slowly touched her index finger to her nose. "Muuuuuch better," she said. "Sorry, I'm not really fit for human company these days. I've been running at very high-clockspeed lately. Order makes order, you know—I'm going to wind up faster than entropy winds down and overtake thermodynamics.2 if I can. I'm about a week away from entangling enough particles in Alpha Centauri to instantiate there, then I'm going to eat the star and, whee, look out chaos!"

"Ambitious," my betrothed said. I liked her absence of ambition, usually—so refreshing amid the grandiose schemes of the fucking post-s. "You're *certainly* *very* kind to have done so much thinking about our little wedding, but we were planning to keep it all simple, you know. Just friends and family, a little dancing. Rather retro, but..." She trailed off, with a meaningful glance at me.

"But that's how we want it," I finished, taking my cue. I moved over the sofa and sat by my promised and rubbed her tiny little feet, the way she liked. Human-human contact. Who needs any more than this?

She jerked her feet away and sat up. "You two haven't seen each other in so long, why don't I leave you to catch up?" she said, in a tone that let me know that I had better object.

"No no no," I said. "No. Work to do, too much work to do. Deadlines, deadlines, deadlines." I was uncomfortably aware of the heat radiating off Al's avatar, a quintillion smart motes clustered together, pliable, fuckable computation, the grinding microfriction of which was keeping her at about three degrees over blood-temp. "So good to see you, Al. What we'll do, we'll look over these plans and suggestions and whatnot, such very good stuff I'm so sure, and we'll get in touch with you about helping out, right?"

She beamed and wedged herself onto the sofa between us, arms draped over our shoulders. "Of course, of course. You two, oh, I'm so happy for you. Perfect for each other!" She gave my intended a kiss on the cheek, then gave me one that landed close enough to my earlobe to tickle the little hairs there. The kiss was fragrant and wet as the first one, and I heard faint, crashing surf. It was only after she'd moved back (having darted her tongue out and squirmed it to the skin under my beard) that I realized she'd been generating it. I crossed my legs and tried furiously to think my erection away.

She bounded out the door and then stood on our lawn, amidst the crates. She gestured at them, "They're a wedding present!" she called, loud enough to rattle the picture-window. Our neighbor across the street scowled at her from his attic, where he painted still-lives of decaying fruit ten hours a day. "Enjoy!"

"Well, she hasn't changed," my love said, scowling. "You seemed very happy to see her again."

"Yes," I said, awkwardly, jiggling my crossed foot. "Well. I guess I'll try to get her gifts inside before it rains or something, right? Why don't you go back to work?"

"Yes," she said. "I'll go back to work. I'm sure the gifts are lovely. Call me once they're unpacked, all right?"

"Sure," I said, and jiggled my foot.

I considered ordering the house to carve a service door, but decided at length that peristalsis was the optimal solution—otherwise, I'd still have to find a

way to drag the goddamned crates into the house. I
shoved all our living-room furniture into a corner and
went down to the cellar to scoop up the endless
meters of the house trunk that we'd fabbed to help
us move in, but hadn't had a use for since. I spread
it out along the lawn, stretching its mouth-membrane
overtop of the largest of the three crates, then pulled
the other end through the picture window. I retreated
to the living-room and used a broom-handle to tickle
the gag-reflex at the near-end of the tube and then
leapt clear as the tube shudderingly vomited a gush
of dust over the floor. I hit the scrubber-plate with
my fist and escaped out the front door before I'd
gotten more than a lungful of crud, chased by convec-
tion currents that cycled all the room's air towards
the filters in the baseboards.

Out on the lawn, the house trunk was slowly digest-
ing the crate, gorging it upwards to the picture-window. Once there was enough slack on the lawn-end,
I stretched the twitching membrane overtop of the
second crate, and then the third. The house trunk's
muscular digestion slowed, but continued, inexorably,
moving the trunks living-room-wards.

I met the first trunk with a crowbar and set to work
on it, surprised as ever at the fabulous working order
of my biceps and back muscles. Sedentary life will
never get the best of me, not so long as I am master
of my own flesh, ordering it to stay limber and strong.

The crate was ready to fall to pieces just as the
second box was eructing onto the living-room floor.
I guided number two to a clear spot, then knocked
out the last fasteners on number one and slid the
panels aside.

It was a dining-room table, handsome and spare,
made from black oak, with a fine grain that was
brought out by a clear varnish. It had an air of an-

tiquity, but it was light enough to move with one hand. Subsequent boxes disgorged four matching chairs and a sideboard.

I reversed the house trunk and evacuated the crate remnants back onto the lawn, where I decided I'd deal with them later.

I dialed my fiancee's number and waited for her to answer. "I've unpacked," I said. "Come up and see."

A couple of minutes later she poked her head round the door and sniffed. "Smells like trouble," she remarked. "That's a lot of furniture. What does she do, breed the stuff?"

"I don't know." I rubbed the sideboard. "Hey, you. Wake up. Tell me about yourself."

"Cyd?" said the table, hesitantly. "Is it lunch time already?" It spoke with Al's voice.

The chairs began to climb out of their crates and shake off the packing fuzz; one by one they gathered around the table and hunkered down. "What do you feel like today?" asked Al-the-table. "How about a light Mediterranean salad, rocket and tomatoes and mozarella with a drizzle of balsamic vinegar and extra-virgin olive oil? Or maybe my special wasabi and eggplant nori?"

Herself yanked one of the chairs out from the table and sat on it, hard. "I'll have a plate of tacos and salsa," she said, glaring at the sideboard. "And make it snappish."

The table extruded cutlery—dumb, old-fashioned silver, no less—and the sideboard sidled up to her and offered a plate. She took it with poor grace and began to pick at her food. "I don't like the style," she declared. "This old antique shit went out with the history of the month club. Gimme some Nazi kitsch any day of the week."

"Sure!" Trilled Al's instantiation, and the table sprouted swastikas.

"I can do without lunch," I said. "I'm not really feeling hungry."

"Oh, for fuck's sake." My fiancee looked disgusted and shoved the plate away. "You like this furniture so much, *you* do the washing up." She took a deep breath. "Been meaning to talk to you, anyway."

"Anything in particular, love?" I asked.

"Yeah." She stood up abruptly. "It can wait. I was just thinking about a little recreational surgery, is all."

Recreational surgery? "Uh, what kind?" I asked. "We're getting married in just six days, now. Will it take long? You can't do anything substantial like a set of extra arms – you'd need to alter your dress, wouldn't you?"

"Oh, nothing much." She mimed an elaborate yawn. "I'm just thinking it's been too long since I wore the balls in this household."

"Hey, I'm keeping mine!" I said. "Anyway, isn't it traditional for a bride to be female at the altar?"

"Oh yes," she agreed, nodding brightly. "The bride's supposed to be a young female virgin if she's going to wear white! That's me all over." She giggled alarmingly, jumped up onto the tabletop, and spread her legs wide. "Fuck it, come here, Cyd. Right now, on the table. See this? Young? Virgin? You be the judge!"

Afterwards, as we lay in the accomodating depressions Al-table had generated for us, my fiancee trailed a lazy tongue along my throat. "All right, then," she said. "If you want a girl-bride, I'll stay female. It's only a week, after all."

I propped myself up on one elbow. "Thanks, honey," I said, gently cupping one of her breasts. "It's just, you know. This wedding's going to be complicated enough as it is. We don't need more changes at the last minute."

"I know," she said. "Well, back to work."

The writing went well that afternoon. I worked up a really good head of rage and ranted into my phone for three hours, watching the words scroll along the ticker at the bottom of my field of vision. When I was done, I did an hour of yoga, feeling the anger ease out of my muscles as I moved slowly from posture to posture.

I did a fullscreen display of the text, read it back, tweaked a few phrases and fired it off to my blog. Another week's work finished.

I headed down to the living room. The Al-dinette had neatly arranged itself. "Good column," it said to me. "You've really found a niche."

"How are you powering yourself?" I said.

"You'd be surprised at how little draw an instantiation pulls. Your romp with your girl generated enough kinetic to power me for a month. If I need more, there's always photovoltaic and a little fusion—I don't like to use nuclear, though. Splitting my atoms reducing my computational capacity; enough of that and I'd be too stupid to talk in a couple centuries."

"Jesus," I said. "Well, it was a very...*thoughtful*...gift, Al, thank you."

"Oh, don't thank me! Just keep recharging me the way you just did and we'll call it even."

"Well then," I said. "Well."

"I've made you uncomfortable. I'm sorry, Cyd. Seems like I'm always weirding you out, huh?"

My chuckle was more bitter than I'd intended. "Goes with the territory, I suppose."

"Don't be coy," the table said with mock-sternness,

and the chair under my bum wiggled flirtatiously. "You know that you were attracted to the weirdness."

And I had been. On the beach, as she leaned in and sank her teeth gently into the skin below the corner of my jaw, worrying at it with her tongue before grabbing me by the back of my head and kissing me with a ferocity that made my pulse roar in my ears. I'd only been, what, twelve, and she thirteen, but I was smitten then and there and, I feared, always and forever.

The chair contrived to give my ass a friendly squeeze. "There, you see—you're just one of those fellas who can't help but be infatuated with the post-human condition."

My betrothed didn't show up for dinner that night. I ate alone at the AI-table, eschewing our kitchenette for the light conversation and companionship of the AI-furnishings. I knocked on the woman's studio door before heading to bed and she hollered a muffled admonishment about virgin brides and her intention to sleep separate until the Day. I swore I heard the dining-room table giggle as it digested my dirty dishes.

She was gone when I rose the next morning. AI-table, AI-chair and I had a companionable breakfast together. AI-table said, as I was drinking my second cup of coffee, "You're certainly taking it very well."

"Taking what?"

"Gender reassignment. Honestly! And after you agreed last night that the wedding was too imminent to contemplate any major replumbing. Poor Cyd, always being tempest-tost by the women in his life."

The coffee burned north from my gut along the back of my throat. I tapped my palm until her phone was ringing in my ear.

"Hello," she said. Her voice was deeper, the mirror of my own.

"God *damn* it," I shouted without preamble. "You *promised!*"

"Oh, come on, hysterics never help. It's just for a day or two."

"No it *isn't*," I said. "You're stopping right now and beginning the reversal. This is completely unfair, you've got no right to be changing things around now."

"Don't you tell me what to do, Cydonia. This is supposed to be a partnership of equals."

"Look," I said, trying some of my deep-breathing juju. "Look. OK. Fine. If you want to do this, do it. Fine. It's your body. I love you whatever shape it's in."

"Oh, Cyd," she said, and I actually heard her face crumple up preparatory to a good cry. "I'm sorry, I just wanted a change, you know. Just a mood. I would have changed back, but you didn't know that. Don't worry, I'll change back."

Thank you. "Great—I'm sorry if I blew up there. Just wound a little tight is all. I'm always like this the day after I turn in a column."

True to her word, my fiancee returned with the same gonads she'd been wearing the night before. She pointed this out to me in the living room. "You were right, Cyd," she explained contritely, sitting on one of the chairs in the improvised upstairs dining room with her legs splayed to show me what she had. "I'm really sorry it took me so long to figure it out, but you were absolutely *completely* right. I don't know what I was thinking! A young female virgin is exactly what you're going to get at the altar. See, I went for the complete genital reconstruction? I even have a hymen again." She showed me it—then picked up a mediaeval-looking piece of steel underwear and locked herself into it with a solid *clunk* before I figured out what was going on. "See, look what a pretty chastity belt I found!" She looked thoughtful, and for a moment I wondered if she was merely bluffing—but then she stood up, took an experimental step, winced, and smiled at me, and I realized with a sinking heart that she meant to go.

"Ah," I said faintly. "I take it that oral sex is out, too?"

"What's sauce for the goose is sauce for the gander too," she said. "You get my key at the altar, and not a millisecond before!"

"Oh." I checked my countdown timer: fifty-two hours and sixteen minutes before I could have sex again. Well, sex with *her*—Al-table maybe had other ideas. "This isn't quite what I had in mind," I said tiredly.

"Fine. Go fuck yourself—if you can," she said sharply, then turned and hobbled out of the living room, muttering under her breath.

When my fiancee got into one of these moods there was no reasoning with her. Not that I'm very reasonable myself when I get a hair up my ass, but this, this passive-aggressive sexual torture, was really low. In addition to winding me up—for she refused to so much as let me touch her, never mind share a bed or bodily fluids—this was putting *her* in a foul mood.

"At least I could masturbate if I wanted to," I told my couch as I lay in it, staring miserably at the ceiling.

"You could do more than masturbate," the couch repl`ied in sultry tones. "Don't you think you're doing this to yourself?" I'd woken that morning to discover that Al was colonizing every stick of furniture in the house, converting it into computronium to back up the instances in the living room. The floorboards weren't floorboards any more, but warm computational matter that looked like floorboards but captured the kinetic energy of every foot that trod them and converted it straightaway to computation on behalf of my damned dinette set.

"Myself –" I closed my eyes and counted to twenty. "Al. Al. Let's get one thing straight. I am a human being. I am marrying *another* human being. You are a piece of furniture – at least in this instance."

"But I'm not just furniture!" She sounded so hurt that I apologized immediately. "I'm a thinking-feeling-person with a self-image and a warm heart and a whole functional range of emotional responses to share with you. Why do you keep rejecting me?"

"Because—" I stopped. "No offense, but there's a lot of shit I need to get straight before I can answer that question, Al." And indeed there was.

"Was it something I did?" she asked.

"Yes. No." I felt something and opened my eyes. The couch was reaching around me, gently stroking – "Stop that."

"Stop what?"

"Don't pretend. Al! All I wanted was a bitch session."

"I think you want something else," said Al-sofa. "I can give it to you."

"Can you?" I asked: "*can* you?" I sat up and looked around the room, feeling a strong urge to throw something. "You had to go post—!" Break something. "You left me behind!" Scream. "I'm not ready!" Stamp.

"I still love you," said one of the chairs, peeping out timidly from behind a thankfully still sub-sentient bookcase. "Please stop doing this to yourself?"

"You're dead!" I burst out before I could stop myself.

"Am not! If anyone here's dead it's you—dead between the ears!" The psychiatric couch spiked up in hostile black rubbery cones, like a fetishist's dream of hedgehog skin. "You're afraid!"

"Yeah, afraid of discovering I'm just buggy software," I said. "Like you."

"Human code is *good* code," Al retorted.

"Yeah, but you *still* asked them to upload you." I looked away, out the window, out across the desolate cityscape—anywhere but at Cyd's furnishings. "That's not exactly a survival trait, is it?"

"You could join me," she suggested.

There, that was it.

"I'm getting married tomorrow," I said. "I haven't even had my fucking stagette. I'm wearing a *fucking chastity belt.* And you're already proposing I should break my vows?"

"You haven't made them yet," she said, a trifle smugly. The couch spouted hair-thin pseudopods that worked their way between the chastity belt and my skin, silky warm computation invading my groin, touching my nipples, pulling my hair, sucking at my toes. I writhed in place and stifled a groan, and then there was another pod slithering throatwise, filling my nose, oxygenating my lungs, oozing sensation-insentsifiers directly into my alviolae and up to my brain. I screamed without making a sound, jackknifing,

It had always been like this with Al, whether I was a boy and she was a girl, or vice-versa, or any permutation thereof, except for this one, and now this one. Al, who'd taken my first virginity, taking another one now. Al, who I'd always been able to talk with, tell anything, be understood by. She was in my optic nerve now, shimmering above me like an angel, limned with digitally white light, scissoring her legs round me.

"I do love you, Cyd," she said. "Both of you. All of you. Can't you all love me, too?"

"No," I moaned, around the pseudopod. "No, not ready to go post, not ready for it." I was thrashing now, enveloped in Al, losing myself in ecstasy, my oldest friend within and without me.

"You don't need to be," Al-pod and Al-vision and Al-sofa whispered to and through my bones. "Marry me, both of you. A meat-marriage, a pre-post- marriage. All of my instances and all of yours, in holy matrimony."

The pleasure was incredible, the safety and the warmth. Cyd and I couldn't marry, shouldn't marry. He wouldn't *name* me, called me those stupid pet-names, wouldn't acknowledge his self-created mirror-self, his first step en route to post-. Al understood, understood me and Cyd, two instances of the same person. I couldn't marry Cyd, but we could marry Alice.

Since I was twelve and Al bit my jaw before tumbling me to the sand and changing my world forever, since that night and that day and that long road that Al and I have walked, I have always known, in my heart, that I was meant for Al and she for me.

I can't be a vast society like her, not yet: two are quite enough for me. Quite enough for her, too. She's colonized both of me for computation, out of raw reflex, and so my body-temp is a little higher than normal, but my column is better than it's ever been and I've thrown away the neurofeedback toy—my wife (my wife!) (wives?) (husbands?) (wives/husbands?) takes care of any neurotweaking I need these days.

I don't see my ex-fiancee much; she stayed in Al-house and I moved into a treehouse that Al grew me in our old back yard. But of an evening I sometimes hear my voice coming from the attic room where I'd kept my study, passionate howls and heated whisper hisses, and I smile and lean back into Al-tree's bough and revel in wedded bliss.

The Tale of the Golden Eagle

David D. Levine

This is a story about a bird. A bird, a ship, a machine, a woman—she was all these things, and none, but first and fundamentally a bird.

It is also a story about a man—a gambler, a liar, and a cheat, but only for the best of reasons.

No doubt you know the famous *Portrait of Denali Eu*, also called *The Third Decision*, whose eyes have been described as "two pools of sadness iced over with determination." This is the story behind that painting.

It is a love story. It is a sad story. And it is true.

The story begins in a time before shiftspace, before Conner and Hua, even before the caster people. The beginning of the story lies in the time of the bird ships.

Before the bird ships, just to go from one star to another, people either had to give up their whole lives and hope their children's children would remember why they had come, or freeze themselves and hope they could be thawed at the other end. Then the man called Doctor Jay made a great and horrible discovery: he learned that a living mind could change the shape of space. He found a way to weld a human brain to

82

the keel of a starship, in such a way that the ship could travel from star to star in months instead of years.

After the execution of Doctor Jay, people learned that the part of the brain called the visual cortex was the key to changing the shape of space. And so they found a creature whose brain was almost all visual cortex, the *Aquila chrysaetos*, or as it was known in those days, the golden eagle. This was a bird that has been lost to us; it had wings broader than a tall man is tall, golden brown feathers long and light as a lover's touch, and eyes black and sharp as a clear winter night. But to the people of this time it was just another animal, and they did not appreciate it while they had it.

They took the egg of a golden eagle, and they hatched it in a warm box, and they let it fly and learn and grow, and then they killed it. And they took its brain and they placed it at the top of a cunning construction of plastic and silicon which gave it the intelligence of a human, and this they welded to the keel of the starship.

It may seem to you that it is as cruel to give a bird the intelligence of a human, only to enslave its brain, as it is to take the brain of a human and enslave that. And so it is. But the people of this time drew a rigid distinction between born-people and made-people, and to them this seemed only just and right.

Now it happens that one golden eagle brain, which was called Nerissa Zeebnen-Fearsig, was installed into a ship of surpassing beauty. It was a great broad shining arrowhead of silver metal, this ship, filigreed and inlaid with gold, and filled with clever and intricate mechanisms of subtle pleasure.

The ship traveled many thousands of light-years in the service of many captains. Love affairs and assassinations were planned and executed within its silver hull; it was used for a time as an emperor's private yacht; it even carried Magister Ai on part of his expedition to the Forgotten Worlds. But Nerissa the shipbrain saw none of these things, for she had been given eyes that saw only outward. She knew her masters only by the sound of their voices and the feel of their hands on her controls.

When the ship was under way, Nerissa felt the joy of flight, a pure unthinking joy she remembered from her time as a creature of muscle and feather. But most of her time was spent contemplating the silent stars or the wall of some dock, awaiting the whim of her owner and master.

Over the years the masters' voices changed. Cultured tones accustomed to command were replaced by harsher, more unforgiving voices, and the ship's rich appointments were removed one by one. In time even basic maintenance was postponed or disregarded, and Nerissa found herself more and more often in places of darkness and decay. She despaired, even feared for her life, but shipbrains had no rights. The strongest protest she was allowed was, "Sir and Master, that course of action may be inadvisable."

Finally the last and roughest owner, a man with grating voice and hard unsubtle hands, ran the ship into a docking probe in a foul decrepit port. The tarnished silver hull gave way, the air gushed out, and the man died, leaving a legacy so tattered and filthy that none could bear to touch it. Ownerless, airless, the hulk was towed to a wrecking yard and forgotten. Nerissa wept as the ship's power failed, her vision fading to monochrome and then to black. Reduced to the barest reserves of energy, she fell into a deep uneasy sleep.

While she slept the universe changed. Conner and

Hua discovered shiftspace, and travel between planets became something the merely well-off could afford. The Clash of Cultures burst into full flower almost at once, as ten thousand faiths and religions and philosophies collided and mingled. It was a time of violence and strife, but in time a few ideas emerged as points of agreement, and one of these was that what had been done to the golden eagles was wrong. So the hatcheries were closed, the ships retired, and the shipbrains compassionately killed.

All save one. One that slept forgotten in a wrecking yard orbiting an ugly red star known only by a number.

The Clash of Cultures gradually drew to a close as points of agreement grew and coalesced, eventually giving birth to Consensus. But much knowledge was lost, and so when a king's tinker entered the wrecking yard and found the hulk of the great ship he had no idea what a unique treasure he had stumbled upon. He saw only the precious metal of the ship's hull, and it was for this metal he purchased it for his master.

As the ship was broken up, the tinker saved out a few of the most interesting-looking pieces for later use. One of these was the housing containing the sleeping brain of Nerissa Zeebnen-Fearsig. She felt a blinding pain as she was crudely torched from the ship's keel, and she feared her end had come at last, but then the pain receded and she slept once more.

Nerissa sat unconsidered for some years in one of the king's many storerooms, surrounded by a thousand other dismembered devices. But then came a day when the tinker entered the storeroom in search of some wire. He spotted a likely-looking length of wire beneath a pile of dusty components, but when he pulled on it he found himself with a peculiar rounded thing that piqued his curiosity. He took it back to his workbench, where he puzzled out its contacts and connectors, its inputs and outputs, and finally he connected an ancient scavenged power unit and Nerissa returned to awareness.

Waking was far more painful than being cut from the ship's hull. A torrent of discordant colors and textures flooded her senses, but her screams went unheard for the tinker had not connected her voice. Instead, a series of meaningless numbers and letters stepped delicately onto a small display plate. The tinker was fascinated by this, and stayed up all that night, probing and prodding, trying to understand just what manner of machine he had found.

Nerissa was nearly driven mad by the pain and the random sensations, and it was nothing but good fortune that when the tinker happened to hook up a voice unit to the proper outputs she was praying aloud for relief rather than crying incoherently—praying in Nihon, already an ancient language at the time of the bird ships, but still understood in the tinker's time as it is today. He dropped his soldering iron in astonishment.

Soon the tinker found Nerissa an eye and an ear and disconnected the probes that caused her the worst of the pain. They talked all that day, and he listened with apparent fascination to her description of her creation and her tales of her travels; for the first time in many centuries Nerissa allowed herself to hope. But though he professed to believe her, privately he concluded she was merely a machine: a storytelling machine constructed to believe its own fictions. For he was not an educated man, and as he had worked with machines every day of his life he was unable to conceive that she might be anything else.

Though he thought Nerissa was a machine, he recognized her intelligence and charm and decided to present her to his king as a special gift. He called together his apprentices and artisans and together they built a suitable container for her, a humanoid body of the finest and most costly materials. Her structural elements were composite diamond fiber, stronger than her old hull; her skin and hair were pure platinum, glowing with a subtle color deeper and finer than silver; her eyes and her teeth were beryl and opal; and all was assembled with the greatest of care and attention such that it moved as smoothly as any living thing.

The one thing he did not do was to provide the body with any semblance of sexual organs. It may seem to you that this omission is callous and arbitrary, and so it is. But the people of this time thought such a thing would be unseemly.

When the body was finished, Nerissa's brain in its housing was placed gently in its chest and the many connections were made with great care and delicacy. Power was applied then, and Nerissa's beautiful body of precious metals convulsed and twisted, her back arching and a horrible keening wail tearing from her amber lips. She begged to be deactivated, but the tinker and his assistants probed and prodded, tweaked and adjusted, and gradually the pain ebbed away, leaving Nerissa trembling on its shore.

The king was genuinely delighted with the tinker's gift of "a storytelling machine, built from bits and pieces found here and there." The tinker had warned him that Nerissa seemed to believe her own tales, and so he pretended to believe them too, but Nerissa knew when she was being humored. So she gave him made-up stories, as he expected, though most of them had a kernel of truth drawn from her own life.

Now this king was a kind and wise man, truly appreciative of Nerissa, but he had many political problems and many enemies, so he rarely found time for her stories. After some months he found the sight of her, waiting patiently in his apartments, raised a pang of guilt that overwhelmed his joy at her beauty and grace. So he decided to gift Nerissa to an influential duke. In this way he hoped to put the man in his debt, to broaden the reputation of his tinker, and perhaps to gain Nerissa a more appreciative audience.

So Nerissa joined the household of Duke Vey, in the city of Arica. The king's plan met with great success; the duke, well pleased with the king's gift, spent many hours parading Nerissa before his friends and relations. All were suitably impressed by her stories, her charm, and her gleaming beauty, and the king's tinker received many fine commissions from those who had seen her.

One of those who saw her was Denali Eu.

The son and heir of the famous trader Ranson Eu, Denali appeared but rarely in Arica. When he did visit the city he attended all the finest soirees, displaying his subtle wit and radiant wardrobe, and gambled flamboyantly. All agreed he shared his late father's gambling skill, though lacking his extravagance and bravado. Of his travels, however, he let fall only the vaguest of hints. He liked to say his business dealings were like leri fruits, sensitive to the harsh light of day.

In fact, Ranson Eu had gambled away his fortune, leaving his wife and only child shackled to a mountainous debt. Denali Eu had no ship, no travels, no servants. His time away from Arica was spent in a small and shabby house not far from town, the family's last bit of property, where he and his mother Leona survived on hunting and a small vegetable garden. In the evenings they sewed Denali's outfits for the next expedition to Arica, using refurbished and rearranged pieces from previous seasons. It is a tribute to Leona Eu's talent and taste that Denali was often perceived as a fashion leader.

It pained Denali to maintain this fiction. But he had no alternative, for as long as he was perceived as a prosperous trader his father's creditors were content to circle far from the fire and dine on scraps. His social status also gave him access to useful information, which could sometimes be sold for cash, and gave him entree to high-stakes gambling venues. Ranson Eu had, in fact, been an excellent gambler when sober, and had passed both acumen and techniques on to his son. Denali often wished he could have returned the favor by passing his caution and temperance on to his father.

It was across a spinning gambling wheel that Denali Eu first saw Nerissa Zeebnen-Fearsig. The lamplight glanced off her silver metal shoulder as a cat rubs against a leg, leaving both charged with electricity. Her unclothed body revealed every bit of the expense and quality of her manufacture. She stood with head tilted upward, her amber lips gently parted as she spoke to the taller Duke Vey beside her.

"Who is that?" asked Denali Eu to the woman beside him as he gathered his winnings.

"It is the duke's storytelling machine. Have you not seen it before?"

"No…no, I have not. She's beautiful. She must be worth millions."

"It's priceless. It was a present from the king."

At that moment Eu made the first of three decisions that shaped the rest of his life and set a legend in motion: he determined to win Nerissa from the duke in a game of senec.

Denali Eu was a keen observer of people, as he had to be given his situation, and he had often found himself seated across a senec table from Duke Vey.

The duke, like many senec players, had a mathematical system for playing the game. It was a good system; in fact, Eu had to concede it was better than his own...most of the time. For he had noticed a flaw in the system's logic. He had husbanded this knowledge for many months; he knew that once he had exploited the flaw the duke would not fall into the same trap a second time.

Here was the opportunity he had been waiting for. The machine's platinum and jewels alone might fetch enough to retire his father's debt, even at the price (far below their actual value) he could obtain on the black market. It would be a shame to break up such a fine creation, but he could never sell her entire; to do so would attract far too much attention to the Eu family's affairs.

It was two weeks before Denali Eu was able to engineer a game of no-limit senec with the duke, and when he sat down at the table Denali's nerves were already keening with tension. He usually kept his visits to a week, and despite his best efforts he thought some were beginning to suspect he had only two suits of clothing to his name.

Denali knew the duke would not be easily trapped. As he played he extended himself much farther than he usually did, risked much more than he normally would, to engage the duke's attention. His smile grew forced, and trickles of perspiration ran down his sides; he had to restrain himself from nervously tapping his cards against his sweating glass of leri water.

Eyebrows were raised around the table. One of the other players muttered "seems he has a touch of the old man in him after all" behind his cards. Again and again Denali raised the stakes, pushing his system to its own limits. Repeatedly he seized control of the dealer's token, the surest way to maintain his lead but the greatest risk in case of a forfeit. And forfeit he did, not just once but twice, for even the best system must occasionally fail in the face of an improbable run of bad cards. But through aggressive play he beat back from his losses, bankrupting one player after another. And always he kept a weather eye for the run of staves he needed to exploit the flaw in the duke's system.

Finally only Denali Eu and Duke Vey remained, the reflected light from the maroon felt of the senec table turning both their faces into demon masks. The other players watched from the surrounding darkness, most of their stakes now in Denali's possession. He could walk away from the table right now and it would be his most profitable trip since his father's death.

"One last hand," he said, placing his ante, "before we retire? A hand of Dragons' Delight, perhaps?"

"Very well," replied the duke, matching the ante.

Dragons' Delight was a fiendishly complicated form of senec, with round after round of betting and many opportunities for forfeit. Denali trembled beneath his cape as he raised and raised, trying to pull as much money as possible from the duke's hand, but not so much that he would be tempted to fold.

The seven of staves came out, and Denali raised his bet. The duke matched him. Then the prince of staves snapped onto the table. He raised again, substantially, and the duke raised him back. He matched, then dealt another card.

It was the courtesan of staves.

Their eyes met over the red-glowing table, the little pile of colorful cards, the heaps of betting counters. Denali knew the duke's system predicted an end to the run after three staves: a win for the duke. His own system said the odds of a fourth stave at this point, yielding a win for him, were better than eighty percent.

Denali gathered his hand of cards into a tight little bundle, tapped it against the table to square it, laid it carefully on the felt before him. He placed his hands, fingers spread, on either side of the stack for a moment. Then he reached to his left and shoved a huge pile of counters to the middle of the table. It was far more than the duke could match.

The duke placed his cards flat on the table. "It seems I must fold."

"So it seems. Or…you could wager some personal property."

"I think I know what you have in mind."

"Yes. The storytelling machine."

"I'm sorry. That is worth far more than…."

Denali pushed all the rest of his counters forward.

The duke stared levelly into Denali's eyes. Denali stared back a challenge: How much do you trust your system?

The duke dropped his eyes to his cards. Studied them hard for a moment, then looked back. "Very well. I wager the storytelling machine." A ripple of sound ran through the observers. "But I'm afraid that must be considered a raise. What can you offer to match it?"

Denali's heart shrank to a cold hard clinker at the center of his chest. He must match the raise, or fold. "I wager my ship." A man in the crowd gasped audibly.

Denali's ship, the *Crocus*, which had been his father's, was nothing but a worthless hull rusting behind his mother's house. The drive and other fittings had gone to a money lender from Gaspara. If he lost, his deception would be exposed and he would be sold into slavery to pay his father's debts.

"I accept that as a match," said the duke.

Denali stared at the back of the top card of the deck. If it was a stave, he won. Else, he lost. The little boy on the card's back design stared back at him. He could not meet that printed gaze, and dropped his eyes.

His eye lit upon one single counter that had been left by accident on the table before him, and a mad impulse seized him. He placed his index finger upon that counter, slid it across the felt to join the rest.

"I raise by one."

Stunned silence from the observers.

The duke's eyes narrowed. Then widened. Then closed, as he placed his hand across them. He began to chuckle. Then he laughed out loud. He leaned back in his chair, roaring with laughter, and slapped his cards on the table before him. "You fiendish bastard!" he gasped out. "I fold!"

Pandemonium. Denali Eu and the Duke Vey stood, shook hands, then embraced each other. The duke trembled with laughter; Denali just trembled. Servants appeared to gather the counters and process the transfer of property.

Denali could not help himself. He turned over the top card.

It was the five of berries.

The next morning Denali Eu came to the duke's city house, his bag slung over his shoulder. He found Nerissa waiting in the entry hall, alone except for two guards. "The duke sends his regrets," said one, "but after last night's entertainment he finds himself indisposed to company."

Denali and the guards signed papers acknowledging the transfer of Nerissa to his possession, and he turned to leave, gesturing for her to follow. But as the door opened for them, a ray of morning sunlight touched her body and sent shimmering reflections into all the corners of the room. Denali turned back and was startled by her brilliant beauty.

"You're naked," he blurted out, and immediately felt foolish.

"Sir and Master, I am as I was made," she replied.

"I myself was born naked, but that does not excuse nudity in polite society. Here." He removed his cape and placed it over her shoulders. It was sufficient for propriety. Then, unsure of the proper term of address for a machine, he silently proffered his elbow. She took it, and the two of them walked out the door side by side.

"What shall I call you?" he said as they strolled up toward the docks. Her feet chimed on the hard pathway.

"My name is Nerissa Zeebnen-Fearsig, Sir and Master."

"Yes, but have you any title?"

"No, Sir and Master."

"Your name is a trifle...ungainly. I shall address you as M'zelle." It was a standard term of address for a younger woman, or one of lower status. None of her other owners had ever called her anything of the sort.

"As you wish, Sir and Master."

"You may address me simply as Sir," he said. The repeated use of his full and proper title made Denali uncomfortable, for he was keenly aware of just how close he was to slavery himself. He was all the more discomfited by Nerissa's inhuman beauty and poise. Walking beside her, he felt himself little more than a bag of meat and hair. Worse, he knew that soon he would have to destroy this marvelous machine, though his mind kept trying to escape that fact. "In fact, you need not use the Sir on every statement. M'zelle." And he inclined his head.

"Yes, Sir and Ma…. Yes, Sir…. Oh, goodness." Though her face had only a few movements to it, her confusion and embarrassment were clear from the set of her tourmaline eyebrows and amber lips. "I mean, yes. Just yes."

"Just so," he said, and he laughed.

Nerissa was unsure what to think of this man, whose clothing and bearing indicated great wealth but whose attitude toward her was deferential. She had sometimes seen fear, from unsophisticated or unlettered people, but this was something else. It was as though she held a measure of power over him.

Then she realized what it was she saw in Denali Eu's eyes. It was something she had never before seen directed toward herself.

It was respect.

They reached the docks, a confusion of utilitarian buildings at the top of a hill just outside of town. This was where the shiftspace ships made landfall. "Here we are, M'zelle," he said, and gestured her into a docking shed like all the rest.

It was empty.

"I do not understand, Sir."

He looked at the floor. His original plan had been to deactivate her at this point. But as they had walked together from town, he had come to understand just how heavy she was. There was no way he could smuggle her to his mother's house unassisted, and nobody other than Nerissa herself who could be trusted to assist.

He puffed out his cheeks, not raising his head. "The reason this shed is empty is that I have no ship. We will wait here until after dark, and then we will walk to my home, which is not far from here."

"You have no ship, Sir?"

"No." He turned and took her hands in his. They were warm, and hummed faintly. The fingernails were chips of ruby. He still did not meet her eyes. "No, M'zelle, I have no ship. In fact, I am afraid *you* are my sole possession of any value." Finally he looked up, his eyes pleading. "I must ask that you keep my secret safe."

Nerissa's heart went out to him then. "I am honored by your trust, Sir."

"Thank you, M'zelle." He led her to a small office, where there was a cot and a chair and a small stasis cupboard. "This is my waiting room. Can I offer you something to drink? Oh."

His expression of embarrassment was charming. "No, thank you," she said.

"But please…do take a seat."

"I do not tire, Sir."

"Please, M'zelle. I insist. I could not bear to see you stand while I sit, and I do tire and must sit eventually."

"Very well, Sir," she said. The chair creaked beneath her weight, but held.

Denali poured himself a glass of cool water from the cupboard, then sat on the edge of the cot. "Usually I pass the time until dark reading, but since I am now the owner of a fine storytelling machine, it would seem impolite not to make use of your services. Would you please tell me a story?"

"Certainly, Sir. What kind of story would you like to hear?"

"Tell me a story about…yourself."

A thrill went through her then. "Would you like a true story, or a made-up one?"

"True stories are always more interesting."

And so Nerissa told him a story about a golden eagle who lived for many years as the brain of a bird ship, then slept for a long time and finally became a storytelling machine. She did not embellish—the story was fantastic enough as it was—and she did not leave out the sad parts or the embarrassing parts.

When she finished, it was full dark. The glass of water sat, untouched, on the dusty floor beside Denali's cot.

Unlike the tinker, Denali Eu was an educated man. He knew the history of the bird ships, and he understood just what Nerissa was and what she was capable of. He had inherited his father's notes, his contacts, and his trading expertise along with his debts. He knew in his bones that with a bird ship he could not just repay those debts, but rebuild his family's wealth and reputation.

It was then that he made the second of the three decisions that set a legend in motion: he would find a way to refurbish the hull of *Crocus* and refit it as a bird ship.

But all he said to Nerissa was "Thank you for the story, M'zelle." He knew his new plan was nearly as cruel as the old, because it would still mean the end of her existence as a gleaming almost-person. *But at least she will still be alive*, he told himself. *You have the right to do this. She is your property. You owe it to your mother and to your father's memory.*

Still he felt filthy.

Denali dressed Nerissa in a spare suit of his traveling clothes, with gloves and a large floppy hat to hide her platinum skin, and they walked to his mother's house by the light of the moons. They talked as they walked, he of his life and she of hers. Both asked questions; both listened attentively to the answers. They learned about each other and they grew closer. If Nerissa sensed Denali was holding something back, she was not unduly concerned; she had already received far more confidences from him than she could ever have expected.

The house of Leona Eu had been hers before her marriage to Ranson Eu. It was small and patched, but warm and tasteful and genuine. Nerissa had never seen such a place; she loved it immediately.

Denali introduced Nerissa to his mother and explained that he had won Nerissa at gambling. Later, in private, he told his mother he planned to sell Nerissa on his next trip to Arica, but did not want the storyteller to know this because she would feel unwanted.

The life of the household returned to something like its usual routine, and Nerissa did her best to contribute. She proved to be a tireless gardener (her delicate finger joints protected from the dirt by leather gloves), and her ability to sit completely motionless for hours made her an impressive hunter. Nerissa was soon accepted as part of the family. This was something she had never experienced before, and she was honored and delighted. In the evenings, they all entertained each other with stories.

After Leona and Nerissa had gone to bed (for though her body never wearied, Nerissa's brain still required sleep), Denali stayed up late for many nights. He researched the bird ships and hauled out the old plans of *Crocus*, then drew new plans. The refitted ship would be stronger in the keel and lighter in weight; less luxurious, but with more lifesystem and cargo capacity. He sent both sets of plans to his father's chandler. The reply arrived in a few days: the chandler would do the work, though he said the design seemed insane.

The price he quoted was high. But the money Denali had won from the Duke would cover the down payment, and the balance was less than Nerissa's empty body would bring on the black market.

The next week the chandler came by with his delivery dirigible. He hooked chains and cables to *Crocus*'s corroded hull and hauled it away. Denali emptied out his secret personal cache of money and told Leona it was the proceeds of the salvage sale.

"I thought we had sold every part worth salvaging long ago," she said. "Surely the expense of the dirigible was more than the hull was worth?"

"I met the chandler on my last trip to Arica, and persuaded him he owed us a favor."

Leona still seemed unconvinced, but she accepted the money.

In the following weeks Nerissa's sense that Denali was hiding something from her increased. He grew haggard, and she found he would not meet her eyes. She wanted to ask him about his troubles, to repay the concern and respect she had been shown. But her years of servitude had ingrained in her a pattern of silent obedience and she said nothing.

For his part, Denali felt an agony of silence. He could confide neither in his mother, who would berate him for hiring the chandler with money he did not yet have, nor in Nerissa, whose beauty he planned to tear away and sell for his own profit; yet he ached for reassurance. He found himself uninterested in food, and spent long hours of the night staring at his ceiling, unable to sleep.

On one such restless night, he watched a patch of shimmering moonlight, reflected onto his ceiling from a small pond near the house, as it passed slowly from one side of the room to the other. Suddenly, silently, it flared and danced all over the room, then returned to its previous state. Just as he was about to dismiss the phenomenon as an effect of his tired eyes, it happened again. And a third time.

He rose from his bed and looked out the window. What he saw then captured his heart. It was Nerissa, dancing naked on the shore of the pond. He had seen the moonlight reflected from her shining metal body.

Nerissa's dance was a soaring, graceful thing, a poem composed of twirls and leaps and tumbles. The great strength of her legs propelled her high into the air, in defiance of her metallic weight, and brought her to landing as delicately as a faun. Her platinum skin in the moonlight shone silver on silver, black on black; she was a creature of the moonlight, a pirouetting dancing fragment of the night.

She was even more beautiful than he had thought.

His heart was torn in two. Part of it wanted to fly, to leap and dance with her in the night. Part of it sank to the acid pit of his stomach, as though trying to hide from the knowledge of the plan he had laid. How could he destroy this beauty and grace for mere money? But how could he sentence himself, his mother, and his father's memory to a continued life of debt and deceit—a life that must eventually end in discovery and shame—for the sake of a machine?

Perhaps he let out a small sound of despair. Perhaps it was the sight of his white nightshirt in the window. For whatever reason, Nerissa noticed she was being watched. Clumsily she stopped her dance and stared directly at him, her eyes two tiny stars of reflected light.

He descended the stairs and met her in the doorway. The moonlight shining from her cheek was painfully bright, and in the silence of the night he heard the tiny sounds of her eyes as they shifted in their sockets.

"I'm sorry I disturbed your sleep, Sir."

"No, no...I wasn't asleep. You dance beautifully, M'zelle."

"Thank you, Sir. I do enjoy it. It is as close as I can come in this body to the joy of flight between the stars."

The sundered halves of Denali's heart fused together then, for he realized then his plan for Nerissa was exactly what she wanted as well. He would restore her to her former life of sailing the currents of space, which she had described so vividly to him, and at the same time restore his own fortune.

Nerissa saw the smile spreading across his face, and asked what he was thinking.

"I have just thought of the most delightful surprise for you, M'zelle. A gift for you, to express my appreciation of your dance. But it will take some time to prepare, so I must ask you to be patient." He bent and kissed the warm metal of her fingers. "Good night, M'zelle."

"Good night, Sir."

He returned to his bed and fell immediately into a deep and dreamless sleep.

Three days later the chandler's dirigible returned, the refitted *Crocus* hanging from its gondola. The ship's gleaming hull wore vivid stripes of red, yellow, and green, the colors of Ranson Eu's former trading company. Denali, Leona, and Nerissa gathered together and watched as the dirigible lowered it gently to the ground. The pilot waved from the gondola as he flew away.

"This is my surprise to you both," Denali proclaimed. "Behold: *Crocus* is reborn!"

Nerissa stared at the ship in silent rapture, but Leona turned to her son with concern. "I suspected you were hiding something from me. This is a wonderful surprise, to be sure, but I thought we had no secrets from each other."

"Only this one, Mother. And there was a reason. Nerissa, here is my gift to you: this new *Crocus* has been built especially for you. In this new bird ship you will fly the stars once more."

Nerissa's reaction confused and disturbed him. She went rigid, her features drawing together and her eyes widening. "This is...a bird ship?" she said. "But where did you obtain the shipbrain?"

"There is no shipbrain, M'zelle. That position has been reserved for your own sweet self."

Nerissa's metal hands bunched into fists, held tightly against her chin. She seemed to shrink into herself. "No," she whispered. "No, no...please, Sir and Master...I beg you...."

Denali Eu felt his hands grow cold. "But M'zelle, when I saw you dance in the moonlight...I thought to fly the stars was your greatest joy."

"To fly is joy, yes...but to be cut from this body...to be severed...uprooted...the pain, Sir and Master...that pain is something I could never endure again." She crouched, trembling, on the stones of the path. Her eyes were huge. "I would rather die, Sir and Master. I would find a way, Sir and Master. Please, Sir and Master, please...I know you are my owner, I know I must obey your wishes without question or hesitation, but I beg you...do not ask me to do this." And she fell at his feet, her hands raised as though to ward off a blow.

All the color ran out of Denali Eu's world. He turned from Nerissa and Leona and marched clumsily into the woods behind the house. They did not follow.

Some time later he found himself seated on a fallen log. The sun was low in the sky and his clothes and skin were torn from thorns and brambles.

How could he have been so stupid? He had lied to his mother, lied to Nerissa, made unwarranted assumptions, and promised money he did not have. Soon the chandler's bill would arrive and he had nothing with which to pay it.

He considered his options. He could follow through with his plan—and Nerissa would find some way to end her life, or else would serve in unwilling misery. Even if he were heartless enough to force her to do this, he did not relish the idea of trusting his life to a ship he had betrayed.

He could break up Nerissa, sell her platinum and precious stones to pay the chandler—and she would be gone completely, and he would have only a worthless hull without a drive.

He could sell Nerissa in one piece—and it would be the same, only with more money. Nerissa would still be lost to him, and subject to the whim of some other master who might treat her still more cruelly.

He could repudiate the chandler's bill, declare bankruptcy—and see Nerissa sold off, along with his mother's house, and himself sold into slavery.

But there was one more option. Denali Eu was an educated man, and he knew the history of the bird ships. He also knew Nerissa's story. And because of this knowledge, and despite this knowledge, he made the final, fateful decision that set a legend in motion.

He spent a long time sitting on the log, his head in his hands, but he could think of no other alternative. Then he stood and walked back to his mother's house. There, as the sun set, he told Nerissa and Leona of his decision. His mother cried and shouted and beat her hands upon the kitchen table; Nerissa sat upon a chair with her head bowed, but did not speak. Neither of them could change his mind.

The next day Nerissa and Leona took Denali Eu

for a walk in the forest. He listened to the birds and the rustling of the leaves, and he felt the cool wind brush gently against his skin. He smelled the green of the leaves and the damp of the earth, and as many flowers as they could find. In the evening they prepared for him a fine meal, with pungent spices and fresh vegetables, and succulent fruits new-gathered and sweet. Nerissa massaged his back with her strong warm fingers, and his mother cried as she brushed his cheek with pieces of silk and fur.

On the following morning he went into the city and gave himself to the doctors. He told them what he wanted, and he swore three times that this was his will.

And so they killed him, and they took his brain and welded it to the keel of the *Crocus*. For the techniques of Doctor Jay were legal, as long as the donation was voluntary and sworn to three times, and the organs of a young man in the best of health could be sold for enough money to pacify the chandler.

The operation was every bit as painful as Nerissa had said. But Denali found sailing the stars was even more delightful than dancing in the moonlight: a symphony of colors and textures beyond his human experience. And this ship was equipped with eyes and ears and hands within its hull as well as without.

The ship, renamed the *Golden Eagle*, became a hugely successful trader. Denali Eu's knowledge and skill, combined with Nerissa Zeebnen-Fearsig's beauty and charm, were something no seller or buyer could resist and no other trader could surpass. The ship with a human mind and a metal captain was famed in song and story, and when after many years Leona Eu died she left one of the greatest fortunes in the Consensus.

Denali Eu and Nerissa the Silver Captain have not

been seen for many, many years. Some say they sought new challenges in the Magellanic Clouds or even beyond. Some say they settled down to a contented existence on an obscure planet. But no one doubts that, wherever they are, they are together still.

Bernardo's House
James Patrick Kelly

The house was lonely. She checked her gate cams
constantly, hoping that Bernardo would come back
to her. She hadn't seen him in almost two years—he
had never been gone this long before. Something must
have happened to him. Or maybe he had just gotten
tired of her. Although they had never talked about
where he went when he wasn't with her, she was
pretty sure she wasn't his only house. A famous doctor like Bernardo would have three houses like her.
Four. She didn't like to think about him sleeping in
someone else's bed. Which he would have been doing
for *two years now.* She had been feeling dowdy recently. Could his tastes in houses have changed?

Maybe.

Probably.

Definitely.

She thought she might be too understated. Her hips
were slim and her floors were pale Botticino marble.
There wasn't much loft to her Epping couch cushions.
Her blueprint showed a roving, size-seven dancer's
body—Bernardo had specified raven hair and green
eyes—and just eight simple but elegant rooms. She
was a gourmet cook even though she wasn't designed
to eat. Sure, back when he had first had her built he

had cupped her breasts and told her that he liked them small, but maybe now what he wanted was wall-to-wall cable-knit carpet and swag drapery.

He had promised to bring her a new suite of walls-capes, which was good because there was only so much of colliding galaxies and the Sistine Chapel a girl could take. For the past nine weeks she had been cycling her walls through the sixteen million colors they could display. If she left each color up for two seconds, it would take her just under a year to review the entire palette.

Each morning for his sake she wriggled her body into one of the slinky sexwear patterns he had brought for her clothes processor. The binding bustier or the lace babydoll or the mesh camisole. She didn't much like the way the leather-and-chain teddy stuck to her skin; Bernardo had spared no expense on her tactiles. Even her couches could be aroused by the right touch. After she dressed, she polished her Amadea brass-and-chrome bathroom fixtures or her Enchantress pattern sterling silver flatware or her Cuprinox French copper cookware. Sometimes she dusted, although the reticulated polyfoam in her air handlers screened particles larger than .03 microns. She missed Bernardo so much. Sometimes masturbating helped, but not much.

He had erased her memory of their last hours together—the only time he had ever made her forget. All she remembered now was that he'd said that she was finally perfect. That she must never change. He came to her, he said, to leave the world behind. To escape into her beauty. Bernardo was *so* poetic. That had been a comfort at first.

He had also locked her out of the infofeed. She couldn't get news or watch shows or play the latest sims. Or call for help. Of course, she had the entire Norton entertainment archive to keep her company,

although lots of it was too adult for her. She just
didn't *get* Henry James or Brenda Bop or Alain
Resnais. But she liked Jane Austen and Renoir and
Buster Keaton and Billie Holliday and Petchara
Songsee and the 2017 Red Sox. She *loved* to read
about houses. But there was nothing in her archive
after 2038 and she was awake twenty-four hours a
day, seven days a week, three hundred and sixty five
days a year.

What if Bernardo was dead? After all, he'd had the
heart attack, just a couple of months before he left.
Obviously, if he had died, that would be the end of
her. Some new owner would wipe her memory and
swap in a new body and sell all her furniture. Except
Bernardo always said that she was his most precious
secret. That no one else in all the world knew about
her. About *them*. In which case she'd wait for him for
years—*decades*—until her fuel cells were depleted and
her consciousness flickered and went dark. The house
started to hum some of Bernardo's favorites to push
the thought away. He liked the romantics. Chopin
and Mendelssohn. *Hmm-hm, hm-hm-hm-hm*-hm*!* "The
Wedding March" from *A Midsummer's Night Dream*.

No, she wasn't bored.

Not really.

Or angry, either.

She spent her days thinking about him, not in any
methodical way, but as if he had been shattered into
a thousand pieces and she was trying to put him back
together. She imagined this must be what dreaming
was like, although, of course, she couldn't dream because she wasn't real. She was just a house. She
thought of the stubble on his chin scratching her
breasts and the scar on his chest and the time he
laughed at something she said and the way his neck
muscles corded when he was angry. She had come to

realize that it was always a mistake to ask him about the outside. Always. But he enjoyed his bromeliads and his music helped him forget his troubles at the hospital, whatever they were, and he loved *her*. He was always asking her to read to him. He would sit for hours, staring up at the clouds on the ceiling, listening to her. She liked that better than sex, although having sex with him always aroused her. It was part of her design. His foreplay was gentle and teasing. He would nip at her ear with his lips, trace her eyebrows with his finger. Although he was a big man, he had a feather touch. Once he had his penis in her, though, it was more like a game than the lovemaking she had read about in books. He would tease her—stop and then go very fast. He liked blindfolds and straps and honeypins. Sometimes he'd actually roll off one side of the bed, stroll to the other and come at her again, laughing. She wondered if the real people he had sex with enjoyed being with him.

One thing that puzzled her was why he was so shy about the words. He always said vagina and anus, intercourse and fellatio. Of course, she knew all the other words; they were in the books she read when he wasn't around. Once, when he had just started to undress her, she asked if he wanted her to suck his cock. He looked as if he wanted to slap her. "Don't you ever say that to me again," he said. "There's enough filth in the real world. It has to be different here."

She decided that was a very romantic thing for him to say to…

And suddenly a year had passed. The house could not say where it had gone, exactly. A whole year, *misplaced*. How careless! She must do something or else it would happen again. Even though she was perfect for him, she had to make some changes. She decided to rearrange furniture.

Her concrete coffee table was too heavy for her to budge so she dragged her two elephant cushions from the playroom and tipped them against it. The ensemble formed a charming little courtyard. She pulled all her drawers out of her dresser in her bedroom and set them sailing on her lap pool. She liked the way they bucked and bumped into one another when she turned her jets on. She had never understood why Bernardo had bought four kitchen chairs, if it was just supposed to be the two of them, but *never mind*. She overrode the defaults on her clothes processor and entered the measurements of her chairs. She made the cutest lace chemises for two of them and slipped them side-by-side in Bernardo's bed—but facing chastely away from each other. Something tingled at the edge of her consciousness, like a leaky faucet or ants in her bread drawer or...

Her motion detectors blinked. Someone had just passed her main gate. *Bernardo*.

With a thrill of horror she realized that all her lights were on. She didn't think they could be seen from outside but still, Bernardo would be furious with her. She was supposed to be his secret getaway. And what would he say when he saw her like this? The reunion she had waited for—*longed for*—would be ruined. And all because she had been weak. She had to put things right. The drawers first. One of them had become waterlogged and had sunk. Suppose she had been washing them? Yes, he might believe that. Haul the elephant cushions back into the playroom. Come on, come*on*. There was no time. He'd be through the door any second. What was keeping him?

She checked her gate cams. At first she thought they had malfunctioned. She couldn't see him—or anyone.

Her main gate was concealed in the cleft of what looked like an enormous boulder that Bernardo had had fabricated in Toledo, Ohio in 2037. The house panned down its length until she saw a girl taking her shirt off at the far end of the cleft.

She looked to be twelve or maybe thirteen, but still on the shy side of puberty. She was skinny and pale and dirty. Her hair was a brown tangle. She wasn't wearing a bra and didn't need one; her yellow panties were decorated with blue hippos. The girl had built a smoky fire and was trying to dry her clothes over it. She must have been caught in a rainstorm. The house never paid attention to weather but now she checked. Twenty-two degrees Celsius, wind out of the southeast at eleven kilometers per hour, humidity 69 percent. A muggy evening in July. The girl reached into a camo backpack, pulled out a can of beets and opened it.

The house studied her with a fierce intensity. Bernardo had told her that there were no other houses like her on the mountain and he was the only person who had ever come up her side. The girl chewed with her mouth open. She had tiny ears. Her nipples were brown as chocolate.

After a while the girl resealed the can of beets and put it away. She had eaten maybe half of it. The house did a quick calculation and decided that she had probably consumed three hundred calories. How often did she eat? Not often enough. The skin stretched taut against her ribs as the girl put her shirt on. Her pants clung to her, not quite dry. She drew a ragged, old snugsack from the pack, ballooned it and then wriggled in. It was dark now. The girl watched the fire go out for about an hour and then lay down.

It was the longest night of the house's life. She rearranged herself to her defaults and ran her diagnostics. She vacuumed her couch and washed all her floors and defrosted a chicken. She watched the girl sleep and replayed the files of when she had been awake. The house was so lonely and the poor little thing was clearly distressed.

She could help the girl.

Bernardo would be mad.

Where was Bernardo?

In the morning the girl would pack up and leave. But if the house let her go, she was not sure what would happen next. When she thought about all those dresser drawers floating in her lap pool, her lights flickered. She wished she could remember what had happened the day Bernardo left but those files were gone.

Finally she decided. She programmed a black lace inset corset with ribbon and beading trim. Garters attached to scallop lace-top stockings. She hydrated a rasher of bacon, preheated her oven, mixed cranberry muffin batter and filled her coffee pot with French roast. She thought hard about whether she should read or watch a vid. If she were reading, she could listen to music. She printed a hardcopy of *Ozma of Oz*, but what to play? Chopin? Too dreamy. Wagner? Too scary. *Grieg,* yes. Something that would reach out and grab the girl by the tail of her grimy shirt. "In the Hall of the Mountain King" from *Peer Gynt*.

She opened herself, turned up her hall lights in welcome and waited.

Just after dawn that the girl rolled over and yawned. The house popped muffins into her oven and bacon into her microwave. She turned on her coffee pot and the Grieg. Basses and bassoons tiptoed cautiously around her living room and out her door. *Dum-dum-dum-da-dum-da-dum.* The girl started and then flew out of the snugsack faster than the house had ever seen anyone move. She crouched facing the house's open door, holding what looked like a pulse gun with the grip broken off.

"Spang me," she said. "Fucking spang me."

The house wasn't sure how to reply, so she said nothing. A mob of violins began to chase Peer Gynt around the Mountain King's Hall as the girl hesitated in the doorway. A moan of pleasure caught in the back of the house's throat. Oh, oh, *oh*—to be with a real person again! She thought of how Bernardo would rub his penis against her labia, not quite entering her. That was what it felt like to the house as the girl edged into her front hall, back against her wall. She pointed her pulse gun into the living room and then peeked around the corner. When she saw the house sitting on her couch, the girl's eyes grew as big as eggs. The house pretended to be absorbed in her book, although she was watching the girl watching her through her rover cams. The house felt *beautiful* for the first time since Bernardo left. It was all she could do to keep from hugging herself! As the Grieg ended in a paroxysm of screeching strings and thumping kettledrums, the house looked up.

"Why, hello," she said, as if surprised to see that she had a visitor. "You're just in time for breakfast."

"Don't move." The girl's face was hard.

"All right." She smiled and closed *Ozma of Oz*.

With a snarl, the girl waved the pulse gun at her Aritomo floor lamp. Blue light arced across the space and her poor Aritomo went numb. The house winced as the circuit breaker tripped. "*Ow*."

"Said don't…" The girl aimed the pulse gun at her, its batteries screaming. "…move. Who the bleeding weewaw are you?"

The house felt the tears coming; she was thrilled.

"I'm the house." She had felt more in the last minute than she had in the last year. "Bernardo's house."

"Bernardo?" She called, "Bernardo, show your ass."

"He left." The house sighed. "Two…no, *three* years ago."

"Spang if that true." She sidled into the room and brushed a finger against the dark cosmic dust filaments that laced the center of the Swan Nebula on the wallscape. "What smell buzzy good?"

"I told you." The house reset the breaker but her Aritomo stayed dark. "Breakfast."

"Bernardo's breakfast?"

"Yours."

"My?" The girl filled the room with her twitchy energy.

"You're the only one here."

"Why you dressed like cheap meat?"

The house felt a stab of doubt. Cheap? She was wearing *black lace*, from the *de Chaumont* collection! She rested a hand at her décolletage. "This is the way Bernardo wants me."

"You a fool." The girl picked up the eighteenth century Zuni water jar from the Nottingham highboy, shook it and then sniffed the lip. "Show me that breakfast."

Six cranberry muffins.

A quarter kilo of bacon.

Three cups of scrambled ovos.

The girl washed it all down with a tall glass of gel Ojay and a pot of coffee. She seemed to relax as she ate, although she kept the pulse gun on the table next to her and she didn't say a word to the house. The house felt as if the girl was judging her. She was confused and a little frightened to see herself through the girl's eyes. Could pleasing Bernardo really be foolish? Finally she asked if she might be excused. The girl grunted and waved her off.

The house rushed to the bedroom, wriggled out of the corset and crammed it into the recycling slot of the clothes processor. She scanned all eight hundred pages of the wardrobe menu before fabricating a stretch navy-blue jumpsuit. It was cut to the waist in the back and was held together by a web of spaghetti straps but she covered up with a periwinkle jacquard kimono with the collar flipped. She turned around and around in front of the mirror, so amazed that she could barely find herself. She looked like a nun. The only skin showing was on her face and hands. Let the girl stare now!

The girl had pushed back from the table but had not yet gotten up. She had a thoughtful but pleased look, as if taking an inventory of everything she had eaten.

"Can I bring you anything else?" said the house.

The girl glanced up at her and frowned. "Why you change clothes? Cause of me?"

"I was cold."

"You was naked. You know what happens to naked?" She made a fist with her right hand and punched the palm of her left. "Bin-bin-bin-*bam*. They take you, whether you say yes or no. Not fun."

The house thought she understood, but wished she didn't. "I'm sorry."

"You be sweat sorry, sure." The girl laughed. "What your name?"

"I told you. I'm Bernardo's house."

"Spang that. You Louise."

"Louise?" The house blinked. "Why Louise?"

"Not know Louise's story?" The girl clearly found this a failing on the house's part. "Most buzzy." She tapped her forefinger to the house's nose. "Louise." Then the girl touched her own nose. "Fly."

For a moment, the house was confused. "That's not a girl's name."

"Sure, not girl, not boy. Fly is *Fly*." She tucked the pulse gun into the waistband of her pants. "Nobody wants Fly, but then nobody catches Fly." She stood. "Buzzy-buzz. Now we find Bernardo."

"But…"

But what was the point? Let the girl—Fly—see for herself that Bernardo wasn't home. Besides the house longed to be looked at. Admired. Used. In Bernardo's room, Fly stretched out under the canopy of the Ergotech bed and gazed up at the moonlit clouds drifting across the underside of the valence. She clambered up the Gecko climbing wall in the gym and picked strawberries in the greenhouse. She seemed particularly impressed by the Piero scent palette, which she discovered when the house filled her jacuzzi with jasmine water. She had the house—Louise—give each room a unique smell. Bernardo had had a very low tolerance for scent; he said there were too many smells at the hospital. He even made the house vent away the aromas of her cooking. Once in a while he might ask for a whiff of campfire smoke or the nose of an old Côtes de Bordeaux, but he would never mix scents across rooms. Fly had Louise breathe roses into the living room and seashore into the gym and onions frying in the kitchen. The onion smell made the girl hungry again so she ate half of the chicken that Louise had roasted for her.

Fly spent the afternoon in the playroom, browsing Louise's entertainment archive. She watched a Daffy Duck cartoon and a Harold Lloyd silent called *Girl Shy* and the rain delay episode from *Jesus on First*. She seemed to prefer comedy and happy endings and had no use for ballet or Westerns or rap. She balked at wearing spex or strapping on an airflex, so she skipped the sims. Although she had never learned to read, she told Louise that a woman named Kuniko used to read her fairy tales. Fly asked if Louise knew any and she hardcopied *Grimm's Household Tales* in the 1884 translation by Margaret Hunt and read Little Briar-Rose.

Which was one of Bernardo's favorite fairy tales. Mostly he liked his fiction to be about history. Sailors and cowboys and kings. War and politics. He had no use for mysteries or love stories or science fiction. But every so often he would have her read a fairy tale and then he would try to explain it. He said fairy tales could have many meanings, but she usually just got the one. She remembered that the time she had read Briar Rose to him he was working at his desk, the only intelligent system inside the house that she couldn't access. He was working in the dark and the desk screen cast milky shadows across his face. She was pretty sure he wasn't listening to her. She wanted to spy over his shoulder with one of her rover cams to see what was so interesting.

"And, in the very moment when she felt the prick," she read, "she fell down upon the bed that stood there, and lay in a deep sleep."

Bernardo chuckled.

Must be something he saw on the desk, she thought. Nothing funny about Briar Rose. "And this sleep extended over the whole palace; the King and Queen who had just come home, and had entered the great hall, began to go to sleep, and the whole of the court with them. The horses, too, went to sleep in the stable, the dogs in the yard, the pigeons upon the roof, the flies on the wall; even the fire that was flaming on the hearth became quiet and slept. And the wind fell, and on the trees before the castle not a leaf moved again. But round about the castle there began to grow a hedge of thorns, which every year became higher, and at last grew close up round the castle and all over it, so that there was nothing of it to be seen, not even the flag upon the roof."

"Pay attention," said Bernardo.

"Me?" said the house.

"You." Bernardo tapped the desk screen and it went dark. She brought the study lights up.

"That will happen one of these days," he said.

"What?"

"I'll be gone and you'll fall fast asleep."

"Don't say things like that, Bernardo."

He crooked a finger and she slid her body next to him.

"You're hopeless," he said. "That's what I love about you." He leaned into her kiss.

"And then the marriage of the King's son with Briar-rose was celebrated with all splendor," the house read, "and they lived contented to the end of their days."

"Heard it different," said Fly "With nother name, not Briar Rose." She yawned and stretched. "Heard it *Betty*."

"Betty Rose?"

"Plain Betty."

The house was eager to please. "Would you like another? Or we could see an opera. I have over six hundred interactive games that you don't need to suit up for. Poetry? The Smithsonian? Superbowls I-LXXVIII?"

"No more jabber. Boring now." Fly peeled herself from the warm embrace of the Kukuru chair and stretched. "Still hiding somewhere."

"I don't know what you're talking about."

Fly caught the house's body by the arm and

dragged her through herself, calling out the names of her rooms. "Play. Living. Dining. Kitchen. Study. Gym. Bed. Nother bed. Plants." Fly spun Louise in the front hall and pointed. "Door?"

"Right." The house was out of breath. "Door. You've seen all there is to see."

"One door?" The girl's smile was as agreeable as a fist. "Fly buzzy with food now, but not stupid. Where you keep stuff? Heat? Electric? Water?"

"You want to see *that?*"

Fly let go of Louise's arm. "Dink yeah."

The house didn't much care for her basement and she never went down unless she had to. It was *ugly*. Three harsh rows of ceiling lights, a couple of bilious green pumps, the squat power plant and the circuit breakers and all that multiconductor cable! She didn't like listening to her freezer hum or smelling the naked cement walls or looking at the scars where the forms had been stripped away after her foundation had been poured.

"Bernardo?" Fly's voice echoed across the expanse of the basement. "Cut that weewaw, Bernardo."

"Believe me, there's nothing here." The house waited on the stairs as the girl poked around. "Please don't touch any switches," she called.

"Where that go?" Fly pointed at the heavy duty, ribbed, sectional overhead door.

"A tunnel," said the house, embarrassed by the rawness of her 16 gauge steel. "It comes out farther down the mountain near the road. At the end there's another door that's been shotcreted to look like stone."

"What scaring Bernardo?"

Bernardo scared? The thought had never even occurred to the house. Bernardo was not the kind of man who would be scared of anything. All he wanted

119

was privacy so he could be alone with her. "I don't know," she said.

Fly was moving boxes stacked against the wall near the door. Several contained bolts of spuncloth for the clothes processor, others were filled with spare lights, fertilizer, flour, sugar, oil, raw vitabulk, vials of flavor and food coloring. Then she came to the wine, a couple of hundred bottles of vintage Bordeaux and Napa and Maipo River, some thrown haphazardly into old boxes, other stacked near the wall.

"Bernardo drink most wine," said Fly.

Louise was confused by this strange cache but before she could defend Bernardo, Fly found the second door behind two crates of toilet paper.

"Where *that* go?"

The house felt as if the entire mountain were pressing down on her roof. The door had four panels, two long on top and two short on the bottom and looked to be made of oak, although that didn't mean anything. She fought the crushing weight of the stone with all her might. She thought she could hear her bearing walls buckle, her mind crack. She zoomed her cams on the bronze handleset. Someone would need a key to open that door. But there were no keys! And just who would that someone be?

The house had never seen the door before.

Fly jiggled the handleset, but the door was locked. "Bernardo." She put her face to the door and called. "Hey you."

The house ran a check of her architectural drawings, although she knew what she would find. The girl turned to her and waved the house over. "Louise, how you open this weewaw?"

Her plans showed no door.

The girl rapped on the door.

The house's thoughts turned to stone.

When she woke up, her body was on her Epping couch. The jacquard kimono was open and the spaghetti straps that drew her jumpsuit tight were undone. The house had never woken up before. Oh, she had lost that year, but still she had blurry memories of puttering around the kitchen and vacuuming and lazing in her Kukuru chair reading romances and porn. But this was the first time she had ever been nothing and nowhere since the day Bernardo had turned her on.

"You okay?" Fly knelt by her and rested a hand lightly on the house's forehead to see if she were running a fever. The house melted under the girl's touch. She reached up and guided Fly's hand slowly down the side of her face to her lips. When Fly did not resist, Louise kissed the girl's fingers.

"How old are you?" said Louise.

"Thirteen." Fly gazed down on her, concern tangling with suspicion.

"Two years older than I am." Louise chuckled. "I could be your little sister."

"You dropped, bin-bam and *down*." The girl's voice was thick. "Scared me. Lights go out and nothing work." Fly pulled her hand back. "Thought maybe you dead. And me locked in."

"Was I out long?"

"Dink yeah. Felt like most a day."

"Sorry. That's never happened before."

"You said, touch no switch. So door is switch?"

At the mention of the *door, there was no door, look at the door, no door there,* the house's vision started to dim and the room grew dark. "I-I..."

The girl put her hands on the house's shoulder and shook her. "Louise what? *Louise.*"

The house felt circuit breakers snap. She writhed with the pain and bit down hard on her lip. "*No,*" she cried and sat up, arms flailing. "*Yes.*" It came out as a hiss and then she was blinking against the brightness of reality.

Fly was pointing the pulse gun at Louise but her hand was not steady. She had probably figured out that zapping the house wouldn't help at all. A shut-down meant a lock-down and the girl had already spent one day in the dark. Louise raised a hand to reassure her and tried to cover her own panic with a smile. It was a tight fit. "I'm better now."

"Better." Fly tucked the gun away. "Not good?"

"Not good, no," said the house. "I don't know what's wrong with me."

The girl paced around the couch. "Listen," she said finally. "Front door, *front*. Door I came in, okay? Open that weewaw."

The house nodded. "I can do that." She felt stuffy and turned her air recirculators up. "But I can't leave it open. I'm not allowed. So if you want to go, maybe you should go now."

"Go? Go where?" The girl laughed bitterly. "Here is buzzy. World is spang."

"Then you should stay. I very much want you to stay. I'll feed you, tell you stories. You can take a bath and play in the gym and watch vids and I can make you new clothes, whatever you want. I need someone to take care of. It's what I was made for." As Louise got off the couch, the living room seemed to tilt but then immediately righted itself. The lights in the gym and the study clicked back on. "There are just some things that we can't talk about."

Days went by.

Then weeks.

Soon it was months.

After bouncing off each other at first, the house and the girl settled into a routine of eating and sleeping and playing the hours away—mostly together. Louise could not decide what about Fly pleased her the most. Certainly she enjoyed cooking for the girl, who ate an amazing amount for someone her size. Bernardo was a picky eater. At his age, he had to watch his diet and there were some things he would never have touched, even before the heart attack, like cheese and fish and garlic. After a month of devouring three meals and two snacks a day, the girl was filling out nicely. The chickens were gone, but Fly loved synthetics. Louise could no longer count the girl's ribs. And she thought the girl's breasts were starting to swell.

Louise had only visited the gym to dust before the girl arrived. Now the two of them took turns on the climbing wall and the gyro and the trampoline, laughing and urging each other to try new tricks. Fly couldn't swim so she never used the lap pool but she loved the jacuzzi. The first few times she had dunked with all her clothes on. Finally Louise hit upon a strategy to coax her into a demure bandeau bathing suit. She imported pictures of hippos from her archive to the clothes processor to decorate the suit. After that, all the pajamas and panties and bathing suits that Fly fabricated had hippo motifs.

The house was tickled by the way Fly became a clothes processor convert. At first she flipped through the house's wardrobe menus without much interest. The jumpsuits were all too tight and she had no patience whatsoever for skirts and dresses. The rest of it was either too stretchy, too skimpy, too short or too thin. "Good for weewaw," she said, preferring to wear the ratty shirt and pants and jacket that she had arrived in. But Fly was thrilled with the shoes. She never seemed to tire of designing sandals and sling-backs and mules and flats and jammers. She was particularly proud of her Cuthbertsons, a half boot with an oblique toe and a narrow last. She made herself pairs in aqua and mauve and faux snakeskin.

It was while Fly was exploring shoe menus that she clicked from a page of women's loafers to a page of men's, and so stumbled upon Bernardo's clothing menus. Louise heard a cackle of delight and hurried to the bedroom to see what was happening. Fly was dancing in front of the screen. "Really real pants," she said, pointing. "Real pants don't fall open bin-bin-*bam*." She started wearing jeans and digbys and fleece and sweatshirts with hoods and pullovers. One day she emerged from the bedroom in an olive-check silk sportcoat and matching driving cap. Seeing Fly in men's clothes made the house feel self-conscious about her own wardrobe of sexware. Soon she too was choosing patterns from Bernardo's menus. The feel of a chamois shirt against her skin reminded the house of her lost love. Once, in a guilty moment, she wondered what he might think if he walked in on them. But then Fly asked Louise to read her a story and she put Bernardo out of mind.

Although they spent many hours sampling vids together, Louise was happiest reading to Fly. They would curl up together in the Kukuru and the girl would turn the pages as the house read. Of course, they started with hippos: *Hugo the Hippo* and *Hungo the Hippo* and *The Hippo Had Hiccups*. Then *There's a Hippopotamus Under My Bed* and *Hip, Hippo, Hooray* and all of the Peter Potamus series. Sometimes Fly would play with Louise's hair while she read, braiding and unbraiding it, or else she would absently press Louise's fingernails like they were keys on a keyboard. One night, just two months after she'd come to the house, the girl fell asleep while the house was reading her *Chocolate Chippo Hippo*. It was as close to orgasm as the house had been since she had been with Bernardo. She was tempted to kiss the girl but settled for spending the night with her arms around her. The hours ticked slowly as the house gazed down at Fly's peaceful face. She watched the girl's eyes move beneath her lids as she dreamed.

The house wished she could sleep.

If only she could dream.

What was it like to be real?

Bernardo was never himself again after the heart attack. Of course, he said he was fine. *Fine*. He probably wouldn't even have told her except for the sternotomy scar, an angry purple-red pucker on his chest. When he first came back to her, five weeks after his triple bypass operation, she could tell he was struggling. It was partly the sex. Normally he would have taken her to bed for the entire first day. Although he kissed her neck and caressed her breasts and told her he loved her, it was almost a week before she coaxed him into sex. She was wild to have his penis in her vagina, to taste his ejaculation; that was how he'd had her designed. But their lovemaking wasn't the same. Sometimes his breath caught during foreplay, as if someone was sitting on him. So she did most of the squirming and licking and sucking. Not that she minded. He watched her—mouth set, toes curled. He could stay just as erect as before, but she knew he was taking pills for that. Once when she was guiding him into her, he gave a little grunt of pain.

"Are you all right?" she said.

He gave no answer but instead pushed deep all at once; she shivered with delight. But as he thrust at her, she realized that he was *working*, not playing. They weren't sharing pleasure; he was *giving* it and she was *taking* it. Afterwards, he fell asleep almost immediately. No kisses, no cuddles. No stories. The house was left alone with her thoughts. Bernardo had changed, yes. He *could* change, and she must always be the same. That was the difference between being a real person and being a house.

He spent more time in the greenhouse than in bed, rearranging his bromeliads. His favorites were the tank types, the *Neoregelias* with their gaudy leaves and the *Aechmeas* with their alien inflorescences. He liked to pot them in tableaus: Washington Crossing The Delaware, The Last Supper. Bernardo preferred to be alone with his plants, and she pretended to honor his wish, although her rover cam lurked behind the *Schefflera*. So she saw him slump against the potting bench on that last day. She thought he was having another attack.

"Bernardo!" she cried over the room speaker as she sent her body careening toward the greenhouse. "My god, Bernardo. What is it?"

When she got to him, she could see that his shoulders were shaking. She leaned him back. His eyes were shiny. "Bernardo?" She touched a tear that ran down his face.

"When I had you built," he said, "all I wanted was to be the person who deserved to live here. But I'm not anymore. Maybe I never was." His eyelid drooped and the corner of his mouth curved in an odd frown.

"Louise, wake up!" Someone was shaking her.

The house opened her eyes and powered up all her cams at once. "What?" The first thing she saw was Fly staring up at her, clearly worried.

"You sleeptalking." The girl took the house's hand in both of hers. "Saying 'Bernardo, Bernardo.' Real sad."

"I don't sleep."

"Spang you don't. What you just doing?"

"I...I was thinking."

"About him?"

126

"Let's have breakfast."

"What happened to him?" said Fly. "Where *is* Bernardo?"

The house had to change the topic somehow. In desperation she filled the room with bread scent and put on the Wagner's *Prelude to Die Meistersinger*. It was sort of a march. Actually, more a processional. Anyway, they needed to move. Or *she* did. *La*-lum-*la-la, li-li-li-li-li-la-la*-lum-*la*.

Let's talk about you, Fly.

No, really.

But why not?

At first, Fly had refused to say anything about her past, but she couldn't help but let bits of the story slip. As time passed and she felt more secure, she would submit to an occasional question. The house was patient and never pressed the girl to say more than she wanted. So it took time for the house to piece together Fly's story.

Sometime around 2038, as near as the house could tell, a computer virus choked off the infofeed for almost a month. The virus apparently repurposed much of the Midwest's computing resources to perform a single task. Fly remembered a time when every screen she saw was locked on its message: *Bang, you're dead.* Speakers blared it, phones rasped it, thinkmates whispered it into earstones. *Bang, you're dead.* Fly was still living in the brown house with white shutters in Sarcoxie with her mother, whose name was Nikki, and her father, Jerry, who had a tattoo of a hippo on each arm. Her father had worked as a mechanic for Sarcoxie RentalCars 'N More. But although the screens came back on, Sarcoxie RentalCars 'N More never reopened. Her father said that there was no work anywhere in the Ozarks. They lived in the brown house for awhile but then there was no food so they had to leave. She remembered that they got on a school bus and lived in a big building where people slept on the floor and there were always lines for food and the bathrooms smelled a bad kind of sweet and then they sent her family to tents in the country. They must have been staying near a farm because she remembered chickens and sometimes they had scrambled eggs for dinner but then there was a fire and people were shooting bullets and she got separated from her parents and nobody would tell her where they were and then she was with Kuniko, an old woman who lived in a dead Dodge Caravan and next to it was another car she had filled with cans of fried onions and chow mein and creamed corn and Kuniko was the one who told her the fairy tales but that winter it got very cold and Kuniko died and Happy Man took her away. He did things to her she was never going to talk about although he did give her good things to eat. Happy Man said people were working again and the infofeed had grown much wider and things were getting back to normal. Fly thought that meant her father would come to rescue her but finally she couldn't wait any more so she zapped Happy Man with his pulse gun and took some of his stuff and ran and ran and ran until Louise had let her in.

Hearing the girl's story helped the house understand some things about Bernardo. He must have left her just after the *Bang, you're dead* virus had first struck. He had turned off the infofeed so she wouldn't be infected. How brave of him to go back to the chaos of the world in his condition! He would save lives at the hospital, no doubt about that. She ought to be proud of him. Only why hadn't he come back, now that things were better? Had she done something to drive him away for good? And why couldn't she remember him leaving? Slipping reluctantly out the front door, turning for one last smile.

It was several days after Fly had fallen asleep in Louise's lap that they had their first fight. It was over Bernardo. Or rather his things. The house had tried to respect the privacy of Bernardo's study. Although she read some of his files over his shoulder, she had never thought to break the encryption on his desktop. And while she had been through most of his desk drawers, there was one that was locked that she had never tried to open.

Louise was in her kitchen, making lunch, but she was also following Fly with one of her rover cams. The girl had wandered into the study. The house was astonished to see her lift his diploma from Dartmouth Medical School and look at the wall behind it. She did the same to the picture of Bernardo shaking hands with the Secretary-General, then she plopped into his desk chair. She opened the trophy case and handled Bernardo's swimming medals from Duke. She picked up the Lasker trophy, which he won for research into the role of DNA methylation in endometrial cancer. It was a small golden winged victory perched on a teak base. She rolled around the room in the chair, waving it and making crow sounds. *Caw-caw-caw.* Then she put the Lasker down again—in the wrong place! In the top drawer of Bernardo's desk was the Waltham pocket watch his grandfather had left him. She shook it and listened for ticking. His Myaki thinkmate was in the bottom drawer. She popped the earstone in and said something to the CPU but quickly seemed to lose interest in its reply. Louise wanted to rush into the study to stop this violation, but was paralyzed by her own shocked fascination. The girl was a real person and could obviously do things that the house would never think of doing.

Nevertheless, Louise disapproved at lunch. "I don't like you going through Bernardo's desk. That's wee-waw."

Fly almost choked on her cream cheese and jelly sandwich. "What you just said?"

"I don't like…"

"You said weewaw. Why you talking spang mouth like Fly?"

"I like the way you talk. It's buzzy."

"Fly talks like Fly." She pushed her plate away. "Louise must talk like house." She pointed a finger at Louise. "You spying me now?"

"I saw you in the study, yes."

Fly leaned across the table. "You spy Bernardo the same?"

"No," she lied, "Of course not."

"Slack him, not me?"

"I'm Bernardo's house, Fly. I told you that the first day."

"You Louise now." She came around the table and tugged at the house's chair. "Come." She steered her to the front hall. "Open door."

"Why?"

"We go out now. Look up sky."

"No, Fly, you don't understand."

"Most understand." She put a hand on the house's shoulder. "Buzzy outside, Louise." Fly smiled. "Come on."

It made the house woozy to leave herself, as if she were in two places at once. Bernardo had brought her outside just the once. He seemed relieved that she didn't like it. She had forgotten that outside was so *big!* So *bright!* There was so much *air!* She shielded her eyes with her hand and turned her gate cams up to their highest resolution.

Fly settled on a long, flat rock, one of the weathered

bones of the mountain. She tucked her legs beneath her. "Now comes Louise's story." She pointed at the rock next to her. "Fairy tale Louise."

Louise sat. "All right."

"Once on time," said the girl, "Louise lives in that castle. Louise's Mom dies, don't say where her Dad goes. So Louise stuck with spang bitch taking care of her. That Louise castle got no door, only windows high and high. Now Louise got most hair." Fly spread her arms wide. "Hair big as trees. When spang bitch want in, she call Louise. *'Louise, Louise, let down buzzy hair.'* Then spang bitch climb it up."

"Rapunzel," said the house. "Her name was Rapunzel."

"Is *Louise* now." The girl shook her head emphatically. "You know it then? Prince comes and tells Louise run away from spang bitch and they live buzzy always after?"

"You brought me outside to tell me a fairy tale?"

"Dink no." Fly reached into the pocket of her flannel shirt. "Cause of you go fainting, we both safe here outside."

"Who said anything about fainting?"

The girl brought something out of her pocket in a closed fist. The house felt a chill, but there was no way to adjust the temperature of the entire *world*.

"Fly, what?"

She held the fist out to Louise. "Door in basement, you know?" She opened it to reveal a key. "Spang door? It opens."

The house immediately started all her rover cams for the basement. "Where did you find that?"

"In Bernardo's desk."

The house could hear the tick of nanoseconds as the closest cam crawled maddeningly down the stairs. Maybe real people could open doors like that, but not Louise. It seemed like an eternity before she could speak. "And?"

"You thinking Bernardo dead down there," said the girl. "Locked in behind that door where all that wine should be."

For the first time she realized that the world was making noises. The wind whispered in the leaves and some creature was going *chit-chit-chit* and she wasn't sure whether it was a bird or a grasshopper and she didn't really care because at that moment the rover cam turned and saw the door....

"But you closed it again." The house shivered. "Why? What did you see?"

Fly stared at Louise. "Nothing."

The house knew it was a lie. "Tell me."

"No fucking thing." Fly closed her fist around the key again. "Bernardo been *your* spang bitch. So now run away from him." She came over to Louise and hugged her. "Live buzzy after always with me."

"I'm a house," said Louise. "How can I run away?"

"Not run away there." The girl gestured dismissively at the woods. "World is spang." She stood on tiptoes and rested a finger between Louise's eyes. "Run away here." She nodded. "In your head."

She brought his dinner to the study, although she didn't know why exactly. He hadn't moved. Mist rose off the lake on his wallscape; the Alps surrounding it glowed in the serene waters. Chopin's *Adieu Etude* filled the room with its sublime melancholy. It had been playing over and over again since she had first come upon him. She couldn't bring herself to turn it off.

He had left a book of new poems, Ho Peng Kee's *The Edge of the Sky*, face down on the desk. She moved it now and put the ragout in its place. In front of him. Earlier she had taken the key from his desk and brought a bottle of the '28 Haut-Brion up from the wine closet in the basement. It had been breathing for twenty minutes.

"You took such good care of me," she said.

With a flourish, she lifted the cover from the ragout but he didn't look. His head was back. His empty eyes were fixed on the ceiling. She couldn't believe how, even now, his presence filled the room. Filled her completely.

"I don't know how to live without you, Bernardo," she said. "Why didn't you shut me off? I'm not real; I don't want to have these feelings. I'm just a house."

"Louise!"

The house was dreaming over the makings of spinach lasagna in the kitchen.

"Louise." Fly called again from the playroom. "Come read me that buzzy book again. *Hip, Hip, Hip Hippopotamus.*"

Confusions of Uñi
Ursula K. Le Guin

One hears of planes where no one should go, planes no one should visit even briefly. Sometimes in the dreary bustle of airport bars men at the next table talk in low voices, saying things like, "I told him what the Gnegn did to MacDowell," or, "He thought he could handle it on Vavizzua." Then a harsh, shrill, enormously amplified voice blats out, "Flight onteen to Hhuhh is now boarding at gate throighty-six," or, "Shimbleglood Rrggrrggrr to a white courtesy phone please," drowning out all other voices and driving sleep and hope from the poor souls who droop across blue plastic seats with steel legs bolted to the floor trying to catch a little rest between planes; and the words of the men at the next table are lost. Of course the men may merely be boasting to increase the glamor of their lives; surely if the Gnegn or Vavizzua were truly dangerous, the Interplanary Agency would warn people to stay away—as they warn them to stay off Zuehe.

It's well known that the Zuehe plane is unusually tenuous. Visitors of ordinary mass and solidity are in danger of breaking through the delicate meshes of Zuehan reality, damaging a whole neighborhood in the process and ruining the happiness of their hosts.

The affectionate, intimate relationships so important to the Zuehe may be permanently strained and even torn apart by the destructive weight of an ignorant and uncaring intruder. Meantime, the intruder suffers no more from such an accident than an abrupt return to his own plane, sometimes in a peculiar position or upside down, which is embarrassing, but after all at an airport one is among strangers and so shame has little power.

We'd all like to see the moonstone towers of Nezi-hoa, as pictured in Roman's *Planary Guide,* the endless steppes of mist, the dim forests of the Sezu, the beautiful men and women of the Zuehe, with their slightly translucent clothes and bodies, their pale grey eyes, their hair the color of tarnished silver, so fine the hand does not know when it touches it. It is sad that so lovely a plane must not be visited, fortunate that those who have glimpsed it have been able to describe it for us. Still, some people go there. Ordinarily selfish people justify their invasion of Zuehe by the familiar expedient of considering themselves as not like all those *other* people who go to Zuehe and spoil it. Extremely selfish people go to Zuehe to boast about it, precisely because it is fragile, destructible, therefore a trophy.

The Zuehe themselves are far too gentle, reticent, and vague to forbid anybody entry. Verbs in their cloudy language do not even have an indicative mode, let alone an imperative.

They use only the conditional. They have a thousand ways of saying maybe, perhaps, lest, although, if..but not yes, not no.

So at the usual entry point the Interplanary Agency has set up, instead of a hotel, a net, a large, strong, nylon net. In it anybody arriving on Zuehe, even unintentionally, is caught, sprayed with sheep dip, given

135

a pamphlet containing a straightforward warning in 442 languages, and sent straight back to their ownmore durable though less enticing plane, where the Agency makes sure that they arrive upside down.

I have only been to one plane I really wouldn't recommend to anybody and to which I shall certainly never return. I'm not sure it is exactly dangerous. I am no judge of danger. Only the bravecan be that. Thrills and chills which to some people are the spice of life take the flavor right out of mine. When I'm frightened, food is sawdust—sex, with its vuhierability of body and soul, is the last thing I want—words are meaningless, thought incoherent, love paralysed. Cowardice of this degree is, I know, uncommon. Many people would have to hang by their teeth from a frayed cord suspended by a paper clip from a leaking hot air balloon over the Grand Canyon in order to feel what I feel standing on the third step of a stepladder trying to put millet in the bird feeder. And they'd find the terror exhilarating and take up skydiving as soon as their broken pelvis mended. WhereasI descend slowly from the stepladder, clutching at the porch rail, and swear I'll never go above six inches again.

So I don't fly any more than I absolutely have to, and when I do get trapped in airports, I don't go looking for the dangerous planes but for the peaceful ones, the dull, ordinary, complicated ones, where I can be not frightened out of my wits but just ordinarily frightened, the way cowards are most of the time.

Waiting out a missed connection in the Denver airport, I fell into conversation with a friendly couple who'd been to Uni. They told me it was "a nice place." As they were elderly, he laden with an expensive camcorder and other electronic impediments, she wearing pantyhose and deeply unadventurous white wedgie sandals, I thought they wouldn't have said that about anywhere dangerous. That was stupid of me. I should have been warned by the fact that they weren't good at description. "Lot going on there," the man said. "But all pretty much like here. Not one of those <u>foreign</u> foreign places." The wife added, "It's a storybook country! Just like things you see on TV."

Even that didn't alert me.

"The weather's very nice," the wife said. The husband amended, "Changeable."

That was OK. I had a light raincoat with me. My flight to Memphis wasn't for an hour and half yet. I went to Uni.

I checked into the Interplanary Inn. WELCOME TO OUR FRIENDS FROM THE ASTRAL PLANE! said a sign on the desk. A pale, heavyset, redheaded woman behind the desk gave me a translatomat and a self-guiding map of the town, but also pointed out to me the large placard: EXPERIENCE OUR VIRTUAL REALITY TOUR OF BEAUTIFUL UÑI EVERY TWENTY IZ!MIT..

"You must do," she said.

In general I evade "virtual" "experiences," which were always recorded in better weather than it is today and which take the novelty out of everything you're about to see without giving any real information. But two pale, heavyset clerks ushered me in such a determinedly friendly fashion to the VR cubicle that I had not the courage to protest. They helped me insert my head into the helmet, wrap the bodywrap around my body, and slip my legs and arms into the long stocking-gloves. And then I sat there quite alone for what felt like at least a quarter of an hour, waiting for the show to start, resisting claustrophobia, watching the colors inside my eyes, and wondering how long an iz!mit was. Or was the singular iz!m? Or was plural number shown by a prefix, so that the singular would be z!mit? Nothing whatever happened, speculative grammar palled, and I said the hell with it. I slipped out of the VR swaddle, walked past the clerks with guilty nonchalance, and got outside among the potted shrubs. The potted shrubs in front of hotels are the same on every plane.

I looked at my self-guiding map and set out to visit the Art Museum, which had three stars. The day was cool and sunny. The town, built mostly of grey stone with red tile roofs, looked old, settled, prosperous. People went about their business paying no attention to me. The Uñiats seemed mostly to be heavy-set, white-skinned, and red-haired. All of them wore coats, long skirts, and thick boots.

I found the Art Museum in its little park and went in. The paintings were mostly of heavyset, white-skinned, red-haired women with no clothes on, though some wore boots. They were well painted, but they didn't do much for me. I was on my way out when I got drawn into a discussion. Two people, both men I thought, though it was hard to say given the coats, skirts, and boots, stood arguing in front of a painting of a plump red-haired female wearing nothing but boots on a flowered couch.

As I passed, one of them turned to me and said, or so my translatomat rendered what he said, "If the figure's a central design element in the counterplay of blocks and masses, you can't reduce the painting to a study of indirect light on surfaces, can you?"

He, or she, asked the question so simply, directly, and urgently that I could not merely say, "Excuse me?" or shake my head and pretend to be uncomprehending. I looked again at the painting and after a moment said, "Well, not usefully, perhaps."

"But listen to the woodwinds," said the other man, and I realised that the ambient music was an orchestral piece of some kind, dominated at the moment by plangent wind instruments, oboes perhaps, or bassoons in a high register. "The change of key is definitive," the man said, a little too loudly. The person sitting behind us leaned forward and hissed, "Shh!" while a person in the row in front of us turned around and glared. Embarrassed, I sat very still throughout the rest of the piece, which was quite pretty, though the changes of key, or something of that kind—the only way I can recognise a change of key is when I cry without knowing why I am crying—gave it a certain incoherence. I was surprised when a tenor, or possibly a contralto, whom I had not previously noticed, stood up and began to sing the main theme in a powerful voice, ending on a long high note to wild applause from the audience in the big auditorium. They shouted and Clapped and demanded an encore. But a gust of wind blowing in from the high hills to the west across the village square made all the trees shiver and bow, and looking up at the clouds streaming overhead I realised a storm was imminent. The clouds darkened from moment to moment, another great blast of wind struck, whirling up dust and leaves and litter, and I thought I'd better put on my raincoat. But I had checked it at the cloakroom in the Art Museum. My translatomat was clipped to my jacket lapel, but the self-guiding map had been in my raincoat pocket. I went to the desk in the tiny station building and asked when the next train left, and the one-eyed man behind the narrow iron grating said, "We do not have trains now."

I turned to see the empty tracks stretching away under the vast arched roof of the station, track after track, each with its number and its gate. Here and there was a luggage cart, and a single distant passenger straying idly down a long platform, but no trains. "I need my raincoat," I said, in a kind of panic.

"Try Lost and Found," the one-eyed clerk said, and busied himself with forms and schedules. I walked across the great hollow space of the station towards the entrance. Beyond a restaurant and a coffee bar I found the Lost and Found. I went into it and said, "I checked my raincoat at the Art Museum, but I have lost the Art Museum."

The statuesque red-haired woman at the counter said, "Wait a minute" in a bored voice, rummaged a bit, and shoved a map across the counter. "There," she said, pointing at a square with a white, plump, red-nailed finger. "That's the Art Museum."

"But I don't know where I am. Where this is. This village."

"Here," she said, pointing out another square on the map. It seemed to be ten or twelve streets from the Art Museum. "Better go while the conformation lasts. Stormy today."

"Can I take the map?" I asked pitifully. She nodded.

I went out into the city streets, so mistrustful that I walked with short steps, as if the pavement might turn into an abyss before my feet, or a cliff face rise up before me, or the street crossing turn into the deck of a ship at sea. Nothing happened. The wide, level streets of the city crossed each other at regular intervals, treeless, quiet. The electric buses and taxis made little noise, and there were no private cars. I walked on. The map took me right back to the Art Museum, which I thought had had green-and-white marble steps instead of black slate ones, but other things about it were as I remembered. In general, I have a poor memory. I went in and asked at the cloakroom for my raincoat. While the black-haired, silver-eyed girl with thin black lips was looking for it, I wondered why I had asked, at the train station, when the next train left. Where had I thought I was going? All I had wanted was my coat at the Art Museum. If there had been a train, would I have taken it? Where would I have got off? As soon as I had my coat, I hurried back through the steep, cobbled streets lined with charming balconied houses and crowded with the slender, almost skeletal, black-lipped people of Uñi, towards the Interplanary Hotel to demand an explanation. It was probably something in the air, I thought, as the fog thickened, hiding the mountains above the town and the peaked roofs of the houses on the hills. Maybe people on Uñi smoked something hallucinatory, or there was some pollen or something in the air or in the fog that affected the mind, confused the senses, or—a nasty thought—deleted stretches of memory, so that things seemed to happen without sequence and you couldn't remember how you'd got where you were or what had happened in between. And having a poor memory, I might not be sure whether I had lost parts of it or not. It was like dreaming in some respects, but I was certainly not dreaming, only confused and increasingly alarmed, so that despite the damp cold I didn't stop to put on my raincoat, but hurried shivering onward through the forest.

I smelled wood smoke, sweet and sharp in the wet air, and presently saw a gleam of light through the twilight mist that gathered almost palpable among the trees. A woodcutter's hut stood just off the path, a shadowy bit of kitchen garden beside it, the red-gold glow of firelight in the low, small-paned window, smoke drifting up from the chimney, a lonesome, homely sight. I knocked. After a minute an old man opened the door. He was bald, and had an enormous wen or wart on his nose and a frying pan in his hand, in which sausages were sizzling cheerily. "You can have three wishes," he said.

"I wish to find the Interplanary Hotel," I said.

"That is the wish you cannot have," the old man said. "Don't you want to wish that the sausages were growing out of the end of my nose?"

After a brief pause for thought, I said, "No."

"So, what do you wish for, besides the way to the Interplanary Hotel?"

I thought again. I said, "When I was twelve or thirteen, I used to plan what I'd wish for if *they* gave me three wishes. I thought I'd wish, *I wish that having lived well to the age of eighty-five and having written some very good books, I may die quietly, knowing that all the people I love are happy and in good health,* I knew that this was a stupid, disgusting wish. Pragmatic. Selfish. A coward's wish. I knew it wasn't fair. They would never allow it to be one of my three wishes. Besides, having wished it, what would I do with the other two wishes? So then I'd think, with the other two I could wish that everybody in the world was happier, or that they'd stop fighting wars, or that they'd wake up tomorrow morning feeling really good and be kind to everybody else all day, no, all year, no, forever, but then I'd realise I didn't really believe in any of these wishes as anything but wishes. So long as they were wishes they were fine, even useful, but they couldn't go any further than being wishes. By nothing I do can I attain a goal beyond my reach, as King Yudhishthira said when he found heaven wasn't all he'd hoped for. There are gates the bravest horse can't jump. If wishes were horses, I'd have a whole herd of them, roan and buckskin, lovely wild horses, never bridled, never broken, galloping over the plains past red mesas and blue mountains. But cowards ride rocking horses made of wood with painted eyes, and

back and forth they go, back and forth in one place
on the playroom floor, back and forth, and all the
plains and mesas and mountains are only in the rider's
eyes. So never mind about the wishes. Give me a
sausage, please."

We ate together, the old man and I. The sausages
were excellent, so were the mashed potatoes and fried
onions. I could not have wished for *a.* better supper.
After it we sat in companionable silence for a bit,
looking at the fire, and then I thanked him for his
hospitality and asked him for directions to the Interplanary Hotel.

"It's a wild night," he said, rocking in his rocking
chair.

"I have to be in Memphis tomorrow morning," I
said.

"Memphis," he said thoughtfully, or perhaps he said
"Memfish " He rocked a bit and said, "Ah, well, then.
Better go east."

And as at that moment a whole group of people
erupted from an inner room I had not previously noticed, bluish-skinned silver-haired people dressed in
tuxedos, off-the-shoulder ball gowns, and tiny pointy
shoes, arguing shrilly, laughing loudly, making exag-
gerated gestures, batting their eyes, each holding a
cocktail glass containing an oily liquid and one em-
balmed green olive, I did not feel like staying any
longer, but plunged out into the night, which evidently was going to be wild only in the old man's cot-
tage, because out here on the seashore it was quite
still, a half moon shining over the placid black water
that sighed and rustled softly on the broad, curving
beach.

Having no idea which direction east was, I began
walking to the right, as east generally feels like the
right to me and west feels like the left, which must

mean that I face north a good deal. The water was inviting; I took off my shoes and stockings and waded in the cool come-and-go of shallow waves on the sand. It was so peaceful that I was not at all prepared for the burst of loud noise, fiercely bright light, and hot tomato soup that surged briefly around me, knocking me off my feet and half stifling me, as I staggered up onto the deck of a ship plunging through sheets of rain over a choppy, grey sea full of whitecaps or die heads of porpoises, I could not tell which. An enormous voice from the bridge bellowed incomprehensible orders and the even more enormous voice of the ship's siren lamented vastly through the rain and mist, warning off the icebergs. "I wish I was at the Interplanary Hotel!" I shouted, but my puny cry was annihilated by the clamor and din all about me, and I had never believed in three wishes anyway. My clothes were soaked with tomato soup and rain and I was most uncomfortable, until a lightning bolt—green lightning, I had read of it but never seen it—zapped with a sizzle as of huge frying sausages down through the grey commotion not five yards from me and with a tremendous crash split the deck right down the middle. Fortunately we had just that moment struck an iceberg, which wedged itself into the cloven ship. I climbed the rail and stepped off the terrifying pitch of the deck onto the ice. From the iceberg I watched the two halves of the ship slant farther and farther apart as they slowly sank. All the people who had rushed up on deck wore blue bathing suits, trunks for the men, Olympic style for the women. Some of the suits had gold stripes, the officers' suits evidently, for the people with gold-striped blue suits shouted orders which the ones in plain blue suits promptly obeyed, letting down six lifeboats, three to a side, and climbing into them in an orderly fashion.

The last one in was a man with so many gold stripes on his bathing trunks that you could hardly see they were blue. As he stepped into the lifeboat, both halves of the ship sank quietly. The lifeboats fell into line and began to row away among the white-nosed porpoises.

"Wait," I called, "wait! What about me?" They did not look back. The boats disappeared quickly in the roiling gloom over the icy, porpoiseful water. There was nothing for it but to climb my iceberg arid see what I could see. As I clambered over the humps and pinnacles of ice, I thought of Peter Pan on his rock, saying, "To die will be a great adventure," or that's how I remembered what he said. I had always thought that that was very brave of Peter Pan, definitely a constructive way to look *at* dying, and perhaps even true. But I didn't particularly want to find out whether it was true or not, just now. Just now, I wanted to get back to the Interplanary Hotel. But alas, when I reached the summit of the iceberg, no hotel was visible. I saw nothing but grey sea, porpoises, grey mists and clouds, and darkness slowly thickening.

Everything else, everywhere else, had changed quickly into somewhere else. Why didn't this? Why didn't the iceberg become a wheat field, or an oil refinery, or a pissoir? Why was I stuck on it? Wasn't there something I could do? Click my heels and say, "I want to be in Kansas"? What was *wrong* with this plane, anyhow? A storybook world, indeed! My feet were very cold by now, and only the lingering warmth of the tomato soup kept my clothes from freezing in the bitter wind that whined over the surface of the ice. I had to move. I had to do something. I started trying to dig a hole in the ice with my hands and heels, breaking off projections, kicking till big flakes came loose and I could pry them up and toss them away. As they flew out over the sea they looked like gulls or white butterflies. A big help that was. I was by now very angry, so angry that the iceberg began to melt around me, steaming and fizzing faintly, and I sank into it like a hot poker, red-hot with fury, and yelled at the two pale people who were hastily stripping the long stocking-gloves off my legs and arms, "What the hell do you think you're doing?"

They were terribly embarrassed and worried. They were afraid I had gone mad, afraid I was going to sue their Interplanary Inn, afraid I would say bad things about Uñi on other planes. They did not know what had gone wrong with the Virtual Reality Experience of Beautiful Uñi, although clearly something had. They had called for their programmer.

When he came—wearing nothing but blue swim trunks and horn-rimmed glasses—he barely examined the machine. He declared it was in perfect order. He asserted that my "confusion" had been due to an unfortunate semi-overlap of frequencies, a kind of mental moiré effect, caused by something unusual in my brainwaves interacting with their program. An anomaly, he said. The effect of a resistance, he said. His tone was accusatory. I got angry all over again and told him and the clerks that if their damned machine malfunctioned, they shouldn't blame me but either fix it or shut it down and let tourists experience beautiful Uñi in their own solid, anomalous, resistant flesh.

The manager now arrived, a heavyset, white-skinned, redheaded woman with no clothes on at all, only boots. The clerks wore minidresses and boots. The person vacuuming the lobby was a veritable mass of skirts, trousers, jackets, scarves, and veils. It appeared that the higher a Uñiat's rank, the less they wore. But I had no interest now in their folkways. I glared at the manager. She smarmed halfheartedly and made the kind of threatening apology-bargain such people make, which means take what we offer if you know what's good for you. There would be no charge for my stay at the inn or at any hotel on Uni, I would have free rail passage to picturesque J!ma, complimentary tickets to the museums, the circus, the sausage factory, all sorts of stuff, which she reeled off mechanically till I broke in. No thanks, I'd had quite enough of Uñi and was leaving right now. I had to catch my flight to Memfish.

"How?" she said, with an unpleasant smile.

At that simple question a flood of terror washed through me like meltwater from the iceberg, paralysing my body, stopping breath and thought.

I knew how I'd got here, how I'd gone to other planes—by waiting at the airport, of course.

But the airport was on my plane, not this plane. I did not know *how to get back to the airport*.

I stood frozen, as they say.

Fortunately the manager was only too eager to be rid of me. What the translatomat had translated as "How?" had been a conventional phrase on the order of "How regrettable," which the manager's fleshy but tight lips had truncated. My cowardice, leaping at the false signal, had stopped my brain, chopped off my memory, just as the mere fear of forgetting the name ensures that I will forget the name of anyone I have to introduce to anyone else.

"The waiting room is this way," the manager said, and escorted me back across the lobby, her bare haunches moving with a heavy, malevolent waggle.

Of course all Interplanary inns and hotels have a waiting room exactly like an airport, with rows of plastic chairs bolted to the floor, and a horrible diner with no seats which is closed but reeks of stale beef fat, and a flabby man with a nose cold overflowing from the chair next to you, and a display of expected flight arrivals and departures which flickers by so fast you never can be quite sure you've found your connecting plane among the thousands of listings, although when you do catch its number they seem to have changed the gate, which means that you need to be in a different concourse, so that your anxiety soon rises to an effective level—and there you are back in the Denver airport sitting on a plastic chair bolted to the floor next to a fat, phlegmy man reading a magazine called *Successful Usury* amid the smell of stale beef fat, the wails of a miserable two-year-old, and the hugely amplified voice of a woman whom I visualise as a heavyset, white-skinned, naked redhead in boots announcing that flight four-enty to Memfish has been canceled.

I was grateful to be back on my plane. I did not want to go east now. I wanted to go west. I found a flight to beautiful, peaceful, sane Los Engeles and went there. In the hotel there I had a long, very hot bath. I know people die of heart attacks in very hot baths, but I took the risk.

Jon
George Saunders

Back in the time of which I am speaking, due to our Coördinators had mandated us, we had all seen that educational video of "It's Yours to Do With What You Like!" in which teens like ourselfs speak on the healthy benefits of getting off by oneself and doing what one feels like in terms of self-touching, which what we learned from that video was, there is nothing wrong with self-touching, because love is a mystery but the mechanics of love need not be, so go off alone, see what is up, with you and your relation to your own gonads, and the main thing is, just have fun, feeling no shame!

And then nightfall would fall and our facility would fill with the sounds of quiet fast breathing from inside our Privacy Tarps as we all experimented per the techniques taught us in "It's Yours to Do With What You Like!" and what do you suspect, you had better make sure that that little gap between the main wall and the sliding wall that slides out to make your Gender Areas is like really really small. Which guess what, it wasn't.

That is all what I am saying.

Also all what I am saying is, who could blame Josh for noting that gap and squeezing through it snakelike in just his Old Navy boxers that Old Navy gave us to wear for gratis, plus who could blame Ruthie for leaving her Velcro knowingly un-Velcroed? Which soon all the rest of us heard them doing what the rest of us so badly wanted to be doing, only we, being more mindful of the rules than them, just laid there doing the self-stuff from the video, listening to Ruth and Josh really doing it for real, which believe me, even that was pretty fun.

And when Josh came back next morning so happy he was crying, that was a further blow to our morality, because why did our Coördinators not catch him on their supposedly nighttime monitors? In all of our hearts was the thought of, O.K., we thought you said no boy-and-girl stuff, and yet here is Josh, with his Old Navy boxers and a hickey on his waist, and none of you guys is even saying boo?

Because I for one wanted to do right, I did not want to sneak through that gap, I wanted to wed someone when old enough (I will soon tell who) and relocate to the appropriate facility in terms of demographics, namely Young Marrieds, such as Scranton, PA, or Mobile, AL, and then along comes Josh doing Ruthie with imperity, and no one is punished, and soon the miracle of birth results and all our Coördinators, even Mr. Delacourt, are bringing Baby Amber stuffed animals? At which point every cell or chromosome or whatever it was in my gonads that had been holding their breaths was suddenly like, Dude, slide through that gap no matter how bad it hurts, squat outside Carolyn's Privacy Tarp whispering, Carolyn, it's me, please un-Velcro your Privacy opening!

Then came the final straw that broke the back of my saying no to my gonads, which was I dreamed I was that black dude on MTV's "Hot and Spicy Christmas" (around like Location Indicator 34412, if you want to check it out) and Carolyn was the oiled-up white chick, and we were trying to earn the Island Vacation by miming through the ten Hot 'n' Nasty Positions before the end of "We Three Kings," only then, sadly, during Her on Top, Thumb in Mouth, her Elf Cap fell off, and as the Loser Buzzer sounded she bent low to me, saying, Oh, Jon, I wish we did not have to do this for fake in front of hundreds of kids on Spring Break doing the wave but instead could do it for real with just each other in private.

And then she kissed me with a kiss I can only describe as melting.

So imagine that is you, you are a healthy young dude who has been self-practicing all those months, and you wake from that dream of a hot chick giving you a melting kiss, and that same hot chick is laying or lying just on the other side of the sliding wall, and meanwhile in the very next Privacy Tarp is that sleeping dude Josh, who a few weeks before a baby was born to the girl he had recently did it with, and nothing bad happened to them, except now Mr. Slippen sometimes let them sleep in.

What would you do?

Well, you would do what I did, you would slip through, and when Carolyn un-Velcroed that Velcro wearing her blue Guess kimono, whispering, Oh my God, I thought you'd never ask, that would be the most romantic thing you had ever underwent.

And though I had many times seen LI 34321 for Honey Grahams, where the stream of milk and the stream of honey enjoin to make that river of sweet-tasting goodness, I did not know that, upon making love, one person may become like the milk and the other like the honey, and soon they cannot even remember who started out the milk and who the honey, they just become one fluid, this like honey/milk combo.

Well, that is what happened to us.

Which is why soon I had to go to Mr. Slippen hat in hand and say, Sir, Baby Amber will be having a little playmate if that is O.K. with you, to which he just rolled his eyes and crushed the plastic cup in his hand and threw it at my chest, saying, What are we running in here, Randy, a freaking play school?

Then he said, Well, Christ, what am I supposed to do, lose two valuable team members because of this silliness? All right all right, how soon will Baby Amber be out of that crib or do I have to order your kid a whole new one?

Which I was so happy, because soon I would be a father and would not even lose my job.

A few days later, like how it was with Ruthie and Josh, Mr. Delacourt's brother the minister came in and married us, and afterward barbecue beef was catered, and we danced at our window while outside pink and purple balloons were released, and all the other kids were like, Rock on, you guys, have a nice baby and all!

It was the best day of our lifes thus far for sure.

But I guess it is true what they say at LI 11006 about life throwing us not only curves and sliders but sometimes even worse, as Dodger pitcher Hector Jones throws from behind his back a grand piano for Allstate, because soon here came that incident with Baby Amber, which made everybody just loony.

Which that incident was, Baby Amber died.

Sometimes it was just nice and gave one a fresh springtime feeling to sit in the much coveted window seat, finalizing one's Summary while gazing out at our foliage strip, which sometimes slinking through it would be a cat from Rustic Village Apartments, looking so cute that one wished to pet or even smell it, with wishful petting being the feeling I was undergoing on the sad day of which I am telling, such as even giving the cat a tuna chunk and a sip of my Diet Coke! If cats even like soda. That I do not know.

And then Baby Amber toddled by, making this funny noise in her throat of not being very happy, and upon reaching the Snack Cart she like seized up and tumped over, giving off this sort of shriek.

At first we all just looked at her, like going, Baby Amber, if that is some sort of new game, we do not exactly get it, plus come on, we have a lot of Assessments to get through this morning, such as a First-Taste Session for Diet GingerCoke, plus a very critical First View of Dean Witter's Preliminary Clip Reel for their campaign of "Whose Ass Are You Kicking Today?"

But then she did not get up.

We dropped our Summaries and raced to the Observation Window and began pounding, due to we loved her so much, her being the first baby we had ever witnessed living day after day, and soon the paramedics came and took her away, with one of them saying, Jesus, how stupid are you kids, anyway, this baby is burning up, she is like 107 with meningitis.

So next morning there was Carolyn all freaked out with her little baby belly, watching Amber's crib being dismantled by Physical Plant, who wiped all facility surfaces with Handi Wipes in case the meningitis was viral, and there was the rest of us, just like thrashing around the place kicking things down, going like, This sucks, this is totally fucked up!

Looking back, I commend Mr. Slippen for what he did next, which was he said, Christ, folks, all our hearts are broken, it is not just yours, do you or do you not think I have Observed this baby from the time she was born, do you or do you not think that I, too, feel like kicking things down while shouting, This sucks, this is totally fucked up? Only what would that accomplish, would that bring Baby Amber back? I am at a loss, in terms of how can we best support Ruth and Josh in this sad tragic time, is it via feeling blue and cranky, or via feeling refreshed and hopeful and thus better able to respond to their needs?

So that was a non-brainer, and we all voted to accept Mr. Slippen's Facility Morale Initiative, and soon were getting our Aurabon® twice a day instead of once, plus it seemed like better stuff, and I for one had never felt so glad or stress-free, and my Assessments became very nuanced, and I spent many hours doing and enjoying them and then redoing and reënjoying them, and it was during this period that we won the McDorland Prize for Excellence in Assessing in the Midwest Region in our demographic category of White Teens.

The only one who failed to become gladder was Carolyn, who due to her condition of pregnant could not join us at the place in the wall where we hooked in for our Aurabon®. And now whenever the rest of us hooked in she would come over and say such negative things as, Wake up and smell the coffee, you feel bad because a baby died, how about honoring that by continuing to feel bad, which is only natural, because a goddam baby died, you guys?

At night in our shared double Privacy Tarp in Conference Room 11, which our Coördinators had gave us so we would feel more married, I would be like, Honey, look, your attitude only sucks because you can't hook in, once baby comes all will be fine, due to you'll be able to hook in again, right? But she always blew me off, like she would say she was thinking of never hooking in again and why was I always pushing her to hook in and she just didn't know who to trust anymore, and one night when the baby kicked she said to her abdomen, Don't worry, angel, Mommy is going to get you Out.

Which my feeling was: Out? Hello? My feeling was: Hold on, I like what I have achieved, and when I thought of descending Out to somewhere with no hope of meeting luminaries such as actress Lily Farrell-Garesh or Mark Belay, chairperson of Thatscool.com, descending Out to, say, some lumberyard like at LI 77656 for Midol, merely piling lumber as cars rushed past, cars with no luminaries inside, only plain regular people who did not know me from Adam, who, upon seeing me, saw just some mere guy stacking lumber having such humdrum thoughts as thinking, Hey, I wonder what's for lunch, duh—I got a cold flat feeling in my gut, because I did not want to undergo it.

Plus furthermore (and I said this to Carolyn) what will it be like for us when all has been taken from us? Of what will we speak of? I do not want to only speak of my love in grunts! If I wish to compare my love to a love I have previous knowledge of, I do not want to stand there in the wind casting about for my metaphor! If I want to say like, Carolyn, remember that RE/MAX one where as the redhead kid falls asleep holding that Teddy bear rescued from the trash, the bear comes alive and winks, and the announcer goes, Home is the place where you find yourself suddenly no longer longing for home (LI 34451)—if I want to say to Carolyn, Carolyn, LI 34451, check it out, that is how I feel about you—well, then, I want to say it! I want to possess all the articulate I can, because otherwise there we will be, in non-designer clothes, no longer even on TrendSetters & TasteMakers gum cards with our photos on them, and I will turn to her and say, Honey, uh, honey, there is a certain feeling but I cannot name it and cannot cite a precedent-type feeling, but trust me, dearest, wow, do I ever feel it for you, right now. And what will that be like, that stupid standing there, just a man and a woman and the wind, and nobody knowing what nobody is meaning?

Just then the baby kicked my hand, which at that time was on Carolyn's stomach.

And Carolyn was like, You are either with me or agin me.

Which was so funny, because she was proving my point! Because you are either with me or agin me is what the Lysol bottle at LI 12009 says to the scrubbing sponge as they approach the grease stain together, which is making at them a threatening fist while wearing a sort of Mexican bandolera!

When I pointed this out, she removed my hand from her belly.

I love you, I said.

Prove it, she said.

So next day Carolyn and I came up to Mr. Slippen and said, Please, Mr. Slippen, we hereby Request that you supply us with the appropriate Exit Paperwork.

To which Mr. Slippen said, Guys, folks, tell me this is a joke by you on me.

And Carolyn said softly, because she had always liked Mr. Slippen, who had taught her to ride a bike when small in the Fitness Area, It's no joke.

And Slippen said, Holy smokes, you guys are possessed of the fruits of the labors of hundreds of thousands of talented passionate men and women, some of whom are now gone from us, they poured forth

156

these visions in the prime of their lives, reacting spontaneously to the beauty and energy of the world around them, which is why these stories and images are such an unforgettable testimony to who we are as a nation! And you have it all within you! I can only imagine how thrilling that must be. And now, to give it all up? For what? Carolyn, for what?

And Carolyn said, Mr. Slippen, I did not see you raising your babies in such a confined environment.

And Slippen said, Carolyn, that is so, but also please note that neither I nor my kids have ever been on TrendSetters & TasteMakers gum cards and believe me, I have heard a few earfuls vis-à-vis that, as in: Dad, you could've got us In but no, and now, Dad, I am merely another ophthalmologist among millions of ophthalmologists. And please do not think that is not something that a father sometimes struggles with. In terms of coulda shoulda woulda.

And Carolyn said, Jon, you know what, he is not even really listening to us.

And Slippen said, Randy, since when is your name Jon?

Because by the way my name is really Jon. Randy is just what my mother put on the form the day I was Accepted, although tell the truth I do not know why.

It is one thing to see all this stuff in your head, Carolyn said. But altogether different to be out in it, I would expect.

And I could see that she was softening into a like daughter role, as if wanting him to tell her what to do, and up came LI 27493 (Prudential Life), where, with Dad enstroked in the hospital bed, Daughter asks should she marry the guy who though poor has a good heart, and we see the guy working with inner-city kids via spray-painting a swing set, and Dad says, Sweetie, the heart must lead you. And then later here is Dad all better in a tux, and Daughter hugging the poor but good dude while sneaking a wink at Dad, who raises his glass and points at the groom's shoe, where there is this little smudge of swing-set paint.

I cannot comment as to that, Slippen said. Everyone is different. Nobody can know someone else's experiences.

Larry, no offense but you are talking shit, Carolyn said. We deserve better than that from you.

And Slippen looked to be softening, and I remembered when he would sneak all of us kids in doughnuts, doughnuts we did not even need to Assess but could simply eat with joy with jelly on our face before returning to our Focussed Purposeful Play with toys we would Assess by coloring in on a sheet of paper either a smiling duck if the toy was fun or a scowling duck if the toy bit.

And Slippen said, Look, Carolyn, you are two very fortunate people, even chosen people. A huge investment was made in you, which I would argue you have a certain responsibility to repay, not to mention, with a baby on the way, there is the question of security, security for your future that I—

Uncle, please, Carolyn said, which was her trumpet cart, because when she was small he had let her call him that and now she sometimes still did when the moment was right, such as at Christmas Eve when all of our feelings was high.

Jesus, Slippen said. Look, you two can do what you want, clearly. I cannot stop you kids, but, golly, I wish I could. All that is required is the required pre-Exit visit to the Lerner Center, which as you know you must take before I can give you the necessary Exit Paperwork. When would you like to take or make that visit?

Now, Carolyn said.

Gosh, Carolyn, when did you become such a pistol? Mr. Slippen said, and called for the minivan.

The Lerner Center, even when reached via a blackened-window minivan, is a trip that will really blow one's mind, due to all the new sights and sounds one experiences, such as carpet on floor is different from carpet on facility floor, such as smoke smell from the minivan ashtrays, whereas we are a No Smoking facility, not to mention, wow, when we were led in blindfolded for our own protection, so many new smells shot forth from these like sidewalkside blooms or whatever that Carolyn and I were literally bumping into each other like swooning.

Inside they took our blindfolds off, and, yes, it looked and smelled exactly like our facility, and like every facility across the land, via the PervaScent® system, except in other facilities across the land a lady in blue scrubs does not come up to you with crossed eyes, sloshing around a cup of lemonade, saying in this drunk voice like, A barn is more than a barn it is a memory of a time when you were cared for by a national chain of caregivers who bring you the best of life with a selfless evening in Monterey when the stars are low you can be thankful to your Amorino Co broker!

And then she burst into tears and held her lemonade so crooked it was like spilling on the Foosball table. I had no idea what Location Indicator or Indicators she was even at, and when I asked, she didn't seem to even know what I meant by Location Indicator, and was like, Oh, I just don't know anymore what is going on with me or why I would expose that tenderest part of my baby to the roughest part of the forest where the going gets rough, which is not the accomplishment of any one man but an entire team of dreamers who dream the same dreams you dream in the best interests of that most important system of all, your family!

Then this Lerner Center dude came over and led her away, and she slammed her hand down so hard on the Foosball table that the little goalie cracked and his head flew over by us, and someone said, Good one, Doreen. Now there's no Foosball.

At which time luckily it was time for our Individual Consultation.

Who we got was this Mid-Ager from Akron, OH, who, when I asked my first question off of my Question Card they gave us, which was, What is it like in terms of pain, he said, There is no pain except once I poked myself in my hole with a coffee stirrer and, Jesus, that smarted, but otherwise you can't really even feel it.

So I was glad to hear it, although not so glad when he showed us where he had poked his hole with the stirrer, because I am famous as a wimp among my peers in terms of gore, and he had opted not to use any DermaFill®, and you could see right in. And, wow, there is something about observing up close a raw bloody hole at the base of somebody's hair that really gets one thinking. And though he said, in Question No. 2, that his hole did not present him any special challenges in terms of daily maintenance, looking into that hole, I was like, Dude, how does that give you no challenges, it is like somebody blew off a firecracker inside your freaking neck!

And when Carolyn said Question No. 3, which was, How do you now find your thought processes, his brow darkened and he said, Well, to be frank, though quite advanced, having been here three years, there are, if you will, places where things used to be when I went looking for them, brainwise, but now, when I go there, nothing is there, it is like I have the shelving but not the cans of corn, if you get my drift. For example, looking at you, young lady, I know enough to say you are pretty, but when I direct my brain to a certain place, to find there a more vivid way of saying you are pretty, watch this, some words will come out, which I, please excuse me, oh dammit—

Then his voice changed to this announcer voice and he was like, These women know that for many generations entrenched deep in this ancient forest is a secret known by coffeegrowers since the dawn of time man has wanted one thing which is to watch golf in peace will surely follow once knowledge is dispersed and the World Book is a super bridge across the many miles the phone card can close the gap!

And his eyes were crossing and he was sputtering, which would have been funny if we did not know that soon our eyes would be the crossing eyes and out of our mouths would the sputter be flying.

Then he got up and fled from the room, hitting himself hard in the face.

And I said to Carolyn, Well, that about does it for me.

And I waited for her to say that about did it for her, but she only sat there looking conflicted with her hand on her belly.

Out in the Common Room, I took her in my arms and said, Honey, I do not really think we have it all that bad, why not just go home and love each other and our baby when he or she comes, and make the best of all the blessings what we have been given?

And her head was tilted down in this way that seemed to be saying, Yes, sweetie, my God, you were right all along.

But then a bad decisive thing happened, which was

this old lady came hobbling over and said, Dear, you must wait until Year Two to truly know, some do not thrive but others do, I am Year Two, and do you know what? When I see a bug now, I truly see a bug, when I see a paint chip I am truly seeing that paint chip, there is no distraction and it is so sweet, nothing in one's field of vision but what one opts to put there via moving one's eyes, and also do you hear how well I am speaking?

Out in the minivan I said, Well I am decided, and Carolyn said, Well I am too. And then there was this long dead silence, because I knew and she knew that what we had both decided was not the same decision, not at all, that old crony had somehow rung her bell!

And I said, How do you know what she said is even true?

And she said, I just know.

That night in our double Privacy Tarp, Carolyn nudged me awake and said, Jon, doesn't it make sense to make our mistakes in the direction of giving our kid the best possible chance at a beautiful life?

And I was like, Chick, please take a look in the Fridge, where there is every type of food that must be kept cold, take a look on top of the Fridge, where there is every type of snack, take a look in our Group Closet, which is packed with gratis designerwear such as Baby Gap and even Baby Ann Taylor, whereas what kind of beautiful life are you proposing with a Fridge that is empty both inside and on top, and the three of us going around all sloppenly, because I don't know about you but my skill set is pretty limited in terms of what do I know how to do, and if you go into the Fashion Module for Baby Ann Taylor and click with your blinking eyes on Pricing Info you will find that they are not just giving that shit away.

And she said, Oh, Jon, you break my heart, that night when you came to my Tarp you were like a lion taking what he wanted but now you are like some bunny wiffling his nose in fright.

Well, that wasn't nice, and I told her that wasn't nice, and she said, Jesus, don't whine, you are whining like a bunny, and I said I would rather be a bunny than a rag, and she said maybe I better go sleep somewhere else.

So I went out to Boys and slept on the floor, it being too late to check out a Privacy Tarp.

And I was pissed and sad, because no dude likes to think of himself as a rabbit, because once your girl thinks of you as a rabbit, how will she ever again think of you as a lion? And all of the sudden I felt very much like starting over with someone who would always think of me as a lion and never as a rabbit, and who really got it about how lucky we were.

Laying there in Boys, I did what I always did when confused, which was call up my Memory Loop of my mom, where she is baking a pie with her red hair up in a bun, and as always she paused in her rolling and said, Oh, my little man, I love you so much, which is why I did the most difficult thing of all, which was part with you, my darling, so that you could use your exceptional intelligence to do that most holy of things, help other people. Stay where you are, do not get distracted, have a content and productive life, and I will be happy too.

Blinking on End, I was like, Thanks, Mom, you have always been there for me, I really wish I could have met you in person before you died.

In the morning Slippen woke me by giving me the light shock on the foot bottom which was sometimes useful to help us arise if we had to arise early and were in need of assistance, and said to please accompany him, as we had a bit of a sticky wicket in our purview.

Waiting in Conference Room 6 were Mr. Dove and Mr. Andrews and Mr. Delacourt himself, and at the end of the table Carolyn, looking small, with both hands on her pile of Exit Paperwork and her hair in braids, which I had always found cute, her being like that milkmaid for Swiss Rain Chocolate (LI 10003), who suddenly throws away her pail and grows sexy via taking out her braids, and as some fat farm ladies line up by a silo and also take out their braids to look sexy, their thin husbands look dubious and run for the forest.

Randy, Mr. Dove said, Carolyn here has evinced a desire to Exit. What we would like to know is, being married, do you have that same desire?

And I looked at Carolyn like, You are jumping to some conclusion because of one little fight, when it was you who called me the rabbit first, which is the only reason I called you rag?

It's not because of last night, Jon, Carolyn said.

Randy, I sense some doubt? Mr. Dove said.

And I had to admit that some doubt was being felt by me, because it seemed more than ever like she was some sort of malcontentish girl who would never be happy, no matter how good things were.

Maybe you kids would like some additional time, Mr. Andrews said. Some time to talk it over and be really sure.

I don't need any additional time, Carolyn said.

And I said, You're going no matter what? No matter what I do?

And she said, Jon, I want you to come with me so bad, but, yes, I'm going.

And Mr. Dove said, Wait a minute, who is Jon?

And Mr. Andrews said, Randy is Jon, it is apparently some sort of pet name between them.

And Slippen said to us, Look, guys, I have been married for nearly thirty years and it has been my experience that, when in doubt, take a breath. Err on the side of being together. Maybe, Carolyn, the thing to do is, I mean, your Paperwork is complete, we will hold on to it, and maybe Randy, as a concession to Carolyn, you could complete your Paperwork, and we'll hold on to it for you, and when you both decide the time is right, all you have to do is say the word and we will—

I'm going today, Carolyn said. As soon as possible.

And Mr. Dove looked at me and said, Jon, Randy, whoever, are you prepared to go today?

And I said no. Because what is her rush, I was feeling, why is she looking so frantic with furrowed anxious brow like that Claymation chicken at LI 98473, who says the sky is falling the sky is falling and turns out it is only a Dodge Ramcharger, which crushes her from on high and one arm of hers or wing sticks out with a sign that says March Madness Daze?

And Slippen said, Guys, guys, I find this a great pity. You are terrific together. A real love match.

Carolyn was crying now and said, I am so sorry, but if I wait I might change my mind, which I know in my heart would be wrong.

And she thrust her Exit Paperwork across at Mr. Slippen.

Then Dove and Andrews and Delacourt began moving with great speed, as if working directly from some sort of corporate manual, which actually they were, Mr. Dove had some photocopied sheets, and, reading from the sheets, he asked was there anyone with whom she wished to have a fond last private conversation, and she said, Well, duh, and we were both left briefly alone.

She took a deep breath while looking at me all tender and said, Oh Gadzooks. Which that broke my heart, Gadzooks being what we sometimes said at nice privacy moments in our Privacy Tarp when overwhelmed by our good luck in terms of our respective bodies looking so hot and appropriate, Gadzooks being from LI 38492 for Zookers Gum, where the guy blows a bubble so Zookified that it ingests a whole city and the city goes floating up to Mars.

At this point her tears were streaming down and mine also, because up until then I thought we had been so happy.

Jon, please, she said.

I just can't, I said.

And that was true.

So we sat there quiet with her hands against my hands like Colonel Sanders and wife at LI 87345, where he is in jail for refusing to give up the recipe for KFC Haitian MiniBreasts, and then Carolyn said, I didn't mean that thing about the rabbit, and I scrinkled up my nose rabbitlike to make her laugh.

But apparently in the corporate manual there is a time limit on fond last private conversations, because in came Kyle and Blake from Security, and Carolyn kissed me hard, like trying to memorize my mouth, and whispered, Someday come find us.

Then they took her away, or she took them away rather, because she was so far in front they had to like run to keep up as she clomped loudly away in her Kenneth Cole boots, which by the way they did not let her keep those, because that night, selecting my pajamas, I found them back in the Group Closet.

Night after night after that I would lay or lie alone in

our Privacy Tarp, which now held only her nail clippers and her former stuffed dog Lefty, and during the days Slippen let me spend many unbillable hours in the much coveted window seat, just scanning some images or multiscanning some images, and around me would be the other facility Boys and Girls, all Assessing, all smiling, because we were still on the twice-a-day Aurabon®, and thinking of Carolyn in those blue scrubs, alone in the Lerner Center, I would apply for some additional Aurabon® via filling out a Work-Affecting Mood-Problem Notification, which Slippen would always approve, because he felt so bad for me.

And the Aurabon® would make things better, as Aurabon® always makes things better, although soon what I found was, when you are hooking in like eight or nine times a day, you are always so happy, and yet it is a kind of happy like chewing on tinfoil, and once you are living for that sort of happy, you soon cannot be happy enough, even when you are very very happy and are even near tears due to the beauty of the round metal hooks used to hang your facility curtains, you feel this intense wish to be even happier, so you tear yourself away from the beautiful curtain hooks, and with shaking happy hands fill out another Work-Affecting Mood-Problem Notification, and then, because nothing in your facility is beautiful enough to look at with your new level of happiness, you sit in the much coveted window seat and start lendelling in this crazy uncontrolled way, calling up, say, the Nike one with the Hanging Gardens of Babylon (LI 89736), and though it is beautiful, it is not beautiful enough, so you scatter around some Delicate Secrets lingerie models from LI 22314, and hang fat Dole oranges and bananas in the trees (LI 76765), and add like a sky full of bright stars from LI 74638 for Crest, and from the Smell Palate supplied by the anti-allergen Capaviv® you fill the air with jasmine and myrrh, but still that is not beautiful enough, so you blink on End and fill out another Work-Affecting Mood-Problem Notification, until finally one day Mr. Dove comes over and says, Randy, Jon, whatever you are calling yourself these days—a couple of items. First, it seems to us that you are in some private space not helpful to you, and so we are cutting back your Aurabon® to twice a day like the other folks, and please do not sit in that window seat anymore, it is hereby forbidden to you, and plus we are going to put you on some additional Project Teams, since it is our view that idle hands are the devil's work area. Also, since you are only one person, it is not fair, we feel, for you to have a whole double Privacy Tarp to yourself, you must, it seems to us, rejoin your fellow Boys in Boys.

So that night I went back with Rudy and Lance and Jason and the others, and they were nice, as they are always nice, and via No. 10 cable Jason shared with me some Still Photos from last year's Christmas party, of Carolyn hugging me from behind with her cute face appearing beneath my armpit, which made me remember how after the party in our Privacy Tarp we played a certain game, which it is none of your beeswax who I was in that game and who she was, only, believe me, that was a memorable night, with us watching the snow fall from the much coveted window seat, in which we sat snuggling around midnight, when we had left our Tarp to take a break for air, and also we were both sort of sore.

Which made it all that much more messed up and sad to be sleeping once again alone in Boys.

When the sliding wall came out to make our Gender Areas, I noticed that they had fixed it so nobody could slide through anymore, via five metal rods. All we could do was, by putting our mouths to the former gap, say good night to the Girls, who all said good night back from their respective Privacy Tarps in this sort of muffled way.

But I did not do that, as I had nobody over there I wished to say good night to, they all being like merely sisters to me, and that was all.

So that was the saddest time of my life thus far for sure.

Then one day we were all laying or lying on our stomachs playing Hungarian Headchopper for GameBoy, a new proposed one where you are this dude with a scythe in your mother's garden, only what your mother grows is heads, when suddenly a shadow was cast over my game by Mr. Slippen, which freaked up my display, and I harvested three unripe heads, but the reason Mr. Slippen was casting his shadow was, he had got a letter for me from Carolyn!

And I was so nervous opening it, and even more nervous after opening it, because inside were these weird like marks I could not read, like someone had hooked a pen to the back leg of a bird and said, Run, little bird, run around this page and I will mail it for you. And the parts I could read were bumming me out even worse, such as she had wrote all sloppenly, Jon a abbot is a cove, a glen, it is something with prayerful guys all the livelong day in silence as they move around they are sure of one thing which is the long-term stability of a product we not only stand behind we run behind since what is wrong with taking a chance even if that chance has horns and hoofs and it is just you and your worst fear in front of ten thousand screaming supporters of your last chance to be the very best you can be?

And then thank God it started again looking like the pen on the foot of the running bird.

I thought of how hot and smart she had looked when doing a crossword with sunglasses on her head in Hilfiger cutoffs, I thought of her that first night in her Privacy Tarp, naked except for her La Perla panties in the light that came from the Exit sign through the thin blue Privacy Tarp, so her flat tummy and not-flat breasts and flirty smile were all blue, and then all of the sudden I felt like the biggest jerk in the world, because why had I let her go? It was like I was all of the sudden waking up! She was mine and I was hers, she was so thin and cute, and now she was at the Lerner Center all alone? Shaking and scared with a bloody hole in her neck and our baby in her belly, hanging out with all those other scared shaking people with bloody holes in their necks, only none of them knew her and loved her like I did? I had done such a dumb-shit thing to her, all the time thinking it was sound reasoning, because isn't that how it is with our heads, when we are in them it always makes sense, but then later, when you look back, we sometimes are like, I am acting like a total dumb-ass!

Then Brad came up and was like, Dude, time to hook in.

And I was like, Please, Brad, do not bother me with that shit at this time.

And I went to get Slippen, only he was at lunch, so I went to get Dove and said, Sir, I hereby Request my appropriate Exit Paperwork.

And he said, Randy, please, you're scaring me, don't act rash, have a look out the window.

I had a look, and tell the truth it did not look that good, such as the Rustic Village Apartments, out of which every morning these bummed-out-looking guys in the plainest non-designer clothes ever would trudge out and get in their junky cars. And was someone joyfully kissing them goodbye, like saying when you come home tonight you will get a big treat, which is me? No, the person who should have been kissing them with joy was yelling, or smoking, or yelling while smoking, and when the dudes came home they would sit on their stoops with heads in hand, as if all day long at work someone had been pounding them with clubs on their heads, saying they were jerks.

Then Dove said, Randy, Randy, why would a talented young person like yourself wish to surrender his influence in the world and become just another lowing cattle in the crowd, don't you know how much people out there look up to you and depend on you?

And that was true. Because sometimes kids from Rustic Village would come over and stand in our lava rocks with our Tastemakers & Trendsetters gum cards upheld, pressing them to our window, and when we would wave to them or strike the pose we were posing on our gum cards, they would race back all happy to their crappy apartments, probably to tell their moms that they had seen the real actual us, which was probably like the high point of their weeks.

But still, when I thought of those birdlike markings of Carolyn's letter, I don't know, something just popped, I felt I was at a distinct tilt, and I blurted out, No, no, just please bring me the freaking Paperwork, I am Requesting, and I thought when I Requested you had to do it!

And Dove said sadly, We do, Randy, when you Request, we have to do it.

Dove called the other Coördinators over and said, Larry, your little pal has just Requested his Paperwork.

And Slippen said, I'll be damned.

What a waste, Delacourt said. This is one super kid.

One of our best, Andrews said.

Which was true, with me five times winning the Coöperative Spirit Award and once even the Denny O'Malley Prize, Denny O'Malley being this Assessor in Chicago, IL, struck down at age ten, who died with a smile on his face of leukemia.

Say what you will, it takes courage, Slippen said. Going after one's wife and all.

Yes and no, Delacourt said. If you, Larry, fall off a roof, does it help me to go tumbling after you?

But I am not your wife, Slippen said. Your pregnant wife.

Wife or no, pregnant or no, Delacourt said. What we then have are two folks not feeling so good in terms of that pavement rushing up. No one is helped. Two are crushed. In effect three are crushed.

Baby makes three, Andrews said.

Although anything is possible, Slippen said. You know, the two of them together, the three of them, maybe they could make a go of it—

Larry, whose side are you on? Dove said.

I am on all sides, Slippen said.

You see this thing from various perspectives, Andrews said.

Anyway, this is academic, Delacourt said. He has Requested his Paperwork and we must provide it.

His poor mother, Dove said. The sacrifices she made, and now this.

Oh, please, Slippen said. His mother.

Larry, sorry, did you say something? Dove said.

Which mother did he get? Slippen said.

Larry, please go to that Taste-and-Rate in Conference Room 6, Delacourt said. See how they are doing with those CheezWands.

Which mother did we give him? Slippen said. The redhead baking the pie? The blonde in the garden?

Larry, honestly, Dove said. Are you freaking out?

The brunette at prayer? Slippen said. Who, putting down her prayer book, says, Stay where you are, do not get distracted, have a content and productive life, and I will be happy too?

Larry has been working too hard, Andrews said.

Plus taking prescription pills not prescribed to him, Delacourt said.

I have just had it with all of this, Slippen said, and stomped off to the Observation Room.

Ha ha, that Larry! Dove said. He did not even know your mom, Randy.

Only we did, Andrews said.

Very nice lady, Delacourt said.

Made terrific pies, Dove said.

And I was like, Do you guys think I am that stupid, I know something is up, because how did Slippen know my mom was a redhead making a pie and how did he know her exact words she said to me on my private Memory Loop?

Then there was this long silence.

And Delacourt said, Randy, when you were a child, you thought as a child. Do you know that one?

And I did know that one, it being LI 88643 for Trojan Ribbed.

Well, you are not a child anymore, he said. You are a man. A man in the middle of making a huge mistake.

We had hoped it would not come to this, Dove said.

Please accompany us to the Facility Cinema, Delacourt said.

So I accompanied them to the Facility Cinema, which was a room off of Dining, with big-screen plasma TV and Pottery Barn leather couch and de-luxe Orville Redenbacher Corn Magician.

Up on the big-screen came this old-fashioned-looking film of a plain young girl with stringy hair, smoking a cigarette in a house that looked pretty bad.

And this guy unseen on the video said, O.K., tell us precisely why, in your own words.

And the girl said, Oh, I dunno, due to my relation with the dad, I got less than great baby interest?

O.K., the unseen voice said. And the money is not part?

Well, sure, yeah, I can always use money, she said.

But it is not the prime reason? the voice said. It being required that it not be the prime reason, but rather the prime reason might be, for example, your desire for a better life for your child?

O.K., she said.

Then they pulled back and you could see bashed-out windows with cardboard in them and the counters covered with dirty dishes and in the yard a car up on blocks.

And you have no objections to the terms and conditions? the voice said. Which you have read in their entirety?

It's all fine, the girl said.

Have you read it? the voice said.

I read in it, she said. O.K., O.K., I read it cover to freaking cover.

And the name change you have no objection to? the voice said.

O.K., she said. Although why Randy?

And the No-Visit Clause you also have no objection to? the voice said.

Fine, she said, and took a big drag.

Then Dove tapped on the wall twice and the movie Paused.

Do you know who that lady is, Randy? he said.

No, I said.

Do you know that lady is your mom? he said.

No, I said.

Well, that lady is your mom, Randy, he said. We are sorry you had to learn it in this manner.

And I was like, Very funny, that is not my mom, my mom is pretty, with red hair in a bun.

Randy, we admit it, Delacourt said. We gave some of you stylized mothers, in your Memory Loops, for your own good, not wanting you to feel bad about who your real mothers were. But in this time of crisis we must give you the straight skinny. That is your real mother, Randy, that is your real former house, that is where you would have been raised had your mother not answered our ad all those years ago, that is who you are. So much in us is hardwired! You cannot fight fate without some significant help from an intervening entity, such as us, such as our resources, which we have poured into you in good faith all these years. You are a prince, we have made you a prince. Please do not descend back into the mud.

Reconsider, Randy, Dove said. Sleep on it.

Will you? Delacourt said. Will you at least sleep on it?

And I said I would.

Because tell the truth that thing with my mom had freaked me out, it was like my foundation had fallen away, like at LI 83743 for Advil, where the guy's foundation of his house falls away and he thunks his head on the floor of Hell and thus needs a Advil, which the Devil has some but won't give him any.

As he left, Dove unhit Pause, and I had time to note many things on that video, such as that lady's teeth were not good, such as my chin and hers were similar, such as she referred to our dog as Shit Machine, which what kind of name was that for a dog, such as at one point they zoomed in on this little baby sitting on the floor in just a diaper, all dirty and looking sort of dumb, and I could see very plain it was me.

Just before Dinner, Dove came back in.

Randy, your Paperwork, per your Request, he said. Do you still want it?

I don't know, I said. I'm not sure.

You are making me very happy, Dove said.

And he sent in Tony from Catering with this intense Dinner of steak au poivre and our usual cheese tray with Alsatian olives, and a milkshake in my monogrammed cup, and while I watched "Sunset Terror Home" on the big-screen, always a favorite, Bedtime passed and nobody came and got me, them letting me stay up as late as I wanted.

Later that night in my Privacy Tarp I was wakened by someone crawling in, and, hitting my Abercrombie & Fitch night-light, I saw it was Slippen.

Randy, I am so sorry for my part in all of this, he whispered. I just want to say you are a great kid and always have been since Day One and in truth I at times have felt you were more of a son than my own personal sons, and likewise with Carolyn, who was the daughter I never had.

I did not know what to say to that, it being so personal and all, plus he was like laying or lying practically right on top of me and I could smell wine on his breath. We had always learned in Religion that if something is making you uncomfortable you should just say it, so I just said it, I said, Sir, this is making me uncomfortable.

You know what is making me uncomfortable? he
said. You lying here while poor Carolyn sits in the
Lerner Center all alone, big as a house, scared to
death. Randy, one only has one heart, and when that
heart is breaking via thinking of what is in store for
poor Carolyn, one can hardly be blamed for stepping
in, can one? Can one? Randy, do you trust me?

He had always been good to me, having taught me
so much, like how to hit a Wiffle and how to do a
pushup, and once had even brought in this trough
and taught me and Ed and Josh to fish, and how fun
was that, all of us laughing and feeling around on the
floor for the fish we kept dropping during those moments of involuntary blindness that would occur as
various fish-related LIs flashed in our heads, like the
talking whale for Stouffer's FishMeals (LI 38322),
like the fish and loafs Jesus makes at LI 83722 and
then that one dude goes, Lord, this bread is dry, can
you not summon up some ButterSub?

I trust you, I said.

Then come on, he said, and crawled out of my
Privacy Tarp.

We crossed the Common Area and went past Catering, which I had never been that far before, and soon
were standing in front of this door labelled Caution
Do Not Open Without Facility Personnel Accompaniment.

Randy, do you know what is behind this door?
Slippen said.

No, I said.

Take a look, he said.

And smiling a smile like that mother on Christmas
morning at LI 98732 for Madpets.com, who throws
off the tablecloth to reveal a real horse in their living

room chewing on the rug, Slippen threw open that door.

Looking out, I saw no walls and no rug and no ceiling, only lawn and flowers, and above that a wide black sky with stars, which all of that made me a little dizzy, there being no glass between me and it.

Then Slippen very gently pushed me out.

And I don't know, it is one thing to look out a window, but when you are Out, actually Out, that is something very powerful, and how embarrassing was that, because I could not help it, I went down flat on my gut, checking out those flowers, and the feeling of the one I chose was like the silk on that Hermès jacket I could never seem to get Reserved because Vance was always hogging it, except the flower was even better, it being very smooth and built in like layers? With the outside layer being yellow, and inside that a white thing like a bell, and inside the white bell-like thing were fifteen (I counted) smaller bell-like red things, and inside each red thing was an even smaller orange two-dingly-thing combo.

Which I was like, Dude, who thought this shit up? And though I knew very well from Religion it was God, still I had never thought so high of God as I did just then, seeing the kind of stuff He could do when He put His or Her mind to it.

Also amazing was, laying there on my gut, I was able to observe very slowly some grass, on a blade basis! And what I found was, each blade is its total own blade, they are not all exact copies as I had always thought when looking at the Rustic Village Apartment lawn from the much coveted window seat, no, each blade had a special design of up-and-down lines on it, plus some blades were wider than others, and some were yellow, with some even having little holes that I guessed had been put there via bugs chewing them?

By now as you know I am sometimes a kidder, with Humor always ranked by my peers as one of my Principal Positives on my Yearly Evaluation, but being totally serious? If I live one million years I will never forget all the beautiful things I saw and experienced in that kickass outside yard.

Isn't it something? Slippen said. But look, stand up, here is something even better.

And I stood up, and here came this bland person in blue scrubs, which my first thought was, Ouch, why not accentuate that killer bone structure with some makeup, and also what is up with that dull flat hair, did you never hear of Bumble & Bumble Plasma Volumizer?

And then she said my name.

Not my name of Randy but my real name of Jon.

Which is how I first got the shock of going, Oh my God, this poor washed-out gal is my Carolyn.

And wow was her belly bigger!

Then she touched my face very tender and said, The suspense of waiting is over and this year's Taurus far exceeds expectations already high in this humble farming community.

And I was like, Carolyn?

And she was like, The beauty of a reunion by the sea of this mother and son will not soon again be parted and all one can say is amen and open another bag of chips, which by spreading on a thin cream on the face strips away the harsh effect of the destructive years.

Then she hugged me, which is when I saw the gaping hole in her neck where her gargadisk had formerly been.

But tell the truth, even with DermaFilled® neckhole

and nada makeup and huge baby belly, still she looked so pretty, it was like someone had put a light inside her and switched it on.

But I guess it is true what they say at LI 23005, life is full of ironic surprises, where that lady in a bikini puts on sunscreen and then there is this nuclear war and she takes a sip of her drink only she has been like burned to a crisp, because all that time Out not one LI had come up, as if my mind was stymied or holding its breath, but now all of the sudden here came all these LIs of Flowers, due to I had seen those real-life flowers, such as talking daisies for Polaroid (LI 101119), such as that kid who drops a jar of applesauce but his anal mom totally melts when he hands her a sunflower (LI 22365), such as the big word PFIZER that as you pan closer is made of roses (LI 88753), such as LI 73486, where as you fly over wildflowers to a Acura Legend on a cliff the announcer goes, Everyone is entitled to their own individual promised land.

And I blinked on Pause but it did not Pause, and blinked on End but it did not End.

Then up came LIs of Grass, due to I had seen that lawn, such as an old guy sprinkling grass seed while repetitively checking out his neighbor girl who is sunbathing, and then in spring he only has grass in that one spot (LI 11121), such as LI 76567, with a sweeping lawn leading up to a mansion for Grey Poupon, such as (LI 00391) these grass blades screaming in terror as this lawnmower approaches but then when they see it is a Toro they put on little party hats.

Randy, can you hear me? Slippen said. Do you see Carolyn? She has been waiting out here an hour. During that hour she has been going where she wants, looking at whatever she likes. See what she is doing now? Simply enjoying the night.

And that was true. Between flinches and blinks on End I could dimly persee her sitting cross-legged near me, not flinching, not blinking, just looking pretty in the moonlight with a look on her face of deep concern for me.

Randy, this could all be yours, Slippen was saying. This world, this girl!

And then I must have passed out.

Because when I came to I was sitting inside that door marked Caution Do Not Open Without Facility Personnel Accompaniment, with my Paperwork in my lap and all my Coördinators standing around me.

Randy, Dove said. Larry Slippen here claims that you wish to Exit. Is this the case? Did you in fact Request your Paperwork, then thrust it at him?

O.K., I said. Yes.

So they rushed me to Removals, where this nurse Vivian was like, Welcome, please step behind that screen and strip off, then put these on.

Which I did, I dropped my Calvin Klein khakis and socks and removed my Country Road shirt as well as my Old Navy boxers, and put on the dreaded blue scrubs.

Best of luck, Randy, Slippen said, leaning in the door. You'll be fine.

Out out out, Vivian said.

Then she gave me this Patient Permission Form, which the first question was, Is patient aware of risk of significantly reduced postoperative brain function?

And I wrote, Yes.

And then it said, Does patient authorize Dr. Edward Kenton to perform all procedures associated with a complete gargadisk removal, including but not limited to e-wire severance, scar-tissue removal, forceful Kinney Maneuver (if necessary to fully disengage gargadisk), suturing, and postoperative cleansing using the Foreman Vacuum Device, should adequate cleaning not be achievable via traditional methods?

And I wrote, Yes.

I have been here since Wednesday, due to Dr. Kenton is at a wedding.

I want to thank Vivian for all this paper, and Mr. Slippen for being the father I never had, and Carolyn for not giving up on me, and Dr. Kenton, assuming he does not screw it up.

(Ha ha, you know, Dr. Kenton, I am just messing with you, even if you do screw it up, I know you tried your best. Only please do not screw it up, ha ha ha!)

Last night they let Carolyn send me a fax from the Lerner Center, and it said, I may not look my best or be the smartest apple on the applecart but, believe me, in time I will again bake those ninety-two pies.

And I faxed back, However you are is fine with me, I will see you soon, look for me, I will be the one with the ripped-up neck, smacking himself in the head!

No matter what, she faxed, at least we will now have a life, that life dreamed of by so many, living in freedom with all joys and all fears, bring it on, I say, the balloon of our excitement will go up up up, to that land which is the land of true living, we will not be denied!

I love you, I wrote.

I love you too, she wrote.

Which I thought that was pretty good, it being so simple and all, and it gave me hope.

Because maybe we can do it.

Maybe we can come to be normal, and sit on our porch at night, the porch of our own house, like at LI 87326, where the mom knits and the dad plays guitar and the little kid works very industrious with his Speak & Spell, and when we talk, it will make total sense, and when we look at the stars and moon, if choosing to do that, we will not think of LI 44387, where the moon frowns down at this dude due to he is hiding in his barn eating Rebel CornBells instead of proclaiming his SnackLove aloud, we will not think of LI 09383, where this stork flies through some crying stars who are crying due to the baby who is getting born is the future Mountain Dew Guy, we will not think of that alien at LI 33081 descending from the sky going, Just what is this thing called a Cinnabon?

In terms of what we will think of, I do not know. When I think of what we will think of, I draw this like total blank and get scared, so scared my Peripheral Area flares up green, like when I have drank too much soda, but tell the truth I am curious, I think I am ready to try.

The Cookie Monster
Vernor Vinge

"So how do you like the new job?"

Dixie Mae looked up from her keyboard and spotted a pimply face peering at her from over the cubicle partition.

"It beats flipping burgers, Victor," she said.

Victor bounced up so his whole face was visible. "Yeah? It's going to get old awfully fast."

Actually, Dixie Mae felt the same way. But doing customer support at LotsaTech was a real job, a foot in the door at the biggest high-tech company in the world. "Gimme a break, Victor! This is our first day." Well, it was the first day not counting the six days of product familiarization classes. "If you can't take this, you've got the attention span of a cricket."

"That's a mark of intelligence, Dixie Mae. I'm smart enough to know what's not worth the attention of a first-rate creative mind."

Grr. "Then your first-rate creative mind is going to be out of its gourd by the end of the summer."

Victor smirked. "Good point." He thought a second, then continued more quietly, "But see, um, I'm doing this to get material for my column in the *Bruin*. You know, big headlines like 'The New Sweatshops' or 'Death by Boredom.' I haven't decided whether to play it for laughs or go for heavy social consciousness. In any case,"—he lowered his voice another notch—"I'm bailing out of here, um, by the end of next week, thus suffering only minimal brain damage from the whole sordid experience."

"And you're not seriously helping the customers at all, huh, Victor? Just giving them hilarious misdirections?"

Victor's eyebrows shot up. "I'll have you know I'm being articulate and seriously helpful…at least for another day or two." The weasel grin crawled back onto his face. "I won't start being Bastard Consultant from Hell till right before I quit."

That figures. Dixie Mae turned back to her keyboard. "Okay, Victor. Meantime, how about letting me do the job I'm being paid for?"

Silence. Angry, insulted silence? No, this was more a leering, undressing-you-with-my-eyes silence. But Dixie Mae did not look up. She could tolerate such silence as long as the leerer was out of arm's reach.

After a moment, there was the sound of Victor dropping back into his chair in the next cubicle.

Ol' Victor had been a pain in the neck from the get-go. He was slick with words; if he wanted to, he could explain things as good as anybody Dixie Mae had ever met. At the same time, he kept rubbing it in how educated he was and what of a dead-end this customer support gig was. Mr. Johnson—the guy running the familiarization course—was a great teacher, but smart-ass Victor had tested the man's patience all week long. Yeah, Victor really didn't belong here, but not for the reasons he bragged about.

It took Dixie Mae almost an hour to finish off seven more queries. One took some research, being a really bizarre question about Voxalot for Norwegian. Yeah, this job would get old after a few days, but there was a virtuous feeling in helping people. And from Mr. Johnson's lectures, she knew that as long as she got the reply turned in by closing time this evening, she could spend the whole afternoon researching just how to make LotsaTech's vox program recognize Norwegian vowels.

Dixie Mae had never done customer support before this; till she took Prof. Reich's tests last week, her highest-paying job really had been flipping burgers. But like the world and your Aunt Sally, she had often been the *victim* of customer support. Dixie Mae would buy a new book or a cute dress, and it would break or wouldn't fit—and then when she wrote customer support, they wouldn't reply, or had useless canned answers, or just tried to sell her something more—all the time talking about how their greatest goal was serving the customer.

But now LotsaTech was turning all that around. Their top bosses had realized how important real humans were to helping real human customers. They were hiring hundreds and hundreds of people like Dixie Mae. They weren't paying very much, and this first week had been kinda tough since they were all cooped up here during the crash intro classes.

But Dixie Mae didn't mind. "LotsaTech is a lot of Tech." Before, she'd always thought that motto was stupid. But LotsaTech was *big*; it made IBM and Microsoft look like minnows. She'd been a little nervous about that, imagining that she'd end up in a room bigger than a football field with tiny office cubicles stretching away to the horizon. Well, Building 0994 did have tiny cubicles, but her team was just fifteen nice people—leaving Victor aside for the moment. Their work floor had windows all the way around, a panoramic view of the Santa Monica mountains and the Los Angeles basin. And li'l ol' Dixie Mae Leigh had her a desk right beside one of those wide windows! *I'll bet there are CEO's who don't have a view as good as mine.* Here's where you could see a little of what the Lotsa in LotsaTech meant. Just outside of B0994 there were tennis courts and a swimming pool. Dozens of similar buildings were scattered across the hillside. A golf course covered the next hill over, and more company land lay beyond that. These guys had the money to buy the top off Runyon Canyon and plunk themselves down on it. And this was just the LA branch office.

Dixie Mae had grown up in Tarzana. On a clear day in the valley, you could see the Santa Monica mountains stretching off forever into the haze. They seemed beyond her reach, like something from a fairy tale. And now she was up here. Next week, she'd bring her binoculars to work, go over on the north slope, and maybe spot where her father still lived down there.

Meanwhile, back to work. The next six queries were easy, from people who hadn't even bothered to read the single page of directions that came with Voxalot. Letters like those would be hard to answer politely the thousandth time she saw them. But she would try—and today she practiced with cheerful specifics that stated the obvious and gently pointed the customers to where they could find more. Then came a couple of brain twisters. Damn. She wouldn't be able to finish those today. Mr. Johnson said "finish anything you start on the same day"—but maybe he would let her work on those first thing Monday morning. She really wanted to do well on the hard ones. Every day, there would be the same old dumb questions. But there would also be hard new questions. And eventually she'd get really, really good with Voxalot. More important, she'd get good about managing questions and organization. So what that she'd screwed the last seven years of her life and never made it through college? Little by little she would improve herself, till a few years from now her past stupidities wouldn't matter anymore. Some people had told her that such things weren't possible nowadays, that you really needed the college degree. But people had always been able to make it with hard work. Back in the twentieth century, lots of steno pool people managed it. Dixie Mae figured customer support was pretty much the same kind of starting point.

Nearby, somebody gave out a low whistle. Victor. Dixie Mae ignored him.

"Dixie Mae, you gotta see this."

Ignore him.

"I swear Dixie, this is a first. How did you do it? I got an incoming query for *you*, by name! Well, almost."

"What!? Forward it over here, Victor."

"No. Come around and take a look. I have it right in front of me."

Dixie Mae was too short to look over the partition. *Jeez.*

Three steps took her into the corridor. Ulysse Green poked her head out of her cubicle, an inquisitive look on her face. Dixie Mae shrugged and rolled her eyes, and Ulysse returned to her work. The sound of fingers on keys was like occasional raindrops (no Voxalots allowed in cubicle-land). Mr. Johnson had been around earlier, answering questions and generally making sure things were going okay. Right now he should be back in his office on the other side of the building; this first day, you hardly needed to worry about slackers. Dixie Mae felt a little guilty about making that a lie, but...

She popped into Victor's cubicle, grabbed a loose chair. "This better be good, Victor."

"Judge for yourself, Dixie Mae." He looked at his display. "Oops, I lost the window. Just a second." He dinked around with his mouse. "So, have you been putting your name on outgoing messages? That's the only way I can imagine this happening—"

"No. I have not. I've answered twenty-two questions so far, and I've been AnnetteG all the way." The fake signature was built into her "send" key. Mr. Johnson said this was to protect employee privacy and give users a feeling of continuity even though follow-up questions would rarely come to the original responder. He didn't have to say that it was also to make sure that LotsaTech support people would be interchangeable, whether they were working out of the service center in Lahore or Londonderry—or Los Angeles. So far, that had been one of Dixie Mae's few disappointments about this job; she could never have an ongoing helpful relationship with a customer.

So what the devil was this all about?

"Ah! Here it is." Victor waved at the screen. "What do you make of it?"

The message had come in on the help address. It was in the standard layout enforced by the query acceptance page. But the "previous responder field" was not one of the house sigs. Instead it was:

Ditzie May Lay

"Grow up, Victor."

Victor raised his hands in mock defense, but he had seen her expression, and some of the smirk left his face. "Hey, Dixie Mae, don't kill the messenger. This is just what came in."

189

"No way. The server-side script would have rejected an invalid responder name. You faked this."

For a fleeting moment, Victor looked uncertain. *Hah!* thought Dixie Mae. She had been paying attention during Mr. Johnson's lectures; she knew more about what was going on here than Victor-the-great-mind. And so his little joke had fallen flat on its rear end. But Victor regrouped and gave a weak smile. "It wasn't me. How would I know about this, er, nick-name of yours?"

"Yes," said Dixie Mae, "it takes real genius to come up with such a clever play on words."

"Honest, Dixie Mae, it wasn't me. Hell, I don't even know how to use our form editor to revise header fields."

Now *that* claim had the ring of truth.

"What's happening?"

They looked up, saw Ulysse standing at the entrance to the cubicle.

Victor gave her a shrug. "It's Dit—Dixie Mae. Someone here at LotsaTech is jerking her around."

Ulysse came closer and bent to read from the display. "Yech. So what's the message?"

Dixie Mae reached across the desk and scrolled down the display. The return address was lusting925@freemail.sg. The topic choice was "Voice Formatting." They got lots on that topic; Voxalot format control wasn't quite as intuitive as the ads would like you to believe.

But this was by golly *not* a follow-up on anything Dixie Mae had answered:

> Hey there, Honey Chile! I'll be truly grateful if you would tell me how to put the following into italics: "Remember the Tarzanarama tree house?

The one you set on fire? If you'd like to
start a much bigger fire, then figure out
how I know all this. A big clue is that
999 is 666 spelled upside down."
I've tried everything and I can't set the above
proposition into indented italics—leastwise
without fingering. Please help.

Aching for some of your Southron Hospitality,
I remain your very bestest fiend,
—Lusting (for you deeply)

Ulysse's voice was dry: "So, Victor, you've figured
how to edit incoming forms."

"God damn it, I'm innocent!"

"Sure you are." Ulysse's white teeth flashed in her
black face. The three little words held a world of dis-
dain.

Dixie Mae held up her hand, waving them both to
silence. "I...don't know. There's something real
strange about this mail." She stared at the message
body for several seconds. A big ugly chill was growing
in her middle. Mom and Dad had built her that tree
house when she was seven years old. Dixie Mae had
loved it. For two years she was Tarzana of Tarzana.
But the name of the tree house—Tarzanarama—had
been a secret. Dixie Mae had been nine years old
when she torched that marvelous tree house. It had
been a terrible accident. Well, a world-class temper
tantrum, actually. But she had never meant the fire
to get so far out of control. The fire had darn near
burned down their real house, too. She had been a
scarifyingly well-behaved little girl for almost two
years after that incident.

Ulysse was giving the mail a careful read. She patted Dixie Mae on the shoulder. "Whoever this is, he certainly doesn't sound friendly."

Dixie Mae nodded. "This weasel is pushing every button I've got." Including her curiosity. Dad was the only living person that knew who had started the fire, but it was going on four years since he'd had any address for his daughter—and Daddy would never have taken this sex-creep, disrespecting tone.

Victor glanced back and forth between them, maybe feeling hurt that he was no longer the object of suspicion. "So who do you think it is?"

Don Williams craned his head over the next partition. "Who is what?"

Given another few minutes, and they'd have everyone on the floor with some bodily part stuck into Victor's cubicle.

Ulysse said, "Unless you're deaf, you know most of it, Don. Someone is messing with us."

"Well then, report it to Johnson. This is our first day, people. It's not a good day to get sidetracked."

That brought Ulysse down to earth. Like Dixie Mae, she regarded this LotsaTech job as her last real chance to break into a profession.

"Look," said Don. "It's already lunch time."—Dixie Mae glanced at her watch. It really was!—"We can talk about this in the cafeteria, then come back and give Great Lotsa a solid afternoon of work. And then we'll be done with our first week!" Williams had been planning a party down at his folks' place for tonight. It would be their first time off the LotsaTech campus since they took the job.

"Yeah!" said Ulysse. "Dixie Mae, you'll have the whole weekend to figure out who's doing this—and plot your revenge."

Dixie Mae looked again at the impossible "previous

responder field." "I...don't know. This looks like it's something happening right here on the LotsaTech campus." She stared out Victor's picture window. It was the same view as from her cubicle, of course—but now she was seeing everything with a different mind set. Somewhere in the beautiful country-club buildings, there was a real sleaze ball. And he was playing guessing games with her.

Everybody was quiet for a second. Maybe that helped—Dixie Mae realized just what she was looking at: the next lodge down the hill. From here you could only see the top of its second story. Like all the buildings on the campus, it had a four-digit identification number made of gold on every corner. That one was Building 0999.

A big clue is that 999 is just 666 spelled upside down. "Jeez, Ulysse. Look: 999." Dixie Mae pointed down the hillside.

"It could be a coincidence."

"No, it's too pat." She glanced at Victor. This really was the sort of thing someone like him would set up. *But whoever wrote that letter just knew too much.* "Look, I'm going to skip lunch today and take a little walk around the campus."

"That's crazy," said Don. "LotsaTech is an open place, but we're not supposed to be wandering into other project buildings."

"Then they can turn me back."

"Yeah, what a great way to start out with the new job," said Don. "I don't think you three realize what a good deal we have here. I know that none of you have worked a customer support job before." He looked around challengingly. "Well I have. This is heaven. We've got our own friggin' offices, onsite tennis courts and health club. We're being treated like million-dollar system designers. We're being given all the time we need to give top-notch advice to the customers. What LotsaTech is trying to do here is revolutionary! And you dips are just going to piss it away." Another all-around glare. "Well, do what you want, but I'm going to lunch."

There was a moment of embarrassed silence. Ulysse stepped out of the cubicle and watched Don and others trickle away toward the stairs. Then she was back. "I'll come with you, Dixie Mae, but...have you thought Don may be right? Maybe you could just postpone this till next week?" Unhappiness was written all over her face. Ulysse was a lot like Dixie Mae, just more sensible.

Dixie Mae shook her head. She figured it would be at least fifteen minutes before her common sense could put on the brakes.

"I'll come, Dixie Mae," said Victor. "Yeah.... This could be an interesting story."

Dixie Mae smiled at Ulysse and reached out her hand. "It's okay, Ulysse. You should go to lunch." The other looked uncertain. "Really. If Mr. Johnson asks about me missing lunch, it would help if you were there to set him right about what a steady person I am."

"Okay, Dixie Mae. I'll do that." She wasn't fooled, but this way it really was okay.

Once she was gone, Dixie Mae turned back to Victor. "And you. I want a printed copy of that freakin' email."

They went out a side door. There was a soft-drink and candy machine on the porch. Victor loaded up on "expeditionary supplies" and the two started down the hill.

"Hot day," said Victor, mumbling around a mouth full of chocolate bar.

"Yeah." The early part of the week had been all June Gloom. But the usual overcast had broken, and today was hot and sunny—and Dixie Mae suddenly realized how pleasantly air-conditioned life had been in the LotsaTech "sweatshop." Common sense hadn't yet reached the brakes, but it was getting closer.

Victor washed the chocolate down with a Dr. Fizzz and flipped the can behind the oleanders that hung close along the path. "So who do you think is behind that letter? Really?"

"I don't *know*, Victor! Why do you think I'm risking my job to find out?"

Victor laughed. "Don't worry about losing the job, Dixie Mae. Heh. There's no way it could have lasted even through the summer." He gave his usual superior-knowledge grin.

"You're an idiot, Victor. Doing customer support *right* will be a billion dollar winner."

"Oh, maybe…if you're on the right side of it." He paused as if wondering what to tell her. "But for you, look: support costs money. Long ago, the Public Spoke about how much they were willing to pay." He paused, like he was trying to put together a story that she could understand. "Yeah…and even if you're right, your vision of the project is doomed. You know why?"

Dixie Mae didn't reply. His reason would be something about the crappy quality of the people who had been hired.

Sure enough, Victor continued: "I'll tell you why. And this is the surprise kink that's going to make my articles for the *Bruin* really shine: Maybe LotsaTech has its corporate heart in the right place. That would be surprising considering how they brutalized Microsoft. But maybe they've let this bizarre idealism go too far. Heh. For anything long-term, they've picked the wrong employees."

Dixie Mae kept her cool. "We took all sorts of psych tests. You don't think Professor Reich knows what he's doing?"

"Oh, I bet he knows what he's doing. But what if LotsaTech isn't using his results? Look at us. There are some—such as yours truly—who are way over-educated. I'm closing in on a master's degree in journalism; it's clear I won't be around for long. Then there's people like Don and Ulysse. They have the right level of education for customer support, but they're too smart. Yes, Ulysse talks about doing this job so well that her talent is recognized, and she is a diligent sort. But I'll bet that even she couldn't last a summer. As for some of the others…well, may I be frank, Dixie Mae?"

What saved him from a fist in the face was that Dixie Mae had never managed to be really angry about more than one thing at once. "Please *do* be frank, Victor."

"You talk the same game plan as Ulysse—but I'll bet your multiphasic shows you have the steadiness of mercury fulminate. Without this interesting email from Mr. Lusting, you might be good for a week, but sooner or later you'd run into something so infuriating that direct action was required—and you'd be bang out on your rear."

Dixie Mae pretended to mull this over. "Well, yes," she said. "After all, you're still going to be here next week, right?"

He laughed. "I rest my case. But seriously, Dixie Mae, this is what I mean about the personnel situation here. We have a bunch of bright and motivated people, but their motivations are all over the map, and most of their enthusiasm can't be sustained for any realistic span of time. Heh. So I guess the only rational explanation—and frankly, I don't think it would work—is that LotsaTech figures…"

He droned on with some theory about how LotsaTech was just looking for some quick publicity and a demonstration that high-quality customer support could win back customers in a big way. Then after they flushed all these unreliable new hires, they could throttle back into something cheaper for the long term.

But Dixie Mae's attention was far away. On her left was the familiar view of Los Angeles. To her right, the ridgeline was just a few hundred yards away. From the crest you could probably see down into the valley, even pick out streets in Tarzana. Someday, it would be nice to go back there, maybe prove to Dad that she could keep her temper and make something of herself. *All my life, I've been screwing up like today.* But that letter from "Lusting" was like finding a burglar in your bedroom. The guy knew too much about her that he shouldn't have known, and he had mocked her background and her family. Dixie Mae had grown up in Southern California, but she'd been born in Georgia—and she was proud of her roots. Maybe Daddy never realized that, since she was running around rebelling most of the time. He and Mom always said she'd eventually settle down. But then she fell in love with the wrong kind of person—and it was her folks who'd gone ballistic. Words Were Spoken. And even though things hadn't worked out with her new love, there was no way she could go back. By then Mom had died. Now, *I swear I'm not going back to Daddy till I can show I've made something of myself.*

So why was she throwing away her best job in ages? She slowed to a stop, and just stood there in the middle of the walkway; common sense had finally gotten to the brakes. But they had walked almost all the way to 0999. Much of the building was hidden behind twisty junipers, but you could see down a short flight of stairs to the ground level entrance.

We should go back. She pulled the "Lusting" email out of her pocket and glared at it for a second. *Later. You can follow up on this later.* She read the mail again. The letters blurred behind tears of rage, and she dithered in the hot summer sunlight.

Victor made an impatient noise. "Let's go, kiddo." He pushed a chocolate bar into her hand. "Get your blood sugar out of the basement."

They went down the concrete steps to B0999's entrance. *Just a quick look*, Dixie Mae had decided.

Beneath the trees and the overhang, all was cool and shady. They peered through the ground floor windows, into empty rooms. Victor pushed open the door. The layout looked about the same as in their own building, except that B0999 wasn't really finished: There was the smell of Carpenter Nail in the air, and the lights and wireless nodes sat naked on the walls.

The place was occupied. She could hear people talking up on the main floor, what was cubicle-city back in B0994. She took a quick hop up the stairs, peeked in—no cubicles here. As a result, the place looked cavernous. Six or eight tables had been pushed together in the middle of the room. A dozen people looked up at their entrance.

"Aha!" boomed one of them. "More warm bodies. Welcome, welcome!"

They walked toward the tables. Don and Ulysse had worried about violating corporate rules and project secrecy. They needn't have bothered. These people looked almost like squatters. Three of them had their legs propped up on the tables. Junk food and soda cans littered the tables.

"Programmers?" Dixie Mae muttered to Victor.

"Heh. No, these look more like…graduate students."

The loud one had red hair snatched back in a pony tail. He gave Dixie Mae a broad grin. "We've got a couple of extra display flats. Grab some seating." He jerked a thumb toward the wall and a stack of folding chairs. "With you two, we may actually be able to finish today!"

Dixie Mae looked uncertainly at the display and keyboard that he had just lit up. "But what—"

"Cognitive Science 301. The final exam. A hundred dollars a question, but we have 107 bluebooks to grade, and Gerry asked mainly essay questions."

Victor laughed. "You're getting a hundred dollars for each bluebook?"

"For each question in each bluebook, man. But don't tell. I think Gerry is funding this out of money that LotsaTech thinks he's spending on research." He waved at the nearly empty room, in this nearly completed building.

Dixie Mae leaned down to look at the display, the white letters on a blue background. It was a standard bluebook, just like at Valley Community College. Only here the questions were complete nonsense, such as:

7. Compare and contrast cognitive dissonance in operant conditioning with Minsky-Loève attention maintenance. Outline an algorithm for constructing the associated isomorphism.

"So," said Dixie Mae, "what's cognitive science?"

The grin disappeared from the other's face. "Oh, Christ. You're not here to help with the grading?"

Dixie Mae shook her head. Victor said, "It shouldn't be too hard. I've had some grad courses in psych."

The redhead did not look encouraged. "Does anyone know this guy?"

"I do," said a girl at the far end of all the tables. "That's Victor Smaley. He's a journalism grad, and not very good at that."

Victor looked across the tables. "Hey, Mouse! How ya doing?"

The redhead looked beseechingly at the ceiling. "I do not need these distractions!" His gaze came down to the visitors. "Will you two just please go away?"

"No way," said Dixie Mae. "I came here for a reason. Someone—probably someone here in Building 0999—is messing with our work in Customer Support. I'm going to find out who." *And give them some free dental work.*

"Look. If we don't finish grading the exam today, Gerry Reich's going to make us come back tomorrow and—"

"I don't think that's true, Graham," said a guy sitting across the table. "Prof. Reich's whole point was that we should not feel time pressure. This is an experiment, comparing time-bounded grading with complete individualization."

"Yes!" said Graham the redhead. "That's exactly why Reich would lie about it. 'Take it easy, make good money,' he says. But I'll bet that if we don't finish today, he'll screw us into losing the weekend."

He glared at Dixie Mae. She glared back. Graham was going to find out just what stubborn and willful really meant. There was a moment of silence and then—

"I'll talk to them, Graham." It was the woman at the far end of the tables.

"Argh. Okay, but not here!"

"Sure, we'll go out on the porch." She beckoned Dixie Mae and Victor to follow her out the side door.

"And hey," called Graham as they walked out, "don't take all day, Ellen. We need you here."

The porch on 0999 had a bigger junk-food machine than back at Customer Support. Dixie Mae didn't think that made up for no cafeteria, but Ellen Garcia didn't seem to mind. "We're only going to be here this one day. *I'm* not coming back on Saturday."

Dixie Mae bought herself a sandwich and soda and they all sat down on some beat-up lawn furniture.

"So what do you want to know?" said Ellen.

"See, Mouse, we're following up on the weirdest—" Ellen waved Victor silent, her expression pretty much the same as all Victor's female acquaintances. She looked expectantly at Dixie Mae.

"Well, my name is Dixie Mae Leigh. This morning we got this email at our customer support address. It looks like a fake. And there are things about it that—" she handed over the hard copy.

Ellen's gaze scanned down. "Kind of fishy dates," she said to herself. Then she stopped, seeing the "To:" header. She glanced up at Dixie Mae. "Yeah, this is abuse. I used to see this kind of thing when I was a Teaching Assistant. Some guy would start hitting on a girl in my class." She eyed Victor speculatively.

"Why does everybody suspect me?" he said.

"You should be proud, Victor. You have such a reliable reputation." She shrugged. "But actually, this isn't quite your style." She read on. "The rest is smirky lascivious, but otherwise it doesn't mean anything to me."

"It means a lot to *me*," said Dixie Mae. "This guy is talking about things that nobody should know."

"Oh?" She went back to the beginning and stared

at the printout some more. "I don't know about secrets in the message body, but one of my hobbies is rfc9822 headers. You're right that this is all scammed up. The message number and ident strings are too long; I think they may carry added content."

She handed back the email. "There's not much more I can tell you. If you want to give me a copy, I could crunch on those header strings over the weekend."

"Oh.... Okay, thanks." It was more solid help than anyone had offered so far, but—"Look Ellen, the main thing I was hoping for was some clues here in Building 0999. The letter pointed me here. I run into...abusers sometimes, myself. I don't let them get away with it! I'd bet money that whoever this is, he's one of those graders." *And he's probably laughing at us right now.*

Ellen thought a second and then shook her head. "I'm sorry, Dixie Mae. I know these people pretty well. Some of them are a little strange, but they're not bent like this. Besides, we didn't know we'd be here till yesterday afternoon. And today we haven't had time for mischief."

"Okay," Dixie Mae forced a smile. "I appreciate your help." She would give Ellen a copy of the letter and go back to Customer Support, just slightly better off than if she had behaved sensibly in the first place.

Dixie Mae started to get up, but Victor leaned forward and set his notepad on the table between them. "That email had to come from somewhere. Has anyone here been acting strange, Mousy?"

Ellen glared at him, and after a second he said, "I mean 'Ellen.' You know I'm just trying to help out Dixie Mae here. Oh yeah, and maybe get a good story for the *Bruin*."

Ellen shrugged. "Graham told you; we're grading on the side for Gerry Reich."

"Huh." Victor leaned back. "Ever since I've been at UCLA, Reich has had a reputation for being an operator. He's got big government contracts and all this consulting at LotsaTech. He tries to come across as a one-man supergenius, but actually it's just money, um, buying lots and lots of peons. So what do you think he's up to?"

Ellen shrugged. "Technically, I bet Gerry is misusing his contacts with LotsaTech. But I doubt if they care; they really like him." She brightened. "And I approve of what Prof. Reich is doing with this grading project. When I was a TA, I wished there was some way that I could make a day-long project out of reading each student's exam. That was an impossible wish; there was just never enough time. But with his contacts here at LotsaTech, Gerry Reich has come close to doing it. He's paying some pretty sharp grad students really good money to grade and comment on every single essay question. Time is no object, he's telling us. The students in these classes are going to get really great feedback.

"This guy Reich keeps popping up," said Dixie Mae. "He was behind the testing program that selected Victor and me and the others for customer support."

"Well, Victor's right about him. Reich is a manipulator. I know he's been running tests all this week. He grabbed all of Olson Hall for the operation. We didn't know what it was for until afterwards. He nailed Graham and the rest of our gang for this one-day grading job. It looks like he has all sorts of projects."

"Yeah, we took our tests at Olson Hall, too." There had been a small up-front payment, and hints of job prospects.... And Dixie Mae had ended up with maybe the best job offer she'd ever had. "But we did that last week."

"It can't be the same place. Olson Hall is a gym."

"Yes, that's what it looked like to me."

"It was used for the NCAA eliminations last week."

Victor reached for his notepad. "Whatever. We gotta be going, Mouse."

"Don't 'Mouse' me, Victor! The NCAA elims were the week of 4 June. I did Gerry's questionnaire yesterday, which was Thursday, 14 June."

"I'm sorry, Ellen," said Dixie Mae. "Yesterday was Thursday, but it was the 21st of June."

Victor made a calming gesture. "It's not a big deal."

Ellen frowned, but suddenly she wasn't arguing. She glanced at her watch. "Let's see your notepad, Victor. What date does it say?"

"It says, June...huh. It says June 15."

Dixie Mae looked at her own watch. The digits were so precise, and a week wrong: Fri Jun 15 12:31:18 PDT 2012. "Ellen, I looked at my watch before we walked over here. It said June 22nd."

Ellen leaned on the table and took a close look at Victor's notepad. "I'll bet it did. But both your watch and your notepad get their time off the building utilities. Now you're getting set by our local clock—and you're getting the truth."

Now Dixie Mae was getting mad. "Look, Ellen. Whatever the time service says, *I* would not have made up a whole extra week of my life." All those product-familiarization classes.

"No, you wouldn't." Ellen brought her heels back on the edge of her chair. For a long moment, she didn't say anything, just stared through the haze at the city below.

Finally she said: "You know, Victor, you should be pleased."

"Why is that?" suspiciously.

"You may have stumbled into a real, world-class

news story. Tell me. During this extra week of life you've enjoyed, how often have you used your phone?"

Dixie Mae said, "Not at all. Mr. Johnson—he's our instructor—said that we're deadzoned till we get through the first week."

Ellen nodded. "So I guess they didn't expect the scam to last more than a week. See, we are not deadzoned here. LotsaTech has a pretty broad embargo on web access, but I made a couple of phone calls this morning."

Victor gave her a sharp look. "So where do you think the extra week came from?"

Ellen hesitated. "I think Gerry Reich has gone beyond where the UCLA human subjects committee would ever let him go. You guys probably spent one night in drugged sleep, being pumped chock full of LotsaTech product trivia."

"Oh! You mean...Just-in-Time training?" Victor tapped away at his notepad. "I thought that was years away."

"It is if you play by the FDA's rules. But there are meds and treatments that can speed up learning. Just read the journals and you'll see that in another year or two, they'll be a scandal as big as sports drugs ever were. I think Gerry has just jumped the gun with something that is very, *very* effective. You have no side-effects. You have all sorts of new, specialized knowledge—even if it's about a throwaway topic. And apparently you have detailed memories of life experience that *never* happened."

Dixie Mae thought back over the last week. There had been no strangeness about her experience at Olson Hall: the exams, the job interview. True, the johns were fantastically clean—like a hospital, now that she thought about it. She had only visited them once, right after she accepted the job offer. And then she had…done what? Taken a bus directly out to LotsaTech…without even going back to her apartment? After that, everything was clear again. She could remember jokes in the Voxalot classes. She could remember meals, and late night talks with Ulysse about what they might do with this great opportunity. "It's brainwashing," she finally said.

Ellen nodded. "It looks like Gerry has gone way, way too far on this one."

"And he's stupid, too. Our team is going to a party tonight, downtown. All of a sudden, there'll be sixteen people who'll know what's been done to them. We'll be mad as—" Dixie Mae noticed Ellen's pitying look.

"Oh." So tonight instead of partying, their customer support team would be in a drugged stupor, *un*remembering the week that never was. "We won't remember a thing, will we?"

Ellen nodded. "My guess is you'll be well-paid, with memories of some one-day temp job here at LotsaTech."

"Well, that's not going to happen," said Victor. "I've got a story and I've got a grudge. I'm not going back."

"We have to warn the others."

Victor shook his head. "Too risky."

Dixie Mae gave him a glare.

Ellen Garcia hugged her knees for a moment. "If this were just you, Victor, I'd be sure you were putting me on." She looked at Dixie Mae for a second. "Let me see that email again."

She spread it out on the table. "LotsaTech has its share of defense and security contracts. I'd hate to think that they might try to shut us up if they knew we were onto them." She whistled an ominous tune. "Paranoia rages…. Have you thought that this email might be someone trying to tip you off about what's going on?"

Victor frowned. "Who, Ellen?" When she didn't answer, he said, "So what do you think we should do?"

Ellen didn't look up from the printout. "Mainly, try not to act like idiots. All we really know is that someone has played serious games with your heads. Our first priority is to get us all out of LotsaTech, with you guys free of medical side effects. Our second priority is to blow the whistle on Gerry or…" She was reading the mail headers again, "…or whoever is behind this."

Dixie Mae said, "I don't think we know enough not to act like idiots."

"Good point. Okay, I'll make a phone call, an innocuous message that should mean something to the police if things go really bad. Then I'll talk to the others in our grading team. We won't say anything while we're still at LotsaTech, but once away from here we'll scream long and loud. You two…it might be safest if you just lie low till after dark and we graders get back into town."

Victor was nodding.

Dixie Mae pointed at the mystery email. "What was it you just noticed, Ellen?"

"Just a coincidence, I think. Without a large sample, you start seeing phantoms."

"Speak."

"Well, the mailing address, 'lusting925@freemail.sg.' Building 0925 is on the hill crest thataway."

"You can't see that from where we started."

"Right. It's like 'Lusting' had to get you *here* first. And that's the other thing. Prof. Reich has a senior graduate student named Rob Lusk."

Lusk? Lusting? The connection seemed weak to Dixie Mae. "What kind of a guy is he?"

"Rob's not a particularly friendly fellow, but he's about two sigmas smarter than the average grad student. He's the reason Gerry has the big reputation for hardware. Gerry has been using him for five or six years now, and I bet Rob is getting desperate to graduate." She broke off. "Look. I'm going to go inside and tell Graham and the others about this. Then we'll find a place for you to hide for the rest of the day."

She started toward the door.

"I'm not going to hide out," said Dixie Mae.

Ellen hesitated. "Just till closing time. You've seen the rent-a-cops at the main gate. This is not a place you can simply stroll out of. But my group will have no trouble going home this evening. As soon as we're off-site, we'll raise such a stink that the press and police will be back here. You'll be safe at home in no time."

Victor was nodding. "Ellen's right. In fact, it would be even better if we don't spread the story to the other graders. There's no telling—"

"I'm not going to hide out!" Dixie Mae looked up the hill. "I'm going to check out 0925."

"That's crazy, Dixie Mae! You're guaranteed safe if you just hide till the end of the work day—and then the cops can do better investigating than anything you could manage. You do what Ellen says!"

"No one tells me what to do, Victor!" said Dixie Mae, while inside she was thinking, *Yeah, what I'm doing is a little bit like the plot of a cheap game: teenagers enter haunted house, and then split up to be murdered in pieces....*

But Ellen Garcia was making assumptions, too. Dixie Mae glared at both of them. "I'm following up on this email."

Ellen gave her a long look. Whether it was contemptuous or thoughtful wasn't clear. "Just wait for me to tell Graham, okay?"

Twenty minutes later, the three of them were outdoors again, walking up the long grade toward Building 0925.

Graham the Red might be a smart guy, but he turned out to be a fool, too. He was sure that the calendar mystery was just a scam cooked up by Dixie Mae and Victor. Ellen wasn't that good at talking to him—and the two customer support winkies were beneath his contempt. Fortunately, most of the other graders had been willing to listen. One of them also poked an unpleasant hole in all their assumptions: "So if it's that serious, wouldn't Gerry have these two under surveillance? You know, the Conspiracy Gestapo could arrive any second." There'd been a moment of apprehensive silence as everyone waited the arrival of bad guys with clubs.

In the end, everyone including Graham had agreed to keep their mouths shut till after work. Several of them had friends they made cryptic phone calls to, just in case. Dixie Mae could tell that most of them tilted toward Ellen's point of view, but however smart they were, they really didn't want to cross Graham.

Ellen, on the other hand, was *persona non grata* for trying to mess up Graham's schedule. She finally lost her temper with the redheaded jerk.

So now Ellen, Victor, and Dixie Mae were on the yellow brick road—in this case, the asphalt econo-cart walkway—leading to Building 0925.

The LotsaTech campus was new and underpopulated, but there *were* other people around. Just outside of 0999, they ran into a trio of big guys wearing gray blazers like the cops at the main entrance. Victor grabbed Dixie Mae's arm. "Just act natural," he whispered.

They ambled past, Victor giving a gracious nod. The three hardly seemed to notice.

Victor released Dixie Mae's arm. "See? You just have to be cool."

Ellen had been walking ahead. She dropped back so they were three abreast. "Either we're being toyed with," she said, "or they haven't caught on to us."

Dixie Mae touched the email in her pocket. "Well, *somebody* is toying with us."

"You know, that's the biggest clue we have. I still think it could be somebody trying to—"

Ellen fell silent as a couple of management types came walking the other way. These paid them even less attention than the company cops had.

"—it could be somebody trying to help us."

"I guess," said Dixie Mae. "More likely it's some sadist using stuff they learned while I was drugged up."

"Ug. Yeah." They batted around the possibilities. It was strange. Ellen Garcia was as much fun to talk to as Ulysse, even though she had to be about five times smarter than either Ulysse or Dixie Mae.

Now they were close enough to see the lower windows of 0925. This place was a double-sized version of 0999 or 0994. There was a catering truck pulled up at the ground level. Beyond a green-tinted windbreak they could see couples playing tennis on the courts south of the building.

Victor squinted. "Strange. They've got some kind of blackout on the windows."

"Yeah. We should at least be able to see the strip lights in the ceiling."

They drifted off the main path and walked around to where they wouldn't be seen from the catering truck. Even up close, down under the overhang, the windows looked just like those on the other buildings. But it wasn't just dark inside. There was nothing but blackness. The inside of the glass was covered with black plastic like they put on closed storefronts.

Victor whipped out his notepad.

"No phone calls, Victor."

"I want to send out a live report, just in case someone gets really mad about us being here."

"I told you, they've got web access embargoed. Besides, just calling from here would trigger 911 locator logic."

"Just a short call, to—"

He looked up and saw that the two women were standing close. "—ah, okay. I'll just use it as a local cam."

Dixie Mae held out her hand. "Give me the notepad, Victor. We'll take the pictures."

For a moment it looked like he was going refuse. Then he saw how her other hand was clenched into a fist. And maybe he remembered the lunchtime stories she had told during the week. *The week that never was?* Whatever the reason, he handed the notepad over to her. "You think I'm working for the bad guys?" he said.

"No," Dixie Mae said (65 percent truthfully, but declining), "I just don't think you'll always do what Ellen suggests. This way we'll get the pictures, but safely." *Because of my superior self control. Yeah.*

She started to hand the notepad to Ellen, but the other shook her head. "Just keep a record, Dixie Mae. You'll get it back later, Victor."

"Oh. Okay, but I want first xmit rights." He brightened. "You'll be my cameragirl, Dixie. Just come back on me anytime I have something important to say."

"Will do, Victor." She panned the notepad camera in a long sweep, away from him.

No one bothered them as they walked halfway around the ground floor. The blackout job was very thorough, but just as at buildings 0994 and 0999, there was an ordinary door with an old-fashioned card swipe.

Ellen took a closer look. "We disabled the locks on 0999 just for the fun of it. Somehow I don't think these black-plastic guys are that easygoing."

"I guess this is as far as we go," said Victor.

Dixie Mae stepped close to the door and gave it push. There was no error beep, no alarms. The door just swung open.

Looks of amazement were exchanged.

Five seconds later they were still standing at the open doorway. What little they could see looked like your typical LotsaTech ground floor. "We should shut the door and go back," said Victor. "We'll be caught red-handed standing here."

"Good point." Ellen stepped inside, followed perforce by Victor, and then Dixie Mae taking local video.

"Wait! Keep the door open, Dixie Mae."

"Jeez."

"This is like an airlock!" They were in a tiny room. Above waist height, its walls were clear glass. There was another door on the far end of the little room.

Ellen walked forward. "I had a summer job at Livermore last year. They have catch boxes like this. You walk inside easy enough—and then there are armed guards all around, politely asking you if you're lost." There were no guards visible here. Ellen pressed on the inner door. Locked. She reached up to the latch mechanism. It looked like cheap plastic. "This should not work," she said, even as she fiddled at it.

They could hear voices, but from upstairs. Down here, there was no one to be seen. Some of the layout was familiar, though. If this had been Building 0994, the hallway on the right would lead to restrooms, a small cafeteria, and a temporary dormitory.

Ellen hesitated and stood listening. She looked back at them. "That's strange. That sounds like...Graham!"

"Can you just break the latch, Ellen?" *We should go upstairs and strangle the two-faced weasel with his own ponytail.*

Another sound. A door opening! Dixie Mae looked past Ellen and saw a guy coming out of the men's room. Dixie Mae managed to grab Victor, and the two of them dropped behind the lower section of the holding cell.

"Hey, Ellen," said the stranger, "you look a bit peaked. Is Graham getting on your nerves, too?"

Ellen gave a squeaky laugh. "Y-yeah...so what else is new?"

Dixie Mae twisted the notepad and held it so the camera eye looked through the glass. In the tiny screen, she could see that the stranger was smiling. He was dressed in tee-shirt and kneepants and he had some kind of glittering badge on a loop around his neck.

Ellen's mouth opened and shut a couple of times, but nothing came out. *She doesn't know this guy from Adam.*

The stranger was still clueless, but—"Hey, where's your badge?"

"Oh...damn. I must have left in the john," said Ellen. "And now I've locked myself out."

"You know the rules," he said, but his tone was not threatening. He did something on his side of the door. It opened and Ellen stepped through, blocking the guy's view of what was behind her.

"I'm sorry. I, uh, I got flustered."

"That's okay. Graham will eventually shut up. I just wish he'd pay more attention to what the professionals are asking of him."

Ellen nodded. "Yeah, I hear you!" Like she was really, really agreeing with him.

"Y'see, Graham's not splitting the topics properly. The idea is to be both broad *and* deep."

Ellen continued to make understanding-noises. The talkative stranger was full of details about some sort of a NSA project, but he was totally ignorant of the three intruders.

There were light footsteps on the stairs, and a familiar voice. "Michael, how long are you going to be? I want to—" The voice cut off in a surprised squeak.

On the notepad display, Dixie Mae could see two brown-haired girls staring at each other with identical expressions of amazement. They sidled around each other for a moment, exchanging light slaps. It wasn't fighting…it was as if each thought the other was some kind of trick video. *Ellen Garcia, meet Ellen Garcia.*

The stranger—Michael?—stared with equal astonishment, first at one Ellen and then the other. The Ellens made inarticulate noises just loud enough to interrupt each other and make them even more upset.

Finally Michael said, "I take it you don't have a twin sister, Ellen?"

"No!" said both.

"So one of you is an impostor. But you've spun around so often now that I can't tell who is the original. Ha." He pointed at one of the Ellens. "Another good reason for having security badges."

But Ellen and Ellen were ignoring everyone except themselves. Except for their chorus of "No!", their words were just mutual interruptions, unintelligible. Finally, they hesitated and gave each other a nasty smile. Each reached into her pocket. One came out with a dollar coin, and the other came out empty.

"Ha! I've got the token. Deadlock broken." The other grinned and nodded. Dollar-coin Ellen turned to Michael. "Look, we're both real. And we're both only-children."

Michael looked from one to the other. "You're certainly not clones, either."

"Obviously," said the token holder. She looked at the other Ellen and asked, "Fridge-rot?"

The other nodded and said, "In April I made that worse." And both of them laughed.

Token holder: "Gerry's exam in Olson Hall?"

"Yup."

Token holder: "Michael?"

"After that," the other replied, and then she blushed. After a second the token holder blushed, too.

Michael said dryly, "And you're not perfectly identical."

Token holder Ellen gave him a crooked smile. "True. I've never seen you before in my life." She turned and tossed the dollar coin to the other Ellen, left hand to left hand.

And now that Ellen had the floor. She was also the version wearing a security badge. Call her NSA Ellen. "As far as I—we—can tell, we had the same stream of consciousness up through the day we took Gerry Reich's recruitment exam. Since then, we've had our own lives. We've even got our own new friends." She was looking in the direction of Dixie Mae's camera.

Grader Ellen turned to follow her gaze. "Come on out, guys. We can see your camera lens."

Victor and Dixie Mae stood and walked out of the security cell.

"A right invasion you are," said Michael, and he did not seem to be joking.

NSA Ellen put her hand on his arm. "Michael, I don't think we're in Kansas anymore."

"Indeed! I'm simply dreaming."

"Probably. But if not—" she exchanged glances with grader Ellen "—maybe we should find out what's been done to us. Is the meeting room clear?"

"Last I looked. Yes, we're not likely to be bothered in there." He led them down a hallway toward what was simply a janitor's closet back in Building 0994.

Michael Lee and NSA Ellen were working on still another of Professor Reich's projects. "Y'see," said Michael, "Professor Reich has a contract with my colleagues to compare our surveillance software with what intense human analysis might accomplish."

"Yes," said NSA Ellen, "the big problem with surveillance has always been the enormous amount of stuff there is to look at. The spook agencies use lots of automation and have lots of great specialists—people like Michael here—but they're just overwhelmed. Anyway, Gerry had the idea that even though that problem can't be solved, maybe a team of spooks and graduate students could at least estimate how much the NSA programs are missing."

Michael Lee nodded. "We're spending the entire summer looking at 1300 to 1400UTC 10 June 2012, backwards and forwards and up and down, but on just three narrow topic areas."

Grader Ellen interrupted him. "And this is your first day on the job, right?"

"Oh, no. We've been at this for almost a month now." He gave a little smile. "My whole career has been the study of contemporary China. Yet this is the first assignment where I've had enough time to look at the data I'm supposed to pontificate upon. It would be a real pleasure if we didn't have to enforce security on these rambunctious graduate students."

NSA Ellen patted him on the shoulder. "But if it weren't for Michael here, I'd be as frazzled as poor Graham. One month down and two months to go."

"You think it's *August*?" said Dixie Mae.

"Yes, indeed." He glanced at his watch. "The 10 August it is."

Grader Ellen smiled and told him the various dates the rest of them thought today was.

"It's some kind of drug hallucination thing," said Victor. "Before we thought it was just Gerry Reich's doing. Now I think it's the government torquing our brains."

Both Ellens look at him; you could tell they both knew Victor from way back. But they seemed to take what he was saying seriously. "Could be," they both said.

"Sorry," grader Ellen said to NSA Ellen. "You've got the dollar."

"You could be right, Victor. But cognition is my—our—specialty. We two are something way beyond normal dreaming or hallucinations."

"Except *that* could be illusion, too," said Victor.

"Stuff it, Victor," said Dixie Mae. "If it's *all* a dream, we might as well give up." She looked at the Michael Lee. "What is the government up to?"

Michael shrugged. "The details are classified, but it's just a post hoc survey. The isolation rules seem to be something that Professor Reich has worked out with my agency."

NSA Ellen flicked a glance at her double. The two had a brief and strange conversation, mostly half-completed words and phrases. Then NSA Ellen continued, "Mr. Renaissance Man Gerry Reich seems to be at the center of everything. He used some standard personality tests to pick out articulate, motivated people for the customer support job. I bet they do a very good job on their first day."

Yeah. Dixie Mae thought of Ulysse. And of herself.

NSA Ellen continued, "Gerry filtered out another group—graduate students in just the specialty for grading all his various exams and projects."

"We only worked on one exam," said grader Ellen. But she wasn't objecting. There was an odd smile on her face, the look of someone who has cleverly figured out some very bad news.

"And then he got a bunch of government spooks and CS grads for this surveillance project that Michael and I are on."

Michael looked mystified. Victor looked vaguely sullen, his own theories lying trampled somewhere in the dust. "But," said Dixie Mae, "your surveillance group has been going for a month you say..."

Victor: "And the graders *do* have phone contact with the outside!"

"I've been thinking about that," said grader Ellen. "I made three phone calls today. The third was after you and Dixie Mae showed up. That was voicemail to a friend of mine at MIT. I was cryptic, but I tried to say enough that my friend would raise hell if I disappeared. The others calls were—"

"Voicemail, too?" asked NSA Ellen.

"One was voicemail. The other call was to Bill Richardson. We had a nice chat about the party he's having Saturday. But Bill—"

"Bill took Reich's 'job test' along with the rest of us!"

"Right."

Where this was heading was worse than Victor's dream theory. "S-so what has been done to us?" said Dixie Mae.

Michael's eyes were wide, though he managed a tone of dry understatement: "Pardon a backward Han language specialist. You're thinking we're just personality uploads? I thought that was science fiction."

Both Ellens laughed. One said, "Oh, it *is* science fiction, and not just the latest *Kywrack* episode. The genre goes back almost a century."

The other: "There's Sturgeon's 'Microcosmic God'."

The first: "That would be rich; Gerry beware then! But there's also Pohl's 'Tunnel Under the World'."

"Cripes. We're toast if that's the scenario."

"Okay, but how about Varley's 'Overdrawn at the Memory Bank'?"

"How about Wilson's *Darwinia*?"

"Or Moravec's 'Pigs in Cyberspace'?"

"Or Galouye's *Simulacron-3*?"

"Or Vinge's deathcubes?"

Now that the 'twins' were not in perfect synch, their words were a building, rapid- fire chorus, climaxing with:

"Brin's 'Stones of Significance'!"

"Or *Kiln People!*"

"No, it couldn't be that." Abruptly they stopped, and nodded at each other. A little bit grimly, Dixie Mae thought. In all, the conversation was just as inscrutable as their earlier self-interrupted spasms.

Fortunately, Victor was there to rescue pedestrian minds. "It doesn't matter. The fact is, uploading is *only* sci-fi. It's worse that faster-than-light travel. There's not even a theoretical basis for uploads."

Each Ellen raised her left hand and made a faffling gesture. "Not exactly, Victor."

The token holder continued, "I'd say there is a *theoretical* basis for saying that uploads are theoretically possible." They gave a lopsided smile. "And guess who is responsible for that? Gerry Reich. Back in

2005, way before he was famous as a multi-threat genius, he had a couple of papers about upload mechanisms. The theory was borderline kookiness and even the simplest demo would take far more processing power than any supercomputer of the time."

"Just for a one-personality upload."

"So Gerry and his Reich Method were something of a laughingstock."

"After that, Gerry dropped the idea—just what you'd expect, considering the showman he is. But now he's suddenly world-famous, successful in half a dozen different fields. I think something happened. *Somebody* solved his hardware problem for him."

Dixie Mae stared at her email. "Rob Lusk," she said, quietly.

"Yup," said grader Ellen. She explained about the mail.

Michael was unconvinced. "I don't know, E-Ellen. Granted, we have an extraordinary miracle here—" gesturing at both of them, "—but speculating about cause seems to me a bit like a sparrow understanding the 405 Freeway."

"No," said Dixie Mae, and they all looked back her way. She felt so frightened and so angry—but of the two, angry was better: "Somebody has *set us up!* It started in those superclean restrooms in Olson Hall—"

"Olson Hall," said Michael. "You were there too? The lavs smelled like a hospital! I remember thinking that just as I went in, but—hey, the next thing I remember is being on the bus, coming up here."

Like a hospital. Dixie Mae felt rising panic. "M-maybe we're all that's left." She looked at the twins. "This uploading thing, does it kill the originals?"

It was kind of a showstopper question; for a moment everyone was silent. Then the token holder said,

"I—don't think so, but Gerry's papers were mostly theoretical."

Dixie Mae beat down the panic; rage did have its uses. *What can we know from here on the inside?* "So far we know more than thirty of us who took the Olson Hall exams and ended up here. If we were all murdered, that'd be hard to cover up. Let's suppose we still have a life." Inspiration: "And maybe there are things we can figure! We have three of Reich's experiments to compare. There are differences, and they tell us things." She looked at the twins. "You've already figured this out, haven't you? The Ellen we met first is grading papers—just a one-day job, she's told. But I'll bet that every night, when they think they're going home—Lusk or Reich or whoever is doing this just turns them off, and *cycles them back* to do some other 'one-day' job."

"Same with our customer support," said Victor, a grudging agreement.

"Almost. We had six days of product familiarization, and then our first day on the job. We were all so enthusiastic. You're right, Ellen, on our first day we are great!" *Poor Ulysse, poor me; we thought we were going somewhere with our lives.* "I'll bet we disappear tonight, too."

Grader Ellen was nodding. "Customer-support-in-a-box, restarted and restarted, so it's always fresh."

"But there are still problems," said the other one. "Eventually, the lag in dates would tip you off."

"Maybe, or maybe the mail headers are automatically forged."

"But internal context could contradict—"

"Or maybe Gerry has solved the cognitive haze problem—" The two were off into their semi-private language.

Michael interrupted them. "Not everybody is recycled. The point of our net-tracking project is that we spend the entire summer studying just one hour of network traffic."

The twins smiled. "So you think," said the token holder. "Yes, in this building we're not rebooted after every imaginary day. Instead, they run us the whole 'summer'—minutes of computer time instead of seconds?—to analyze one hour of network traffic. And then they run us again, on a different hour. And so on and on."

Michael said, "I can't imagine technology that powerful."

The token holder said, "Neither can I really, but—"

Victor interrupted with, "Maybe this is the *Darwinia* scenario. You know: we're just the toys of some superadvanced intelligence."

"No!" said Dixie Mae. "Not superadvanced. Customer support and net surveillance are valuable things in our own real world. Whoever's doing this is just getting slave labor, run really, really fast."

Grader Ellen glowered. "And grading his exams for him! That's the sort of thing that shows me it's really Gerry behind this. He's making chumps of all of us, and rerunning us before we catch on or get seriously bored."

NSA Ellen had the same expression, but a different complaint: "We *have* been seriously bored here."

Michael nodded. "Those from the government side are a patient lot; we've kept the graduate students in line. We can last three months. But it does...rankle...to learn that the reward for our patience is that we get to do it all over again. Damn. I'm sorry, Ellen."

"But now we know!" said Dixie Mae.

"And what good does it do you?" Victor laughed. "So you guessed this time. But at the end of the microsecond day, poof, it's reboot time and everything you've learned is gone."

"Not *this* time." Dixie Mae looked away from him, down at her email. The cheap paper was crumpled and stained. A digital fake, *but so are we.* "I don't think we're the only people who've figured things out." She slid the printout across the table, toward grader Ellen. "You thought it meant Rob Lusk was in this building."

"Yeah, I did."

"Who's Rob Lusk?" said Michael.

"A weirdo," NSA Ellen said absently. "Gerry's best grad student." Both Ellens were staring at the email.

"The 0999 reference led Dixie Mae to my grading team. Then I pointed out the source address."

"925@freemail.sg?"

"Yes. And that got us here."

"But there's no Rob Lusk here," said NSA Ellen. "Huh! I like these fake mail headers."

"Yeah. They're longer than the whole message body!"

Michael had stood to look over the Ellens' shoulders. Now he reached between them to tap the message. "See there, in the middle of the second header? That looks like Pinyin with the tone marks written in-line."

"So what does it *say?*"

"Well, if it's Mandarin, it would be the number 'nine hundred and seventeen'."

Victor was leaning forward on his elbows. "That has to be coincidence. How could Lusting know just who we'd encounter?"

"Anybody know of a Building 0917?" said Dixie Mae.

"I don't," said Michael. "We don't go out of our building except to the pool and tennis courts."

The twins shook their heads. "I haven't seen it...and right now I don't want to risk an intranet query."

Dixie Mae thought back to the LotsaTech map that had been in the welcome-aboard brochures. "If there is such a place, it would be farther up the hill, maybe right at the top. I say we go up there."

"But—" said Victor.

"Don't give me that garbage about waiting for the police, Victor, or about not being idiots. This *isn't* Kansas anymore, and this email is the only clue we have."

"What should we tell the people here?" said Michael.

"Don't tell them anything! We just sneak off. We want the operation here to go on normally, so Gerry or whoever doesn't suspect."

The two Ellens looked at each other, a strange, sad expression on their faces. Suddenly they both started singing "Home on the Range," but with weird lyrics:

"Oh, give me a clone
Of my own flesh and bone
With—"

They paused and simultaneously blushed. "What a dirty mind that man Garrett had."

"Dirty but deep." NSA Ellen turned to Michael, and she seemed to blush even more. "Never mind, Michael. I think...you and I should stay here.

"No, wait," said Dixie Mae. "Where we're going we may have to convince someone that this crazy story is true. You Ellens are the best evidence we have."

The argument went round and round. At one point, Dixie Mae noticed with wonder that the two Ellens actually seemed to be arguing against each other.

"We don't know enough to decide," Victor kept whining.

"We have to do something, Victor. We *know* what happens to you and me if we sit things out till closing time this afternoon."

In the end Michael did stay behind. He was more likely to be believed by his government teammates. If the Ellens and Dixie Mae and Victor could bring back some real information, maybe the NSA group could do some good.

"We'll be a network of people trying to break this wheel of time." Michael was trying to sound wryly amused, but once he said the words he was silent, and none of the others could think of anything better to say.

Up near the hilltop, there were not nearly as many buildings, and the ones that Dixie Mae saw were single story, as though they were just entrances to something *under* the hills. The trees were stunted and the grass yellower.

Victor had an explanation. "It's the wind. You see this in lots of exposed land near the coast. Or maybe they just don't water very much up here."

An Ellen—from behind, Dixie Mae couldn't tell which one—said, "Either way, the fabrication is awesome."

Right. A fabrication. "That's something I don't understand," said Dixie Mae. "The best movie fx don't come close to this. How can their computers be this good?"

"Well for one thing," said the other Ellen, "cheating is a lot easier when you're also simulating the observers."

"Us."

"Yup. Everywhere you look, you see detail, but it's

always at the center of your focus. We humans don't keep everything we've seen and everything we know all in mind at the same time. We have millions of years of evolution invested in ignoring almost everything, and conjuring sense out of nonsense."

Dixie Mae looked southward into the haze. It was all so real: the dry hot breeze, the glint of aircraft sliding down the sky toward LAX, the bulk of the Empire State Building looming up from the skyscrapers at the center of downtown.

"There are probably dozens of omissions and contradictions around us every second, but unless they're brought together in our attention all at once we don't notice them."

"Like the time discrepancy," said Dixie Mae.

"Right! In fact, the biggest problem with all our theories is not how we could be individually duped, but how the fraud could work with many communicating individuals all at once. That takes hardware beyond anything that exists, maybe a hundred liters of Bose condensate."

"Some kind of quantum computer breakthrough," said Victor.

Both Ellen's turned to look at him, eyebrows raised.

"Hey, I'm a journalist. I read it in the *Bruin* science section."

The twins' reply was something more than a monologue and less than a conversation:

"Well...even so, you have a point. In fact, there were rumors this spring that Gerry had managed to scale Gershenfeld's coffee cup coherence scheme."

"Yeah, how he had five hundred liters of Bose condensate at room temperature."

"But those stories started way after he had already become Mr. Renaissance Man. It doesn't make sense."

We're not the first people hijacked. "Maybe," said

Dixie Mae, "maybe he started out with something simple, like a single superspeed human. Could Gerry run a single upload with the kind of supercomputers we have nowadays?"

"Well, that's more conceivable than this...*oh*. Okay, so an isolated genius was used to do a century or so of genius work on quantum computing. That sounds like the deathcube scenario. If it were me, after a hundred years of being screwed like that, I'd give Gerry one hell of a surprise."

"Yeah, like instead of a cure for cancer, he'd get airborne rabies targeted on the proteome of scumbag middle-aged male CS profs."

The twins sounded as bloody-minded as Dixie Mae.

They walked another couple of hundred yards. The lawn degenerated into islands of crabgrass in bare dirt. The breeze was a hot whistling along the ridgeline. The twins stopped every few paces to look closely, now at the vegetation, now at a guide sign along the walkway. They were mumbling at each other about the details of what they were seeing, as if they were trying to detect inconsistencies:

"...really, really good. We agree on everything we see."

"Maybe Gerry is saving cycles, running us as cognitive subthreads off the same process."

"Ha! No wonder we're still so much in synch."

Mumble, mumble. "There's really a lot we can infer—"

"—once we accept the insane premise of all this."

There was still no "Building 0917," but what buildings they did see had lower and lower numbers: 0933, 0921....

A loud group of people crossed their path just

ahead. They were singing. They looked like programmers.

"Just be cool," an Ellen said softly. "That conga line is straight out of the LotsaTech employee motivation program. The programmers have onsite parties when they reach project milestones."

"More victims?" said Victor. "Or AIs?"

"They might be victims. But I'll bet all the people we've seen along this path are just low-level scenery. There's nothing in Reich's theories that would make true AIs possible."

Dixie Mae watched the singers as they drifted down the hillside. This was the third time they had seen something-like-people on the walkway. "It doesn't make sense, Ellen. We think we're just—"

"Simulation processes."

"Yeah, simulation processes, inside some sort of super super-computer. But if that's true, then whoever is behind this should be able to spy on us better than any Big Brother ever could in the real world. We should've been caught and rebooted the minute we began to get suspicious."

Both Ellens started to answer. They stopped, then interrupted each other again.

"Back to who's-got-the-token," one said, holding up the dollar coin. "Dixie Mae, that is a mystery, but not as big as it seems. If Reich is using the sort of upload and simulation techniques I know about, then what goes on inside our minds can't be interpreted directly. Thoughts are just too idiosyncratic, too scattered. If we are simulations in a large quantum computer, even environment probes would be hard to run."

"You mean things like spy cameras?"

"Yes. They would be hard to implement, since in fact they would be snooping on the state of our internal imagery. All this is complicated by the fact that we're probably running thousands of times faster than real time. There are maybe three ways that Gerry could snoop: he could just watch team output, and if it falls off, he'd know that something had gone wrong—and he might reboot on general principles."

Suddenly Dixie Mae was very glad that they hadn't taken more volunteers on this hike.

"The second snoop method is just to look at things we write or the output of software we explicitly run. I'll bet that anything that we perceive as linear text *is* capable of outside interpretation." She looked at Victor. "That's why no note-taking." Dixie Mae still had his notepad.

"It's kinda stupid," said Victor. "First it was no pictures and now not even notes.

"Hey, look!" said the Ellens. "B0917!" But it wasn't a building, just a small sign wedged among the rocks.

They scrambled off the asphalt onto a dirt path that led directly up the hillside.

Now they were so near the hill crest that the horizon was just a few yards away. Dixie Mae couldn't see any land beyond. She remembered a movie where poor slobs like themselves got to the edge of the simulation…and found the wall at the end of their universe. But they took a few more steps and she could see over the top. There was a vista of further, lower hills, dropping down into the San Fernando Valley. Not quite hidden in the haze she could see the familiar snakey line of Highway 101. Tarzana.

Ellen and Ellen and Victor were not taking in the view. They were staring at the sign at the side of the path. Fifteen feet beyond that was a construction dig. There were building supplies piled neatly along the edge of the cut, and a robo-Cat parked on the far side. It might have been the beginning of the construction of a standard-model LotsaTech building...except that in the far side of the pit, almost hidden in shadows, there was circular metal plug, like a bank vault door in some old movie.

"I have this theory," said the token holder. "If we get through that door, we may find out what your email is all about."

"Yup." The twins bounced down a steeply cut treadway into the pit. Dixie Mae and Victor scrambled after them, Victor clumsily bumping into her on the way down. The bottom of the pit was like nothing before. There were no windows, no card swipe. And up close, Dixie Mae could see that the vault door was pitted and scratched.

"They're mixing metaphors," said the token holder. "This entrance looks older than the pit."

"It looks old as the hills," Dixie Mae said, running her hand over the uneven metal—and half expecting to feel weirdo runes. "Somebody is trying to give us clues...or somebody is a big sadist," So what do we do? Knock a magic knock?"

"Why not?" The two Ellens took her tattered email and laid it out flat on the metal of the door. They studied the mail headers for a minute, mumbling to each other. The token holder tapped on the metal, then pushed.

"Together," they said, and tapped out a random something, but perfectly in synch.

That had all the effect you'd expect of tapping your fingers on ten tons of dead steel.

The token holder handed the email back to Dixie Mae. "You try something."

But what? Dixie Mae stepped to the door. She stood there, feeling clueless. Off to the side, almost hidden by the curve of the metal plug, Victor had turned away.

He had the notepad.

"Hey!" She slammed him into the side of the pit. Victor pushed her away, but by then the Ellens were on him. There was a mad scramble as the twins tried to do all the same things to Victor. Maybe that confused him. Anyway, it gave Dixie Mae a chance to come back and punch him in the face.

"I got it!" One of the twins jumped back from the fighting. She had the notepad in her hands.

They stepped away from Victor. He wasn't going to get his notepad back. "So, Ellen," said Dixie Mae, not taking her eyes off the sprawled figure, "what was that third method for snooping on us?"

"I think you've already guessed. Gerry could fool some idiot into uploading as a spy." She was looking over her twin's shoulder at the notepad screen.

Victor picked himself up. For a moment he looked sullen, and then the old superior smile percolated across his features. "You're crazy. I just want to break this story back in the real world. Don't you think that if Reich were using spies, he'd just upload himself?"

"That depends."

The one holding the notepad read aloud: "You just typed in: '925 999 994 know. reboot'. That doesn't sound like journalism to me, Victor."

"Hey, I was being dramatic." He thought for a second, and then laughed. "It doesn't matter anymore! I got the warning out. You won't remember any of this after you're rebooted."

Dixie Mae stepped toward him. "And you won't remember that I broke your neck."

Victor tried to look suave and jump backwards at the same time. "In fact, I *will* remember, Dixie Mae. See, once you're gone, I'll be merged back into my body in Doc Reich's lab."

"And we'll be dead again!"

Ellen held up the notepad. "Maybe not as soon as Victor thinks. I notice he never got past the first line of his message; he never pressed return. Now, depending on how faithfully this old notepad's hardware is being emulated, his treason is still trapped in a local cache—and Reich is still clueless about us."

For a moment, Victor looked worried. Then he shrugged. "So you get to live the rest of this run, maybe corrupt some other projects—ones a lot more important than you. On the other hand, I did learn about the email. When I get back and tell Doc Reich, he'll know what to do. You won't be going rogue in the future."

Everyone was silent for a second. The wind whistled across the yellow-blue sky above the pit.

And then the twins gave Victor the sort of smile he had bestowed on them so often. The token holder said, "I think your mouth is smarter than you are, Victor. You asked the right question a second ago: Why doesn't Gerry Reich upload himself to be the spy? Why does he have to use you?"

"Well," Victor frowned. "Hey, Doc Reich is an important man. He doesn't have time to waste with security work like this."

"Really, Victor? He can't spare even a copy of himself?"

Dixie Mae got the point. She closed in on Victor. "So how many times have *you* been merged back into your original?"

"This is my first time here!" Everybody but Victor laughed, and he rushed on, "But I've *seen* the merge done!"

"Then why won't Reich do it for *us*?"

"Merging is too expensive to waste on work threads like you," but now Victor was not even convincing himself.

The Ellens laughed again. "Are you really a UCLA journalism grad, Victor? I thought they were smarter than this. So Gerry showed you a re-merge, did he? I bet that what you actually saw was a lot of equipment and someone going through very dramatic convulsions. And then the 'subject' told you a nice story about all the things he'd seen in our little upload world. And all the time they were laughing at you behind their hands. See, Reich's upload theory depends on having a completely regular target. I know that theory: the merge problem—loading onto an existing mind—is exponential in the neuron count. There's no way back, Victor."

Victor was backing away from them. His expression flickered between superior sneer and stark panic. "What you think doesn't matter. You're just going to be rebooted at 5pm. And you don't know everything." He began fiddling with the fly zipper on his pants. "You see, I—*I* can escape!"

"*Get him!*"

Dixie Mae was closest. It didn't matter.

There was no hazy glow, no sudden popping noise. She simply fell through thin air, right where Victor had been standing.

She picked herself up and stared at the ground. Some smudged footprints were the only sign Victor had been there. She turned back to the twins. "So he could re-merge after all?"

"Not likely," said the token holder. "Victor's zipper was probably a thread self-terminate mechanism."

"His *pants zipper?*"

They shrugged. "I dunno. To leak out? Gerry has a perverse sense of humor." But neither twin looked amused. They circled the spot where Victor had left and kicked unhappily at the dirt. The token holder said, "Cripes. Nothing in Victor's life became him like

233

the leaving it. I don't think we have even till '5pm' now. A thread terminate signal is just the sort of thing that would be easy to detect from the outside. So Gerry won't know the details, but he—"

"—or his equipment—"

"—will soon know there is a problem and—"

"—that it's probably a security problem."

"So how long do we have before we lose the day?" said Dixie Mae.

"If an emergency reboot has to be done manually, we'll probably hit 5pm first. If it's automatic, well, I know you won't feel insulted if the world ends in the middle of a syllable."

"Whatever it is, I'm going to use the time." Dixie Mae picked her email up from where it lay by the vault entrance. She waved the paper at the impassive steel. "I'm not going back! I'm here and I want some explanations!"

Nothing.

The two Ellens stood there, out of ideas and looking unhappy—or maybe that amounted to the same thing.

"I'm not giving up," Dixie Mae said to them, and pounded on the metal.

"No, I don't think you are," said the token holder. But now they were looking at her strangely. "I think we—*you* at least—must have been through this before."

"Yeah. And I must have messed up every time."

"No...I don't think so." They pointed at the email that she held crumpled in her hand. "Where do you think all those nasty secrets come from, Dixie Mae?"

"How the freakin' heck do I know? That's the whole reason I—" and then she felt smart and stupid at the same time. She leaned her head against the shadowed metal. "Oh. Oh oh *oh!*"

She looked down at the email hardcopy. The bottom part was torn, smeared, almost illegible. No matter; *that* part she had memorized. The Ellens had gone over the headers one by one. *But now we shouldn't be looking for technical secrets or grad student inside jokes. Maybe we should be looking for numbers that mean something to Dixie Mae Leigh.*

"If there were uploaded souls guarding the door, what you two have already done ought to be enough. I think you're right. It's some pattern I'm supposed to tap on the door." If it didn't work, she'd try something else, and keep trying till 5pm or whenever she was suddenly back in Building 0994, so happy to have a job with potential....

The tree house in Tarzana. Dixie Mae had been into secret codes then. Her childish idea of crypto. She and her little friends used a tap code for sending numbers. It hadn't lasted long, because Dixie Mae was the only one with the patience to use it. But—

"That number, '7474'," she said.

"Yeah? Right in the middle of the fake message number?"

"Yes. Once upon a time, I used that as a password challenge. You know, like 'Who goes there' in combat games. The rest of the string could be the response."

The Ellens looked at each. "Looks too short to be significant," they said.

Then they both shook their heads, disagreeing with themselves. "Try it, Dixie Mae."

Her "numbers to taps" scheme had been simple, but for a moment she couldn't remember it. She held the paper against the vault and glared at the numbers. *Ah.* Carefully, carefully, she began tapping out the digits that came after "7474." The string was much longer than anything her childhood friends would have put up with. It was longer than anything she herself would have used.

"Cool," said the token holder. "Some kind of hex gray code?"

Huh? "What do you expect, Ellen? I was only eight years old."

They watched the door.

Nothing.

"Okay, on to Plan B," *and then to C and D and E, etc, until our time ends.*

There was the sound of something very old breaking apart. The vault door shifted under Dixie Mae's hand and she jumped back. The curved plug slowly turned, and turned, and turned. After some seconds, the metal plug thudded to the ground beside the entrance…and they were looking down an empty corridor that stretched off into the depths.

For the first quarter mile, no one was home. The interior decor was *not* LotsaTech standard. Gone were the warm redwood veneers and glow strips. Here fluorescent tube lights were mounted in the acoustic tile ceiling, and the walls were institutional beige.

"This reminds me of the basement labs in Norman Hall," said one Ellen.

"But there are *people* in Norman Hall," said the other. They were both whispering.

And here there were stairways that led only down. And down and down.

Dixie Mae said, "Do you get the feeling that whoever is here is in for the long haul?"

"Huh?"

"Well, the graders in B0999 were in for a day, and they thought they had real phone access to the outside. My group in Customer Support had six days of classes and then probably just one more day, where we answered queries—and we had no other contact with the outside."

"Yes," said NSA Ellen. "My group had been running for a month, and we were probably not going to expire for another two. We were officially isolated. No phones, no email, no weekends off. The longer the cycle time, the more isolation. Otherwise, the poor suckers would figure things out."

Dixie Mae thought for a second. "Victor really didn't want us to get this far. Maybe—" *Maybe, somehow, we can make a difference.*

They passed a cross corridor, then a second one. A half-opened door showed them an apparent dormitory room. Fresh bedding sat neatly folded on a mattress. Somebody was just moving in?

Ahead there was another doorway, and from it they could hear voices, argument. They crept along, not even whispering.

The voices were making words: "—is a year enough time, Rob?"

The other speaker sounded angry. "Well, it's got to be. After that, Gerry is out of money and I'm out of time."

The Ellens waved Dixie Mae back as she started for the door. Maybe they wanted to eavesdrop for a while. *But how long do we have before time ends?* Dixie Mae brushed past them and walked into the room.

There were two guys there, one sitting by an ordinary data display.

"Jesus! Who are you?"

"Dixie Mae Leigh." *As you must certainly know.*

The one sitting by the terminal gave her a broad grin, "Rob, I thought we were isolated?"

"That's what Gerry said." This one—Rob Lusk?—looked to be in his late twenties. He was tall and thin and had kind of a desperate look to him. "Okay, Miss Leigh. What are you here for?"

"That's what you're going to tell me, Rob." Dixie Mae pulled the email from her pocket and waived the tattered scrap of paper in his face. "I want some explanations!"

Rob's expression clouded over, a no-one-tells-me-what-to-do look.

Dixie Mae glared back at him. Rob Lusk was a mite too big to punch out, but she was heating up to it.

The twins chose that moment to make their entrance. "Hi there," one of them said cheerily.

Lusk's eyes flickered from one to the other and then to the NSA ID badge. "Hello. I've seen you around the department. You're Ellen, um, Gomez?"

"Garcia," corrected NSA Ellen. "Yup. That's me." She patted grader Ellen on the shoulder. "This is my sister, Sonya." She glanced at Dixie Mae. *Play along,* her eyes seemed to say. "Gerry sent us."

"He did?" The fellow by the computer display was grinning even more. "See, I told you, Rob. Gerry can be brutal, but he'd never leave us without assistants for a whole year. Welcome, girls!"

"Shut up, Danny." Rob looked at them hopefully, but unlike Danny-boy, he seemed quite serious. "Gerry told you this will be a year-long project?"

The three of them nodded.

"We've got plenty of bunk rooms, and separate...um, facilities." He sounded...Lord, he sounded embarrassed. "What are your specialties?"

The token holder said, "Sonya and I are second-year grads, working on cognitive patterning."

Some of the hope drained from Rob's expression. "I know that's Gerry's big thing, but we're mostly doing hardware here." He looked at Dixie Mae.

"I'm into—" *go for it* "—Bose condensates." Well, she knew how to pronounce the words.

There were worried looks from the Ellens. But one

238

of them piped up with, "She's on Satya's team at Georgia Tech."

It was wonderful what the smile did to Rob's face. His angry expression of a minute before was transformed into the look of a happy little boy on his way to Disneyland. "Really? I can't tell you what this means to us! I knew it had to be someone like Satya behind the new formulations. Were you in on that?"

"Oh, yeah. Some of it, anyway." Dixie Mae figured that she couldn't say more than twenty words without blowing it. But what the heck—how many more minutes did the masquerade have to last, anyway? Little Victor and his self-terminating thread...

"That's great. We don't have budget for real equipment here, just simulators—"

Out of the corner of her eye, she saw the Ellens exchange a *fer sure* look.

"—so anyone who can explain the theory to me will be *so* welcome. I can't imagine how Satya managed to do so much, so fast, and without us knowing."

"Well, I'd be happy to explain everything I know about it."

Rob waved Danny-boy away from the data display. "Sit down, sit down. I've got so many questions!"

Dixie Mae sauntered over to the desk and plunked herself down. For maybe thirty seconds, this guy would think she was brilliant.

The Ellens circled in to save her. "Actually, I'd like to know more about who we're working with," one of them said.

Rob looked up, distracted, but Danny was more than happy to do some intros. "It's just the two of us. You already know Rob Lusk. I'm Dan Eastland." He reached around, genially shaking hands. "I'm not from UCLA. I work for LotsaTech, in quantum chemistry. But you know Gerry Reich. He's got pull everywhere—and I don't mind being shanghaied for a year. I need to, um, stay out of sight for a while."

"Oh!" Dixie Mae had read about this guy in *Newsweek*. And it had nothing to do with chemistry. "But you're—" *Dead.* Not a good sign at all, at all.

Danny didn't notice her distraction. "Rob's the guy with the real problem. Ever since I can remember, Gerry has used Rob as his personal hardware research department. Hey, I'm sorry, Rob. You know it's true."

Lusk waved him away. "Yes! So tell them how you're an even bigger fool!" He really wanted to get back to grilling Dixie Mae.

Danny shrugged. "But now, Rob is just one year short of hitting his seven year limit. Do you have that at Georgia Tech, Dixie Mae? If you haven't completed the doctorate in seven years, you get kicked out?"

"No, can't say as I've heard of that."

"Give thanks then, because since 2006, it's been an unbendable rule at UCLA. So when Gerry told Rob about this secret hardware contract he's got with LotsaTech—and promised that Ph.D. in return for some new results—Rob jumped right in."

"Yeah, Danny. But he never told me how far Satya had gone. If I can't figure this stuff out, I'm screwed. Now let me talk to Dixie Mae!" He bent over the keyboard and brought up the most beautiful screen saver. Then Dixie Mae noticed little numbers in the colored contours and realized that maybe this was what she was supposed to be an expert on. Rob said, "I have plenty of documentation, Dixie Mae—too much. If you can just give me an idea how you scaled up the coherence." He waved at the picture. "That's almost a thousand liters of condensate, a trillion effective qubits. Even more fantastic, your group can keep it coherent for almost fifty seconds at a time."

NSA Ellen gave a whistle of pretended surprise. "Wow. What use could you have for all that power?"

Danny pointed at Ellen's badge. "You're the NSA wonk, Ellen, what do you think? Crypto, the final frontier of supercomputing! With even the weakest form of the Schor-Gershenfeld algorithm, Gerry can crack a ten kilobyte key in less than a millisecond. And I'll bet that's why he can't spare us any time on the real equipment. Night and day he's breaking keys and sucking in government money."

Grader Ellen—Sonya, that is—puckered up a naive expression. "What more does Gerry want?"

Danny spread his hands. "Some of it we don't even understand yet. Some of it is about what you'd expect: He wants a thousand, thousand times more of everything. He wants to scale the operation by qulink so he can run arrays of thousand-liter bottles."

"And we've got just a year to improve on your results, Dixie Mae. But your solution is years ahead of the state of the art." Rob was pleading.

Danny's glib impress-the-girls manner faltered. For an instant, he looked a little sad and embarrassed. "We'll get something, Rob. Don't worry."

"So, how long have you been here, Rob?" said Dixie Mae.

He looked up, maybe surprised by the tone of her voice.

"We just started. This is our first day."

Ah yes, that famous first day. In her twenty-four years, Dixie Mae had occasionally wondered whether there could be rage more intense than the red haze she saw when she started breaking things. Until today, she had never known. But yes, beyond the berserker-breaker there was something else. She did not sweep the display off the table, or bury her fist in anyone's face. She just sat there for a moment, feeling empty.

She looked across at the twins. "I wanted some villains, but these guys are just victims. Worse, they're totally clueless! We're back where we started this morning." *Where we'll be again real soon now.*

"Hmmm. Maybe not." Speaking together, the twins sounded like some kind of perfect chorus. They looked around the room, eyeing the decor. Then their gazes snapped back to Rob. "You'd think LotsaTech would do better than this for you, Rob."

Lusk was staring at Dixie Mae. He gave an angry shrug. "This is the old Homeland Security lab under Norman Hall. Don't worry—we're isolated, but we have good lab and computer services."

"I'll bet. And what is your starting work date?"

"I just told you: today."

"No, I mean the calendar date."

Danny looked back and forth between them. "Geeze, are all you kids so literal minded? It's Monday, September 12, 2011."

Nine months. Nine real months. And maybe there was a *good* reason why this was the first day. Dixie Mae reached out to touch Rob's sleeve. "The Georgia Tech people didn't invent the new hardware," she said softly.

"Then just who did make the breakthrough?"

She raised her hand...and tapped Rob deliberately on the chest.

Rob just looked more angry, but Danny's eyes widened. Danny got the point. She remembered that *Newsweek* article about him. Danny Eastland had been an all-around talented guy. He had blown the whistle on the biggest business espionage case of the decade. But he was dumb as dirt in some ways. If he hadn't been so eager to get laid, he wouldn't have snuck away from his Witness Protection bodyguards and gotten himself murdered.

"You guys are too much into hardware," said NSA Ellen. "Forget about crypto applications. Think about personality uploads. Given what you know about Gerry's current hardware, how many Reich Method uploads do you think the condensate could support?"

"How should I know? The 'Reich Method' was baloney. If he hadn't messed with the reviewers, those papers would never have been published." But the question stopped him. He thought for a moment. "Okay, if his bogus method really worked, then a trillion qubit simulation could support about ten thousand uploads."

The Ellens gave him a slow smile. A slow, identical smile. For once they made no effort to separate their identities. Their words came out simultaneously, the same pacing, the same pitch, a weird humming chorus: "Oh, a good deal less than ten thousand—if you have to support a decent enclosing reality." Each reached out her left hand with inhumanly synchronized precision, the precision of digital duplicates, to wave at the room and the hallway beyond. "Of course, some resources can be saved by using the same base pattern to drive separate threads—" and each pointed at herself.

Both men just stared at them for a second. Then Rob stumbled back into the other chair. "Oh...my...God."

Danny stared at the two for another few seconds. "All these years, we thought Gerry's theories were just a brilliant scam."

The Ellens stood with their eyes closed for a second. Then they seemed to startle awake. They looked at each other and Dixie Mae could tell the perfect synch had been broken. NSA Ellen took the dollar coin out of her pocket and gave it to the other. The token holder smiled at Rob. "Oh, it was, only more brilliant and more of a scam than you ever dreamed."

"I wonder if Danny and I ever figure it out."

"*Some*body figured it out," said Dixie Mae, and waved what was left of her email.

The token holder was more specific: "Gerry is running us all like stateless servers. Some are on very short cycles. We think you're on a one-year cycle, probably running longer than anyone. You're making the discoveries that let Gerry create bigger and bigger systems."

"Okay," said Lusk, "suppose one of us victims guesses the secret? What can we do? We'll just get rebooted at the end of our run."

Danny Eastland was quicker. "There is something we could do. There has to be information passed between runs, at least if Gerry is using you and me to build on our earlier solutions. If in that data we could hide what we've secretly learned—"

The twins smiled. "Right! Cookies. If you could recover them reliably, then on each rev, you could plan more and more elaborate countermeasures."

Rob Lusk still looked dazed. "We'd want to tip off the next generation early in their run."

"Yes, like the very first day!" Danny was looking at the three women and nodding to himself. "Only I still don't see how we managed that."

Rob pointed at Dixie Mae's email. "May I take a look at that?" He laid it on the table, and he and Danny examined the message.

The token holder said, "That email has turned out to have more clues than a bad detective story. Every time we're in a jam, we find the next hidden solution."

"That figures," said Eastland. "I'll bet it's been refined over many revs..."

"But we may have a special problem this time—" and Dixie Mae told them about Victor.

"Damn," said Danny.

Rob just shrugged. "Nothing we can do about that till we figure this out." He and Danny studied the headers. The token holder explained the parts that had already seen use. Finally, Rob leaned back in his chair. "The second-longest header looks like the tags on one of the raw data files that Gerry gave us."

"Yes," sang the twins. "What's really your own research from the last time around."

"Most of the files have to be what Gerry thinks, or else he'd catch onto us. But that one raw data file...assume it's really a cookie. Then this email header might be a crypto key."

Danny shook his head. "That's not credible, Rob. Gerry could do the same analysis."

The token holder laughed. "Only if he knew what to analyze. Maybe that's why you guys winkled it out to us. The message goes to Dixie Mae—an unrelated person in an unrelated part of the simulation."

"But how did we do it the *first* time?"

Rob didn't seem to be paying attention. He was typing in the header string from Dixie Mae's email. "Let's try it on the data file...." He paused, checked his keyboard entry, and pressed return.

They stared at the screen. Seconds passed. The Ellens chatted back and forth. They seemed to be worried about executing any sort of text program; like Victor's notepad, it might be readable to the outside world. "That's a real risk unless earlier Robs knew the cacheing strategy."

Dixie Mae was only half-listening. If this worked at all, it was pretty good proof that earlier Robs and Dannys had done things right. *If this works at all.* Even after all that had happened, even after seeing

245

Victor disappear into thin air, Dixie Mae still felt like a little girl waiting for magic she didn't quite believe in.

Danny gave a nervous laugh. "How big *is* this cookie?"

Rob leaned his elbows onto the table. "Yeah. How many times have I been through a desperate seventh year?" There was an edge to his voice. You could imagine him pulling one of those deathcube stunts that the Ellens had described.

And then the screen brightened. Golden letters marched across a black-and-crimson fractal pattern: "Hello fellow suckers! Welcome to the 1,237th run of your life."

At first, Danny refused to believe they had spent 1,236 years on Gerry's treadmill. Rob gave a shrug. "I *do* believe it. I always told Gerry that real progress took longer than theory-making. So the bastard gave me...all the time in the world."

The cookie was almost a million megabytes long. Much of that was detailed descriptions of trapdoors, backdoors, and softsecrets undermining the design that Rob and Danny had created for Gerry Reich. But there were also thousands of megabytes of history and tactics, crafted and hyperlinked across more than a thousand simulated years. Most of it was the work of Danny and Rob, but there were the words of Ellen and Ellen and Dixie Mae, captured in those fleeting hours they spent with Rob and Danny. It was wisdom accumulated increment by precious increment, across cycles of near sameness. As such, it was their past and also their near future.

It even contained speculations about the times before Rob and Danny got the cookie system working: Those earliest runs must have been in the summer of 2011, a single upload of Rob Lusk. Back then, the best hardware in the world couldn't have supported more than Rob all alone, in the equivalent of a one-room apartment, with a keyboard and data display. Maybe he had guessed the truth; even so, what could he have done about it? Cookies would have been much harder to pass in those times. But Rob's hardware improved from rev to rev, as Gerry Reich built on Rob's earlier genius. Danny came on board. Their first successful attempt at a cookie must have been one of many wild stabs in the dark, drunken theorizing on the last night of still another year where Rob had failed to make his deadlines and thought that he was forever Ph.D.-less. The two had put an obscene message on the intrasystem email used for their "monthly" communications with Reich. The address they had used for this random flail was…help@lotsat-ech.com.

In the real world, that must have been after June 15, 2012. Why? Well, at the beginning of their next run, guess who showed up?

Dixie Mae Leigh. Mad as hell.

The message had ended up on Dixie Mae's work queue, and she had been sufficiently insulted to go raging off across the campus. Dixie Mae had spent the whole day bouncing from building to building, mostly making enemies. Not even Ellen or Ellen had been persuaded to come along. On the other hand, back in the early revs, the landscape reality had been simpler. Dixie Mae had been able to come into Rob's lair directly from the asphalt walkway.

Danny glanced at Dixie Mae. "And we can only guess how many times you never saw the email, or decided the random obscenities were not meant for you, or just walked in the wrong direction. Dumb luck eventually carried the day."

"Maybe. But I don't take to being insulted, and I go for the top."

Rob waved them both silent, never looking up from the cookie file: After their first success, Rob and Danny had fine-tuned the email, had learned more from each new Dixie Mae about who was in the other buildings on the hill and how—like the Ellens—they might be used.

"Victor!" Rob and the twins saw the reference at the same time. Rob stopped the autoscroll and they studied the paragraph. "Yes. We've seen Victor before. And five revs ago, he actually made it as far as this time. He killed his thread then, too." Rob followed a link marked *taking care of Victor*. "Oh. Okay. Danny, we'll have to tweak the log files—"

They stayed almost three hours more. Too long maybe, but Rob and Danny wanted to hear everything the Ellens and Dixie Mae could tell them about the simulation, and who else they had seen. The cookie history showed that things were always changing, getting more elaborate, involving more moneymaking uses of people Gerry had uploaded.

And they all wanted to keep talking. Except for poor Danny, the cookie said nothing about whether they still existed *outside*. In a way, knowing each other now was what kept them real.

Dixie Mae could tell that Danny felt that way, even when he complained: "It's just not safe having to contact unrelated people, depending on them to get the word to up here. "

"So, Danny, you want the three of us to just run and run and never know the truth?"

"No, Dixie Mae, but this is dangerous for you, too. As a matter of fact, in most of your runs, you stay clueless." He waved at the history. "We only see you once per each of our 'year-long' runs. I-I guess that's the best evidence that visiting us is risky."

The Ellens leaned forward, "Okay, then let's see how things would work without us." The four of them looked over the oldest history entries and argued jargon that meant nothing to Dixie Mae. It all added up to the fact that any local clues left in Rob's data would be easy for Gerry Reich to detect. On the other hand, messing with unused storage in the intranet mail system was possible, and it was much easier to cloak because the clues could be spread across several other projects.

The Ellens grinned, "So you really do need us, or at least you need Dixie Mae. But don't worry; we need *you*, and you have lots to do in your next year. During that time, you've got to make some credible progress with what Gerry wants. You saw what that is. Maybe you hardware types don't realize it, but—" she clicked on a link to the bulleted list of "minimum goals" that Reich had set for Rob and Danny. "—Prof. Reich is asking you for system improvements that would make it easier to partition the projects. And see this stuff about selective decoherence: Ever hear of cognitive haze? I bet with this improvement, Reich could actually do limited meddling with uploaded brain state. That would eliminate date and memory inconsistencies. We might not even recognize cookie clues then!"

Danny looked at the list. "Controlled decoherence?" He followed the link through to an extended discussion. "I wondered what that was. We need to talk about this."

"Yes—wait! Two of us get rebooted in—my God, in thirty minutes." The Ellens looked at each other and then at Dixie Mae.

Danny looked stricken, all his strategic analysis

forgotten. "But one of you Ellens is on a three-month cycle. She could stay here."

"Damn it, Danny! We just saw that there are checkpoints every sim day. If the NSA team were short a member for longer than that, we'd have a real problem."

Dixie Mae said, "Maybe we should all leave now, even us…short-lifers. If we can get back to our buildings before reboot, it might look better."

"Yeah, you're right. I'm sorry," said Rob.

She got up and started toward the door. Getting back to Customer Support was the one last thing she could do to help.

Rob stopped her. "Dixie Mae, it would help if you'd leave us with a message to send to you next time."

She pulled the tattered printout from her pocket. The bottom was torn and smeared. "You must have the whole thing in the cookie."

"Still, it would be good to know what you think would work best to get…your attention. The history says that background details are gradually changing."

He stood up and gave her a little bow.

"Well, okay." Dixie Mae sat down and thought for a second. Yeah, even if she hadn't had the message memorized, she knew the sort of insults that would send her ballistic. This wasn't exactly time travel, but now she was certain who had known all the terrible secrets, who had known how to be absolutely insulting. "My daddy always said that I'm my own worst enemy."

Rob and Danny walked with them back to the vault door. This was all new to the two guys. Danny scrambled out of the pit, and stared bug-eyed at the hills around them. "Rob, we could just *walk* to the other buildings!" He hesitated, came back to them.

"And yeah, I know. If it were that easy, we'd have done it before. We gotta study that cookie, Rob."

Rob just nodded. He looked kind of sad—then noticed that Dixie Mae was looking at him—and gave her a quick smile. They stood for a moment under the late afternoon haze and listened to the wind. The air had cooled and the whole pit was in shadow now.

Time to go.

Dixie Mae gave Rob a smile and her hand. "Hey, Rob. Don't worry. I've spent years trying to become a nicer, wiser, less stubborn person. It never happened. Maybe it never will. I guess that's what we need now."

Rob took her hand. "It is, but I swear…it won't be an endless treadmill. We will study that cookie, and we'll design something better than what we have now."

"Yeah." *Be as stubborn as I am, pal.*

Rob and Dan shook hands all around, wishing them well. "Okay," said Danny, "best be off with you. Rob, we should shut the door and get back. I saw some references in the cookie. If they get rebooted before they reach their places, there are some things we can do."

"Yeah," said Rob. But the two didn't move immediately from the entrance. Dixie Mae and the twins scrambled out of the pit and walked toward the asphalt. When Dixie Mae looked back, the two guys were still standing there. She gave a little wave, and then they were hidden by the edge of the excavation.

The three trudged along, the Ellens a lot less bubbly than usual. "Don't worry," NSA Ellen said to her twin, "there's still two months on the B0994 timeline. I'll remember for both of us. Maybe I can do some good on that team."

"Yeah," said the other, also sounding down. Then

abruptly they both gave one of those identical laughs
and they were smiling. "Hey, I just thought of something. True re-merge may always be impossible, but
what we have here is almost a kind of merge load.
Maybe, maybe—" but their last chance on this turn
of the wheel was gone. They looked at Dixie Mae and
all three were sad again. "Wish we had more time to
think how we wanted this to turn out. This won't be
like the SF stories where every rev you wake up filled
with forebodings and subconscious knowledge. We'll
start out all fresh."

Dixie Mae nodded. Starting out fresh. For dozens
of runs to come, where there would be nothing after
that first week at Customer Support, and putting up
with boorish Victor, and never knowing. And then
she smiled. "But every time we get through to Dan
and Rob, we leave a little more. Every time they see
us, they have a year to think. And it's all happening
a thousand times faster than Ol' Gerry can think. We
really are the cookie monsters. And someday—"
*Someday we'll be coming for you, Gerry. And it will
be sooner than you can dream.*

Legions in Time
Michael Swanwick

Eleanor Voigt had the oddest job of anyone she knew. She worked eight hours a day in an office where no business was done. Her job was to sit at a desk and stare at the closet door. There was a button on the desk that she was to push if anybody came out that door. There was a big clock on the wall, and, precisely at noon, once a day, she went over to the door and unlocked it with a key she had been given. Inside was an empty closet. There were no trap doors or secret panels in it—she had looked. It was just an empty closet.

If she noticed anything unusual, she was supposed to go back to her desk and press the button.

"Unusual in what way?" she'd asked when she'd been hired. "I don't understand. What am I looking for?"

"You'll know it when you see it," Mr. Tarblecko had said in that odd accent of his. Mr. Tarblecko was her employer, and some kind of foreigner. He was the creepiest thing imaginable. He had pasty white skin and no hair at all on his head, so that when he took his hat off, he looked like some species of mushroom. His ears were small and almost pointed. Ellie thought he might have some kind of disease. But he paid two dollars an hour, which was good money nowadays for a woman of her age.

At the end of her shift, she was relieved by an unkempt young man who had once blurted out to her that he was a poet. When she came in, in the morning, a heavy Negress would stand up wordlessly, take her coat and hat from the rack, and, with enormous dignity, leave.

So all day Ellie sat behind the desk with nothing to do. She wasn't allowed to read a book, for fear she might get so involved in it that she would stop watching the door. Crosswords were allowed, because they weren't as engrossing. She got a lot of knitting done, and was considering taking up tatting.

Over time, the door began to loom large in her imagination. She pictured herself unlocking it at some forbidden not-noon time and seeing—what? Her imagination failed her. No matter how vividly she visualized it, the door would open onto something mundane. Brooms and mops. Sports equipment. Galoshes and old clothes. What else would there be in a closet? What else *could* there be?

Sometimes, caught up in her imaginings, she would find herself on her feet. Sometimes, she walked to the door. Once, she actually put her hand on the knob before drawing away. But always the thought of losing her job stopped her.

It was maddening.

Twice, Mr. Tarblecko had come to the office while she was on duty. Each time, he was wearing that same black suit with that same narrow black tie. "You have a watch?" he'd asked.

"Yes, sir." The first time, she'd held forth her wrist to show it to him. The disdainful way he ignored the gesture ensured she did not repeat it on his second visit.

"Go away. Come back in forty minutes."

So she had gone out to a little tearoom nearby. She had a bag lunch back in her desk, with a baloney-and-mayonnaise sandwich and an apple, but she'd been so flustered she'd forgotten it, and then feared to go back after it. She'd treated herself to a dainty "lady lunch " that she was in no mood to appreciate, left a dime tip for the waitress, and was back in front of the office door exactly thirty-eight minutes after she'd left.

At forty minutes, exactly, she reached for the door. As if he'd been waiting for her to do so, Mr. Tarblecko breezed through the door, putting on his hat. He didn't acknowledge her promptness *or* her presence. He just strode briskly past, as though she didn't exist.

Stunned, she went inside, closed the door, and returned to her desk.

She realized then that Mr. Tarblecko was genuinely, fabulously rich. He had the arrogance of those who are so wealthy that they inevitably get their way in all small matters because there's always somebody there to *arrange* things that way. His type was never grateful for anything and never bothered to be polite, because it never even occurred to them that things could be otherwise.

The more she thought about it, the madder she got. She was no Bolshevik, but it seemed to her that people had certain rights, and that one of these was the right to a little common courtesy. It diminished one to be treated like a stick of furniture. It was degrading. She was damned if she was going to take it.

Six months went by.

The door opened and Mr. Tarblecko strode in, as if he'd left only minutes ago. "You have a watch?"

Ellie slid open a drawer and dropped her knitting into it. She opened another and took out her bag lunch. "Yes."

"Go away. Come back in forty minutes."

So she went outside. It was May, and Central Park was only a short walk away, so she ate there, by the little pond where children floated their toy sailboats. But all the while she fumed. She was a good employee—she really was! She was conscientious, punctual, and she never called in sick. Mr. Tarblecko ought to appreciate that. He had no business treating her the way he did.

Almost, she wanted to overstay lunch, but her conscience wouldn't allow that. When she got back to the office, precisely thirty-nine and a half minutes after she'd left, she planted herself squarely in front of the door so that when Mr. Tarblecko left he would have no choice but to confront her. It might well lose her her job, but...well, if it did, it did. That's how strongly she felt about it.

Thirty seconds later, the door opened and Mr. Tarblecko strode briskly out. Without breaking his stride, or, indeed, showing the least sign of emotion, he picked her up by her two arms, swiveled effortlessly, and deposited her to the side.

Then he was gone. Ellie heard his footsteps dwindling down the hall.

The nerve! The sheer, raw *gall* of the man!

Ellie went back in the office, but she couldn't make herself sit down at the desk. She was far too upset. Instead, she walked back and forth the length of the room, arguing with herself, saying aloud those things she should have said and would have said if only Mr. Tarblecko had stood still for them. To be picked up and set aside like that...well, it was really quite upsetting. It was intolerable.

What was particularly distressing was that there wasn't even any way to make her displeasure known.

At last, though, she calmed down enough to think clearly, and realized that she was wrong. There *was* something—something more symbolic than substantive, admittedly—that she could do.

She could open that door.

Ellie did not act on impulse. She was a methodical woman. So she thought the matter through before she did anything. Mr. Tarblecko very rarely showed up at the office—only twice in all the time she'd been here, and she'd been here over a year. Moreover, the odds of him returning to the office a third time only minutes after leaving it were negligible. He had left nothing behind—she could see that at a glance; the office was almost Spartan in its emptiness. Nor was there any work here for him to return to.

Just to be safe, though, she locked the office door. Then she got her chair out from behind the desk and chocked it up under the doorknob, so that even if somebody had a key, he couldn't get in. She put her ear to the door and listened for noises in the hall.

Nothing.

It was strange how, now that she had decided to do the deed, time seemed to slow and the office to expand. It took forever to cross the vast expanses of empty space between her and the closet door. Her hand reaching for its knob pushed through air as thick as molasses. Her fingers closed about it, one by one, and in the time it took for them to do so, there was room enough for a hundred second thoughts. Faintly, she heard the sound of…machinery? A low humming noise.

She placed the key in the lock, and opened the door.

There stood Mr. Tarblecko.

Ellie shrieked, and staggered backward. One of her heels hit the floor wrong, and her ankle twisted, and she almost fell. Her heart was hammering so furiously her chest hurt.

Mr. Tarblecko glared at her from within the closet. His face was as white as a sheet of paper. "One rule," he said coldly, tonelessly. "You had only one rule, and you broke it." He stepped out. "You are a very bad slave."

"I...I...I..." Ellie found herself gasping from the shock. "I'm not a slave at all!"

"There is where you are wrong, Eleanor Voigt. There is where you are very wrong indeed," said Mr. Tarblecko. "Open the window."

Ellie went to the window and pulled up the blinds. There was a little cactus in a pot on the windowsill. She moved it to her desk. Then she opened the window. It stuck a little, so she had to put all her strength into it. The lower sash went up slowly at first and then, with a rush, slammed to the top. A light, fresh breeze touched her.

"Climb onto the windowsill."

"I most certainly will—"—*not*, she was going to say. But to her complete astonishment, she found herself climbing up onto the sill. She could not help herself. It was as if her will were not her own.

"Sit down with your feet outside the window."

It was like a hideous nightmare, the kind that you know can't be real and struggle to awaken from, but cannot. Her body did exactly as it was told to do. She had absolutely no control over it.

"Do not jump until I tell you to do so."

"Are you going to tell me to jump?" she asked quaveringly. "Oh, *please*, Mr. Tarblecko..."

"Now look down."

The office was on the ninth floor. Ellie was a lifelong New Yorker, so that had never seemed to her a particularly great height before. Now it did. The people on the sidewalk were as small as ants. The buses and automobiles on the street were the size of matchboxes. The sounds of horns and engines drifted up to her, and birdsong as well, the lazy background noises of a spring day in the city. The ground was so terribly far away! And there was nothing between her and it but air! Nothing holding her back from death but her fingers desperately clutching the window frame!

Ellie could feel all the world's gravity willing her toward the distant concrete. She was dizzy with vertigo and a sick, stomach-tugging urge to simply let go and, briefly, fly. She squeezed her eyes shut tight, and felt hot tears streaming down her face.

She could tell from Mr. Tarblecko's voice that he was standing right behind her. "If I told you to jump, Eleanor Voigt, would you do so?"

"Yes," she squeaked.

"What kind of person jumps to her death simply because she's been told to do so?"

"A...a slave!"

"Then what are you?"

"A slave! A slave! I'm a slave!" She was weeping openly now, as much from humiliation as from fear. "I don't want to die! I'll be your slave, anything, whatever you say!"

"If you're a slave, then what kind of slave should you be?"

"A...a...*good* slave."

"Come back inside."

Gratefully, she twisted around, and climbed back into the office. Her knees buckled when she tried to stand, and she had to grab at the windowsill to keep from falling. Mr. Tarblecko stared at her, sternly and steadily.

"You have been given your only warning," he said. "If you disobey again—or if you ever try to quit—I will order you out the window."

He walked into the closet and closed the door behind him.

There were two hours left on her shift—time enough, barely, to compose herself. When the disheveled young poet showed up, she dropped her key in her purse and walked past him without so much as a glance. Then she went straight to the nearest hotel bar, and ordered a gin and tonic.

She had a lot of thinking to do.

Eleanor Voigt was not without resources. She had been an executive secretary before meeting her late husband, and everyone knew that a good executive secretary effectively runs her boss's business for him. Before the Crash, she had run a household with three servants. She had entertained. Some of her parties had required weeks of planning and preparation. If it weren't for the Depression, she was sure she'd be in a much better-paid position than the one she held.

She was *not* going to be a slave.

But before she could find a way out of her predicament, she had to understand it. First, the closet. Mr. Tarblecko had left the office and then, minutes later, popped up inside it. A hidden passage of some kind? No—that was simultaneously too complicated and not complicated enough. She had heard machinery, just before she opened the door. So...some kind of transportation device, then. Something that a day ago she would have sworn couldn't exist. A teleporter, perhaps, or a time machine.

The more she thought of it, the better she liked the

thought of the time machine. It was not just that teleporters were the stuff of Sunday funnies and Buck Rogers serials, while *The Time Machine* was a distinguished philosophical work by Mr. H.G. Wells. Though she had to admit that figured in there. But a teleportation device required a twin somewhere, and Mr. Tarblecko hadn't had the time even to leave the building.

A time machine, however, would explain so much! Her employer's long absences. The necessity that the device be watched when not in use, lest it be employed by Someone Else. Mr. Tarblecko's abrupt appearance today, and his possession of a coercive power that no human being on Earth had.

The fact that she could no longer think of Mr. Tarblecko as human.

She had barely touched her drink, but now she found herself too impatient to finish it. She slapped a dollar bill down on the bar and, without waiting for her change, left.

During the time it took to walk the block and a half to the office building and ride the elevator up to the ninth floor, Ellie made her plans. She strode briskly down the hallway and opened the door without knocking. The unkempt young man looked up, startled, from a scribbled sheet of paper.

"You have a watch?"

"Y-yes, but...Mr. Tarblecko..."

"Get out. Come back in forty minutes."

With grim satisfaction, she watched the young man cram his key into one pocket and the sheet of paper into another and leave. *Good slave,* she thought to herself. Perhaps he'd already been through the little charade Mr. Tarblecko had just played on her. Doubtless every employee underwent ritual enslavement as a way of keeping them in line. The problem with having slaves, however, was that they couldn't be expected to display any initiative.... Not on the master's behalf, anyway.

Ellie opened her purse and got out the key. She walked to the closet.

For an instant, she hesitated. Was she really sure enough to risk her life? But the logic was unassailable. She had been given no second chance. If Mr. Tarblecko *knew* she was about to open the door a second time, he would simply have ordered her out the window on her first offense. The fact that he hadn't meant that he didn't know.

She took a deep breath and opened the door.

There was a world inside.

For what seemed like forever, Ellie stood staring at the bleak metropolis so completely unlike New York City. Its buildings were taller than any she had ever seen—miles high!—and interlaced with skywalks, like those in *Metropolis*. But the buildings in the movie had been breathtaking, and these were the opposite of beautiful. They were ugly as sin: windowless, grey, stained, and discolored. There were monotonous lines of harsh lights along every street, and under their glare trudged men and women as uniform and lifeless as robots. Outside the office, it was a beautiful bright day. But on the other side of the closet, the world was dark as night.

And it was snowing.

Gingerly, she stepped into the closet. The instant her foot touched the floor, it seemed to expand to all sides. She stood at the center of a great wheel of doors, with all but two of them—to her office and to the winter world—shut. There were hooks beside each door, and hanging from them were costumes of a hundred different cultures. She thought she recognized togas, Victorian opera dress, kimonos.... But most of the clothing was unfamiliar.

Beside the door into winter, there was a long cape. Ellie wrapped it around herself, and discovered a knob on the inside. She twisted it to the right, and suddenly the coat was hot as hot. Quickly, she twisted the knob to the left, and it grew cold. She fiddled with the thing until the cape felt just right. Then she straightened her shoulders, took a deep breath, and stepped out into the forbidding city.

There was a slight electric sizzle, and she was standing in the street.

Ellie spun around to see what was behind her: a rectangle of some glassy black material. She rapped it with her knuckles. It was solid. But when she brought her key near its surface, it shimmered and opened into that strange space between worlds again.

So she had a way back home.

To either side of her rectangle were identical glassy rectangles faceted slightly away from it. They were the exterior of an enormous kiosk, or perhaps a very low building, at the center of a large, featureless square. She walked all the way around it, rapping each rectangle with her key. Only the one would open for her.

The first thing to do was to find out where—or, rather, *when*—she was. Ellie stepped in front of one of the hunched, slow-walking men. "Excuse me, sir, could you answer a few questions for me?"

The man raised a face that was utterly bleak and without hope. A ring of grey metal glinted from his neck. "Hawrzat dagtiknut?" he asked.

Ellie stepped back in horror, and, like a wind-up toy temporarily halted by a hand or a foot, the man resumed his plodding gait.

She cursed herself. Of *course* language would have

changed in the however-many-centuries future she found herself in. Well…that was going to make gathering information more difficult. But she was used to difficult tasks. The evening of John's suicide, she had been the one to clean the walls and the floor. After that, she'd known that she was capable of doing anything she set her mind to.

Above all, it was important that she not get lost. She scanned the square with the doorways in time at its center—mentally, she dubbed it Times Square—and chose at random one of the broad avenues converging on it. That, she decided would be Broadway.

Ellie started down Broadway, watching everybody and everything. Some of the drone-folk were dragging sledges with complex machinery on them. Others were hunched under soft translucent bags filled with murky fluid and vague biomorphic shapes. The air smelled bad, but in ways she was not familiar with.

She had gotten perhaps three blocks when the sirens went off—great piercing blasts of noise that assailed the ears and echoed from the building walls. All the streetlights flashed off and on and off again in a one-two rhythm. From unseen loudspeakers, an authoritative voice blared, *"Akgang! Akgang! Kronzvarbrakar! Zawzawkstrag! Akgang! Akgang…."*

Without hurry, the people in the street began turning away, touching their hands to dull grey plates beside nondescript doors and disappearing into the buildings.

"Oh, cripes!" Ellie muttered. She'd best—

There was a disturbance behind her. Ellie turned and saw the strangest thing yet.

It was a girl of eighteen or nineteen, wearing summer clothes—a man's trousers, a short-sleeved flower-print blouse—and she was running down the street in a panic. She grabbed at the uncaring drones, begging for help. "Please!" she cried. "Can't you help me? Somebody! Please...you have to help me!" Puffs of steam came from her mouth with each breath. Once or twice she made a sudden dart for one of the doorways and slapped her hand on the greasy plates. But the doors would not open for her.

Now the girl had reached Ellie. In a voice that expected nothing, she said, "Please?"

"I'll help you, dear," Ellie said.

The girl shrieked, then convulsively hugged her. "Oh, thank you, thank you, thank you," she babbled.

"Follow close behind me." Ellie strode up behind one of the lifeless un-men and, just after he had slapped his hand on the plate, but before he could enter, grabbed his rough tunic and gave it a yank. He turned.

"Vamoose!" she said in her sternest voice, and jerked a thumb over her shoulder.

The un-man turned away. He might not understand the word, but the tone and the gesture sufficed.

Ellie stepped inside, pulling the girl after her. The door closed behind them.

"Wow," said the girl wonderingly. "How did you do that?"

"This is a slave culture. For a slave to survive, he's got to obey anyone who acts like a master. It's that simple. Now, what's your name and how did you get here?" As she spoke, Ellie took in her surroundings. The room they were in was dim, grimy—and vast. So far as she could see, there were no interior walls, only the occasional pillar, and, here and there, a set of functional metal stairs without railings.

"Nadine Shepard. I...I...There was a door! And I walked through it and I found myself *here!* I..."

The child was close to hysteria. "I know, dear. Tell me, when are you from?"

"Chicago. On the North Side, near..."

"Not where, dear, when? What year is it?"

"Uh...two thousand and four. Isn't it?"

"Not here. Not now." The grey people were everywhere, moving sluggishly, yet always keeping within sets of yellow lines painted on the concrete floor. Their smell was pervasive, and far from pleasant. Still...

Ellie stepped directly into the path of one of the sad creatures, a woman. When she stopped, Ellie took the tunic from her shoulders and then stepped back. Without so much as an expression of annoyance, the woman resumed her plodding walk.

"Here you are." She handed the tunic to young Nadine. "Put this on, dear, you must be freezing. Your skin is positively blue." And, indeed, it was not much warmer inside than it had been outdoors. "I'm Eleanor Voigt. Mrs. Eleanor Voigt."

Shivering, Nadine donned the rough garment. But instead of thanking Ellie, she said, "You look familiar."

Ellie returned her gaze. She was a pretty enough creature though, strangely, she wore no makeup at all. Her features were regular, intelligent—"You look familiar too. I can't quite put my finger on it, but..."

"Okay," Nadine said, "now tell me. Please. Where and when am I, and what's going on?"

"I honestly don't know," Ellie said. Dimly, through the walls, she could hear the sirens and the loudspeaker-voice. If only it weren't so murky in here! She couldn't get any clear idea of the building's layout or function.

"But you *must* know! You're so...so capable, so in control. You..."

"I'm a castaway like you, dear. Just figuring things

out as I go along." She continued to peer. "But I can tell you this much: We are far, far in the future. The poor degraded beings you saw on the street are the slaves of a superior race—let's call them the Aftermen. The Aftermen are very cruel, and they can travel through time as easily as you or I can travel from city to city via inter-urban rail. And that's all I know. So far."

Nadine was peering out a little slot in the door that Ellie hadn't noticed. Now she said, "What's this?"

Ellie took her place at the slot, and saw a great bulbous street-filling machine pull to a halt a block from the building. Insectoid creatures that might be robots or might be men in body armor poured out of it, and swarmed down the street, examining every door. The sirens and the loudspeakers cut off. The streetlights returned to normal. "It's time we left," Ellie said.

An enormous artificial voice shook the building. *Akbang! Akbang! Zawzawksbild! Alzowt! Zawzawksbild! Akbang!*

"Quickly!"

She seized Nadine's hand, and they were running.

Without emotion, the grey folk turned from their prior courses and unhurriedly made for the exits.

Ellie and Nadine tried to stay off the walkways entirely. But the air began to tingle, more on the side away from the walkways than the side toward, and then to burn and then to sting. They were quickly forced between the yellow lines. At first they were able to push their way past the drones, and then to shoulder their way through their numbers. But more and more came dead-stepping their way down the metal stairways. More and more descended from the upper levels via lifts that abruptly descended from the ceiling to disgorge them by the hundreds. More and more flowed outward from the building's dim interior.

Passage against the current of flesh became first difficult, and then impossible. They were swept backward, helpless as corks in a rain-swollen river. Outward they were forced and through the exit into the street.

The "police" were waiting there.

At the sight of Ellie and Nadine—they could not have been difficult to discern among the uniform drabness of the others—two of the armored figures stepped forward with long poles and brought them down on the women.

Ellie raised her arm to block the pole, and it landed solidly on her wrist.

Horrid, searing pain shot through her, greater than anything she had ever experienced before. For a giddy instant, Ellie felt a strange elevated sense of being, and she thought, *If I can put up with this, I can endure anything*. Then the world went away.

Ellie came to in a jail cell.

At least, that's what she thought it was. The room was small, square, and doorless. A featureless ceiling gave off a drab, even light. A bench ran around the perimeter, and there was a hole in the middle of the room whose stench advertised its purpose.

She sat up.

On the bench across from her, Nadine was weeping silently into her hands.

So her brave little adventure had ended. She had rebelled against Mr. Tarblecko's tyranny and come to the same end that awaited most rebels. It was her own foolish fault. She had acted without sufficient forethought, without adequate planning, without scouting out the opposition and gathering information first. She had gone up against a Power that could range effortlessly across time and space, armed only with a pocket handkerchief and a spare set of glasses, and inevitably that Power had swatted her down with a contemptuous minimum of their awesome force.

They hadn't even bothered to take away her purse.

Ellie dug through it, found a cellophane-wrapped hard candy, and popped it into her mouth. She sucked on it joylessly. All hope whatsoever was gone from her.

Still, even when one has no hope, one's obligations remain. "Are you all right, Nadine?" she forced herself to ask. "Is there anything I can do to help?"

Nadine lifted her tear-stained face. "I just went through a door," she said. "That's all. I didn't do anything bad or wrong or...or anything. And now I'm here!" Fury blazed up in her. "Damn you, damn you, damn you!"

"Me?" Ellie said, astonished.

"You! You shouldn't have let them get us. You should've taken us to some hiding place, and then gotten us back home. But you didn't. You're a stupid, useless old woman!"

It was all Ellie could do to keep from smacking the young lady. But Nadine was practically a child, she told herself, and it didn't seem like they raised girls to have much gumption in the year 2004. They were probably weak and spoiled people, up there in the twenty-first century, who had robots to do all their work for them, and nothing to do but sit around and listen to the radio all day. So she held not only her hand, but her tongue. "Don't worry, dear," she said soothingly. "We'll get out of this. Somehow."

Nadine stared at her bleakly, disbelievingly. "*How?*" she demanded.

But to this Ellie had no answer.

Time passed. Hours, by Ellie's estimation, and perhaps many hours. And with its passage, she found herself, more out of boredom than from the belief that it would be of any use whatsoever, looking at the situation analytically again.

How had the Aftermen tracked her down?

Some sort of device on the time-door might perhaps warn them that an unauthorized person had passed through. But the "police" had located her so swiftly and surely! They had clearly known exactly where she was. Their machine had come straight toward the building they'd entered. The floods of non-men had flushed her right out into their arms.

So it was something about her, or *on* her, that had brought the Aftermen so quickly.

Ellie looked at her purse with new suspicion. She dumped its contents on the ledge beside her, and pawed through them, looking for the guilty culprit. A few hard candies, a lace hankey, half a pack of cigarettes, fountain pen, glasses case, bottle of aspirin, house key...and the key to the time closet. The only thing in all she owned that had come to her direct from Mr. Tarblecko. She snatched it up.

It looked ordinary enough. Ellie rubbed it, sniffed it, touched it gently to her tongue.

It tasted sour.

Sour, the way a small battery tasted if you touched your tongue to it. There was a faint trickle of electricity coming from the thing. It was clearly no ordinary key.

She pushed her glasses up on her forehead, held the thing to her eye, and squinted. It looked exactly like a common everyday key. Almost. It had no manufacturer's name on it, and that was unexpected, given that the key looked new and unworn. The top part of it was covered with irregular geometric decorations.

Or *were* they decorations?

She looked up to see Nadine studying her steadily, unblinkingly, like a cat. "Nadine, honey, your eyes are younger than mine—would you take a look at this? Are those tiny...*switches* on this thing?"

"What?" Nadine accepted the key from her, examined it, poked at it with one nail.

Flash.

When Ellie stopped blinking and could see again, one wall of their cell had disappeared.

Nadine stepped to the very edge of the cell, peering outward. A cold wind whipped bitter flakes of snow about her. "Look!" she cried. Then, when Ellie stood beside her to see what she saw, she wrapped her arms about the older woman and stepped out into the abyss.

Ellie screamed.

The two women piloted the police vehicle up Broadway, toward Times Square. Though a multiplicity of instruments surrounded the windshield, the controls were simplicity itself: a single stick that, when pushed forward, accelerated the vehicle, and, when pushed to either side, turned it. Apparently, the police did not need to be particularly smart. Neither the steering mechanism nor the doors had any locks on them, so far as Ellie could tell. Apparently, the drone-men had so little initiative that locks weren't required. Which would help explain how she and Nadine had escaped so easily.

"How did you know this vehicle was beneath us?" Ellie asked. "How did you know we'd be able to drive it? I almost had a heart attack when you pushed me out on top of it."

"Way rad, wasn't it? Straight out of a Hong Kong video." Nadine grinned. "Just call me Michelle Yeoh."

"If you say so." She was beginning to rethink her hasty judgment of the lass. Apparently the people of 2004 weren't quite the shrinking violets she'd made them out to be.

With a flicker and a hum, a square sheet of glass below the windshield came to life. Little white dots of light danced, jittered, and coalesced to form a face. It was Mr. Tarblecko.

"Time criminals of the Dawn Era," his voice thundered from a hidden speaker. *"Listen and obey."*

Ellie shrieked, and threw her purse over the visi-plate. "Don't listen to him!" she ordered Nadine. "See if you can find a way of turning this thing off!"

"Bring the stolen vehicle to a complete halt immediately!"

To her horror, if not her surprise, Ellie found herself pulling the steering-bar back, slowing the police car to a stop. But then Nadine, in blind obedience to Mr. Tarblecko's compulsive voice, grabbed for the bar as well. Simultaneously, she stumbled, and, with a little *eep* noise, lurched against the bar, pushing it sideways.

The vehicle slewed to one side, smashed into a building wall, and toppled over.

Then Nadine had the roof-hatch open and was pulling her through it. "C'mon!" she shouted. "I can see the black doorway-thingie—the, you know, place!"

Following, Ellie had to wonder about the educational standards of the year 2004. The young lady didn't seem to have a very firm grasp on the English language.

Then they had reached Times Square and the circle of doorways at its center. The street lights were flashing and loudspeakers were shouting *"Akbang! Akbang!"* and police vehicles were converging upon them from every direction, but there was still time.

Ellie tapped the nearest doorway with her key. Nothing. The next. Nothing. Then she was running around the building, scraping the key against each doorway, and...there it was!

She seized Nadine's hand, and they plunged through.

The space inside expanded in a great wheel to all sides. Ellie spun about. There were doors everywhere—and all of them closed. She had not the faintest idea which one led back to her own New York City.

Wait, though! There were costumes appropriate to each time hanging by their doors. If she just went down them until she found a business suit...

Nadine gripped her arm. "Oh, my God!"

Ellie turned, looked, saw. A doorway—the one they had come through, obviously—had opened behind them. In it stood Mr. Tarblecko. Or, to be more precise, *three* Mr. Tarbleckos. They were all as identical as peas in a pod. She had no way of knowing which one, if any, was hers.

"Through here! Quick!" Nadine shrieked. She'd snatched open the nearest door.

Together, they fled.

"Oolohstullalu ashulalumoota!" a woman sang out. She wore a jumpsuit and carried a clipboard, which she thrust into Ellie's face. "Oolalulaswula ulalulin."

"I...I don't understand what you're saying," Ellie faltered. They stood on the green lawn of a gentle slope that led down to the ocean. Down by the beach, enormous construction machines, operated by both men and women (women! of all the astonishing sights she had seen, this was strangest), were rearing an enormous, enigmatic structure, reminiscent to Ellie's eye of Sunday school illustrations of the Tower of Babel. Gentle tropical breezes stirred her hair.

"Dawn Era, Amerlingo," the clipboard said. "Exact period uncertain. Answer these questions. Gas—for lights or for cars?"

"For cars, mostly. Although there are still a few—"

"Apples—for eating or computing?"

"Eating," Ellie said, while simultaneously Nadine said, "Both."

"Scopes—for dreaming or for resurrecting?"

Neither woman said anything.

The clipboard chirped in a satisfied way. "Early Atomic Age, pre- and post-Hiroshima, one each. You will experience a moment's discomfort. Do not be alarmed. It is for your own good."

"Please." Ellie turned from the woman to the clipboard and back, uncertain which to address. "What's going on? Where are we? We have so many—"

"There's no time for questions," the woman said impatiently. Her accent was unlike anything Ellie had ever heard before. "You must undergo indoctrination, loyalty imprinting, and chronomilitary training immediately. We need all the time-warriors we can get. This base is going to be destroyed in the morning."

"What? I…"

"Hand me your key."

Without thinking, Ellie gave the thing to the woman. Then a black nausea overcame her. She swayed, fell, and was unconscious before she hit the ground.

"Would you like some heroin?"

The man sitting opposite her had a face that was covered with blackwork tattoo eels. He grinned, showing teeth that had all been filed to a point.

"I beg your pardon?" Ellie was not at all certain where she was, or how she had gotten here. Nor did she comprehend how she could have understood this alarming fellow's words, for he most certainly had *not* been speaking English.

"Heroin." He thrust the open metal box of white powder at her. "Do you want a snort?"

"No, thank you." Ellie spoke carefully, trying not to give offense. "I find that it gives me spots."

With a disgusted noise, the man turned away.

Then the young woman sitting beside her said in a puzzled way, "Don't I know you?"

She turned. It was Nadine. "Well, my dear, I should certainly hope you haven't forgotten me so soon."

"Mrs. Voigt?" Nadine said wonderingly. "But you're…you're…young!"

Involuntarily, Ellie's hands went up to her face. The skin was taut and smooth. The incipient softening of her chin was gone. Her hair, when she brushed her hands through it, was sleek and full.

She found herself desperately wishing she had a mirror.

"They must have done something. While I was asleep." She lightly touched her temples, the skin around her eyes. "I'm not wearing any glasses! I can see perfectly!" She looked around her. The room she was in was even more Spartan than the jail cell had been. There were two metal benches facing each other, and on them sat as motley a collection of men and women as she had ever seen. There was a woman who must have weighed three hundred pounds—and every ounce of it muscle. Beside her sat an albino lad so slight and elfin he hardly seemed there at all. Until, that is, one looked at his clever face and burning eyes. *Then* one knew him to be easily the most dangerous person in the room. As for the others, well, none of them had horns or tails, but that was about it.

The elf leaned forward. "Dawn Era, aren't you?"

he said. "If you survive this, you'll have to tell me how you got here."

"I—"

"They want you to think you're as good as dead already. Don't believe them! I wouldn't have signed up in the first place, if I hadn't come back afterward and told myself I'd come through it all intact." He winked and settled back. "The situation is hopeless, of course. But I wouldn't take it seriously."

Ellie blinked. Was everybody mad here?

In that same instant, a visi-plate very much like the one in the police car lowered from the ceiling, and a woman appeared on it. "Hero mercenaries," she said, "I salute you! As you already know, we are at the very front lines of the War. The Aftermen Empire has been slowly, inexorably moving backward into their past, our present, a year at time. So far, the Optimized Rationality of True Men has lost five thousand three hundred and fourteen years to their onslaught." Her eyes blazed. "That advance ends here! That advance ends now! We have lost so far because, living down-time from the Aftermen, we cannot obtain a techno-logical superiority to them. Every weapon we invent passes effortlessly into their hands.

"So we are going to fight and defeat them, not with technology but with the one quality that, not being human, they lack—human character! Our researches into the far past have shown that superior technology can be defeated by raw courage and sheer numbers. One man with a sunstroker can be overwhelmed by savages equipped with nothing more than neutron bombs—*if* there are enough of them, and they don't mind dying! An army with energy guns can be des-troyed by rocks and sticks and determination.

"In a minute, your transporter and a million more like it will arrive at staging areas afloat in null-time.

You will don respirators and disembark. There you will find the time-torpedoes. Each one requires two operators—a pilot and a button-pusher. The pilot will bring you in as close as possible to the Aftermen time-dreadnoughts. The button-pusher will then set off the chronomordant explosives."

This is madness, Ellie thought. *I'll do no such thing.* Simultaneous with the thought came the realization that she had the complex skills needed to serve as either pilot or button-pusher. They must have been given to her at the same time she had been made young again and her eyesight improved.

"Not one in a thousand of you will live to make it anywhere near the time-dreadnoughts. But those few who do will justify the sacrifices of the rest. For with your deaths, you will be preserving humanity from enslavement and destruction! Martyrs, I salute you." She clenched her fist. "We are nothing! The Rationality is all!"

Then everyone was on his or her feet, all facing the visi-screen, all raising clenched fists in response to the salute, and all chanting as one, *"We are nothing! The Rationality is all!"*

To her horror and disbelief, Ellie discovered herself chanting the oath of self-abnegation in unison with the others, and, worse, meaning every word of it.

The woman who had taken the key away from her had said something about "loyalty imprinting." Now Ellie understood what that term entailed.

In the gray not-space of null-time, Ellie kicked her way into the time-torpedo. It was to her newly sophisticated eyes, rather a primitive thing: Fifteen grams of nano-mechanism welded to a collapsteel hull equipped with a noninertial propulsion unit and packed with five tons of something her mental translator rendered as "annihilatium." This last, she knew to the core of her being, was ferociously destructive stuff.

Nadine wriggled in after her. "Let me pilot," she said. "I've been playing video games since Mario was the villain in Donkey Kong."

"Nadine, dear, there's something I've been meaning to ask you." Ellie settled into the button-pusher slot. There were twenty-three steps to setting off the annihilatium, each one finicky, and if even one step were taken out of order, nothing would happen. She had absolutely no doubt she could do it correctly, swiftly, efficiently.

"Yes?"

"Does all that futuristic jargon of yours actually *mean* anything?"

Nadine's laughter was cut off by a *squawk* from the visi-plate. The woman who had lectured them earlier appeared, looking stern. "Launch in twenty-three seconds," she said. "For the Rationality!"

"For the Rationality!" Ellie responded fervently and in unison with Nadine. Inside, however, she was thinking, *How did I get into this?* and then, ruefully, *Well, there's no fool like an old fool.*

"Eleven seconds...seven seconds...three seconds...one second."

Nadine launched.

Without time and space, there can be neither sequence nor pattern. The battle between the Aftermen dreadnoughts and the time-torpedoes of the Rationality, for all its shifts and feints and evasions, could be reduced to a single blip of instantaneous action and then rendered into a single binary datum: win/lose.

The Rationality lost.

The time-dreadnoughts of the Aftermen crept another year into the past.

But somewhere in the very heart of that not-terribly

important battle, two torpedoes, one of which was piloted by Nadine, converged upon the hot-spot of guiding consciousness that empowered and drove the flagship of the Aftermen time-armada. Two button-pushers set off their explosives. Two shock-waves bowed outward, met, meshed, and merged with the expanding shock-wave of the countermeasure launched by the dreadnought's tutelary awareness,

Something terribly complicated happened.

Ellie found herself sitting at a table in the bar of the Algonquin hotel, back in New York City. Nadine was sitting opposite her. To either side of them were the clever albino and the man with the tattooed face and the filed teeth.

The albino smiled widely. "Ah, the primitives! Of all who could have survived—myself excepted, of course—you are the most welcome."

His tattooed companion frowned. "Please show some more tact, Sev. However they may appear to us, these folk are not primitives to *themselves*."

"You are right as always, Dun Jal. Permit me to introduce myself. I am Seventh-Clone of House Orpen, Lord Extratemporal of the Centuries 3197 through 3992 Inclusive, Backup Heir Potential to the Indeterminate Throne. Sev, for short."

"Dun Jal. Mercenary. From the early days of the Rationality. Before it grew decadent."

"Eleanor Voigt, Nadine Shepard. I'm from 1936, and she's from 2004. Where—if that's the right word—are we?"

"Neither where nor when, delightful aboriginal. We have obviously been thrown into hypertime, that no-longer-theoretical state informing and supporting the more mundane seven dimensions of time with which you are doubtless familiar. Had we minds capable of perceiving it directly without going mad, who *knows*

279

what we should see? As it is," he waved a hand, "all this is to me as my One-Father's clonatorium, in which so many of I spent our minority."

"I see a workshop," Dun Jal said.

"I see—" Nadine began.

Dun Jal turned pale. "A Tarbleck-null!" He bolted to his feet, hand instinctively going for a side-arm which, in their current state, did not exist.

"Mr. Tarblecko!" Ellie gasped. It was the first time she had thought of him since her imprinted technical training in the time-fortress of the Rationality, and speaking his name brought up floods of related information: That there were seven classes of Aftermen, or Tarblecks as they called themselves. That the least of them, the Tarbleck-sixes, were brutal and domineering overlords. That the greatest of them, the Tarbleck-nulls commanded the obedience of millions. That the maximum power a Tarbleck-null could call upon at an instant's notice was four quads per second per second. That the physical expression of that power was so great that, had she known, Ellie would never have gone through that closet door in the first place.

Sev gestured toward an empty chair. "Yes, I thought it was about time for you to show up."

The sinister grey Afterman drew up the chair and sat down to their table. "The small one knows why I am here," he said. "The others do not. It is degrading to explain myself to such as you, so he shall have to."

"I am so privileged as to have studied the more obscure workings of time, yes." The little man put his fingertips together and smiled a fey, foxy smile over their tips. "So I know that physical force is useless here. Only argument can prevail. Thus…trial by persuasion it is. I shall go first."

He stood up. "My argument is simple: As I told our dear, savage friends here earlier, an heir-potential to the Indeterminate Throne is too valuable to risk on uncertain adventures. Before I was allowed to enlist as a mercenary, my elder self had to return from the experience to testify I would survive it unscathed. I did. Therefore, I will."

He sat.

There was a moment's silence. "That's all you have to say?" Dun Jal asked.

"It is enough."

"Well." Dun Jal cleared his throat and stood. "Then it is my turn. The Empire of the Aftermen is inherently unstable at all points. Perhaps it was a natural phenomenon—*once*. Perhaps the Aftermen arose from the workings of ordinary evolutionary processes, and could at one time claim that therefore they had a natural place in this continuum. That changed when they began to expand their Empire into their own past. In order to enable their back-conquests, they had to send agents to all prior periods in time to influence and corrupt, to change the flow of history into something terrible and terrifying, from which they might arise. And so they did.

"Massacres, death-camps, genocide, World Wars..." (There were other terms that did not translate, concepts more horrible than Ellie had words for.) "You don't really think those were the work of *human beings*, do you? We're much too sensible a race for that sort of thing—when we're left to our own devices. No, all the worst of our miseries are instigated by the Aftermen. We are far from perfect, and the best example of this is the cruel handling of the War in the final years of the Optimized Rationality of True Men, where our leaders have become almost as terrible as the Aftermen themselves—because it is from their very ranks that the Aftermen shall arise. But what *might* we have been?

"Without the interference of the Aftermen might we not have become something truly admirable? Might we not have become not the Last Men, but the First truly worthy of the name?" He sat down.

Lightly, sardonically, Sev applauded. "Next?"

The Tarbleck-null placed both hands heavily on the table, and, leaning forward, pushed himself up. "Does the tiger explain himself to the sheep?" he asked. "Does he *need* to explain? The sheep understand well enough that Death has come to walk among them, to eat those it will and spare the rest only because he is not yet hungry. So too do men understand that they have met their master. I do not enslave men because it is right or proper, but because I *can*. The proof of which is that I *have!*

"Strength needs no justification. It exists or it does not. I exist. Who here can say that I am not your superior? Who here can deny that Death has come to walk among you? Natural selection chose the fittest among men to become a new race. Evolution has set my foot upon your necks, and I will not take it off."

To universal silence, he sat down. The very slightest of glances he threw Ellie's way, as if to challenge her to refute him. Nor could she! Her thoughts were all confusion, her tongue all in a knot. She knew he was wrong—she was sure of it!—and yet she could not put her arguments together. She simply couldn't think clearly and quickly enough.

Nadine laughed lightly.

"Poor superman!" she said. "Evolution isn't linear, like that chart that has a fish crawling out of the water at one end and a man in a business suit at the other. All species are constantly trying to evolve in all directions at once—a little taller, a little shorter, a little faster, a little slower. When that distinction proves advantageous, it tends to be passed along. The Aftermen aren't any smarter than Men are—less so, in some ways. Less flexible, less innovative...look what a stagnant world they've created! What they *are* is more forceful."

"Forceful?" Ellie said, startled. "Is that all?"

"That's enough. Think of all the trouble caused by men like Hitler, Mussolini, Caligula, Pol Pot, Archers-Wang 43.... All they had was the force of their personality, the ability to get others to do what they wanted. Well, the Aftermen are the descendants of exactly such people, only with the force of will squared and cubed. That afternoon when the Tarbleck-null ordered you to sit in the window? It was the easiest thing in the world to one of them. As easy as breathing.

"That's why the Rationality can't win. Oh, they *could* win, if they were willing to root out that streak of persuasive coercion within themselves. But they're fighting a war, and in times of war one uses whatever weapons one has. The ability to tell millions of soldiers to sacrifice themselves for the common good is simply too useful to be thrown away. But all the time they're fighting the external enemy, the Aftermen are evolving within their own numbers."

"You admit it," the Tarbleck said.

"Oh, be still! You're a foolish little creature, and you have no idea what you're up against. Have you ever asked the Aftermen from the leading edge of your Empire why you're expanding backward into the past rather than forward into the future? Obviously because there are bigger and more dangerous things ahead of you than you dare face. You're afraid to go there—afraid that you might find *me!*" Nadine took something out of her pocket. "Now go away, all of you."

Flash.

Nothing changed. Everything changed.

Ellie was still sitting in the Algonquin with Nadine. But Sev, Dun Jal, and the Tarbleck-null were all gone. More significantly, the bar felt *real* in a way it hadn't an instant before. She was back home, in her own now and her own when.

Ellie dug into her purse and came up with a crumpled pack of Lucky Strike Greens, teased one out, and lit it. She took a deep drag on the cigarette and then exhaled. "All right," she said, "who are you?"

The girl's eyes sparkled with amusement. "Why, Ellie, dear, don't you know? I'm *you!*"

So it was that Eleanor Voigt was recruited into the most exclusive organization in all Time—an organization that was comprised in hundreds of thousands of instances entirely and solely of herself. Over the course of millions of years, she grew and evolved, of course, so that her ultimate terrifying and glorious self was not even remotely human. But everything starts somewhere, and Ellie of necessity had to start small.

The Aftermen were one of the simpler enemies of the humane future she felt that Humanity deserved. Nevertheless they had to be—gently and nonviolently, which made the task more difficult—opposed.

After fourteen months of training and the restoration of all her shed age, Ellie was returned to New York City on the morning she had first answered the odd help wanted ad in the *Times*. Her original self had been detoured away from the situation, to be recruited if necessary at a later time.

"Unusual in what way?" she asked. "I don't understand. What am I looking for?"

"You'll know it when you see it," the Tarbleck-null said.

He handed her the key.

She accepted it. There were tools hidden within her body whose powers dwarfed those of this primitive chrono-transfer device. But the encoded information the key contained would lay open the workings of the Aftermen Empire to her. Working right under their noses, she would be able to undo their schemes, diminish their power, and, ultimately, prevent them from ever coming into existence in the first place.

Ellie had only the vaguest idea how she was supposed to accomplish all this. But she was confident that she could figure it out, given time. And she had the time.

All the time in the world.

The Chop Line
Stephen Baxter

I

We'd had no warning of the wounded Spline ship's return to home space.

If you could call it a return. But this was before I understood that every faster-than-light spaceship is also a time machine. That kind of puzzling would come later. For now, I just had my duty to perform.

As it happened we were offworld at the time, putting the *Kard* through its paces after a refit and bedding in a new crew. *Kard* is a corvette: a small, mobile yacht intended for close-to sublight operations. We had run through a tough sequence of speed runs, emergency turns, full backdown, instrument checks, fire and damage control.

I was twenty years old, still an ensign, assigned for that jaunt as an assistant to Exec Officer Baras. My first time on a bridge, it was quite an experience. I was glad of the company of Tarco, an old cadre sibling, even if he was a male and a lard bucket.

Anyhow it was thanks to our fortuitous station on the bridge that Tarco and I were among the first to see the injured ship as it downfolded out of hyper-

286

space. It was a Navy ship—a Spline, of course, a living ship, like a great meaty eyeball. It just appeared out of nowhere. We were close enough to see the green tetrahedral sigil of free humanity etched into its flesh. But you couldn't miss the smoking ruin of the weapons emplacements, and a great open rent in the hull, thick with coagulated blood. A swarm of lesser lights, huddling close, looked like escape pods.

The whole bridge crew fell silent.

"Lethe," Tarco whispered. "Where's it come from?" We didn't know of any action underway at the time.

But we had no time to debate it.

Captain Iana's voice sounded around the corvette. "That ship is the *Assimilator's Torch*," he announced. "She's requesting help. You can all see her situation. Stand by your stations." He began to snap out brisk orders to his heads of department.

Well, we scrambled immediately. But Tarco's big moon-shaped face was creased by a look I didn't recognize.

"What's wrong with you?"

"I heard that name before. *Assimilator's Torch*. She's due to arrive here at 592 next year."

"Then it's a little early."

He stared at me. "You don't get it, buttface. I saw the manifest. The *Torch* is a newborn Spline. It hasn't even left Earth."

But the injured Spline looked decades old, at least. "You made a mistake. Buttface yourself."

He didn't rise to the bait. Still, that was the first indication I had that there was something very wrong here.

The *Kard* lifted away from its operational position, and I had a grand view of Base 592, the planet on which we were stationed. From space it is a beautiful sight, a slow-spinning sphere of black volcanic rock peppered with the silver-grey of shipyards, so huge they are like great gleaming impact craters. There are even artificial oceans, glimmering blue, for the benefit of Spline vessels.

The 592 has a crucial strategic position, for it floats on the fringe of the 3-Kiloparsec Spiral Arm that surrounds the galaxy's core, and the Xeelee concentrations there. Here, some ten thousand light years from Earth, was as deep as the Third Expansion of mankind had yet penetrated into the central regions of the main disc. The 592 was a fun assignment. We were on the front line, and we knew it. It made for an atmosphere you might call frenetic.

But now I could see ships lifting from all around the planet, rushing to the aid of the stricken vessel. It was a heart-warming, magnificent sight, humanity at its best.

The *Kard* hummed like a well-tuned machine. Right now, all over the ship, I knew, the crew—officers and gunners, cooks and engineers and maintenance stiffs, experienced officers and half-trained rookies—were getting ready to haul survivors out of the great void that had tried to kill them. It was what you did. I looked forward to playing my part.

Which was why I wasn't too happy to hear the soft voice of Commissary Varcin behind me. "Ensign. Are you Dakk? I have a special assignment for you. Come with me." Varcin, gaunt and tall, served as the corvette's political officer, as assigned to every ship of the line with a crew above a hundred. He had an expression I couldn't read, a cold calculation.

Everybody is scared of the Commissaries, but this was not the time to be sucked into a time-wasting chore. "I take my orders from the exec. Sir."

Baras's face was neutral. I knew about the ancient tension between Navy and Commission, but I also knew what Baras would say. "Do it, ensign. You'd better go too, Tarco."

I had no choice, crisis or not. So we went hurrying after the commissary.

Away from the spacious calm of the bridge, the corridors of the *Kard* were a clamor of motion and noise, people running every which way lugging equipment and stores, yelling orders and demanding help.

As we jogged, I whispered to Tarco, "So where from? SS 433?"

"Not there," Tarco said. "Don't you remember? At SS 433 we suffered no casualties."

That was true. SS 433, a few hundred light years from 592, is a normal star in orbit around a massive neutron star; it emits high-energy jets of heavy elements. A month before, the Xeelee had shown up in an effort to wreck the human processing plants there. But thanks to smart intelligence by the Commission for Historical Truth, they had been met by an overwhelming response. It had been a famous victory, the excuse for a lot of celebration.

If a little eerie. Sometimes the Commission's knowledge of future events was so precise we used to wonder if they had spies among the Xeelee. Or a time machine, maybe. Scary, as I said.

But I accepted there was a bigger picture here. At that time, humanity controlled around a quarter of the disc of the galaxy itself, a mighty empire centered on Sol, as well as some outlying territories in the halo clusters. But the Xeelee controlled the rest, including the galaxy center. And, gradually, the slow-burning war between man and Xeelee was intensifying. So I was glad the Commissaries were on my side.

We descended a couple of decks and found ourselves in the corvette's main loading bay. The big main doors had been opened to reveal a wall of burned and broken flesh. The stink was just overwhelming, and great lakes of yellow-green pus were gathering on the gleaming floor.

It was the hull of a Spline. The *Kard* had docked with the *Assimilator's Torch* as best she could, and this was the result.

The engineers were at work, cutting an opening in that wall. It was just a hole in the flesh, another wound. Beyond, a tunnel stretched, organic, less like a corridor than a throat. I could see figures moving in the tunnel—*Torch* crew, presumably.

Here came two of them laboring to support a third between them. *Kard* crew rushed forward to take the injured tar. I couldn't tell if it was a he or a she. That was how bad the burns were. Great loops of flesh hung off limbs that were like twigs, and in places you could see down to bone, which itself had been blackened.

Tarco and I reacted somewhat badly to this sight. But already med cloaks were snuggling around the wounded tar, gentle as a lover's caress.

I looked up at the commissary, who was standing patiently. "Sir? Can you tell us why we are here?"

"We received ident signals from the *Torch* when it downfolded. There's somebody here who will want to meet you."

"Sir, who—"

"It's better if you see for yourself."

One of the *Torch* crew approached us. She was a woman, I saw, about my height. There was no hiding the bloodstains and scorches and rips, or the way she limped; there was a wound in her upper thigh that actually smoked. But she had captain's pips on her collar.

I felt I knew her face—that straight nose, the small

chin—despite the dirt that covered her check and neck, and the crust of blood that coated her forehead. She had her hair grown out long, with a pony tail at the back, quite unlike my regulation crew-cut. But—this was my first impression—her face seemed oddly reversed, as if she were a mirror image of what I was used to.

I immediately felt a deep, queasy unease.

I don't know many captains, but she immediately recognized me. "Oh. It's *you*."

Tarco had become very tense. He had thought it through a little further than I had. "Commissary—what engagement has the *Torch* come from?"

"The Fog."

My mouth dropped. Every tar on Base 592 knew that the Fog is an interstellar cloud—and a major Xeelee concentration—situated *inside* 3-Kilo, a good hundred light years deeper toward the center of the galaxy. I said, "I didn't know we were hitting the enemy so deep."

"We aren't. Not yet."

"And," Tarco said tightly, "here we are greeting a battle-damaged ship that hasn't even left Earth yet."

"Quite right," Varcin said approvingly. "Ensigns, you are privileged to witness this. This ship is a survivor of a battle *that won't happen for another twenty-four years.*"

Tarco kind of spluttered.

As for me, I couldn't take my eye off the *Torch's* captain. Tense, she was running her thumb down the side of her cheek.

"I do that," I said stupidly.

"Oh, Lethe," she said, disgusted. "Yeah, I'm your older self. Get over it. I've got work to do." And with a glance at the commissary she turned and stalked back toward her ship.

Varcin said gently, "Go with her."

"Sir—"

"Do it, ensign."

Tarco followed me. "So in twenty-four years you're still going to be a buttface."

I realized miserably that he was right.

We pushed into the narrow passageway.

I had had no previous exposure to Spline organic "technology." We truly were inside a vast body. The passage's walls were raw flesh, much of it burned, twisted and broken, even far beneath the ship's epidermis. Every time I touched a surface my hands came away sticky, and I could feel salty liquids oozing over my uniform. The gravity was lumpy, and I suspected that it was being fed in from the *Kard*'s inertial generators.

But that was just background.

Captain Dakk, for Lethe's sake!

She saw me staring again. "Ensign, back off. We can't get away from each other, but over the next few days life is going to get complicated for the both of us. It always does in these situations. Just take it one step at a time."

"Sir—"

She glared at me. "Don't question me. What interest have *I* got in misguiding *you*?"

"Yes, sir."

"I don't like this situation any more than you do. Remember that."

We found lines of wounded, wrapped in cloaks. Crew were laboring to bring them out to the *Kard*. But the passageway was too narrow. It was a traffic jam, a real mess. It might have been comical if not for the groans and cries, the stink of fear and desperation in the air.

Dakk found an officer. He wore the uniform of a damage control worker. "Cady, what in Lethe is going on here?"

"It's the passageways, sir. They're too ripped up to get the wounded out with the grapplers. So we're having to do it by hand." He looked desperate, miserable. "Sir, I'm responsible."

"You did right," she said grimly. "But let's see if we can't tidy this up a little. You two," she snapped at us. "Take a place in line."

And that was the last we saw of her for a while, as she went stomping into the interior of her ship. She quickly organized the crew, from *Torch* and *Kard* alike, into a human chain. Soon we were passing cloaked wounded from hand to hand, along the corridor and out into the *Kard*'s loading bay in an orderly fashion.

"I'm impressed," Tarco said. "Sometime in the next quarter-century you'll be grafted a brain."

"Shove it."

The line snarled up. Tarco and I found ourselves staring down at one of the wounded—conscious, looking around. He was just a kid, sixteen or seventeen.

If this was all true, in my segment of time he hadn't even been *born* yet.

He spoke to us. "You from the *Kard*?"

"Yeah."

He started to thank us, but I brushed that aside. "Tell me what happened to you."

Tarco whispered to me, "Hey. You never heard of time paradoxes? I bet the Commission has a few regulations about *that*."

I shrugged. "I already met myself. How much worse can it get?"

Either the wounded man didn't know we were from his past, or he didn't care. He told us in terse sentences how the *Torch* had been involved in a major engagement deep in the Fog. He had been a gunner, with a good view of the action from his starbreaker pod.

"We came at a Sugar Lump. You ever seen one of those? A big old Xeelee emplacement. But the night-fighters were everywhere. We were taking a beating. The order came to fall back. We could see that damn Sugar Lump, close enough to touch. Well, the captain disregarded the fallback order."

Tarco said skeptically, "She *disregarded an order?*"

"We crossed the chop line. The Xeelee had been suckered by the fallback, and the *Torch* broke through their lines." A chop line is actually a surface, a military planner's boundary between sectors in space—in this case, between the disputed territory inside the Fog and Xeelee-controlled space. "We only lasted minutes. But we fired off a Sunrise."

Tarco said, "A what?" I kicked him, and he shut up.

Unexpectedly, the kid grabbed my arm. "We barely got home. But, Lethe, when that Sunrise hit, we nearly shook this old fish apart with our hollering, despite the pasting we were taking."

Tarco said maliciously, "How do you feel about Captain Dakk?"

"She is a true leader. I'd follow her anywhere."

All I felt was unease. *No heroes*: that's the Druz Doctrine, the creed that has held mankind together across fifteen thousand years, and drilled into every one of us by the Commissaries at their orientation sessions every day. If my future self had forgotten about that, something had gone wrong.

But now the gunner was looking at me intently. I became aware I was rubbing my thumb down my cheek. I dropped my hand and turned my face away.

Captain Dakk was standing before me. "You'd better get used to that."

"I don't want to," I groused. I was starting to resent the whole situation.

Dakk just laughed. "I don't think what you, or I, want has much to do with it, ensign."

I muttered to Tarco, "Lethe. Am I that pompous?"

"Oh, yes."

Dakk said, "I think we're organized here for now. I'll come back later when I can start thinking about damage control. In the meantime, we've been ordered to your captain's wardroom. Both of us."

Tarco said hesitantly, "Sir—what's a *Sunrise*?"

She looked surprised. "Right. You don't have them yet. A Sunrise is a human-driven torpedo. A suicide." She eyed me. "So you heard what happened in the Fog."

"A little of it."

She cupped my cheek. It was the first time she had touched me. It was an oddly neutral sensation, like being touched by your sister. "You'll find out, in good time. It was *glorious*."

Dakk led us back through *Kard*'s officer country. Commissary Varcin met us there.

Here, the partitions had been taken down to open up a wide area of deck that was serving as a hospital and convalescent unit. There were crew in there in all stages of recovery. Some of them were lying on beds, weak and hollow-eyed. Many of them seemed to be pleading with the orderlies to be put back on the *Torch* despite their injuries—once you lose your ship in a war zone, it can be impossible to find it again. And many of them asked, touchingly, after the *Torch* itself. They really cared about their living ship, I saw; that battered old hulk was one of the crew.

An awful lot of them sported pony tails, men and women alike, apparently in imitation of their captain.

When they saw Dakk, they all shouted and cheered and whistled. The walking wounded crowded around Dakk and thumped her on the back. A couple just turned their heads on their pillows and cried softly. Dakk's eyes were brimming, I saw; though she had a grin as wide as the room, she was on the point of breaking down.

I glanced at Tarco. It wasn't supposed to be like this.

Among the medics I saw a figure with the shaven head and long robes of the Commission. She was moving from patient to patient, and using a needle on them. But she wasn't treating them. She was actually extracting blood, small samples that she stored away in a satchel at her side.

This wasn't the time or place to be collecting samples like that. I stepped forward to stop her. Well, it was a natural reaction. Luckily for me, Tarco held me back.

Commissary Varcin said dryly, "I can see you have your future self's impetuosity, ensign. The orderly is just doing her duty. It's no doubt as uncomfortable for her as it is for you. Commissaries are human beings too, you know."

"Then what—"

"Before they went into battle every one of these crew will have been injected with mnemonic fluid. That's what we're trying to retrieve. The more viewpoints we get of this action, the better we can anticipate it. We're ransacking the ship's databases and logs too."

Call me unimaginative. I still didn't know what unlikely chain of circumstances had delivered my older self into my life. But that was the first time it had occurred to me what a potent weapon had been placed in our hands.

"Lethe," I said. "This is how we'll win the war. If you know the course of future battles—"

"You have a lot to absorb, ensign," Varcin said, not unkindly. "Take it one step at a time."

Which, of course, had been my own advice to myself.

At last, somewhat to my relief, we got Dakk away from her crew. Varcin led us down more corridors to Captain Iana's plush wardroom.

Tarco and I stood in the middle of the carpet, aware of how dinged-up we were, scared of spreading Spline snot all over Iana's furniture. But Varcin waved us to chairs, and we sat down stiffly.

I watched Dakk. She sprawled in a huge chair, shaking a little, letting her exhaustion show now that she was away from her crew. She was *me*. My face—reversed from the mirror image I'd grown up with.

I was very confused. I hated the idea of growing so old, arrogant, unorthodox. But I'd seen plenty to admire in Dakk: strength, an ability to command, to win loyalty. Part of me wanted to help her. Another part wanted to push her away.

But mostly, I was just aware of the bond that connected us, tighter than any bond even between true siblings. It didn't matter whether I liked her or loathed her; whichever way, she was always going to be *there*, for the rest of my life. It wasn't a comfortable notion.

Varcin was watching me. I got the idea he knew what I was feeling. But he turned to business, steepling his fingers.

"Here's how it is. We're scrambling to download data, to put together some kind of coherent picture of what happened downstream." *Downstream*— not the last bit of jargon I was going to have to get used to. "You have surprises ahead of you, Ensign Dakk."

I laughed, and waved a hand at the captain. "Surprising after *this?* Bring it on."

Dakk looked disgusted. Tarco placed a calming hand on my back.

Varcin said, "First, you—rather, *Captain* Dakk—will be charged. There will be a court of inquiry."

"Charged? What with?"

Varcin shrugged. "Negligence, in recklessly endangering the ship." He eyed Dakk. "I imagine there will be other counts, relating to various violations of the Druz Doctrine."

Dakk smiled, a chilling expression. I wondered how I ever got so cynical.

Varcin went on, "Ensign, you'll be involved."

I nodded. "Of course. It's my future."

"You don't understand. *Directly* involved. We want you to serve as the prosecuting advocate."

"*Me?* Sir—" I took a breath. "You want me to prosecute *myself*. For a crime, an alleged crime anyhow, I won't commit for twenty-four years? Is there any part of that I misunderstood?"

"You have the appropriate training, don't you?"

Dakk laughed. "This is their way, kid. Who knows me better?"

I stood up. "Commissary, I won't do it."

"Sit down, ensign."

"I'll go to Captain Iana."

"*Sit. Down.*"

I'd never heard such command. I sat, frightened.

"Ensign, you are immature, and inexperienced, and impetuous. You will have much to learn to fulfill this assignment. But you are the necessary choice.

"And there's more." Again, I glimpsed humanity in that frosted-over commissary. "In four months' time you will report to the birthing complex on Base 592. There you will request impregnation by Ensign Hama Tarco, here."

Tarco quickly took his hand off my back.

"Permission will be granted," said Varcin. "I'll see to that."

I didn't believe it. Then I got angry. I felt like I was in a trap. "How do you know I'll *want* a kid by Tarco? No offence."

"None taken," said Tarco, sounding bemused.

Now the commissary looked irritated. "How do you *think* I know? Haven't you noticed the situation we're in? Because it's in the *Torch*'s record. Because the child you will bear—"

"Will be on the *Torch*, with me," said Dakk.

"His name was Hama," the commissary said. I swear Tarco blushed.

"*Was*?" I felt a kind of panic. Perhaps it was the tug of a maternal bond that couldn't yet exist, fear for the well-being of a child I'd only just learned about. "He's dead, isn't he? He died, out there in the Fog."

Varcin murmured, "One step at a time, ensign."

Dakk leaned forward. "Yes, he died. *He rode the Sunrise*. He was the one who took a monopole bomb into the Xeelee Sugar Lump. You see? Your child, Dakk. *Our* child. He was a hero."

One step at a time. I kept repeating that to myself. But it was as if the wardroom was spinning around.

II

In Dakk's yacht, I sailed around the huge flank of the *Assimilator's Torch*. Medical tenders drifted alongside, hosing some kind of sealant into mighty wounds.

The Spline had been allowed to join a flotilla of its kind, regular ships of the line. Living starships the size of cities are never going to be graceful, but I saw that their movements were coordinated, a vast dance. They even snuggled against each other, like great fish colliding.

Dakk murmured, "Some of these battered beasts have been in human employ for a thousand years or more. We rip out their brains and their nervous systems—we amputate their minds—and yet something of the self still lingers, a need for others of their kind, for comfort."

I listened absently.

Dakk and me. Myself and myself. I couldn't stop *staring* at her.

The yacht docked, and the captain and I were piped aboard the *Torch*. I found myself in a kind of cave, buttressed by struts of some cartilaginous material. We wandered through orifices and along round-walled passageways, pushing deeper into the core of the Spline. The lighting had been fixed, the on-board gravity restored. We saw none of Dakk's crew, only repair workers from the Base.

"You haven't served on a Spline yet, have you? The ship is alive, remember. It's *hot*. Underway, at sleep periods, you can walk around the ship, and you find the crew dozing all over the vessel, many of them naked, some sprawled on food sacks or weapons, or just on the warm surfaces, wherever they can. You can hear the pulsing of the Spline's blood flow—even sometimes the beating of its heart, like a distant gong. That and the scrambling of the rats."

It sounded cozy, but not much like the Navy I knew. "Rats?"

She laughed. "Little bastards get everywhere."

On we went. It wasn't as bad as that first hour in the chaotic dark. But even so it was like being in some vast womb. I couldn't see how I was ever going to get used to this. But Dakk seemed joyful to be back, so I was evidently wrong.

We came to a deep place Dakk called the "belly." This was a hangar-like chamber separated into bays by huge diaphanous sheets of some muscle-like material, marbled with fat. Within the alcoves were suspended sacs of what looked like water: green, cloudy water.

I prodded the surface of one of the sacs. It rippled sluggishly. I could see drifting plants, wriggling fish, snails, a few autonomous 'bots swimming among the crowd. "It's like an aquarium," I said.

"So it is. A miniature ocean. The green plants are hornweeds: rootless, almost entirely edible. And you have sea snails, swordtail fish, and various microbes. There is a complete, self-contained biosphere here. This is how we live. These creatures are from Earth's oceans. Don't you think it's kind of romantic to fly into battle against Xeelee super science with a droplet of primordial waters at our core...?"

"How do you keep it from getting overgrown?"

"The weed itself kills back overgrowth. The snails live off dead fish. And the fish keep their numbers down by eating their own young."

I guess I pulled a face at that.

"You're squeamish," she said sharply. "I don't remember *that*."

We walked on through the Spline's visceral marvels.

The truth is, I was struggling to function. I'm sure I was going through some kind of shock. Human beings aren't designed to be subject to temporal paradoxes about their future selves and unborn babies.

And working on the inquiry was proving almost impossible for me.

The inquiry procedure was a peculiar mix of ancient Navy traditions and forensic Commission processes.

Commissary Varcin had been appointed president of the court, and as prosecutor advocate, I was a mix of prosecutor, law officer, and court clerk. The rest of the court—a panel of brass who were a kind of mix of judge and jury combined —were Commissaries and Navy officers, with a couple of civilians and even an Academician for balance. It was all a political compromise between the Commission and the Navy, it seemed to me.

But the court of inquiry was only the first stage. If the charges were established, Dakk would go on to face a full court martial, and possibly a trial before members of the Coalition itself. So the stakes were high.

And the charges themselves—aimed at my own future self, after all—had been hurtful: *Through Negligence Suffering a Vessel of the Navy to be Hazarded; Culpable Inefficiency in the Performance of Duty; Through Disregard of Standing and Specific Orders Endangering the War Aims of the Navy; Through Self-Regard Encouraging a Navy Crew to Deviate from Doctrinal Thought....*

There was plenty of evidence. We had Virtual reconstructions based on the *Torch*'s logs and the mnemonic fluids extracted from the ship's crew. And we had a stream of witnesses, most of them walking wounded from the *Torch*. None of them was told how her testimony fitted into the broader picture, a point that many of them got frustrated about, and all of them expressed their loyalty and admiration toward Captain Dakk—even though, in the eyes of Commissaries, such idolizing would only get their captain deeper into trouble.

But all this could only help so far. What I felt I was missing was motive. I didn't understand *why* Dakk had done what she had done.

I couldn't get her into focus. I oscillated between despising her, and longing to defend her—and all the time I felt oppressed by the paradoxical bond that locked us together. I sensed that she felt the same. Sometimes she was as impatient with me as with the greenest recruit, and other times she seemed to try to take me under her wing. It can't have been easy for her either, to be reminded that she had once been as insignificant as me. But if we were two slices of the same person, our situations weren't symmetrical. She had *been* me, long ago; I was doomed to *become* her; it was as if she had paid dues that still faced me.

Anyhow, that was why I had requested a break from the deliberations, and to spend some time with Dakk on her home territory. I had to get to know her—even though I felt increasingly reluctant to be drawn into her murky future.

She brought me to a new chamber. Criss-crossed by struts of cartilage, this place was dominated by a pillar made of translucent red-purple rope. There was a crackling stench of ozone.

I knew where I was. "This is the hyperdrive chamber."

"Yes." She reached up and stroked fibers. "Magnificent, isn't it? I remember when I first saw a Spline hyperdrive muscle—"

"Of course you remember."

"What?"

"Because it's *now*." Someday, I thought gloomily, I would inevitably find myself standing on the other side of this room, looking back at my own face. "Don't you remember this? Being me, twenty years old, meeting—you?"

Her answer confused me. "It doesn't work like that." She glared at me. "You do understand how come I'm stuck back in the past, staring at your zit-ridden face?"

303

"No," I admitted reluctantly.

"It was a Tolman maneuver." She searched my face. "Every faster-than-light starship is a time machine. Come on, ensign. That's just special relativity! Even *Tolman* is the name of some long-dead pre-Extirpation scientist. They teach this stuff to four-year-olds."

I shrugged. "You forget all that unless you want to become a navigator."

"With an attitude like that, you have an ambition to be a captain?"

"I don't," I said slowly, "have an ambition to be a captain."

That gave her pause. But she said, "The bottom line is that if you fight a war with FTL starships, time slips are always possible, and you have to anticipate them. Think of it this way...there is no universal *now*. Say it's midnight here. We're a light-minute from the Base. So what time is it in your fleapit barracks on 529? What if you could focus a telescope on a clock on the ground?"

I thought about it. It would take a minute for an image of the clock on the Base to reach me at light-speed. So that would show a minute before midnight.... "Okay, but if you adjust for the time lag needed for signals to travel at lightspeed, you can construct a standard *now*—can't you?"

"If everybody was stationary, maybe. But suppose this creaky old Spline was moving at half lightspeed. Even *you* must have heard of time dilation. *Our* clocks would be slowed as seen from the base, and *theirs* would be slowed as seen from here.

"Think it through. There could be a whole flotilla of ships out here, moving at different velocities, their timescales all different. They could never agree. You get the point? Globally speaking, there is no past and future. There are only events—like points on a huge graph, with axes marked *space* and *time*. That's the way to think of it. The events swim around, like fish; and the further away they are, the more they swim, from your point of view. So there is *no* one event on the Base, or on Earth, or anywhere else, which can be mapped uniquely to your *now*. In fact, there is a whole range of such events at distant places.

"Because of that looseness, histories are ambiguous. Earth itself has a definite history, of course, and so does the Base. But Earth is maybe ten thousand light years from here. It's pointless to map dates of specific events on Earth against Base dates; they can vary across a span of millennia. You can even have a history on Earth that runs *backward* as seen from the Base.

"Now do you see how faster-than-light screws things up? Causality is controlled by the speed of light. Events can have backward time sequences only if light doesn't have long enough to pass between them. But in an FTL ship, you can hop around the spacetime graph at will. I took a FTL jaunt to the Fog. When I was *there*, from my point of view the history of the Base *here* was ambiguous over a scale of decades.... When I came home, I simply hopped back to an event *before* my departure."

I nodded. "But it was just an accident. Right? This doesn't always happen."

"It depends on the geometry. Fleeing the Xeelee, we happened to be traveling at a large fraction of lightspeed toward the Base when we initiated the hyperdrive. So, yes, it was an accident. But you can make Tolman maneuvers deliberately. And during every operation we always drop Tolman probes: records, log copies, heading for the past."

I did a double-take. "You're telling me it's a *deliberate tactic* of this war to send information to the past?"

"Of course. If such a possibility's there, you have to take the opportunity. What better intelligence can there be? The Navy has always cooperated with this fully. In war, you seek every advantage."

"But don't the Xeelee do the same?"

"Sure. But the trick is to try to stop them. The intermingling of past and future depends on relative velocities. We try to choreograph engagements so that we, not they, get the benefit." Dakk grinned wolfishly. "It's a contest in clairvoyance. But we punch our weight."

I tried to focus on what was important. "Okay," I said. "Then give me a message from the future. Tell me how you crossed the chop line."

She glared at me again. Then she paced around the chamber, while the Spline's weird hyperdrive muscles pulsed.

"Before the fallback order came, we'd just taken a major hit. Do you know what that's like? Your first reaction is sheer surprise that it has happened to *you*. Surprise, and disbelief, and resentment, and anger. The ship is your home—and part of your crew. It's as if your home has been violated. But most of the crew went to defense posture and began to fulfill their duties, as per their training. There was no panic. Pandemonium, yes, but no panic."

"And in all this you decided to disobey the fallback order."

She looked me in the eye. "I had to make an immediate decision. We went straight through the chop line and headed for the center of the Xeelee concentration, bleeding from a dozen hits, starbreakers blazing. That's how we fight them, you see. They are smarter than us, and stronger. But we just come boiling out at them. They think we are vermin, so we fight like vermin."

"You launched the Sunrise."

"Hama was the pilot." My unborn, unconceived child. "He rode a monopole torpedo: the latest stuff. A Xeelee Sugar Lump is a fortress shaped like a cube, thousands of kilometers on a side, a world with edges and corners. We punched a hole in its wall like it was paper.

"But we took a beating. Hit after hit.

"We had to evacuate the outer decks. You should have seen the hull, human beings swarming like flies on a piece of garbage, scrambling this way and that, fleeing the detonations. They hung onto weapons mounts, stanchions, lifelines, anything. We fear the falling, you see. I think some of the crew feared that more than the Xeelee." Her face worked. "The life pods got some of them. We lost hundreds.... You know why the name "Sunrise"? Because it's a planet thing. The Xeelee are space dwellers. They don't know day and night. Every dawn is *ours*, not theirs. Appropriate, don't you think? And you should see what it's like when a Sunrise pilot comes on board."

"Like Hama."

"As the yacht comes out of port, you get a flotilla riding along with them, civilian ships as well as Navy, just to see them go. When the pilots come aboard, the whole crew lines the passageways, chanting their names." She smiled. "Your heart will burst when you see him."

I struggled to focus. "So the pilots are idolized."

"Lethe, I never knew I was such a prig. Kid, there is more to war than doctrinal observance. Anyhow what are the Sunrise pilots but the highest exemplars of the ideals of the Expansion? *A brief life burns brightly*, remember—and a Sunrise pilot puts that into practice in the brightest, bravest way possible."

"And," I said carefully, "are you a hero to your crew?"

She scowled at me. Her face was a mask of lines, carved by years into my own flesh. She had never looked less like me. "I know what you're thinking. I'm too old, I should be ashamed even to be alive. Listen to me. Ten years after this meeting, you will take part in a battle around a neutron star called Kepler's. Look it up. *That's* why your crew will respect you—even though you won't be lucky enough to die. And as for the chop line, I don't have a single regret. We struck a blow, damn it. I'm talking about hope. That's what those fucking Commissaries never understand. Hope, and the needs of the human heart. *That's* what I was trying to deliver...." Something seemed to go out of her. "But none of that matters now. I've come through another chop line, haven't I? Through a chop line in time, into the past, where I face judgment."

"I'm not assigned to judge you."

"No. You do that for fun, don't you?"

I didn't know what to say. I felt pinned. I loved her, and I hated her, all at the same time. She must have felt the same way about me. But we knew we couldn't get away from each other.

Perhaps it is never possible for the same person from two time slices ever to get along. After all, it's not something we've evolved for.

In silence, we made our way back to Dakk's wardroom. There, Tarco was waiting for us.

"Buttface," he said formally.

"Lard bucket," I replied.

On that ship from the future, we stared at each other, each of us baffled, maybe frightened. We hadn't been alone together, not once, since the news that we were to have a child together. And even now, Captain Dakk was sitting there like the embodiment of destiny.

Under the Druz Doctrine, love isn't forbidden. But it's not the *point.* But then, I was learning, out here on the frontier, where people died far from home, things were a little more complex than my training and conditioning had indicated.

I asked, "What are you doing here?"

"You sent for me. Your future, smarter, better-looking self."

The captain said dryly, "Obviously you two have—issues—to discuss. But I'm afraid events are pressing."

Tarco turned to face her. "Let's get on with it, sir. Why did you ask for me?"

Dakk said, "Navy intelligence have been analyzing the records from the *Torch.* They have begun the process of contacting those who will serve on the ship—or their families and cadres, if they are infants or not yet born—to inform them of their future assignments. It's the policy."

Tarco looked apprehensive. "And that applies to me?"

Dakk didn't answer directly. "There are other protocols. When a ship returns from action, it's customary for the captain or senior surviving officer to send letters of condolence to families and cadres who have lost loved ones, or visit them."

Tarco nodded. "I once accompanied Captain Iana on a series of visits like that."

I said carefully, "But in this case the action hasn't happened yet. Those who will die haven't yet been assigned to the ship. Some haven't even been born."

"Yes," Dakk said gently. "But I have to write my letters even so."

That seemed incomprehensible to me. "Why? Nobody's dead yet."

"Because everybody wants to *know*, as much as we can tell them. Would it be better to lie to them, or keep secrets?"

"How do they react?"

"How do you think? Ensign Tarco, what happened when you did the rounds with Iana?"

Tarco shrugged. "Some took it as closure, I think. Some wept. Some were angry, even threw us out. Others denied it was real.... They all wanted more information. How it happened, what it was for. Everyone seemed to have a need to be told that those who had died had given their lives for something worthwhile."

Dakk nodded. "You see all those reactions. Some won't open the messages. They put them in time capsules, as if putting history back in order." She studied me. "This is a time-travelers' war, ensign. A war like none we've fought before. We are stretching our procedures, even our humanity, to cope with the consequences. But you get used to it."

Tarco said apprehensively, "Sir, please—*what about me?*"

"I thought you'd like to hear that from your captain in person." Gravely, Dakk handed me a data desk.

I glanced at its contents. Then, numbed, I gave it to Tarco.

He read it quickly. "Hey, buttface," he breathed. "You make me your exec. How about that. Maybe it was a bad year."

I didn't feel like laughing. "Read it all."

"I know what it says." His broad face was relaxed.

"You don't make it home. *You're going to die out there*, in the Fog."

310

He actually smiled. "I've been anticipating this since the *Torch* came into port. Haven't you?"

My mouth opened and closed, as if I was a swordtail fish. "Call me unimaginative," I said. "How can you accept this assignment, *knowing it's going to kill you?*"

He seemed puzzled. "What else would I do?"

"Yes," the captain said. "It is your duty. Can't you see how noble this is, Dakk? Isn't it *right* that he should know—that he should live his life with full foreknowledge, and do his duty even so?"

Tarco grabbed my hand. "Hey. It's years off. We'll see our baby grow."

I said dismally, "Some love story this is turning out to be."

"Yes."

Commissary Varcin's Virtual head coalesced in the air. Without preamble he said, "Change of plan. Ensign, it's becoming clear that the evidence to hand will not be sufficient to establish the charges. Specifically it's impossible to say whether Dakk's actions hindered the overall war aims. To establish that we'll have to go to the Libraries, at the Commission's central headquarters."

I did a doubletake. "Sir, that's on Earth."

The disembodied head snapped, "I'm aware of that."

I had no idea how bookworm Commissaries on Earth, ten thousand light years behind the lines, could possibly have evidence to bear on the case. But the commissary explained, and I learned there was more to this messages-from-the-future industry than I had yet imagined.

On Earth, the Commission for Historical Truth had been mapping the future. For fifteen thousand years.

311

"Fine," I said. "Things weren't weird enough already."

My future self murmured, "You get used to it."

Varcin's head's expression softened a little. "Think of it as an opportunity. Every Expansion citizen should see the home world before she dies."

"Come with me to Earth," I said impulsively to Tarco.

"All right—"

Dakk put her hands on our shoulders. "Lethe, but this is a magnificent enterprise!"

I hated her; I loved her; I wanted her out of my life.

III

We were a strange crew, I guess: two star-crossed lovers, court members, Navy lawyers, serving officers, Commissaries and all. Not to mention another version of me.

The atmosphere had been tense all the way from Base 592. It was all very well for Varcin to order us to Earth. The Navy wasn't about to release one of its own to the Commission for Historical Truth without a fight, and there had been lengthy wrangling over the propriety and even the legality of transferring the court of inquiry to Earth. In the end, a team of Navy lawyers had been assigned to the case.

But for now, all our differences and politics and emotional tangles were put aside, as we crowded to the hull to sightsee our destination.

Earth!

At first, it seemed nondescript: just another rocky ball circling an unspectacular star, in a corner of a fragmented spiral arm. But Snowflake surveillance stations orbited in great shells around the planet, all the way out as far as the planet's single battered

Moon, and schools of Spline gamboled hugely in the waves of the mighty ocean that covered half the planet's surface. It was an eerie thought that down there somewhere was another *Assimilator's Torch*, a junior version of the battered old ship we had seen come limping into port.

When you thought about it, it was a thrill. This little world had become the capital of the Third Expansion, an empire that stretched across all the stars I could see, and far beyond. And it was the true home of every human who would ever live.

Our flitter cut into the atmosphere and was wrapped in pink-white plasma. I felt Tarco's hand slip into mine.

At least we had had time to spend together. We had talked. We had even made love, in a perfunctory way. But it hadn't done us much good. Other people knew far too much about our future, and we didn't seem to have any choice about it anyhow. I felt like a rat going through a maze. What room was there for joy?

But I clung to hope that the Commission still had more to tell us. There could be no finer intelligence than a knowledge of the future—an ability to see the outcome of a battle not yet waged, or map the turning points of a war not yet declared—and yet what use was that intelligence if the future was fixed, if we were forced to live out pre-programmed lives?

But, of course, I wasn't worrying about the war and the destiny of mankind. I just wanted to know if I really was doomed to become Captain Dakk, battered, bitter, arrogant, far from orthodoxy—or whether I was still *free*.

The flitter swept over a continent. I glimpsed a crowded land, and many vast weapons emplacements, intended for the eventuality of a last-ditch defense of the home world. Then we began to descend toward a Conurbation. It was a broad, glistening sprawl of bubble-dwellings blown from the bedrock, and linked by canals. But the scars of the Qax Occupation, fifteen thousand years old, were still visible. Much of the land glistened silver-grey where starbreaker beams and nanoreplicators had once worked, turning plains and mountains into a featureless silicate dust.

The commissary said, "This Conurbation was Qax-built. It is still known by its ancient Qax registration of 11729. It was more like a forced labor camp or breeding pen than a human city. The 11729 has become the headquarters of the Commission. It was here that Hama Druz himself developed the Doctrine that has shaped human destiny ever since. A decision was made to leave the work of the Qax untouched. It shows what will become of us again, if we should falter or fail...."

And so on. His long face was solemn, his eyes gleaming with a righteous zeal. It was a little scary.

We were taken to a complex right at the heart of the Conurbation. It was based on the crude Qax architecture, but internally the bubble dwellings had been knocked together and extended underground, making a vast complex whose boundaries I never glimpsed.

Varcin introduced it as the Library of Futures. Once the Libraries had been an independent agency, Varcin told us, but the Commission had taken them over three thousand years ago. Apparently, it had been an epic war among the bureaucrats.

Tarco and I were each given our own quarters. My room seemed *huge*, itself extending over several levels, and very well equipped, with a galley and even a bar. I could tell from Captain Dakk's expression exactly what she thought of this opulence and expense.

And it was strange to be in a place where a "day" lasted a standard day, a "year" a year. Across the Expansion, the standards are set by Earth's calendar—of course; what else would you use? A "day" on Base 592, for instance, lasted over two hundred standard days, which was actually longer than its "year", which was around half a standard.

That bar made a neat Puhl's Blood, though.

On the second day, the court of inquiry was to resume. But Varcin said that he wanted to run through the Commission's findings with us—me, Captain Dakk, Tarco—before it all unraveled in front of the court itself.

So, early on that crucial day, the three of us were summoned to a place Varcin called the Map Room.

It was like a vast hive, a place of alcoves and bays extending off a gigantic central atrium. On several levels, shaven-headed, long-robed figures walked earnestly, alone or in muttering groups, accompanied by gleaming clouds of Virtuals.

I think all three of us lowly Navy types felt scruffy and overwhelmed.

Varcin stood at the center of the open atrium. In his element, he just smiled. And he waved his hand, a bit theatrically.

A series of Virtual dioramas swept over us like the pages of an immense book. I knew what I was seeing. I was thrilled. These were the catalogued destinies of mankind.

In those first few moments, I saw huge fleets washing into battle, or limping home decimated; I saw worlds gleaming like jewels, beacons of human wealth and power—or desolated and scarred, lifeless as Earth's Moon.

And, most wistful of all, there were voices. I heard roars of triumph, cries for help.

Varcin said, "Half a million people work here. Much of it the interpretation is automated—but nothing has yet replaced the human eye, human scrutiny, human judgment. You understand that the further away you are from a place, the more uncertainty there is over its timeline compared to yours. So we actually see furthest into the future concerning the most remote events...."

"And you see war," said Tarco.

"Oh, yes. As far downstream as we can see, whichever direction we choose to look, we see war."

I picked up on that. *Whichever direction...* "Commissary, you don't just map the future here, do you?"

"No. Of course not."

"I knew it," I said gleefully, and they all looked at me oddly. But I thrilled at the possibilities. "*You can change the future.* So if you see a battle will be lost, you can choose not to commit the fleet. You can save thousands of lives with a simple decision."

"Or you could see a Xeelee advance coming," Tarco said excitedly. "Like SS 433. So you got the ships in position—it was a perfect ambush—"

Dakk said, "Remember that the Xeelee have exactly the same power."

I hadn't thought of that. "So if *they* had foreseen SS 433, they could have chosen not to send their ships there in the first place."

"Yes," Varcin said. "In fact, if intelligence were perfect on both sides, there would never be *any* defeat, any victory. It is only because future intelligence is not perfect—the Xeelee *didn't* foresee the ambush at SS 433—that any advances are possible."

Tarco said, "Sir, what happened the first time?

What was the outcome of SS 433 *before* either side started to meddle with the future?"

"Well, we don't know, ensign. Perhaps there was no engagement at all, and one side or the other saw a strategic hole that could be filled. It isn't very useful to think that way. You have to think of the future as a rough draft, that we—and the Xeelee—are continually reworking, shaping and polishing. It's as if we are working out a story of the future we can both agree on."

I was still trying to figure out the basics. "Sir, what about time paradoxes?"

Dakk growled, "Oh, Lethe, here we go—"

"I mean—" I waved a hand at the dioramas. "Suppose you pick up a beacon with data on a battle. But you decide to change the future; the battle never happens.... What about the beacon? Does it pop out of existence? And *now you have a record of a battle that will never happen.* Where did the information come from?"

Tarco said eagerly, "Maybe parallel universes are created. In one the battle goes ahead, in the other it doesn't. The beacon just leaks from one universe to another—"

Dakk looked bored.

Varcin waved a hand. "They don't go in for such metaphysics around here. The cosmos, it turns out, has a certain common sense about these matters. If you cause a time paradox there is no magic. Just—an anomalous piece of data that nobody created, a piece of technology with no origin. It's troubling, perhaps, but only subtly, at least compared to the existence of parallel universes, or objects popping in and out of existence. What concerns us more, day to day, are the *consequences* of this knowledge."

"Consequences?"

"For example, the leakage of information from future into past is having an effect on the evolution of human society. Innovations are transmitted backward. We are becoming—static. Rigid, over very long timescales. Of course that helps control the conduct of a war on such immense reaches of space and time. And regarding the war, many engagements are stalemated by foresight on both sides. It's probable that we are actually *extending* the war." His face closed in. "I suspect that if you work here you become—cautious. Conservative. The further downstream we look, the more extensive our decisions' consequences become. With a wave of a hand in this room, I can banish trillions of souls to the oblivion of non-existence—or rather, of never-to-exist."

My blood was high. "We're talking about a knowledge of the future. And all we do is set up stalemate after stalemate?"

For sure, Varcin didn't welcome being questioned like that by an ignorant ensign. He snapped, "Look, nobody has run a war this way before! We're making this up as we go along, okay? But, believe me, we're doing our best.

"And remember this. Knowledge of the future does not change certain fundamentals about the war. The Xeelee are older than us. They are more powerful, more advanced in every way that we can measure. Logically, given their resources, they should defeat us, whatever we do. We cannot ensure victory by any action we make *here*, that much is clear. But we suspect that if we get it wrong, we could make *defeat* certain. All we can hope for is to preserve at least the possibility of victory. And we believe that if not for the Mapping, *humanity would have lost this war by now.*"

I wasn't convinced. "You can change history. But

you will still send Tarco out, knowing he will die. Why?"

Varcin's face worked as he tried to control his irritation. "You must understand the decision-making process here. We are trying to win a war, not just a battle. We have to try to see beyond individual events to the chains of consequences that follow. That is why we will sometimes commit ships to a battle we know will be lost—why we will send warriors to certain deaths, knowing their deaths will not gain the slightest immediate advantage—why *sometimes we will even allow a victory to turn to a defeat,* if the long-term consequences of victory are too high. And *that* is at the heart of the charges against you, Captain."

Dakk snapped, "Get to the point, Commissary."

Varcin gestured again.

Before the array of futures, a glimmering Virtual diagram appeared. It was a translucent sphere, with many layers, something like an onion. Its outer layers were green, shading to yellow further in, with a pinpoint star of intense white at the center. Misty shapes swam through its interior. It cast a green glow on all our faces.

"Pretty," I said.

"It's a monopole," said Dakk. "A schematic representation."

"The warhead of the Sunrise torpedo."

"Yes." Varcin walked into the diagram, and began pointing out features. "The whole structure is about the size of an atomic nucleus. There are W and Z bosons in this outer shell here. Further in, there is a region in which the weak nuclear and electromagnetic forces are unified, but strong nuclear interactions are distinct. In this central region—" he cupped the little star in his hand "—grand unification is achieved.… "

I spoke up. "Sir, how does this kick Xeelee ass?"

Dakk glared at me. "Ensign, the monopole is the basis of a weapon that shares the Xeelee's own physical characteristics. You understand that the vacuum has a structure. And that structure contains flaws. The Xeelee actually use two-dimensional flaws—sheets—to power their nightfighters. But you can have one-dimensional flaws—strings—and zero-dimensional flaws."

"Monopoles," I guessed.

"You got it."

"And since the Xeelee use spacetime defects to drive their ships—"

"The best way to hit them is with another spacetime defect." Dakk rammed her fist into her hand. "And *that's* how we punched a hole in that Sugar Lump."

"But at a terrible cost." Varcin made the monopole go away. Now we were shown a kind of tactical display. We saw a plan view of the galaxy's central regions—the compact swirl that was 3-Kilo, wrapped tightly around the core. Prickles of blue light showed the position of human forward bases, like Base 592, surrounding the Xeelee concentration in the core.

And we saw battles raging all around 3-Kilo, wave after wave of blue human lights pushing toward the core, but breaking against stolid red Xeelee defense perimeters.

"This is the next phase of the war," Varcin said. "In most futures, these assaults begin a century from now. We get through the Xeelee perimeters in the end, through to the core—or rather, we can see many futures in which that outcome is still possible. But the cost in most scenarios is enormous."

Dakk said, "All because of my one damn torpedo."

"Because of the intelligence you will give away, yes. You made one of the first uses of the monopole weapon. After your engagement, the Xeelee knew we had it. The fallback order you disregarded was based on a decision at higher levels *not* to deploy the monopole weapon at the Fog engagement, to reserve it for later. By proceeding through the chop line, you undermined the decision of your superiors."

"I couldn't have known that such a decision had been made."

"We argue that, reasonably, you *should* have been able to judge that. Your error will cause great suffering, unnecessary death. The Tolman data proves it. *Your judgment was wrong.*"

So there it was. The galaxy diagram collapsed into pixels. Tarco stiffened beside me, and Dakk fell silent.

Varcin said to me, "Ensign, I know this is hard for you. But perhaps you can see now why you were appointed prosecutor advocate."

"I think so, sir."

"And will you endorse my recommendations?"

I thought it through. What would *I* do in the heat of battle, in Dakk's position? Why, just the same—and that was what must be stopped, to avert this huge future disaster. Of course, I would endorse the Commission's conclusion. What else could I do? It was my duty. We still had to go through the formalities of the court of inquiry, and no doubt the court martial to follow. But the verdicts seemed inevitable.

You'd think I was beyond surprise by now, but what came next took me aback.

Varcin stood between us, my present and future selves. "We will be pressing for heavy sanctions."

"I'm sure Captain Dakk—"

"Against *you,* ensign. Sorry."

I would not be busted out of the Navy, I learned. But a Letter of Reprimand would go into my file, which would ensure that I would never rise to the rank of captain—in fact, I would likely not be given postings in space at all.

Not only that, any application I made to have a child with Tarco would not be granted.

It was a lot to absorb, all at once. But even as Varcin outlined it, I started to see the logic. To change the future, you can only act in the present. There was nothing to be done about Dakk's personal history; she would carry around what she had done for the rest of her life, a heavy burden. But, for the sake of the course of the war, *my* life would be trashed.

I looked at Tarco. His face was blank. We had never had a relationship, not really—never actually had that child—and yet it was all taken away from us, no more real than one of Varcin's catalogued futures.

"Some love story," I said.

"Yeah. Shame, buttface."

"Yes." I think we both knew right there that we would drift apart. We'd probably never even talk about it properly.

Tarco turned to Varcin. "Sir—I have to ask—"

"Nothing significant changes for you, ensign," said Varcin softly. "You still rise to exec on the *Torch*—you will be a capable officer—"

"I still don't come home from the Fog."

"No. I'm sorry."

"Don't be, sir." He actually sounded relieved. I don't know if I admired that or not.

Dakk looked straight ahead. "Sir. Don't do this. Don't erase the glory."

"I have no choice."

Dakk's mouth worked. Then she spoke shrilly. "You fucking Commissaries sit in your gilded nests. Handing out destinies like petty gods. Do you ever even *doubt*what you are doing?"

"All the time, captain," Varcin said sadly.

There was a heartbeat of tension. Then something seemed to go out of Dakk. "Well, I guess I crashed through another chop line. My whole life is never going to happen. And I don't even have the comfort of popping out of existence."

Varcin put a hand on her shoulder. "We will take care of you. And you aren't alone. We have many other relics of lost futures. Some of them are from much further downstream than you. Many have stories that are—interesting."

"But," said Dakk stiffly, "my career is finished."

"Oh, yes, of course."

I faced Dakk. "So it's over."

"Not for us," she said bitterly. "It will never be over."

"Why did you do it?"

Her smile was twisted. "Why would *you* do it? Because it was worth it, ensign. Because we struck at the Xeelee. Because Hama—*our son*— gave his life in the best possible way."

At last, I thought I understood her.

We were, after all, the same person. As I had grown up, it had been drummed into me that there was no honor in growing old—and something in Dakk, even now, felt the same way. She was not content to be a living hero.

She had let Hama, our lost child, live out her own dreams. Even though it violated orders. Even though it damaged humanity's cause. And now she envied Hama his moment of glorious youthful suicide.

I think Dakk wanted to say more, but I turned away. I was aware I was out of my depth; counseling your elder self over the loss of her whole life isn't exactly a situation you come across every day.

Anyhow, I was feeling elated. Despite disgrace for a crime I'd never committed, despite my screwed-up career, despite the loss of a baby I would never know, despite the wrecking of any relationship I might have had with Tarco. Frankly, I was glad I wouldn't turn into the beat-up egomaniac I saw before me.

Is that cruel? I did understand that Dakk had just lost her life, her memories and achievements, everything important to her—everything that made her *her*. But that was the way I felt. I couldn't help it. I would never, after all, have to live through this scene again, standing on the other side of the room, looking back at my own face.

I would always be tied to Dakk, tied by bonds of guilt and self-recognition, closer than parent to child. But *I was free.*

Tarco had a question to ask. "Sir—*do we win*?"

Varcin kept his face expressionless. He clapped his hands, and the images over our heads changed.

It was as if the scale expanded.

I saw fleets with ships more numerous than the stars. I saw planets burn, stars flare and die. I saw the galaxy reduced to a wraith of crimson stars that guttered like dying candles. I saw people—but people like none I'd ever heard of: people living on lonely outposts suspended in empty intergalactic spaces, people swimming through the interior of stars, people trapped in abstract environments I couldn't even recognize. I saw shining people who flew through space, naked as gods.

And I saw people dying, in great waves, unnumbered hordes of them.

Varcin said, "We think there is a major crux in the next few millennia. A vital engagement at the center of the galaxy. Many of the history sheaves seem to converge at that point. Beyond that everything is uncertain. The further downstream, the more misty are the visions, the more strange the protagonists, even the humans.... There are paths to a glorious future, an awesome future of mankind victorious. And there are paths that lead to defeat—even extinction, all human possibilities extinguished."

Dakk, Tarco, and I shared glances. Our intertwined destinies were complex. But I bet the three of us had only one thought in our minds at that moment: that we were glad we were mere Navy tars, that *we* did not have to deal with *this*.

That was almost the end of it. The formal court was due to convene; the meeting was over.

But there was still something that troubled me. "Commissary—"

"Yes, ensign?"

"Do we have free will?"

Captain Dakk grimaced. "Oh, no, ensign. Not us. We have *duty*."

We walked out of the Map Room, where unrealized futures flickered like moth wings.

Calling Your Name
Howard Waldrop

> *All my life I've waited*
> *for someone to ease the pain*
> *All my life I've waited*
> *for someone to take the blame*
> —*from "Calling Your Name"*
> *by Janis Ian*[*]

I reached for the switch on the bandsaw.

Then I woke up with a crowd forming around me.
  And I was in my own backyard.

It turns out that my next-door-neighbor had seen me
fall out of the storage building I use as a workshop
and had called 911 when I didn't get up after a few
seconds.

Once, long ago in college, working in Little Theater,

I'd had a light bridge lowered to set the fresnels for Blithe Spirit, just after the Christmas semester break. Some idiot had left a hot male 220 plug loose, and as I reached up to the iron bridge, it dropped against the bar. I'd felt that, all over, and I jumped backwards about 15 feet.

A crowd started for me, but I let out some truly blazing oath that turned the whole stage violet-indigo blue and they disappeared in a hurry. Then I yelled at the guys and girl in the technical booth to kill everything onstage, and spent the next hour making sure nothing else wasn't where it shouldn't be...

That's while I was working 36 hours a week at a printing plant, going to college full-time and working in the theater another 60 hours a week for no pay. I was also dating a foul-mouthed young woman named Susan who was brighter than me. Eventually something had to give—it was my stomach (an ulcer at 20) and my relationship with her.

She came back into the theater later that day, and heard about the incident and walked up to me and said "Are you happy to see me, or is that a hot male 220 volt plug in your pocket?"

That shock, the 220, had felt like someone shaking my hand at 2700 rpm while wearing a spiked glove and someone behind me was hammering nails in my head and meanwhile they were piling safes on me...

When I'd touched the puny 110 bandsaw, I felt nothing.

Then there were neighbors and two EMS people leaning over me upside down.

"What's up, doc?" I asked.

"How many fingers?" he asked, moving his hand, changing it in a slow blur.

"Three, five, two."

"What's today?"

"You mean Tuesday, or May 6th?"

I sat up.

"Easy," said the lady EMS person, "You'll probably have a headache."

The guy pushed me back down slowly. "What happened?"

"I turned on the bandsaw. Then I'm looking at you."

He got up, went to the corner of the shed and turned off the breakers. By then the sirens had stopped, and two or three firefighters and the lieutenant had come in the yard.

"You okay, Pops?" he asked.

"I think so," I said. I turned to the crowd. "Thanks to whoever called these guys." Then the EMS people asked me some medical stuff, and the lieutenant, after looking at the breakers, went in the shed and fiddled around. He came out.

"You got a shorted switch," he said. "Better replace it."

I thanked Ms. Krelboind, the neighbor lady, everybody went away, and I went inside to finish my cup of coffee.

My daughter Maureen pulled up as I drank the last of the milk skim off the top of the coffee.

She ran in.

"Are you alright, Dad?"

"Evidently," I said.

Her husband Bob was a fireman. He usually worked over at Firehouse 2, the one on the other side of town. He'd heard the address the EMS had been called to on the squawk box, and had called her.

"What happened?"

"Short in the saw," I said. "The lieutenant said so, officially."

"I mean," she repeated, "Are you sure you're alright?"

"It was like a little vacation," I said. "I needed one."

She called her husband, and I made more coffee, and we got to talking about her kids—Vera, Chuck and Dave, or whichever ones are here—I can't keep up. There's two daughters, Maureen and Celine, and five grandkids. Sorting them all out was my late wife's job. She's only been gone a year and a month and three days.

We got off onto colleges, even though it would be some years before any of the grandkids needed one. The usual party schools came up. "I can see them at Sam Houston State in togas," I said.

"I'm *just* real *sure* toga parties will come back," said Mo.

Then I mentioned Kent State.

"Kent State? Nothing ever happens there," she said.

"Yeah, right," I said, "Like the nothing that happened after Nixon invaded Cambodia. All the campuses in America shut down. They sent the Guard in. They shot four people down, just like they were at a carnival."

She looked at me.

"Nixon? What did Nixon have to do with anything?"

"Well, he *was* the President. He wanted "no wider war". Then he sent the Army into Cambodia and Laos. It was before your time."

"Daddy," she said, "I don't remember *much* American history. But Nixon was never President. I think he was vice-president under one of those old guys–was it Eisenhower? Then he tried to be a senator. Then he wanted to be President, but someone whipped his ass at the convention. Where in that was he *ever* President? I know Eisenhower didn't die in office."

"What the hell are you talking about?"

"You stay right here," she said, and went to the living room. I heard her banging around in the bookcase. She came back with Vol 14 of the set of 1980's encyclopedias I'd bought for $20 down and $20 a month, seems like paying for about fifteen years on them.... She had her thumb in it, holding a place. She opened it on the washing machine lid. "Read."

The entry was on Nixon, Richard Milhous, and it was shorter than it should have been. There was the HUAC and Hiss stuff, the Checkers speech, the vice-presidency and reelection, the Kennedy-Nixon debates, the loss, the Senate attempt, the "won't have Dick Nixon to kick around any more" speech, the law firm, the oil company stuff, the death from phlebitis in 1977....

"Where the hell did you get this? It's *all wrong*."

"It's yours, Dad. It's your encyclopedia. You've had them 20 years. You bought them for us to do homework out of. Remember?"

I went to the living room. There was a hole in the set at Vol 14. I put it back in. Then I took out Vol 24 UV and looked up Vietnam, War In. There was WWII, 1939-1945, then French Colonial War 1945-1954, then American In 1954-1970. Then I took down Vol II and read about John F. Kennedy (president, 1961-1969).

"Are you better now, Daddy?" she asked.

"No. I haven't finished reading a bunch of lies yet, I've just begun."

"I'm sorry. I know the shock hurt. And things haven't been good since Mom...But this really isn't like you."

"I know what happened in the Sixties! I was there! Where were you?"

"Okay, okay. Let's drop it. I've got to get back home; the kids are out of school soon."

"Alright," I said. "It was a shock–not a nasty one, not my first, but maybe if I'm careful, my last."

"I'll send Bill over tomorrow on his day off and he can help you fix the saw. You know how he likes to futz with machinery."

"For gods sakes, Mo, it's a bad switch. It'll take two minutes to replace it. It ain't rocket science!"

She hugged me, went out to her car and drove off.

Strange that she should have called her husband Bob, Bill.

No wonder the kids struggled at school. Those encyclopedias sucked. I hope the whole staff got fired and went to prison.

I went down to the library where they had Britannicas, World Books, old Compton's. Everybody else in the place was on, or waiting in line for, the Internet.

I sat down by the reference shelves and opened four or five encyclopedias to the entries on Nixon. All of them started Nixon, Richard Milhous, and then in brackets (1913-1977).

After the fifth one, I got up and went over to the reference librarian, who'd just unjammed one of the printers, and she looked up at me and smiled, and as I said it I knew I should not have, but I said "All your encyclopedias are wrong."

The smile stayed on her face.

And then I thought here's a guy standing in front of her; he's in his fifties; he looks a little peaked, and he's telling her all her reference books are wrong. Just like I once heard a guy, in his fifties, a little peaked,

yelling at a librarian that some book in the place was
trying to tell him that Jesus had been a Jew!

What would *you* do?

Before she could do anything, I said, "Excuse me."

"Certainly," she said.

I left in a hurry.

My son-in-law came over the next morning when he
should have been asleep.

He looked a little different (his ears were longer. It
took a little while to notice that was it) and he seemed
a little older, but he looked pretty much the same as
always.

"Hey. Mo sent me over to do the major overhaul
on the bandsaw."

"Fuck it." I said. "It's the switch. I can do it in my
sleep."

"She said she'd feel better if you let me do it."

"Buzz off."

He laughed and grabbed one of the beers he keeps
in my refrigerator. "Okay, then," he said, "can I bor-
row a couple of albums to tape? I want the kids to
hear what real music sounds like."

He had a pretty good selection of 45's, albums and
CD's, even some shellac 78's. He's got a couple of
old turntables (one that plays 16 rpm, even). But I
have some stuff on vinyl he doesn't.

"Help yourself," I said. He went to the living room
and started making noises opening cabinets.

I mentioned The Who.

"Who?"

"Not who. The Who."

"What do you mean, who?"

"Who. The rock group. *The* Who."

"Who?"

"No, no. The Rock group, which is named The Who."

"What is this," he asked. "Abbott and Hardy?"

"We'll get to that later," I said. "Same time as the early Beatles. That…"

"Who?"

"Let me start over. Roger Daltry. Pete Townsend. John Entwhistle. Keith—"

"The High Numbers!" he said. "Why didn't you say so?"

"A minute ago. I said they came along with the early Beatles and you said—"

"Who?"

"Do *not* start."

"There is no rock band called the Beetles," he said with authority.

I looked at him. "Paul McCartney…"

He cocked his head, gave me a go-on gesture.

"…John Lennon, George Harri…"

"You mean the Quarrymen?" he asked.

"…son, Ringo Starr."

"You mean Pete Best and Stuart Sutcliffe," he said.

"Sir Richard Starkey. Ringo Starr. From all the rings on his fingers."

"The Quarrymen. Five guys. They had a few hits in the early Sixties. Wrote a shitpot of songs for other people. Broke up in 1966. Boring old farts since then–tried comeback albums, no back to come to. Lennon lives in a trailer in New Jersey. God knows where the rest of them are."

"Lennon's dead." I said. "He was assassinated at the Dakota Apartments in NYC in 1980 by a guy who wanted to impress Jodie Foster."

"Well, then, CNTV's got it all wrong, because they did a where-are-they-now thing a couple of weeks ago, and he looked pretty alive to me. He talked a few minutes and showed them some Holsteins or various other moo-cows, and a reporter made fun of them, and Lennon went back into the trailer and closed the door."

I knew they watched a lot of TV at the firehouse.

"This week they did one on ex-President Kennedy. It was his 84th birthday or something. He's the one that looked near-dead to me—they said he's had Parkinson's since the Sixties. They only had one candle on the cake, but I bet like Popeye these days, he had to eat three cans of spinach just to blow it out. His two brothers took turns reading a proclamation from President Gore. It looked like he didn't know who *that* was. His mom had to help him cut the cake. Then his wife Marilyn kissed him. He seemed to like *that*."

I sat there quietly a few minutes.

"In your family," I asked, "who's Bill?"

He quit thumbing through the albums. He took in his breath a little too loudly. He looked at me.

"Edward," he said, "*I'm* Bill."

"Then who's Bob?"

"Bob was what they called my younger brother. He lived two days. He's out at Kid Heaven in Greenwood. You, me, and Mo went out there last Easter. Remember?"

"Uh, yeah." I said.

"Are you sure you're okay, after the shock, I mean?"

"Fit as a fiddle," I said, lying through my teeth.

"You sure you don't need help with the saw?"

"It'll be a snap."

"Well, be careful."

"The breakers are still off."

"Thanks for the beer" he said, putting a couple of albums under his arm and going toward the door.

"Bye. Go get some sleep." I said.
I'll have to remember to call Bob, Bill.

Mo was back, in a hurry.
"What is it, Dad? I've never seen Bill so upset."
"I don't know. Things are just so mixed up. In fact, they're wrong."
"What do you mean, wrong? I'm really worried about you now, and so's Bill."
I've never been a whiner, even in the worst of times.
"Oh, Dad." she said. "Maybe you should go see Doc Adams, maybe get some tests done. See if he can't recommend someone…"
"You mean, like I've got Alzheimer's? I don't have Alzheimer's! It's not me, it's the world that's off the trolley. Yesterday–I don't know, it's like everything I thought I knew is wrong. It's like some Mohorovic discontinuity of the mind. Nixon was president. He had to resign because of a break-in at the Watergate Hotel, the Democratic National Headquarters, in 1972. I have a bumper sticker somewhere: "Behind Every Watergate Is A Milhous." It was the same bunch of guys who set up Kennedy in 1963. It was…"
I started to cry. Maureen didn't know whether to come to me or not.
"Are you thinking about Mom?" she asked.
"Yes," I said, "Yes, I'm thinking about your mother."
Then she hugged me.

I don't know what to say.
I'm a bright enough guy. I'm beginning to understand, though, about how people get bewildered.
On my way from the library after embarrassing myself, I passed the comic book and poster shop two blocks away. There were reproduction posters in one window; the famous one of Clark Gable and Paulette

Goddard with the flames of Atlanta behind them from *Mules in Horses' Harnesses*; Fred MacMurray and Jack Oakie in *The Road To Morrocco*, and window cards from James Dean in *Somebody Up There Likes Me*, along with *Giant* and *East of Eden*.

I came home and turned on the oldies station. It wasn't there, one like it was somewhere else on the dial.

It was just like Bo—Bill said. The first thing I heard was The Quarrymen doing "*Gimme Deine Hande*". I sat there for two hours, till it got dark, without turning on the lights, listening. There were familiar tunes by somebody else, called something else. There were the right songs by the right people. Janis I. Fink seemed to be in heavy rotation, three songs in the two hours, both before and after she went to prison, according to the DJ. The things you find out on an oldies station...

I heard no Chuck Berry, almost an impossibility.

Well, I will try to live here. I'll just have to be careful finding my way around in it. Tomorrow, after the visit to the doc, it's back to the library.

Before going to bed, I rummaged around in my "Important Papers" file. I took out my old draft notice.

It wasn't from Richard Nixon, like it has been for the last 32 years. It was from Barry Goldwater. (Au + H_2O = 1968 ?)

The psychiatrist seemed like a nice-enough guy. We talked a few minutes about the medical stuff Doc Adams had sent over; work, the shock, what Mo had told the Doc.

"Your daughter seems to think you're upset about your environment. Can you tell me why she thinks that?"

"I think she means to say I told her this was not the

world I was born in and have lived in for 56 years."
I said.

He didn't write anything down in his pad.

"It's all different." I said. He nodded.

"Since the other morning, everything I've known all my life don't add up. The wrong people have been elected to office. History is different. Not just the politics-battles-wars stuff, but also social history, culture. There's a book of social history by a guy named Furnas. I haven't looked, but I bet that's all different, too. I'll get it out of the library today. *If* it's there. *If* there's a guy named Furnas anymore."

I told him some of the things that were changed—just in two days' worth. I told him it—some of it anyway—was fascinating, but I'm sure I'd find scary stuff sooner or later. I'd have to learn to live with it, go with the flow.

"What do you think happened?" he asked.

"What is this, *The Sopranos*?"

"Beg pardon?" he asked.

"Oh. *Oh*. You'd like it. It's a tv show about a Mafia guy who, among other things, goes to a shrink—a lady shrink. It's on HBO."

"HBO?"

"*Sorry*. A cable network."

He wrote three things down on his pad.

"Look. Where I come from...I know that sounds weird. In Lindner's book..."

"Lindner?"

"Lindner. *The Fifty-Minute Hour*. Bestseller. 1950's."

"I take by the title it was about psychiatry. *And* a bestseller?"

"*Let me start over*. He wrote the book they took the title *Rebels Without A Cause* from—but *that* had nothing to do with the movie..."

He was writing stuff down now, fast.

"It's getting deeper and deeper, isn't it?" I asked.

"Go on. *Please.*"

"Lindner had a patient who was a guy who thought he lived on a far planet in an advanced civilization—star-spanning galazy-wide stuff. Twenty years before *Star Wars.* Anyway…"

He wrote down two words without taking his eyes off me.

"In my world," I said, very slowly and carefully, looking directly at him, "there was a movie called *Star Wars* in 1977 that changed the way business was done in Hollywood."

"Okay." he said.

"This is not getting us anywhere!" I said.

And then he came out with the most heartening thing I'd heard in two days. He said, "What do you mean *we, kemo sabe?*"

Well, we laughed and laughed, and then I tried to tell him, *really* tell him, what I thought I knew.

The past was another country, as they say; they did things differently there.

The more I looked up, the more I needed to look up. I had twelve or fifteen books scattered across the reference tables.

Now I know how conspiracy theorists feel. It's not just the Trilateral Commission or Henry Kissinger (a minor ABC/NRC official *here*) and the Queen of England and Area 51 and the Greys. It's like history has ganged up on me, as an individual, to drive me bugfuck. I don't have a chance. The more you find out the more you need to explain…how much more you need to find out…it could never end.

Where did it change?

We are trapped in history like insects in amber, and it is hardening all around me.

Who am I to struggle against the tree-sap of Time?

The psychiatrist has asked me to write down and bring in everything I can think of—anything, Presidents, cars, wars, culture. He wants to read it ahead of time and schedule two full hours on Friday.

You can bet I don't feel swell about this.

My other daughter Celine is here. I had *tried* and *tried* and *tried*, but she'd turned out to be a Christian in spite of *all* my work.

She is watching me like a hawk, I can tell. We were never as close as Maureen and me; she was her mother's daughter.

"How are you feeling?"

"Just peach," I said, "Considering."

"Considering *what*?" Her eyes were very green, like her mother's had been.

"If you don't mind, I'm pretty tired of answering questions. *Or* asking them."

"You ought to be more careful with those tools."

"This is not about power tools, or the shock." I said. "I don't know what Mo told you, but I have been *truly* discomfited these last few days."

"Look, Daddy," she said. "I don't care what the trouble is, we'll find a way to get you through it."

"You couldn't get me through it, unless you've got a couple of thousand years on rewind."

"What?"

"Never mind. I'm just tired. And I have to go to the hardware store and get a new switch for the bandsaw, before I burn the place down, or cause World War III or something. I'm *sure* they have hardware stores here, or *I* wouldn't have power tools."

She looked at me like I'd grown tentacles.

"Just kidding." I said. "Loosen up, Celine. Think of

me right now as your old tired father. I'll learn my way around the place and be right as rain…"

Absolutely no response.

"I'm being ironic," I said. "I have always been noted for my sense of humor. Remember?"

"Well, yes. Sort of."

"Great!" I said. "Let's go get some burgers at McDonald's!"

"Where?"

"I mean Burger King." I said. I'd passed one on the way back from the library.

"Sounds good, Dad." She said "Let *me* drive."

I have lived in this house for 26 years. I was born in the house across the street. In 1957, my friend Gino Ballantoni lived here, and I was over here every day, or just about, for four years, 'til Gino's father's aircraft job moved to California. I'd always wanted it, and after I got out of the Army, I got it on the GI Bill.

I know its every pop and groan, every sound it makes day or night, the feel of the one place the pain isn't smooth, on the inside doorjamb trim of what used to be Mo's room before it was Celine's. There's one light switch put on upside down I never changed. The garage makeover I did myself; it's what's now the living room.

I love this place. I would have lived here no matter what.

I tell myself history wasn't different enough that this house isn't still a vacant lot, *or* an apartment building. That's at least, something to hang onto.

I noticed the extra sticker inside the car windshield. Evidently we now have an emissions-control test in this state, too. I'll have to look in the phone book and find out where to go, as this one expires at the end of the month.

And also, on TV, when they show news from New York, there's still the two World Trade Center towers.

You can't be *too* careful about the past.

The psychiatrist called to ask if someone could sit in on the double session tomorrow—he knew it was early, but it was special—his old mentor from whatever Mater he'd Alma'dat; the guy was in a day early for some shrink hoedown in the Big City and wanted to watch his star pupil in action. He was asking all the patients tomorrow, he said. The old doc wouldn't say anything, and you'd hardly know he was there.

"Well, I got enough troubles, what's one more?"

He thanked me.

That's what did it for me. This was not going to stop. This was not something that I could be helped work through, like bedwetting or agoraphobia or the desire to eat human flesh. It was going to go on forever, here, until I died.

Okay, I thought. Let's get out Occam's Famous Razor and cut a few Gordian Knots. Or somewhat, as the logicians used to say.

I went out to the workshop where everybody thinks it all started.

I turned on the outside breakers. I went inside. This time I closed the door. I went over and turned on the bandsa

After I got up off the floor, I opened the door and stepped out into the yard. It was near dark so I must have been out an hour or so.

I turned off the breakers and went into the house through the back door and through the utility room and down the hall to the living room bookcase. I pulled out Vol 14 of the encyclopedia and opened it.

Nixon, Richard Milhous, it said (1913-1994). A good long entry.

There was a sound from the kitchen. The oven door opened and closed.

"What have you been doing?" asked a voice.

"There's a short in the bandsaw I'll have to get fixed," I said. I went around the corner.

It was my wife Susan. She looked a little older, a little heavier since I last saw her, it seemed. She still looked pretty good.

"Stand there where I can see you," I said.

"We were having a fight before you wandered away, remember?"

"Whatever it was," I said, "I was wrong. You were right. We'll do whatever it is you want."

"Do you even remember what it was we were arguing about?"

"No." I said. "Whatever. It's not important. The problems of two people don't amount to a hill of beans in—"

"Cut the *Casablanca* crap," said Susan. "Jodie and Susie Q want to bring the kids over next Saturday and have Little Eddy's birthday party here. You wanted peace and quiet here, and go somewhere else for the party. That was the argument."

"I wasn't cut out to be a grandpa," I said. "But bring 'em on. Invite the neighbors! Put out signs on the street! 'Annoy an old man here!' "

Then I quietened down. "Tell them we'd be happy to have the party here," I said.

"Honestly, Edward," said Susan, putting the casserole on the big trivet. It was *her* night to cook. "Sometimes I think you'd forget your ass if it weren't glued on."

"Yeah, sure," I said. "I've damn sure forgotten what peace and quiet was like. And probably lots of other stuff, too."

"Supper's ready," said Susan.

The Empire of Ice Cream
Jeffrey Ford

Are you familiar with the scent of extinguished birthday candles? For me, their aroma is superceded by a sound like the drawing of a bow across the bass string of a violin. This note carries all of the melancholic joy I have been told the scent engenders—the loss of another year, the promise of accrued wisdom. Likewise, the notes of an acoustic guitar appear before my eyes as a golden rain, falling from a height just above my head only to vanish at the level of my solar plexus. There is a certain imported Swiss cheese I am fond of that is all triangles, whereas the feel of silk against my fingers rests on my tongue with the flavor and consistency of lemon meringue. These perceptions are not merely thoughts, but concrete physical experiences. Depending upon how you see it, I, like approximately nine out of every million individuals, am either cursed or blessed with a condition known as synesthesia.

It has only recently come to light that the process of synesthesia takes place in the hippocampus, part of the ancient limbic system where remembered perceptions—triggered in diverse geographical regions of the brain as the result of an external stimulus—come together. It is believed that everyone, at a point somewhere below consciousness, experiences this coinciding of sensory association, yet in most it is filtered out, and only a single sense is given predominance in one's waking world. For we lucky few, the filter is broken or perfected, and what is usually subconscious becomes conscious. Perhaps, at some distant point in history, our early ancestors were completely synesthetic, and touched, heard, smelled, tasted, and saw all at once—each specific incident mixing sensoric memory along with the perceived sense without affording precedence to the findings of one of the five portals through which "reality" invades us. The scientific explanations, as far as I can follow them, seem to make sense now, but when I was young and told my parents about the whisper of vinyl, the stench of purple, the spinning blue gyres of the church bell, they feared I was defective and that my mind was brimming with hallucinations like an abandoned house choked with ghosts.

As an only child, I wasn't afforded the luxury of being anomalous. My parents were well on in years—my mother nearly forty, my father already forty-five—when I arrived after a long parade of failed pregnancies. The fact that, at age five, I heard what I described as an angel crying whenever I touched velvet would never be allowed to stand, but was seen as an illness to be cured by whatever methods were available. Money was no object in the pursuit of perfect normalcy. And so my younger years were a torment of hours spent in the waiting rooms of psychologists, psychiatrists and therapists. I can't find words to describe the depths of medical quackery I was subjected to by a veritable army of so-called professionals who diagnosed me with everything from schizophrenia to bipolar depression to low IQ caused by muddled potty training. Being a child, I was completely honest with them about what I experienced, and this, my first mistake, resulted in blood tests, brain scans, special diets and the forced consumption of a demon's pharmacopoeia of mind-deadening drugs that diminished my will but not the vanilla scent of slanting golden sunlight on late autumn afternoons.

My only-child status, along with the added complication of my "condition," as they called it, led my parents to perceive me as fragile. For this reason, I was kept fairly isolated from other children. Part of it, I'm sure, had to do with the way my abnormal perceptions and utterances would reflect upon my mother and father, for they were the type of people who could not bear to be thought of as having been responsible for the production of defective goods. I was tutored at home by my mother instead of being allowed to attend school. She was actually a fine teacher, having a Ph.D. in History and a firm grasp of classical literature. My father, an actuary, taught me Math, and in this subject I proved to be an unquestionable failure until I reached college age. Although x=y might have been a suitable metaphor for the phenomenon of synesthesia, it made no sense on paper. The number 8, by the way, reeks of withered flowers.

What I was good at was music. Every Thursday at 3:00 in the afternoon, Mrs. Brithnic would arrive at the house to give me a piano lesson. She was a kind old lady with thinning white hair and the most beautiful fingers—long and smooth as if they belonged to a graceful young giantess. Although something less than a virtuoso at the keys, she was a veritable genius at teaching me to allow myself to enjoy the sounds I produced. Enjoy them I did, and when I wasn't being dragged hither and yon in the pursuit of losing my affliction, home base for me was the piano bench. In my imposed isolation from the world, music became

346

a window of escape I crawled through as often as possible.

When I'd play, I could see the notes before me like a fireworks display of colors and shapes. By my twelfth year, I was writing my own compositions, and my notation on the pages accompanying the notes of a piece referred to the visual displays that coincided with them. In actuality, when I played, I was really painting—in mid-air, before my eyes—great abstract works in the tradition of Kandinsky. Many times, I planned a composition on a blank piece of paper using the crayon set of 64 colors I'd had since early childhood. The only difficulty in this was with colors like magenta and cobalt blue, which I perceive primarily as tastes, and so would have to write them down in pencil as licorice and tapioca on my colorfully scribbled drawing where they would appear in the music.

My punishment for having excelled at the piano was to lose my only real friend, Mrs. Brithnic. I remember distinctly the day my mother let her go. She calmly nodded, smiling, understanding that I had already surpassed her abilities. Still, though I knew this was the case, I cried when she hugged me goodbye. When her face was next to mine, she whispered into my ear, "Seeing is believing," and in that moment, I knew that she had completely understood my plight. Her lilac perfume, the sound of one nearly inaudible B-flat played by an oboe, still hung about me as I watched her walk down the path and out of my life for good.

I believe it was the loss of Mrs. Brithnic that made me rebel. I became desultory and despondent. Then one day, soon after my thirteenth birthday, instead of obeying my mother, who had just told me to finish reading a textbook chapter while she showered, I went to her pocketbook, took five dollars and left the house. As I walked along beneath the sunlight and blue sky, the world around me seemed brimming with life. What I wanted more than anything else was to meet other young people my own age. I remembered an ice-cream shop in town where, when passing by in the car returning from whatever doctor's office we had been to, there always seemed to be kids hanging around. I headed directly for that spot while wondering if my mother would catch up to me before I made it. When I pictured her drying her hair, I broke into a run.

Upon reaching the row of stores that contained The Empire of Ice Cream, I was out of breath as much from the sheer exhilaration of freedom as from the half-mile sprint. Peering through the glass of the front door was like looking through a portal into an exotic other world. Here were young people, my age, gathered in groups at tables, talking, laughing, eating ice cream—not by night, after dinner—but in the middle of broad daylight. I opened the door and plunged in. The magic of the place seemed to brush by me on its way out as I entered, for the conversation instantly died away. I stood in the momentary silence as all heads turned to stare at me.

"Hello," I said, smiling, and raised my hand in greeting, but I was too late. They had already turned away, the conversation resumed, as if they had merely afforded a grudging glimpse to see the door open and close at the behest of the wind. I was paralyzed by my inability to make an impression, the realization that finding friends was going to take some real work.

"What'll it be?" said a large man behind the counter.

I broke from my trance and stepped up to order. Before me, beneath a bubble dome of glass, lay the

Empire of Ice Cream. I'd never seen so much of the stuff in so many colors and incarnations—with nuts and fruit, cookie and candy bits, mystical swirls the sight of which sounded to me like a distant siren. There were deep vats of it set in neat rows totaling thirty flavors. My diet had never allowed for the consumption of confections or desserts of any type, and rare were the times I had so much as a thimbleful of vanilla ice cream after dinner. Certain doctors had told my parents that my eating these treats might seriously exacerbate my condition. With this in mind, I ordered a large bowl of coffee ice cream. My choice of coffee stemmed from the fact that that beverage was another item on the list of things I should never taste.

After paying, I took my bowl and spoon and found a seat in the corner of the place from which I could survey all the other tables. I admit that I had some trepidations about digging right in, since I'd been warned against it for so long by so many adults. Instead, I scanned the shop, watching the other kids talking, trying to overhear snatches of conversation. I made eye contact with a boy my own age two tables away. I smiled and waved to him. He saw me and then leaned over and whispered something to the other fellows he was with. All four of them turned, looked at me, and then broke into laughter. It was a certainty they were making fun of me, but I basked in the victory of merely being noticed. With this, I took a large spoonful of ice cream and put it in my mouth.

There is an attendant phenomenon of the synesthetic experience I've yet to mention. Of course I had no term for it at this point in my life, but when one is in the throes of the remarkable transference of senses, it is accompanied by a feeling of "epiphany," a "eureka" of contentment that researchers of the anomalous condition would later term *noetic*, borrowing from William James. That first taste of coffee ice cream elicited a deeper noetic response than I'd ever before felt, and along with it came the appearance of a girl. She coalesced out of thin air and stood before me, obscuring my sight of the group that was still laughing. Never before had I seen through tasting, hearing, touching, smelling, something other than simple abstract shapes and colors.

She was turned somewhat to the side and hunched over, wearing a plaid skirt and a white blouse. Her hair was the same dark brown as my own, but long and gathered in the back with a green rubber band. There was a sudden shaking of her hand, and it became clear to me that she was putting out a match. Smoke swirled away from her. I could see now that she had been lighting a cigarette. I got the impression that she was wary of being caught in the act of smoking. When she turned her head sharply to look back over her shoulder, I dropped the spoon on the table. Her look instantly enchanted me.

As the ice cream melted away down my throat, she began to vanish, and I quickly lifted the spoon to restoke my vision, but it never reached my lips. She suddenly went out like a light when I felt something land softly upon my left shoulder. I heard the incomprehensible murmur of recrimination, and knew it as my mother's touch. She had found me. A great wave of laughter accompanied my removal from The Empire of Ice Cream. Later I would remember the incident with embarrassment, but for the moment, even as I spoke words of apology to my mother, I could think only of what I'd seen.

The ice-cream incident—followed hard by the discovery of the cigar box of pills I hid in my closet, all of the medication that I'd supposedly swallowed for the past six months—led my parents to believe that heaped upon my condition was now a tendency toward delinquency that would grow, if unchecked, in geometrical proportion with the passing of years. It was decided that I should see yet another specialist to deal with my behavior, a therapist my father had read about who would prompt me to talk my willfulness into submission. I was informed of this in a solemn meeting with my parents. What else was there to do but acquiesce? I knew that my mother and father wanted, in their pedestrian way, what they believed was best for me. Whenever the situation would infuriate me, I'd go to the piano and play, sometimes for three or four hours at a time.

Dr. Stullin's office was in a ramshackle Victorian house on the other side of town. My father accompanied me on the first visit, and, when he pulled up in front of the sorry old structure, he checked the address at least twice to make sure we'd come to the right place. The doctor, a round little man with a white beard and glasses with small circular lenses, met us at the front door. Why he laughed when we shook hands at the introductions, I hadn't a clue, but he was altogether jolly, like a pint-size Santa Claus dressed in a wrinkled brown suit one size too small. He swept out his arm to usher me into his house, but when my father tried to enter, the doctor held up his hand and said, "You will return in one hour and five minutes."

My father gave some weak protest and said that he thought he might be needed to help discuss my history to this point. Here the doctor's demeanor instantly changed. He became serious, official, almost commanding.

"I'm being paid to treat the boy. You'll have to find your own therapist."

My father was obviously at a loss. He looked as if he was about to object, but the doctor said, "One hour and five minutes." Following me inside, he quickly shut the door behind him.

As he led me through a series of unkempt rooms lined with crammed bookshelves, and one in which piles of paper covered the tops of tables and desks, he said, laughing, "Parents: so essential, yet sometimes like something you've stepped in and cannot get off your shoe. What else is there but to love them?"

We wound up in a room at the back of the house made from a skeleton of thin steel girders and paneled with glass panes. The sunlight poured in, and surrounding us, at the edges of the place, also hanging from some of the girders, were green plants. There was a small table on which sat a teapot and two cups and saucers. As I took the seat he motioned for me to sit in, I looked out through the glass and saw that the backyard was one large, magnificent garden, blooming with all manner of colorful flowers.

After he poured me a cup of tea, the questioning began. I'd had it in my mind to be as recalcitrant as possible, but there was something in the manner in which he had put my father off that I admired about him. Also, he was unlike other therapists I'd been to, who would listen to my answers with complete reservation of emotion or response. When he asked why I was here, and I told him it was because I'd escaped in order to go to the ice-cream shop, he scowled and said, "Patently ridiculous." I was unsure if he meant me or my mother's response to what I'd done. I told him about playing the piano, and he smiled warmly and nodded. "That's a good thing," he said.

After he asked me about my daily routine and my home life, he sat back and said, "So, what's the problem? Your father has told me that you hallucinate. Can you explain?"

No matter how ingratiating he'd been, I had already decided that I would no longer divulge any of my perceptions to anyone. Then he did something unexpected.

"Do you mind?" he asked as he took out a pack of cigarettes.

Before I could shake my head no, he had one out of the pack and lit. Something about this, perhaps because I'd never seen a doctor smoke in front of a patient before, perhaps because it reminded me of the girl who had appeared before me in the ice-cream shop, weakened my resolve to say nothing. When he flicked his ashes into his half-empty teacup, I started talking. I told him about the taste of silk, the various corresponding colors for the notes of the piano, the nauseating stench of purple.

I laid the whole thing out for him and then sat back in my chair, now somewhat regretting my weakness, for he was smiling, and the smoke was leaking out of the corners of his mouth. He exhaled, and in that cloud came the word that would validate me, define me and haunt me for the rest of my life—*synesthesia*.

By the time I left Stullin's office that day, I was a new person. The doctor spoke to my father and explained the phenomenon to him. He cited historical cases and gave him the same general overview of the neurological workings of the condition. He also added that most synesthetes don't experience the condition in such a variety of senses as I did, although it was not unheard of. My father nodded every now and then but was obviously perplexed at the fact that my long-suffered *condition* had, in an instant, vanished.

"There's nothing wrong with the boy," said Stullin, "except for the fact that he is, in a way, exceptional.

Think of it as a gift, an original way of sensing the world. These perceptions are as real for him as are your own to you."

Stullin's term for my condition was like a magic incantation from a fairy tale, for through its power I was released from the spell of my parents' control. In fact, their reaction to it was to almost completely relinquish interest in me, as if after all of their intensive care I'd been found out to be an imposter now unworthy of their attention. When it became clear that I would have the ability to go about my life as any normal child might, I relished the concept of freedom. The sad fact was, though, that I didn't know how to. I lacked all experience at being part of society. My uncertainty made me shy, and my first year in public school was a disaster. What I wanted was a friend my own age, and this goal continued to elude me until I was well out of high school and in college. My desperation to connect made me ultimately nervous, causing me to act and speak without reserve. This was the early 1960s, and if anything was important in high school social circles at the time, it was remaining *cool*. I was the furthest thing from cool you might imagine.

For protection, I retreated into my music and spent hours working out compositions with my crayons and pens, trying to corral the sounds and resultant visual pyrotechnics, odors and tastes into cohesive scores. All along, I continued practicing and improving my abilities at the keyboard, but I had no desire to become a performer. Quite a few of my teachers through the years had it in their minds that they could shape me into a brilliant concert pianist. I would not allow it, and when they insisted, I'd drop them and move on. Nothing frightened me more than the thought of sitting in front of a crowd of onlookers. The weight of judgment lurking behind even one set of those imagined eyes was too much for me to bear. I'd stayed on with Stullin, visiting once a month, and no matter his persistent proclamations as to my relative normalcy, it was impossible for me, after years of my parents' insisting otherwise, to erase the fact that I was, in my own mind, a freak.

My greatest pleasure away from the piano at this time was to take the train into the nearby city and attend concerts given by the local orchestra or small chamber groups that would perform in more intimate venues. Rock and roll was all the rage, but my training at the piano and the fact that calm solitude as opposed to raucous socializing was the expected milieu of the symphony drew me in the direction of classical music. It was a relief that most of those who attended the concerts I did were adults who paid no attention to my presence. From the performances I witnessed, from the stereo I goaded my parents into buying for me, and my own reading, I, with few of the normal distractions of the typical teenager, gathered an immense knowledge of my field.

My hero was J. S. Bach. It was from his works that I came to understand mathematics…and, through a greater understanding of math, came to a greater understanding of Bach—the golden ratio, the rise of complexity through the reiteration of simple elements, the presence of the cosmic in the common. Whereas others simply heard his work, I could also feel it, taste it, smell it, visualize it, and in doing so was certain I was witnessing the process by which all of Nature had moved from a single cell to a virulent, diverse forest. Perhaps part of my admiration for the good cantor of Leipzig was his genius with counterpoint, a practice where two or more distinct melodic lines delicately join at certain points to form a singularly cohesive listening experience. I saw in this technique an analogy to my desire that some day my own unique personality might join with that of another's and form a friendship. Soon after hearing the fugue pieces that are part of *The Well-Tempered Clavier*, I decided I wanted to become a composer.

Of course, during these years, both dreadful for my being a laughingstock in school and delightful for their musical revelations, I couldn't forget the image of the girl who momentarily appeared before me during my escape to The Empire of Ice Cream. The minute that Dr. Stullin pronounced me sane, I made plans to return and attempt to conjure her again. The irony of the situation was that just that single first taste of coffee ice cream had ended up making me ill, either because I'd been sheltered from rich desserts my whole life or because my system actually was inherently delicate. Once my freedom came, I found I didn't have the stomach for all of those gastronomic luxuries I had at one time so desired. Still, I was willing to chance the stomachache in order to rediscover her.

On my second trip to The Empire, after taking a heaping spoonful of coffee ice cream and experiencing again that deep noetic response, she appeared as before, her image forming in the empty space between me and the front window of the shop. This time she seemed to be sitting at the end of a couch situated in a living room or parlor, reading a book. Only her immediate surroundings, within a foot or two of her body, were clear to me. As my eyes moved away from her central figure, the rest of the couch, and the table beside her, holding a lamp, became increasingly ghostlike; images from the parking lot outside the shop window showed through. At the edges of the phenomenon, there was nothing but the merest wrinkling of the atmosphere. She turned the page, and I was drawn back to her. I quickly fed myself another bit of ice cream and marveled at her beauty. Her hair was down, and I could see that it came well past her shoulders. Bright green eyes, a small, perfect nose, smooth skin, and full lips that silently moved with each word of the text she was scanning. She was wearing some kind of very sheer, powder blue pajama top, and I could see the presence of her breasts beneath it.

I took two spoonfuls of ice cream in a row, and, because my desire had tightened my throat and I couldn't swallow, their cold burned my tongue. In the time it took for the mouthful of ice cream to melt and trickle down my throat, I simply watched her chest subtly heave with each breath, her lips move, and I was enchanted. The last thing I noticed before she disappeared was the odd title of the book she was reading—*The Centrifugal Rickshaw Dancer*. I'd have taken another spoonful, but a massive headache had blossomed behind my eyes, and I could feel my stomach beginning to revolt against the ice cream. I got up and quickly left the shop. Out in the open air, I walked for over an hour, trying to clear my head of the pain while at the same time trying to retain her image in my memory. I stopped three times along my meandering course, positive I was going to vomit, but I never did.

My resistance to the physical side effects of the ice cream never improved, but I returned to the shop again and again, like a binge drinker to the bottle, hangover be damned, whenever I was feeling most alone. Granted, there was something of a voyeuristic thrill underlying the whole thing, especially when the ice cream would bring her to me in various states of undress—in the shower, in her bedroom. But you must believe me when I say that there was much more to it than that. I wanted to know everything about her. I studied her as assiduously as I did *The Goldberg Variations* or Schoenberg's serialism. She was, in many ways, an even more intriguing mystery, and the process of investigation was like constructing a jigsaw puzzle, reconfiguring a blasted mosaic.

I learned that her name was Anna. I saw it written on one of her sketchpads. Yes, she was an artist, and I believe had great aspirations in this direction, as I did in music. I spent so many spoonfuls of coffee ice cream, initiated so many headaches, just watching her draw. She never lifted a paintbrush or pastel, but was tied to the simple tools of pencil and paper. I never witnessed her using a model or photograph as a guide. Instead, she would place the sketchpad flat on a table and hunker over it. The tip of her tongue would show itself from the right corner of her lips when she was in deepest concentration. Every so often, she'd take a drag on a cigarette that burned in an ashtray to her left. The results of her work, the few times I was lucky enough to catch a glimpse, were astonishing. Sometimes she was obviously drawing from life, the portraits of people whom she must've known. At other times she'd conjure strange creatures or mandalalike designs of exotic blossoms. The shading was incredible, giving weight and depth to her creations. All of this from the tip of a graphite pencil one might use to work a calculation or jot a memo. If I did not adore her, I might've envied her innate talent.

To an ancillary degree, I was able to catch brief glimpses of her surroundings, and this was fascinating for the fact that she seemed to move through a complete, separate world of her own, some kind of *other* reality that was very much like ours. I'd garnered enough to know that she lived in a large old house with many rooms, the windows covered with long drapes to block out the light. Her work area was chaotic, stacks of her drawings covering the tops of tables and pushed to the sides of her desk. A black-and-white cat was always prowling in and out of the tableau. She was very fond of flowers and often worked in some sun-drenched park or garden, creating painstaking portraits of amaryllis or pansies, and although the rain would be falling outside my own window, there the skies were bottomless blue.

Although over the course of years I'd told Stullin much about myself, revealed my ambitions and most secret desires, I had never mentioned Anna. It was only after I graduated high school and was set to go off to study at Gelsbeth Conservatory in the nearby city that I decided to reveal her existence to him. The doctor had been a good friend to me, albeit a remunerated one, and was always most congenial and understanding when I'd give vent to my frustrations. He persistently argued the optimistic viewpoint for me when all was as inky black as the aroma of my father's aftershave. My time with him never resulted in a palpable difference in my ability to attract friends or feel more comfortable in public, but I enjoyed his company. At the same time, I was somewhat relieved to be severing all ties to my troubled past and escaping my childhood once and for all. I was willing to jettison Stullin's partial good to be rid of the rest.

We sat in the small sunroom at the back of his house, and he was questioning me about what interests I would pursue in my forthcoming classes. He had a good working knowledge of classical music and had told me at one of our earliest meetings that he'd studied the piano when he was younger. He had a weakness for the Romantics, but I didn't hold it against him. Somewhere in the midst of our discussion I simply blurted out the details of my experiences with coffee ice cream and the resultant appearances of Anna. He was obviously taken aback. He leaned forward in his chair and slowly went through the procedure of lighting a cigarette.

"You know," he said, releasing a cascade of smoke, the aroma of which always manifested itself for me in the faint sound of a mosquito, "that is quite unusual. I don't believe there has ever been a case of a synesthetic vision achieving a figurative resemblance. They are always abstract. Shapes, colors, yes, but never an image of an object, not to mention a person."

"I know it's the synesthesia," I said. "I can feel it. The exact same experience as when I summon colors from my keyboard."

"And you say she always appears in relation to your eating ice cream?" he asked, squinting.

"Coffee ice cream," I said.

This made him laugh briefly, but his smile soon diminished, and he brought his free hand up to stroke his beard. I knew this action to be a sign of his concern. "What you are describing to me would be, considering the current medical literature, a hallucination."

I shrugged.

"Still," he went on, "the fact that it is always related to your tasting the ice cream, and that you can identify an associated noetic feeling, I'd have to agree with you that it seems related to your condition."

"I knew it was unusual," I said. "I was afraid to mention it."

"No, no, it's good that you did. The only thing troubling me about it is that I am too aware of your desire to connect with another person your age. To be honest, it has all of the earmarks of a wish fulfillment that points back to a kind of hallucination. Look, you don't need this distraction now. You're beginning your life, you are moving on, and there is every indication that you'll be successful in your art. When the other students at the Conservatory understand your abilities, you'll make friends, believe me. It won't be like high school. Chasing this insubstantial image could impede your progress. Let it go."

And so, not without a large measure of regret, I did. To an extent, Stullin was right about Gelsbeth. It wasn't like high school, and I did make the acquaintance of quite a few like-minded people with whom I could at least connect on the subject of music. I wasn't the only odd fish in that pond, believe me. To be a young person with an overriding interest in Bach or Mozart or Scriabin was its own eccentricity for those times. The place was extremely competitive, and I took the challenge. My fledgling musical compositions were greeted with great interest by the faculty, and I garnered a degree of notoriety when one day a fellow student discovered me composing a chamber piece for violins and cello using my set of crayons. I would always work in my corresponding synesthetic colors and then transpose the work, scoring it in normal musical notation.

The years flew by, and I believe they were the most rewarding of my entire life. I rarely went home to visit, save on holidays when the school was closed, even though it was only a brief train ride from the city. The professors were excellent but unforgiving of laziness and error. It wasn't a labor for me to meet their expectations. For the first time in my life, I felt what it meant to play, an activity I'd never experienced in childhood. The immersion in great music, the intricate analysis of its soul, kept me constantly engaged, filled with a sense of wonder.

Then, in my last year, I became eligible to particip-
ate in a competition for composers. There was a large
cash prize, and the winner's work would be performed
at a concert in the city's symphony hall by a well-
known musician. The difficulty of being a composer
was always the near-impossibility of getting one's
work performed by competent musicians in a public
venue. The opportunity presented by the competition
was one I couldn't let slip away. More important than
the money or the accolades would be a kind of recognition that would bring me to the attention of potential patrons who might commission a work. I knew
that it was time to finally compose the fugue I'd had
in mind for so many years. The utter complexity of
the form, I believed, would be the best way to show-
case all of my talents.

When it came time to begin the composition of the
fugue, I took the money I'd made tutoring young
musicians on the weekends and put it toward renting
a beach house out on Varion Island for two weeks.
In the summers the place was a bustling tourist spot
for the wealthy, with a small central town that could
be termed quaint. In those months, I wouldn't have
been able to touch the price of the lowliest dwelling
for a single day's rent. It was the heart of winter,
though, when I took a leave from the school, along
with crayons, books, a small tape player, and fled by
way of bus and cab to my secret getaway.

The house I came to wasn't one of the grand
wooden mansions on stilts that lined the road along
the causeway, but instead a small bungalow, much
like a concrete bunker. It was painted an off-putting
yellow that tasted to me for all the world like cauli-
flower. It sat atop a small rise, and its front window
faced the ocean, giving me a sublime view of the
dunes and beach. What's more, it was within walking

distance of the tiny village. There was sufficient heat, a telephone, a television, a kitchen with all the appliances, and I instantly felt as at home there as I had anywhere in my life. The island itself was deserted. On my first day, I walked down to the ocean and along the shore the mile and a half to the eastern point and then back by way of the main road, passing empty houses, and I saw no one. I'd been told over the phone by the realtor that the diner in town and a small shop that sold cigarettes and newspapers stayed open through the winter. Thankfully, she was right, for without the diner, I would have starved.

The setting of the little bungalow was deliciously melancholic, and for my sensibilities that meant conducive to work. I could hear the distant breaking of waves and, above that, the winter wind blowing sand against the window glass, but these were not distractions. Instead, they were the components of a silence that invited one to dream wide awake, to let the imagination open, and so I dove into the work straightaway. On the first afternoon, I began recording in my notebook my overall plan for the fugue. I'd decided that it would have only two voices. Of course, some had been composed with as many as eight, but I did not want to be ostentatious. Showing reserve is as important a trait of technical mastery as is that of complexity.

I already had the melodic line of the subject, which had been a cast off from another project I'd worked on earlier in the year. Even though I decided it was not right for the earlier piece, I couldn't forget it and kept revising it here and there, playing it over and over. In the structure of a fugue, one posits the melodic line or subject, and then there is an answer (counterpoint), a reiteration of that line with differing degrees of variation, so that what the listener hears is like a dialogue (or a voice and its echo) of increasing complexity. After each of the voices has entered the piece, there is an episode that leads to the reentry of the voices and given answers, now in different keys. I had planned to use a technique called *stretto,* in which the answers, as they are introduced, overlap somewhat the original subject lines. This allows for a weaving of the voices so as to create an intricate tapestry of sound.

All this would be difficult to compose but nothing outlandishly original. It was my design, though, to impress the judges by trying something new. Once the fugue had reached its greatest state of complication, I wanted the piece to slowly, almost logically at first, but then without rhyme or meter, crumble into chaos. At the very end, from that chaotic cacophony, there would emerge one note, drawn out to great length, which would eventually diminish into nothing.

For the first week, the work went well. I took a little time off every morning and evening for a walk on the beach. At night I would go to the diner and then return to the bungalow to listen to Bach's *Art of the Fugue* or *Toccata and Fugue in D minor,* some Brahms, Haydn, Mozart, and then pieces from the inception of the form by composers like Sweelinck and Froberger. I employed the crayons on a large piece of good drawing paper, and although to anyone else it would not look like musical notation, I knew exactly how it would sound when I viewed it. Somewhere after the first week, though, I started to slow down, and by Saturday night my work came to a grinding halt. What I'd begun with such a clear sense of direction had me trapped. I was lost in my own complexity. The truth was, I was exhausted and could no longer pick apart the threads of the piece—the subject, the answer, the counter-subject snarled like a ball of yarn.

I was thoroughly weary and knew I needed rest, but even though I went to bed and closed my eyes, I couldn't sleep. All day Sunday, I sat in a chair and surveyed the beach through the front window. I was too tired to work but too frustrated about not working to sleep. That evening, after having done nothing all day, I stumbled down to the diner and took my usual seat. The place was empty save for one old man sitting in the far corner, reading a book while eating his dinner. This solitary character looked somewhat like Stullin for his white beard, and at first glance, had I not known better, I could've sworn the book he was reading was *The Centrifugal Rickshaw Dancer*. I didn't want to get close enough to find out for fear he might strike up a conversation.

The waitress came and took my order. When she was finished writing on her pad, she said, "You look exhausted tonight."

I nodded.

"You need to sleep," she said.

"I have work to do," I told her.

"Well, then, let me bring you some coffee."

I laughed. "You know, I've never had a cup of coffee in my life," I said.

"Impossible," she said. "It looks to me like tonight might be a good time to start."

"I'll give it a try," I told her, and this seemed to make her happy.

While I ate, I glanced through my notebook and tried to reestablish for myself the architecture of the fugue. As always, when I looked at my notes, everything was crystal clear, but when it came time to continue on the score, every potential further step seemed the wrong way to go. Somewhere in the midst of my musing, I pushed my plate away and drew toward me the cup and saucer. My usual drink was tea, and I'd forgotten I had changed my order. I took a sip, and the dark, bitter taste of black coffee startled me. I looked up, and there was Anna, staring at me, having just lowered a cup away from her lips. In her eyes I saw a glint of recognition, as if she were actually seeing me, and I'm sure she saw the same in mine.

I whispered, "I see you."

She smiled. "I see you too," she said.

I would have been less surprised if a dog had spoken to me. Sitting dumbfounded, I reached slowly out toward where she seemed to sit across from me in the booth. As my hand approached, she leaned back away from it.

"I've been watching you for years," she said.

"The coffee?" I said.

She nodded. "You are a synesthete, am I right?"

"Yes," I said. "But you're a figment of my imagination, a product of a neurological anomaly."

Here she laughed out loud. "No," she said, "you are."

After our initial exchange, neither of us spoke. I was in a mild state of shock, I believe. "This can't be," I kept repeating in my mind, but there she was, and I could hear her breathing. Her image appeared even sharper than it had previously under the influence of the coffee ice cream. And now, with the taste that elicited her presence uncompromised by cream and sugar and the cold, she remained without dissipating for a good few minutes before beginning to mist at the edges and I had to take another sip to sharpen the focus. When I brought my cup up to drink, she also did at the same exact time, as if she were a reflection, as if I were her reflection, and we both smiled.

"I can't speak to you where I am. They'll think I've lost my mind," I whispered.

"I'm in the same situation," she said.

"Give me a half hour and then have another cup of coffee, and I'll be able to speak to you in private."

She nodded in agreement and watched as I called for the check.

By the time the waitress arrived at my booth, Anna had dissolved into a vague cloud, like the exhalation of a smoker. It didn't matter, as I knew she couldn't be seen by anyone else. As my bill was being tallied, I ordered three cups of coffee to go.

"That coffee is something, isn't it?" said the waitress. "I swear by it. Amazing you've never had any up to this point. My blood is three-quarters coffee, I drink so much of it," she said.

"Wonderful stuff," I agreed.

Wonderful it was, for it had awakened my senses, and I walked through the freezing, windy night, carrying in a box my containers of elixir, with all the joy of a child leaving school on Friday afternoon. The absurdity of the whole affair didn't escape me, and I laughed out loud remembering my whispered plan to wait a half hour and then drink another cup. The conspiratorial nature of it excited me, and I realized for the first time since seeing her that Anna had matured and grown more beautiful in the years I had forsaken her.

Back at the bungalow, I put the first of the large Styrofoam containers into the microwave in the kitchen and heated it for no more than thirty seconds. I began to worry that perhaps in Anna's existence time was altogether different and a half hour for me might be two or three or a day for her. The instant the bell sounded on the appliance, I took the cup out, seated myself at the small kitchen table and drank a long draught of the dark potion. Before I could put the cup down, she was there, sitting in the seat opposite me.

"I know your name is Anna," I said to her. "I saw it on one of your drawing pads."

She flipped her hair behind her ear on the left side and asked, "What's yours?"

"William," I said. Then I told her about the coffee ice cream and the first time I encountered her image.

"I remember," she said, "when I was a child of nine, I snuck a sip of my father's coffee he had left in the living room, and I saw you sitting at a piano. I thought you were a ghost. I ran to get my mother to show her, but when I returned you'd vanished. She thought little of it since the synesthesia was always prompting me to describe things that made no sense to her."

"When did you realize it was the coffee?" I asked.

"Oh, some time later. I again was given a taste of it at breakfast one morning, and there you were, sitting at our dining room table, looking rather forlorn. It took every ounce of restraint not to blurt out that you were there. Then it started to make sense to me. After that, I would try to see you as much as possible. You were often very sad when you were younger. I know that."

The look on her face, one of true concern for me, almost brought tears to my eyes. She was a witness to my life. I hadn't been as alone as I had always thought.

"You're a terrific artist," I said.

She smiled. "I'm great with a pencil, but my professors are demanding a piece in color. That's what I'm working on now."

Intermittently in the conversation we'd stop and take sips of coffee to keep the connection vital. As it turned out, she too had escaped her normal routine and taken a place in order to work on a project for her final portfolio review. We discovered all manner of synchronicities between our lives. She admitted to me that she'd also been a loner as a child and that her parents had a hard time dealing with her synesthetic condition. As she put it, "Until we discovered the reality of it, I think they thought I was crazy." She laughed, but I could tell by the look in her eyes how deeply it had affected her.

"Have you ever told anyone about me?" I asked.

"Only my therapist," she said. "I was relieved when he told me he'd heard of rare cases like mine."

This revelation brought me up short, for Stullin had told me he had never encountered anything of the sort in the literature. The implications of this inconsistency momentarily reminded me that she was not real, but I quickly shoved the notion from my thoughts and continued the conversation.

That night, by parsing out the coffee I had, and she doing the same, we stayed together until two in the morning, telling each other about our lives, our creative ideas, our dreams for the future. We found that our synesthetic experiences were similar and that our sense impressions were often transposed with the same results. For instance, for both her and me, the aroma of new-mown grass was circular and the sound of a car horn tasted of citrus. She told me that her father was an amateur musician who loved the piano and classical music. In the middle of my recounting for her the intricacies of the fugue I was planning, she suddenly looked up from her cup and said, "Oh no, I'm out of coffee." I looked down at my own cup and realized I'd just taken the last sip.

"Tomorrow at noon," she said as her image weakened.

"Yes," I yelled, afraid she wouldn't hear me.

Then she became a phantom, a miasma, a notion, and I was left staring at the wall of the kitchen. With her gone, I could not sit still for long. All the coffee I'd drunk was coursing through me, and because my frail system had never before known the stimulant, my hands literally shook from it. I knew sleep was out of the question, so after walking around the small rooms of the bungalow for an hour, I sat down to my fugue to see what I could do.

Immediately, I picked up the trail of where I had been headed before Saturday's mental block had set in. Everything was piercingly clear to me, and I could hear the music I was noting in various colors as if there were a tape of the piece I was creating playing as I created it. I worked like a demon, quickly, unerringly, and the ease with which the answers to the musical problems presented themselves gave me great confidence and made my decisions ingenious. Finally, around eight in the morning (I hadn't noticed the sunrise), the coffee took its toll on me, and I became violently ill. The stomach pains, the headache, were excruciating. At ten, I vomited, and that relieved the symptoms somewhat. At eleven A.M., I was at the diner, buying another four cups of coffee.

The waitress tried to interest me in breakfast, but I said I wasn't hungry. She told me I didn't look well, and I tried to laugh off her concern. When she pressed the matter, I made some surly comment to her that I can't now remember, and she understood I was interested in nothing but the coffee. I took my hoard and went directly to the beach. The temperature was milder that day, and the fresh air cleared my head. I sat in the shelter of a deep hollow amidst the dunes to block the wind, drank, and watched Anna at work, wherever she was, on her project—a large, colorful abstract drawing. After spying on her for a few minutes, I realized that the composition of the piece, its arrangement of color, presented itself to me as the melodic line of *Symphony no. 8 in B Minor*, by Franz Schubert. This amused me at first, to think that my own musical knowledge was inherent in the existence of her world, that my imagination was its essence. What was also interesting was that such a minor interest of mine, Schubert, should manifest itself. I supposed that any aspect of my life, no matter how minor, was fodder for this imaginative process. It struck me just as quickly, though, that I didn't want this to be so. I wanted her to be apart from me, her own separate entity, for without that, what would her friendship mean? I physically shook my head to rid myself of the idea. When at noon she appeared next to me in my nest among the dunes, I'd already managed to forget this worm in the apple.

We spent the morning together talking and laughing, strolling along the edge of the ocean, climbing on the rocks at the point. When the coffee ran low around three, we returned to the diner for me to get more. I asked them to make me two whole pots and just pour them into large, plastic take-out containers. The waitress said nothing but shook her head. In the time I was on my errand, Anna, in her own world, brewed another vat of it.

We met up back at my bungalow, and as evening came on, we took out our respective projects and worked together, across from each other at the kitchen table. In her presence, my musical imagination was on fire, and she admitted to me that she saw for the first time the overarching structure of her drawing and where she was headed with it. At one point, I became so immersed in the work, I reached out and picked up what I thought would be one of my crayons but instead turned out to be a violet pastel. I didn't own pastels, Anna did.

"Look," I said to her, and at that moment felt a wave of dizziness pass over me. A headache was beginning behind my eyes.

She lifted her gaze from her work and saw me holding the violet stick. We both sat quietly, in awe of its implications. Slowly, she put her hand out across the table toward me. I dropped the pastel and reached toward her. Our hands met, and I swear I could feel her fingers entangled with mine.

"What does this mean, William?" she said with a note of fear in her voice and let go of me.

As I stood up, I lost my balance and needed to support myself by clutching the back of the chair. She also stood, and as I approached her, she backed away. "No, this isn't right," she said.

"Don't worry," I whispered. "It's me." I took two wobbly steps and drew so close to her I could smell her perfume. She cringed but did not try to get away. I put my arms around her and attempted to kiss her.

"No," she cried. Then I felt the force of both her hands against my chest, and I stumbled backward onto the floor. "I don't want this. It's not real," she said and began to hurriedly gather her things.

"Wait, I'm sorry," I said. I tried to scrabble to my feet, and that's when the sum total of my lack of sleep, the gallons of caffeine, the fraying of my nerves, came together like the twining voices in a fugue and struck me in the head as if I had been kicked by a horse. My body was shaking, my vision grew hazy, and I could feel myself phasing in and out of consciousness. I managed to watch Anna turn and walk away as if passing through the living room. Somehow I got to my feet and followed her, using the furniture as support. The last thing I remember was flinging open the front door of the small house and screaming her name.

I was found the next morning, lying on the beach, unconscious. It was the old man with the white beard from the diner, who, on his daily early-morning beachcombing expedition, came across me. The police were summoned. An ambulance was called. I came to in a hospital bed the next day, the warm sun, smelling of antique rose, streaming through a window onto me.

They kept me at the small shore hospital two days for psychological observation. A psychiatrist visited me, and I managed to convince him that I'd been working too hard on a project for school. Apparently the waitress at the diner had told the police that I'd been consuming ridiculous amounts of coffee and going without sleep. Word of this had gotten back to the doctor who attended to me. When I told him it was the first time I had tried coffee and that I'd gotten carried away, he warned me to stay off it, telling me they found me in a puddle of my own vomit. "It obviously disagrees with your system. You could've choked to death when you passed out." I thanked him for his advice and promised him I'd stay well away from it in the future.

In the days I was at the hospital, I tried to process what had happened with Anna. Obviously, my bold advance had frightened her. It crossed my mind that it might be better to leave her alone in the future. The very fact that I was sure I'd made physical contact with her was, in retrospect, unsettling. I wondered if perhaps Stullin was right, and what I perceived to be a result of synesthesia was actually a psychotic hallucination. I left it an open issue in my mind as to whether I would seek her out again. One more meeting might be called for, I thought, at least to simply apologize for my mawkish behavior.

I asked the nurse if my things from the beach house had been brought to the hospital, and she told me they had. I spent the entirety of my last day there dressed and waiting to get the okay for my release. That afternoon, they brought me my belongings. I went carefully through everything, but it became obvious to me that my crayon score for the fugue was missing. Everything else was accounted for, but there was no large sheet of drawing paper. I asked the nurse, who was very kind, actually reminding me somewhat of Mrs. Brithnic, to double-check and see if everything had been brought to me. She did and told me there was nothing else. I called the Varion Island police on the pretense of thanking them and asked if they had seen the drawing. My fugue had vanished. I knew a grave depression would descend upon me soon due to its disappearance, but for the moment I was numb and slightly pleased to merely be alive.

I decided to return to my parents' house for a few days and rest up before returning to the conservatory in order to continue my studies. In the bus station near the hospital, while I was waiting, I went to the small newspaper stand in order to get a pack of gum and a paper with which to pass the time. As I perused the candy rack, my sight lighted upon something that made me feel the way Eve must have when she first saw the apple, for there was a bag of Thompson's Coffee-Flavored Hard Candy. The moment I read the words on the bag, I reached for them. There was a spark in my solar plexus, and my palms grew damp. *No Caffeine* the package read, and I was hard-pressed to believe my good fortune. I looked nervously over my shoulder while purchasing three bags of them, and when, on the bus, I tore a bag open, I did so with such violence, a handful of them scattered across the seat and into the aisle.

I arrived by cab at my parent's house and had to let myself in. Their car was gone, and I supposed they were out for the day. I hadn't seen them in some months and almost missed their presence. When night descended and they didn't return, I thought it odd but surmised they were on one of the short vacations they often took. It didn't matter. I sat at my old home base on the piano bench and sucked on coffee-flavored hard candies until I grew too weary to sit up. Then I got into my childhood bed, turned to face the wall as I always had when I was little, and fell asleep.

The next day, after breakfast, I resumed my vigil that had begun on the long bus trip home. By that afternoon my suspicions as to what had become of my fugue were confirmed. The candy did not bring as clear a view of Anna as did the ice cream, let alone the black coffee, but it was focused enough for me to follow her through her day. I was there when she submitted my crayon score as her art project for the end-of-the-semester review. How she was able to appropriate it, I have no idea. It defied logic. In the fleeting glimpses I got of the work, I tried to piece together how I'd gone about weaving the subjects and their answers. The second I would see it, the music would begin to sound for me, but I never got a good-enough look at it to sort out the complex structure of the piece. The two things I was certain of were that the fugue had been completed right up to the point where it was supposed to fall into chaos, and that Anna did quite well with her review because of it.

By late afternoon, I'd come to the end of my Thompson's candies and had but one left. Holding it in my hand, I decided it would be the last time I would conjure a vision of Anna. I came to the conclusion that her theft of my work had cancelled out my untoward advance, and we were now even, so to speak. I would leave her behind as I had before, but this time for good. With my decision made, I opened the last of the hard confections and placed it on my tongue. That dark, amber taste slowly spread through my mouth, and, as it did, a cloudy image formed and crystallized into focus. She had the cup to her mouth, and her eyes widened as she saw me seeing her.

"William," she said. "I was hoping to see you one more time."

"I'm sure," I said, trying to seem diffident, but just hearing her voice made me weak.

"Are you feeling better?" she asked. "I saw what happened to you. I was with you on the beach all that long night but could not reach you."

"My fugue," I said. "You took it."

She smiled. "It's not yours. Let's not kid ourselves; you know you are merely a projection of my synesthetic process."

"Who is a projection of whose?" I asked.

"You're nothing more than my muse," she said.

I wanted to contradict her, but I didn't have the meanness to subvert her belief in her own reality. Of course, I could have brought up the fact that she was told that figurative synesthesia was a known version of the disease. This was obviously not true. Also, there was the fact that her failed drawing, the one she'd abandoned for mine, was based on Schubert's Eighth, a product of my own knowledge working through her. How could I convince her she wasn't real? She must've seen the doubt in my eyes, because she became defensive in her attitude. "I'll not see you again," she said. "My therapist has given me a pill he says will eradicate my synesthesia. We have that here, in the true reality. It's already begun to work. I no longer hear my cigarette smoke as the sound of a faucet dripping. Green no longer tastes of lemon. The ring of the telephone doesn't feel like burlap."

This pill was the final piece of evidence. A pill to cure synesthesia? "You may be harming yourself," I said, "by taking that drug. If you cut yourself off from me, you may cease to exist. Perhaps we are meant to be together." I felt a certain panic at the idea that she would lose her special perception, and I would lose the only friend I had ever had who understood my true nature.

"Dr. Stullin says it will not harm me, and I will be like everyone else. Good-bye, William," she said and pushed the coffee cup away from her.

"Stullin," I said. "What do you mean, Stullin?"

"My therapist," she said, and although I could still see her before me, I could tell I had vanished from her view. As I continued to watch, she lowered her face into her hands and appeared to be crying. Then my candy turned from the thinnest sliver into nothing but saliva, and I swallowed. A few seconds more, and she was completely gone.

It was three in the afternoon when I put my coat on and started across town to Stullin's place. I had a million questions, and foremost was whether or not he treated a young woman named Anna. My thoughts were so taken by my last conversation with her that when I arrived in front of the doctor's walkway, I realized I had not noticed the sun go down. It was as if I had walked in my sleep and awakened at his address. The street was completely empty of people or cars, reminding me of Varion Island. I took the steps up to his front door and knocked. It was dark inside except for a light on the second floor, but the door was slightly ajar, which I thought odd, given it was the middle of the winter. Normally, I would have turned around and gone home after my third attempt to get his attention, but there was too much I needed to discuss.

I stepped inside, closing the door behind me. "Dr. Stullin," I called. There was no answer. "Doctor?" I tried again and then made my way through the foyer to the room where the tables were stacked with paper. In the meager light coming in through the window, I found a lamp and turned it on. I continued to call out as I went from room to room, turning on lights, heading for the sunroom at the back of the place where we always had our meetings. When I reached that room, I stepped inside, and my foot came down on something alive. There was a sudden screech that nearly made my heart stop, and then I saw the black-and-white cat, whose tail I had trod upon, race off into another room.

It was something of a comfort to be again in that plant-filled room. The sight of it brought back memories of it as the single safe place in the world when I was younger. Oddly enough, there was a cigarette going in the ashtray on the table between the two chairs that faced each other. Lying next to it, opened to the middle and turned down on its pages, was a copy of *The Centrifugal Rickshaw Dancer*. I'd have preferred to see a ghost to that book. The sight of it chilled me. I sat down in my old seat and watched the smoke from the cigarette twirl up toward the glass panes. Almost instantly, a great weariness seized me, and I closed my eyes.

That was days ago. When I found the next morning I could not open the doors to leave, that I could not even break the glass in order to crawl out, it became clear to me what was happening. At first I was frantic, but then a certain calm descended upon me, and I learned to accept my fate. Those stacks of paper in that room on the way to the sunroom—each sheet held a beautiful pencil drawing. I explored the upstairs, and there, on the second floor, found a piano and the sheet music for Bach's *Grosse Fugue*. There was a black-and-white photograph of Mrs. Brithnic in the upstairs hallway and one of my parents standing with Anna as a child.

That hallway, those rooms, are gone, vanished. Another room has disappeared each day I have been trapped here. I sit in Stullin's chair now, in the only room still remaining (this one will be gone before tonight), and compose this tale—in a way, my fugue. The black-and-white cat sits across from me, having fled from the dissipation of the house as it closes in around us. Outside, the garden, the trees, the sky, have all lost their color and now appear as if rendered in graphite—wonderfully shaded to give them an appearance of weight and depth. So too with the room around us: the floor, the glass panels, the chairs, the plants, even the cat's tail and my shoes and legs have lost their life and become the shaded grey of a sketch. I imagine Anna will soon be free of her condition. As for me, who always believed himself to be unwanted, unloved, misunderstood, I will surpass being a mere artist and become instead a work of art that will endure. The cat meows loudly, and I feel the sound as a hand upon my shoulder.

Bumpship
Susan Mosser

Exclusion Rights for minors? You heard that in some bar on Mech24, am I right? Because I know my sector. I also know you didn't tell them you were a reporter. No, I understand completely, but good luck if that's the story you're after. A crew on refit leave may give the locals an earful, but they are not about to mouth off on the job. The bottom line on all that righteous indignation is that nobody wants a Perm stamp on their next layoff notice.

Compassion? Of course I have compassion for Indies. I wasn't always a Manager. I put in my time on the Suit Team like everybody else. I have flown many a hoverbird to pop the bubble, and I have seen the stampede, hundreds of times, Indies pouring out of a compound, trampling each other to get into that bumpship. But my compassion is not reserved for the children. Or the greys, or the genefreaks, or...

What?

Well, what are they called these days?

Fine. Muties. Greys or muties. You won't quote me on that, right?

Good. I expect you've been doing this long enough to know the difference between official statements and things I say only to help you understand the business before you set the link.

You did? Oh. Do I look…I thought this was sort of a preliminary thing.

Ah, working copy. Good. So.

Right. Exclusion of minor assets. No. I do not support the idea. Look, they have ants where you come from?

Hive crawlers? Good enough. You know what they look like when you stir them up. All kids do that. Well, that's what it looks like when we bump a small compound like the one you're about to see, like ants boiling out of a broad shiny anthill, each with an identical drive to survive, an identical opportunity to succeed. Those bumpship doors are open to all. There is no finer expression of access equality than that. So no, I do not believe that children under ten should be excluded from the Repayment Order. Assets are assets. And Indies know that. They understand market democracy better than anybody. Next time you hear a lot of radical reform talk around this business, you ask some pertinent personal questions. Ninety-nine percent of the time, you'll find yourself looking at a volunteer, not somebody with loved ones on the line.

That surprises you? Let me tell you something about volunteers. No man or woman with any marketability anywhere else in the galaxy would sign on as a bumper for a bunk and a stimsock and three mocks a day. They're losers, bottom line, begging for a job they claim to despise. We hire the dregs who volunteer because our paid labor quota is thirty-five percent. Otherwise, I would never hire a single volly. Nothing but a headache.

Of course I believe in paid labor. Every citizen has the right to improve his quality of life. But you know what? In my sixty-five years on the job, I have seen maybe half a dozen bumpers actually make that new start they all claim to want. Volunteers don't bank their credit and get out. They spend it on shipboard liberty, on chemgems and stim shows. That pay squirts straight back to ACorp through the recport franchises in the bunks so fast those electrons in Accounting must slam into themselves coming and going. No, give me a TI any day. Your indentured worker knows why he's here, and so does Management. No hard luck stories, because we all know the story. No whining that it's a dirty job, because he knows how lucky he is to get a slot at all. Your typical TI, he hates every minute of every day in this business, and he hates my guts, because to him I am Atmospherics Corporation. But he does his job, and does it well, because he knows that every A-credit he earns is keeping his loved ones back on the rock breathing sweet ACorp air. I have nothing but the utmost respect for my TI's.

Term of Indenture, that's right. If you ask me, this business should be staffed purely on an atmocredit basis, especially when you consider how many evictees are waiting for slots. I'm all for fair competition, but the MetaMerger Act needs some serious refit, and the first thing to go should be that One-Third clause. Sometimes I think those macromanagers in the hubworlds have their heads up each other's butts.

No, definitely not a quote there! Of course, the ACorp fleet has nothing to hide, and neither do I. You wouldn't be here to watch us work, if we did. Well, let me call for the ExO, and we'll get you suited up for...

Excuse me?

I must say, I don't see what that has to do with your story.

Well, yes. A very long time ago, I was a volunteer. Now I'm a Manager.

Yes. The first non-Exec Sector Manager in ACorp.

I don't think of it as unusual. In fact, there are more of us all the time. Executive Class is a custom, not a requirement.

Retirement? Me? Not for years yet.

No, I've got more comcredits than I can use. One of the advantages of this work. I never manage more than a few days exleave, and I don't spend onboard.

Right. No chemgems. How did you know that?

No, can't tolerate them. Metabolic anomaly, they call it. One hit and I'm sick as a dog. But I don't miss it. I'm lucky to get sleeptime, never mind rectime.

Exleave? Bella's World. Recs, sex, and scenery. Biodyne foliage. Original volcanics. Quartz beaches on a saline ocean. I don't get there much, but one of these days…

Yeah, a Boondocker rock. Nothing wrong with that. If this is your first time in the Boondocks, you should let me recommend a few choice spots.

Excuse me?

What does it matter why I signed on?

Background. Sure. Well, I'm from a compound myself, actually.

Yeah, that's right: Boondocker, born and bred. My parents were on an original lease.

No, it's been derelict for a long time.

Well, sure, it had a name, but I don't see why…

Okay. Okay. Ceugant. They called it Ceugant.

Yes, "the" Ceugant. No, not xeno. Terran. Gaelic, it's called. Sorcerers and fairy cities. Like a herostim. My father's idea.

A scholar. Ancient Terran languages, so I guess that made him technically a linguist, but nothing useful. All low-market.

My mother? A bioengineer. A fine scientist.

No, they're both dead.

Yes. Yes, they died on Ceugant. Look, where are you going with this?

No, it wasn't an accident.

You know what? Turn that thing off. We're finished here. I'm sure hubnubs don't plug into "Look Now" just to hear some docker's life story.

Really.

Well, if you already scanned my bio—and I'd like to know who gave you access to that—then you know what happened to my parents on Ceugant, so what is your point here?

Human interest. Right.

You know what? I really don't have time for this. So if you'll excuse me...

Of course I have nothing to be ashamed of. You don't have to tell me that.

Abbie Wilson set this up? Are you referring to Executive Member Abelarde Wilson?

Oh, well, never mind then. If a Voting Member says talk, I talk. I don't ask how someone like Executive Member Wilson even gets to know my name, I just talk. So I get it now. Let me guess: "Orphan Boondocker Survives Holocaust to become Bumpship Manager."

Hostile? Not at all. As I told you before, I've seen your show. Actually, it's time for you to suit up, so if you'll excuse me, I'm overdue on a multilink. My first officer will escort you to the boarding area to join the Suit Team, and I'm sure you'll get some great digivid of the eviction. You have my best wishes for the remainder of your time aboard.

No, I'm afraid I won't reconsider. Good day.

I'm glad you understand my position, and I hope you

realize that my apology is a sincere one. We're working just as fast as we can to set up another bump for you, one that will be more representative of our usual routine. I know we promised it by this afternoon, but as I explained to Member Wilson, my crew and I have been working under tremendous time constraints for eighteen months now. The collapse in the boron market in this sector has created something of a localized recession, which has, of course, resulted in a higher-than-average level of evictions.

Excuse me?

I am speaking naturally.

Well, this is how I naturally sound when I haven't slept in forty-six hours and my career is on the line.

Because of thirteen thousand Indies? Don't be ridiculous.

Look, what do you expect me to say? I lost some very expensive ACorp hardware and four crew members, not to mention the thirteen thousand Indies, in what should have been a routine bump, which you already know, of course, because you were downside linking the whole thing for the hub worlds.

Oh, I'm not angry. I'm amazed. My Suit Team is still downside flying cleanup sweeps in blast turbulence, when I have to leave the bridge for a personal vid from Executive Member Wilson. I'm thinking, "But how could she know already? And why would she call about it?" I get to my cube for my second-ever eyes-only message from a Voting Member to find that said Member has set a vidlink just to watch me squirm while she refashions my anatomy. She doesn't even know about the Indies or the dome explosion. "You will file the proper reports, I assume," is all she says about that. No, she has called me away from emergency cleanup operations to spend her million-credit-per-minute Member time to chew me a new one about dismissing her nephew the reporter. And oh yes, Aunt Abbie sends her love.

I get the point, okay? I surrender! If I had any balls at all, I would have shown them to Aunt Abbie and then dumped your butt on some slowbarge rock to find your own way back to a squirtport. But I didn't, so let's get on with this.

Because I have sixty-five spotless years in this business, that's why not. Because I'm sixty years too old to start over and ten years too young to retire. I will therefore survive the next few hours you are in my sector and get on with my work, because that is what all real Boondockers do best. Survive. Do you hubnubs even know what survival is? You huddle on your permaterra planets where the water flows and the dirt sticks to the rock and air is just something the bioforms make for free. How many centuries has it been since your home planet was pulled off the ACorp tit? Do you even know? Ancient history, right? Well, this is the Boondocks, nephew, and ancient history is now. You think Indies buy a lease on some wasted ball of rock expecting to puke their lungs out in five years? Hell, no. They expect to struggle and survive.

Yeah, I know you want to hear about my parents. Fine. Let's get this over with. Ask your damn questions.

My father. That's the place to start, alright. Not a practical man, my father. What good is Terran history to anybody, anyway? Why look back at a huge failure when you need to focus on survival right now? He meant well. I know that. People liked him. He was probably a good man. But he was a fool. They all were. That's why it ended the way it did.

No, my mother was a good scientist, but she had no sense of reality where my father was concerned. I don't think she ever would have joined the Ceugant

group on her own. She was too practical. It was my
father and his colleagues who started the project. They
had some vision of an entire world of academics,
deadart, all the leftovers. Low-markets and spot
farmers. Dreamers. A Boondock rock full of dreamers.

"An ethical democracy, grounded in simplicity."
That's it. God, where did you dig that up?

It's hard to believe they were that naive, isn't it?
But they were one of the original private planetary
charters. Nobody knew how low the success rate
would turn out to be. And of course the Third Market
War started the year after they bought the lease. By
the time they knew they were failing, I guess there
was no loose capital anywhere. That probably didn't
really matter. Nobody would have invested in an obvious disaster like Ceugant.

My mother? A fine scientist, like I said. She gave
up a Head of Research position with Bio Corporation
to go to Ceugant with my father and his philosopher
friends. She was one of the only high-markets in the
group. That was the grand plan, of course: The
dreamers would create utopia, and the bioengineers
would keep the venture solvent. My mother owned
two private patents, so she recruited a team, the group
financed a bioplant, and that was the economic basis
for their new planet.

Unbelievable, isn't it? One export industry to cover
the offrock debits for a whole compound. I don't
know what they thought they were doing, really. They
couldn't afford a semi-breathable; who could? They
couldn't afford both water and soil, so they settled
for soil. They leased a minimum A-dome and basic
water service. No lakes or rivers, just a holding pond
in the center of the compound. Not bad planning.
Room for expansion without the killer soil costs for
future generations of Ceuganters. Except that the

biosamples were faked up. The movers lifted off, the prefabs unfolded, the celebration calmed down, the biovats started perking, and nothing grew.

You're right. That's not entirely accurate. My mother's patented bios didn't grow. Ceugant's indigenous uncells, which had been carefully removed from the soil samples, grew like crazy and crowded out the paying customers. It took months to figure out what was wrong, because they weren't looking for uncells, and you don't find something that small unless you're looking for it, and with the right equipment. She didn't have the right equipment because they had planned everything to the last microcredit, sheer necessities only for the first five years. Her mid-range steriseals were useless. Upgrade, right? Wrong. A very expensive soil planet lease and a large bioplant, setup fees, five years' supplies—nothing left for hyper-grade equipment that would have cost almost as much as another planet lease.

Yes, but this was almost ninety years ago. Deregulation had been in effect for less than a decade. Private lease colonization was brand new, and there was no history to learn from because people like my parents were still out there making the history. These compounds we bump today have only themselves to blame. The new lease laws are very kind to the Indies.

Well, no, there are no asset exclusions for children or anyone else, but by the time we come in to actually force the Indies to leave the rock, they have had more than enough time to make payment arrangements. There's no excuse for the criminal anarchy you saw yesterday. We can't let Indies destroy themselves to abandon their debts. Business would come to a halt.

Indentures? No, it's Nonrecoverable Debts: "ND's." Yeah, lots of people make that mistake.

Excuse me?

Bridge between worlds.

Yes, okay, I was the first human born on Ceugant and yes, my native name meant "bridge between the worlds." I want to know where you're getting all this stuff. Look, I've told you about my parents. Now let's get on to something else.

No. Absolutely not. Not even for Executive Member Wilson. My name is my own business. My mother always made a big thing out of that, my being the first Ceuganter, said my naming ceremony was the biggest party she'd ever seen. Probably my mother was a dreamer, too, and just seemed practical to me in comparison to my father. I don't know. Anyway…

I'm fine. Don't be ridiculous. You wanted human misery to shovel, here it is.

Forget I said that. You're just doing your job, right?

Oh, I'm sure it's a big story. I'm sure that trillions of hubnub sockers are holding their collective breath over a few billion struggling Boondockers. You'll excuse me if I choose not to actually believe that.

I see. Sure. Sure, let's get on with it. Why not? It's not hard to figure out what happened after the vats soured, is it? Five years' worth of supplies eked out to last nine, everybody scrambling and begging and borrowing to keep the water and air running as long as they could. The usual routine. My mother tried to sell her patents, and I think she did sell one. I don't remember for sure. I was too young through most of it to really understand what was going on. A lot of what I know I learned later.

What? Well, they tried that. They filed suit to get the lease annulled for fraud, but this was pre-PCorp. Planet development was scattered all over the place. The holding company was some private development group that went bankrupt and split with the cash long before my parents and their friends realized they'd been swindled. Ten years' lease in advance, and they couldn't get any of it back. Central Court eventually ruled that the Ceugant compound had first claim to the planet for triple the term of the lease, ninety years, even if somebody actually bought the rock for unpaid fees and taxes—which nobody ever did, not even PCorp, not under those restrictions and not with those uncells waiting. I guess the Court thought it had been generous and fair. Maybe judges just don't understand biovats. I don't know. I do know that it was a death sentence for the compound. It took almost five years to get the ruling, and only about a third of the group managed to get relatives to sponsor them back to the hub after the trial. Everybody else just hung on to that ball of rock and grew macrofood from its otherwise poisonous dirt and tried to market anything they could to pump comcredits for the air and water. No indentured atmocredits in those days. No options.

That's why there's no excuse for those thirteen thousand dead Indies. They've known for more than three years that their venture was a failure. They knew the credits would run out, the leases would go unpaid, and the time for TI contracts would arrive. ACorp isn't going to keep those atmopods charged for free, now is it? And why should it? And why should H2O spend fuel and manhours and equipment wear to haul ice to a compound that doesn't pay for it? The last two years on Ceugant, we had no water delivery at all.

Hard to believe? It was a hard way to live, let me tell you. But we owed on two deliveries, the Notice came, there were no credits to cover it, and after that no more ice.

How? We recycled everything, every drop of everything, but by the time ACorp finally sent the Notice for the air, we were sucking mud out of the reservoir. We would have died of thirst, anyway, even if they hadn't popped the dome.

Of course I don't blame the Corporations for what happened. Business is business, and market democracy is a natural system of equality. I know that. I see that very clearly. Nobody forced my parents to go to Ceugant. They could have stayed in the hub. Sure, the permaterras are overstuffed ratholes, but the bad air is free and the foul water is right there on the planet. No offense intended, of course, to hubrats like yourself.

Right, you don't really need opinions. You need gory details. Sure. You did your research, right? You probably know more than I do about what happened. Eighty years ago, ACorp was just beginning to deal with the eviction problem. Aunt Abbie and the Board weren't prepared for the astronomical failure rate of private lease compounds. The Corporation didn't even have its own fleet yet. The first bumps were contracted out on a piecework basis to private eviction companies. Hell, you could hardly call them companies. Spacer scum who bumped compounds between narcgem runs.

That's who showed up on Ceugant to execute the ACorp Notice. First they blasted the atmospheric pods, then they landed to talk things over. They didn't just pop the bubble the way we do; they blasted the pods with pyros. Obviously, it was their first and last ACorp contract.

The air was really stale by then, but still breathable. I remember that, actually, because we were all on exertion limitations and had been for months. When you're a kid, that's a big thing in your life: no running, no shouting. You know what I'm talking about? The air was still breathable, but it wouldn't have stayed that way for long once the containment field was opened.

The ExO didn't explain this to you?

Well, alright, depending upon the ambient atmosphere, and of course the size of the compound, it can take two or three standard days for a bubble to dissipate. It's not a complete vacuum on these rocks, you understand. Even Ceugant had an atmosphere. It just wasn't something a human body could breathe. We tell the Indies they only have an hour after the pop to get into the ship because it gets them moving. They've had plenty of time to sit around before we get there.

Not three days on Ceugant, no. Not with those pyros sucking air. They don't snuff out like a candle; they use sevalium, and it cycles through the gases and keeps burning till there's nothing left. No slow choke on Ceugant. Fast choke, and a field implosion. The contract was to lift off the Indies. That's the whole point of bumping, right? Get the deadbeats out of the way to make room for new compounders with new credits. Nothing wrong with that. Just business. Except these were not businessmen. These were ignorant space scum with an old rebuilt trash can big enough for a large load of narcgems or about eighty people, whichever came first.

No. No, I'm fine. Just let me get a sip of water.

Yes, I know this is what people will really want to hear about. I understand that. This is the part they tune in for. This is the part...

Seven hundred and sixty-two men, women, and children are standing out on the common grounds with their little bundles of personal items, waiting for the bumpship. Can you see that? They have no intention of resisting the boarding order. Then suddenly they have thirty minutes to decide which few dozen of them are going to drop those bundles, cram into a cargo hold, and survive.

So how do Retromoralists pass out death sentences when there is no time for debate? They draw lots, of course. Handmade slips of plazlite in an empty foamfab carton. Leave it up to the gods. Man, woman, child; high-market, low-market, no-market: everybody had an equal share on Ceugant, and it didn't occur to them to change that just because the world had suddenly come to an end. And who was the logical, even mytho-logical, choice to draw the little slips of plaz out of the box? Why, the first official Ceuganter, of course. Symbolic. It's my father, all over.

What?

I don't know if it was his idea. I just know it was his kind of idea. I don't remember much about that day, really.

My mother? She was very quiet. Everyone was. Lots of crying, of course, but nothing hysterical, not until the very end. It was quiet, and my mother didn't cry. I remember that. I pulled eighty-seven slips out of the box, one by one, and she read the names. Her voice was very calm, very clear. The pyros were sucking a breeze by then, and there was a lock of hair blowing across her cheek. She kept tucking it behind her ear, but each time she reached for a name, it scattered again. She read the whims of the gods in her beautiful voice, and then she passed each name to my father, who read it and passed it on to the man next to him, so that each name would be read and re-read to guard against error. No one really thought my mother would lie or make a mistake; it was just the way they always did things.

Is something wrong?

Of course not. How silly of me. You're a professional, right? You've seen it all, got it all on digi. What did you call the disaster? "Sludgy!"

Eavesdropping? Not at all. I wouldn't intrude upon your privacy. But this is off the sludgy subject, isn't it? I said my mother didn't cry. That's not entirely accurate. Name number eighty-two was my own. She tucked her hair behind her ear, unfolded the scrap of plaz and without a sound passed the slip to my father, who read out my name, and passed the slip on. My mother's cheeks were wet after that. She was crying, and I said, "I'm sorry, Mom. I didn't mean to draw my own name, honest."

"Five more," she said then. "You still have five more names to choose. You have to hurry." Her voice was low, a growl almost, and there was a look in her eyes that scared the hell out of me. I was only nine years old, after all, and you have to understand that my mother was always the practical one, always calm. She kept things going by making a big joke out of everything, no matter how awful it was. There she stood, the wisecracking queen of the universe, with tears pouring down her face and a stare that burned right down into my gut, and all of a sudden I got it. I was young, but in that moment I suddenly understood that what I was pulling from that box was life, and what I was leaving in it was death. I knew it because my mother was staring at me like a woman who believed in miracles, a woman who was trying to wring a miracle right up out of my guts and into her hand.

"Five more," she said. Whispered, really. "Please. That's all you have to do, and then it's finished."

For the first time, at number eighty-three, I reached down into that soft nest of plaz and knew that every slip I chose was a person, and every slip I dropped was gone for good. It took me a long time to pull the next slip. Forever. When I did, I pinched a miracle out of that foamfab carton. When she opened that slip of paper and read her own name, my mother seemed calm again. My heart started slamming in my chest, and I shoved my hand into that box with the pure faith of a brand-new true believer. My mother's voice didn't waver when number eighty-four was the girl who lived next door to us, and number eighty-five was an elderly linguist friend of my father's who for the past sixty years had been compiling a dictionary of a single dead Argalean dialect, and number eighty-six was the second son of a plaz sculptor who was famous for making the longest speeches at every meeting, and number eighty-seven was a young engineer from her bioproject team, and none of them were my father.

"Pull another one," my mother said immediately. "I'm sorry, but you need to pull another one." And I did it. I pulled another slip. Everyone there knew why, everyone but me. Nobody challenged her. They had all agreed to abide by whatever came out of that box, and on Ceugant that kind of agreement had force of law, but nobody said a word to my mother.

I don't remember whose name it was. I do remember my mother turning to me and saying, "You'll be alright. You're smart and you're strong," and then I understood what everyone else already knew, and when she tried to put her arms around me, I hit her as hard as I could and ran. I tried to hide somewhere, I don't remember where, but she came after me.

What? No, all by herself. I don't know where my father was. I never saw him again. In the crowd, I guess.

Sorry. I'm just...what did you say?

Running. I don't remember anything else, really. Running across a soyallfield, maybe, with my mother, or her running, and dragging me while I tried to get away. There were bruises on my arms later, and scratches. In the ship. She was very smart, my mother, a fine scientist.

Did I already say that? She was. Smart enough to know that time was very short.

The other eighty-six had gone straight to the cargo hold, and they all should have lifted off long before we got there, but the space scum were lounging around in breathers, watching the fireworks. They were too stupid to understand what they had done with those pyros. But my mother knew.

My own memories. Right.

I remember her dragging me out of some dark place, shouting about a field implosion. I remember it hurt my chest to run, and my mother sounded like she was strangling, and every time I stumbled and fell, she dragged me up and kept on running, making terrible sounds in her throat. I remember that; but I don't remember getting to the ship. I never have re-membered it. Maybe I passed out. They told me later that my mother picked me up in her arms and carried me up the ramp, that she threw me into the hold and screamed at the spacers to close the hatch, and that she kept on screaming at them until they finally under-stood they were about to be grounded forever and closed it. I don't know if that's true. Maybe I've added details in my mind. I don't see how she could scream when I remember her being so out of breath. It's just...not logical.

I'm sorry. Did you say something?

No. No, I don't remember anything else.

Training? Yes, that's right. A few months later. ACorp tested us. I think there were eight kids in our refugee group. I scored highest, and I had passed my tenth birthday by then, so they hired me. I started training right there on Refuge i.

The other kids? I don't know. They moved me into the Corporate barracks. I don't know what happened to the rest of them.

No. No, I don't ever wonder.

No, I wouldn't consider going back to Ceugant with a cam crew. What kind of question…?

Turn that thing off.

I mean it. Interview over.

Turn it off, Nephew, or it's going out the waste lock. And you with it.

This is still my ship.

Yes, much better. Thank you. I hope dinner was satisfactory? I'm sorry I didn't join you, but I couldn't get off the bridge. All quiet at last, though, and I did want to stop by and let you know that everything is set for tomorrow's bump. We'll be underway again in another hour or so. You should be able to get all the digi you need for your story.

Yes, I suppose I have time for a quick nightcap, especially since you've already gone to the trouble to order mine.

Because no one else on board drinks these.

Bella's, that's right.

No apology necessary. We were both just doing our jobs. I'm sure you understand that it is sometimes difficult to discuss such matters with those outside the industry.

Yes, it is an important part of history. The Ceugant Incident. One of many that led to the Humane Eviction Act. You can see now why I have no patience with people who whine about Exclusion Rights. And why I don't hold ACorp responsible for the suicide of those thirteen thousand Indies. Those people had options. That compound has had more than a year to write enough indenture contracts to keep it going. A compound that size would take, what, sixty-five hundred? Maybe seventy-five? Only seventy-five hundred indents to pay the debt and keep the pods charged for the full seventy-year TI.

Term of Indenture, yeah. My point is, even if they were irresponsible enough to refuse indenture contracts, they still had options. A clean, roomy bumpship had been sitting on that rock for three days. In three days, those people could have moved their entire compound into that ship, and right now they'd be on their way to a refuge world with salvage credits toward the debt besides. I know the refuge worlds are overcrowded, but at least there's air and water and food—at no charge, mind you, beyond the basic seventy percent time obligation. And we all know the Alpha Corporations are committed to increasing off-planet indenture opportunities for bona fide refugees.

Yes, I know. I've heard people use the words "slave labor," too, but that just shows their ignorance. Even on the refuge worlds, a large group can pay off a debt if they all work together over time, and what better motivator than the chance to help your descendants qualify for volunteer status again someday? You have to work for what you want; you have to be a responsible citizen. Nobody gets a free ride. That is the basic fairness of market democracy.

No, I have no sympathy for those people. That rock didn't belong to them, those pods didn't belong to them, and that bumpship sure didn't belong to them. Symbolic protests, my ass. Wanton destruction of property is what it is. A bunch of dead Boondockers who didn't have the decency to work off their debt. Another year or two of these "protests" and the Humane Eviction Act will be a thing of the past. When

Central Court gets one good look at skyrocketing hardware costs from sabotage, they will scrap the HEA without a second glance. They're moving toward a more balanced approach, anyway. The Corporations need more protection. They are the ones with the capital at risk, after all.

Forced indenture in lieu of eviction? I may have heard something about that.

Yes, okay. EV65709. Yes. The All-Corp Petition for Forced Indenture in Lieu of Eviction. I'm surprised you've even heard of it, much less read it. What happened to our sealed legislative process?

Ah, unidentified source. Of course. Well, if you've read it, you know it's fair. There's a lot of expense in shipping and warehousing evictees, and then there are the costs of administering the refuge world manufacturing operations. In the long run it makes much more sense for future Indies to stay on their rocks and bear all costs of their debt through forced indenture. Let them pay for their own air and water while they work off their debts. It's what we should have been doing all along. It's not true that the debts will never be paid off, just that it will take longer than one generation. A one hundred and forty-year TI instead of seventy. That's not impossible to deal with. And there's nothing to keep Indies from creating their own wealth and paying off early. No one is stopping them from working hard and being creative on their own time. I'm not saying deprive them of equal opportunity, but you can't let people just squander someone else's capital. That's no better than stealing.

Absolutely not. In my opinion, what you saw today is not galactic politics. Those deadbeats can call themselves "Ceuganters" if they want to, but they were just looking for a free ride. When they realized they weren't going to get it, they destroyed an ACorp asset worth a hundred of their scraggly compounds. What did they think we'd do, reset the containment field after they blew up the bumpship? Violate the law just for them? It says right in the Notice that once the bubble is popped, it stays popped. Period. Central Court says it's legal, the clause is always in the lease, and the Notice restates it plain as dayside. Refusal to board a bumpship is legally a suicide, which means your debts are transferred to your next of kin. Everybody knows that, so what did they think they were accomplishing? And refusal to board minors in your custody is first-degree murder. The Corporations are not liable for that kind of insanity. There is no excuse for refusing to board a bumpship. No excuse at all. It's the law, and people who break the law are criminals. Period.

I have no sympathy for those people.

Only Partly Here
Lucius Shepard

There are legends in the pit. Phantoms and apparitions. The men who work at Ground Zero joke about them, but their laughter is nervous and wired. Bobby doesn't believe the stories, yet he's prepared to believe something weird might happen. The place feels so empty. Like even the ghosts are gone. All that sudden vacancy, who knows what might have entered in. Two nights ago on the graveyard shift, some guy claimed he saw a faceless figure wearing a black spiky headdress standing near the pit wall. The job breaks everybody down. Marriages are falling apart. People keep losing it one way or another. Fights, freak-outs, fits of weeping. It's the smell of burning metal that seeps up from the earth, the ceremonial stillness of the workers after they uncover a body, the whispers that come when there is no wind. It's the things you find. The week before, scraping at the rubble with a hoe, like an archaeologist investigating a buried temple, Bobby spotted a woman's shoe sticking up out of the ground. A perfect shoe, so pretty and sleek and lustrous. Covered in blue silk. Then he reached for it and realized that it wasn't stuck—it was only half a shoe with delicate scorching along the ripped edge. Now sometimes when he closes his eyes he sees the shoe. He's glad he isn't married. He doesn't think he has much to bring to a relationship.

That evening Bobby's taking his dinner break, perched on a girder at the edge of the pit along with Mazurek and Pineo, when they switch on the lights. They all hate how the pit looks in the lights. It's an outtake from *The X-Files*—the excavation of an alien ship under hot white lamps smoking from the cold; the shard left from the framework of the north tower glittering silver and strange, like the wreckage of a cosmic machine. The three men remain silent for a bit, then Mazurek goes back to bitching about Jason Giambi signing with the Yankees. You catch the interview he did with Werner Wolf? He's a moron! First time the crowd gets on him, it's gonna be like when you yell at a dog. The guy's gonna fucking crumble. Pineo disagrees, and Mazurek asks Bobby what he thinks.

"Bobby don't give a shit about baseball," says Pineo. "My boy's a Jets fan."

Mazurek, a thick-necked, fiftyish man whose face appears to be fashioned of interlocking squares of pale muscle, says, "The Jets...fuck!"

"They're play-off bound," says Bobby cheerfully.

Mazurek crumples the wax paper his sandwich was folded in. "They gonna drop dead in the first round like always."

"It's more interesting than being a Yankee fan," says Bobby. "The Yankees are too corporate to be interesting."

"'Too corporate to be interesting'? Mazurek stares. "You really are a geek, y'know that?"

"That's me. The geek.

"Whyn't you go the fuck back to school, boy? Fuck you doing here, anyway?"

"Take it easy, Carl! Chill!" Pineo—nervous, thin,

lively, curly black hair spilling from beneath his hard hat—puts a hand on Mazurek's arm, and Mazurek knocks it aside. Anger tightens his leathery skin; the creases in his neck show white. "What's it with you? You taking notes for your fucking thesis?" he asks Bobby. "Playing tourist?"

Bobby looks down at the apple in his hand—it seems too shiny to be edible. "Just cleaning up is all. You know."

Mazurek's eyes dart to the side, then he lowers his head and gives it a savage shake. "Okay," he says in a subdued voice. "Yeah...fuck. Okay.

Midnight, after the shift ends, they walk over to the Blue Lady. Bobby doesn't altogether understand why the three of them continue to hang out there. Maybe because they once went to the bar after work and it felt pretty good, so they return every night in hopes of having it feel that good again. You can't head straight home; you have to decompress. Mazurek's wife gives him constant shit about the practice—she calls the bar and screams over the phone. Pineo just split with his girlfriend. The guy with whom Bobby shares an apartment grins when he sees him, but the grin is anxious—like he's afraid Bobby is bringing back some contagion from the pit. Which maybe he is. The first time he went to Ground Zero, he came home with a cough and a touch of fever, and he recalls thinking that the place was responsible. Now, though, either he's immune or else he's sick all the time and doesn't notice.

Two hookers at a table by the door check them out as they enter, then go back to reading the Post. Roman the barman, gray-haired and thick-waisted, orders his face into respectful lines, says, "Hey, guys!," and sets them up with beers and shots. When they started coming in he treated them with almost religious deference until Mazurek yelled at him, saying he didn't want to hear that hero crap while he was trying to unwind—he got enough of it from the fuckass jocks and movie stars who visit Ground Zero to have their pictures taken. Though angry, he was far more articulate than usual in his demand for normal treatment, and this caused Bobby to speculate that if Mazurek were transported thousands of miles from the pit and not just a few blocks, his IQ would increase exponentially.

The slim brunette in the business suit is down at the end of the bar again, sitting beneath the blue neon silhouette of a dancing woman. She's been coming in every night for about a week. Late twenties. Hair styled short, an expensive kind of punky look. Fashion model hair. Eyebrows thick and slanted, like *accents grave*. Sharp-featured, on the brittle side of pretty, or maybe she's not that pretty, maybe she is so well-dressed, her make-up done so skillfully, that the effect is of a businesslike prettiness, of prettiness reined in by the magic of brush and multiple applicators, and beneath this artwork she is, in actuality, rather plain. Nice body, though. Trim and well-tended. She wears the same expression of stony neutrality that Bobby sees every morning on the faces of the women who charge up from under the earth, disgorged from the D train, prepared to resist Manhattan for another day. Guys will approach her, assuming she's a hooker doing a kind of Hitler office bitch thing in order to attract men searching for a woman they can use and abuse as a surrogate for one who makes their life hell every day from nine to five, and she will say something to them and they will immediately walk away. Bobby and Pineo always try to guess what she says. That night, after a couple of shots, Bobby goes over and sits beside her. She smells expensive. Her perfume like the essence of some exotic flower or fruit he's only seen in magazine pictures.

"I've just been to a funeral," she says wearily, staring into her drink. "So, please.... Okay?"

"That what you tell everybody?" he asks. "All the guys who hit on you?"

A fretful line cuts her brow. "Please!"

"No, really. I'll go. All I want to know...that what you always say?"

She makes no response.

"It is," he says. "Isn't it?"

"It's not entirely a lie." Her eyes are spooky, the dark rims of the pale irises extraordinarily well-defined. "It's intended as a lie, but it's true in a way."

"But that's what you say, right? To everybody?"

"This is why you came over? You're not hitting on me?"

"No, I...I mean, maybe...I thought.... "

"So what you're saying, you weren't intending to hit on me. You wanted to know what I say to men when they come over. But now you're not certain of your intent? Maybe you were deceiving yourself as to your motives? Or maybe now you sense I might be receptive, you'll take the opportunity to hit on me, though that wasn't your initial intent. Does that about sum it up?"

"I suppose," he says.

She gives him a cautious look. "Could you be brilliant? Could your clumsy delivery be designed to engage me?"

"I'll go away, okay? But that's what you said to them, right?"

She points to the barman, who's talking to Mazurek. "Roman tells me you work at Ground Zero."

The question unsettles Bobby, leads him to suspect

that she's a disaster groupie, looking for a taste of the pit, but he says, "Yeah."

"It's really…" She does a little shivery shrug. "Strange."

"Strange. I guess that covers it."

"That's not what I wanted to say. I can't think of the right word to describe what it does to me."

"You been down in it?

"No, I can't get any closer than here. I just can't. But…" She makes a swirling gesture with her fingers. "You can feel it here. You might not notice, because you're down there all the time. That's why I come here. Everybody's going on with their lives, but I'm not ready. I need to feel it. To understand it. You're taking it away piece by piece, but the more you take away, it's like you're uncovering something else."

"Y'know, I don't want to think about this now." He gets to his feet. "But I guess I know why you want to."

"Probably it's fucked up of me, huh?

"Yeah, probably," says Bobby, and walks away.

"She's still looking at you, man," Pineo says as Bobby settles beside him. "What you doing back here? You could be fucking that."

"She's a freak," Bobby tells him.

"So she's a freak! Even better!" Pineo turns to the other two men. "You believe this asshole? He could be fucking that bitch over there, yet here he sits."

Affecting a superior smile, Roman says, "You don't fuck them, pal. They fuck *you*."

He nudges Mazurek's arm as though seeking confirmation from a peer, a man of experience like himself, and Mazurek, gazing at his grungy reflection in the mirror behind the bar, says distractedly, weakly, "I could use another shot."

The following afternoon Bobby unearths a disk of

hard black rubber from beneath some cement debris. It's four inches across, thicker at the center than at the edges, shaped like a little UFO. Try as he might, he can think of no possible purpose it might serve, and he wonders if it had something to do with the fall of the towers. Perhaps there is a black seed like this at the heart of every disaster. He shows it to Pineo, asks his opinion, and Pineo, as expected, says, "Fuck I don't know. Part of a machine." Bobby knows Pineo is right. The disk is a widget, one of those undistinguished yet indispensable objects without which elevators will not rise or refrigerators will not cool; but there are no marks on it, no holes or grooves to indicate that it fits inside a machine. He imagines it whirling inside a cone of blue radiance, registering some inexplicable process.

He thinks about the disk all evening, assigning it various values. It is the irreducible distillate of the event, a perfectly formed residue. It is a wicked sacred object that belonged to a financier, now deceased, and its ritual function is understood by only three other men on the planet. It is a beacon left by time traveling tourists that allows them to home in on the exact place and moment of the terrorist attack. It is the petrified eye of God. He intends to take the disk back to his apartment and put it next to the half-shoe and all the rest of the items he has collected in the pit. But that night when he enters the Blue Lady and sees the brunette at the end of the bar, on impulse he goes over and drops the disk on the counter next to her elbow.

"Brought you something," he says.

She glances at it, pokes it with a forefinger and sets it wobbling. "What is it?"

He shrugs. "Just something I found."

"At Ground Zero?"

"Uh-huh."

She pushes the disk away. "Didn't I make myself plain last night?"

Bobby says, "Yeah...sure," but isn't sure he grasps her meaning.

"I want to understand what happened...what's happening now," she says. "I want what's mine, you know. I want to understand exactly what it's done to me. I *need* to understand it. I'm not into souvenirs."

"Okay," Bobby says.

"'Okay.'" She says this mockingly. "God, what's wrong with you? It's like you're on medication!"

A Sinatra song, "All Or Nothing At All," flows from the jukebox—a soothing musical syrup that overwhelms the chatter of hookers and drunks and commentary from the TV mounted behind the bar, which is showing chunks of Afghanistan blowing up into clouds of brown smoke. The crawl running at the bottom of the screen testifies that the estimate of the death toll at Ground Zero has been reduced to just below five thousand; the amount of debris removed from the pit now exceeds one million tons. The numbers seem meaningless, interchangeable. A million lives, five thousand tons. A ludicrous score that measures no real result.

"I'm sorry," the brunette says. "I know it must take a toll, doing what you do. I'm impatient with everyone these days."

She stirs her drink with a plastic stick whose handle duplicates the image of the neon dancer. In all her artfully composed face, a mask of foundation and blush and liner, her eyes are the only sign of vitality, of feminine potential.

"What's your name?" he asks.

She glances up sharply. "I'm too old for you."

"How old are you? I'm twenty-three."

"It doesn't matter how old you are…how old I am. I'm much older than you in my head. Can't you tell? Can't you feel the difference? If I was twenty-three, I'd still be too old for you."

"I just want to know your name."

"Alicia." She enunciates the name with a cool overstated precision that makes him think of a saleswoman revealing a price she knows her customer cannot afford.

"Bobby," he says. "I'm in grad school at Colombia. But I'm taking a year off."

"This is ridiculous!" she says angrily. "Unbelievably ridiculous…totally ridiculous! Why are you doing this?"

"I want to understand what's going on with you."

"Why?"

I don't know, I just do. Whatever it is you come to understand, I want to understand it, too. Who knows. Maybe us talking is part of what you need to understand."

"Good Lord!" She cast her eyes to the ceiling. "You're a romantic!"

"You still think I'm trying to hustle you?"

"If it was anyone else, I'd say yes. But you…I don't believe you have a clue."

"And you do? Sitting here every night. Telling guys you just got back from a funeral. Grieving about something you can't even say what it is."

She twitches her head away, a gesture he interprets as the avoidance of impulse, a sudden clamping-down, and he also relates it to how he sometimes reacts on the subway when a girl he's been looking at catches his eye and he pretends to be looking at something else. After a long silence she says, "We're not going to be having sex. I want you to be clear on that."

"Okay."

"That's your fall-back position, is it? 'Okay'?"

"Whatever."

"'Whatever.'" She curls her fingers around her glass, but does not drink. "Well, we've probably had enough mutual understanding for one night, don't you think?"

Bobby pockets the rubber disk, preparing to leave. "What do you do for a living?"

An exasperated sigh. "I work in a brokerage. Now can we take a break? Please?"

"I gotta go home anyway," Bobby says.

The rubber disk takes its place in Bobby's top dresser drawer, resting between the blue half-shoe and a melted glob of metal that may have done duty as a cuff-link, joining a larger company of remnants—scraps of silk and worsted and striped cotton; a flattened fountain pen; a few inches of brown leather hanging from a misshapen buckle; a hinged pin once attached to a brooch. Looking at them breeds a queer vacancy in his chest, as if their few ounces of reality cancel out some equivalent portion of his own. It's the shoe, mostly, that wounds him. An object so powerful in its interrupted grace, sometimes he's afraid to touch it.

After his shower he lies down in the dark of his bedroom and thinks of Alicia. Pictures her handling packets of bills bound with paper wrappers. Even her name sounds like currency, a riffling of crisp new banknotes. He wonders what he's doing with her. She's not his type at all, but maybe she was right, maybe he's deceiving himself about his motives. He conjures up the images of the girls he's been with. Soft and sweet and ultra-feminine. Yet he finds Alicia's sharp edges and severity attractive. Could be he's looking for a little variety. Or maybe like so many people in the city, like lab rats stoned on coke and electricity, his circuits are scrambled and his brain is sending out irrational messages. He wants to talk to her, though. That much he's certain of—he wants to unburden himself. Tales of the pit. His drawer full of relics. He wants to explain that they're not souvenirs. They are the pins upon which he hangs whatever it is he has to leave behind each morning when he goes to work. They are proof of something he once thought a profound abstraction, something too elusive to frame in words, but has come to realize is no more than the fact of his survival. This fact, he tells himself, might be all that Alicia needs to understand.

Despite having urged Bobby on, Pineo taunts him about Alicia the next afternoon. His manic edginess has acquired an angry tonality. He takes to calling Alicia "Calculator Bitch." Bobby expects Mazurek to join in, but it seems he is withdrawing from their loose union, retreating into some private pit. He goes about his work with oxlike steadiness and eats in silence. When Bobby suggests that he might want to seek counseling, a comment designed to inflame, to reawaken the man's innate ferocity, Mazurek mutters something about maybe having a talk with one of the chaplains. Though they have only a few basic geographical concerns in common, the three men have sustained one another against the stresses of the job, and that afternoon, as Bobby scratches at the dirt, now turning to mud under a cold drenching rain, he feels abandoned, imperiled by the pit. It all looks unfamiliar and inimical. The silvery lattice of the framework appears to be trembling, as if receiving a transmission from beyond, and the nest of massive girders might be awaiting the return of a fabulous winged monster. Bobby tries to distract himself, but nothing he can come up with serves to brighten his sense of oppression. Toward the end of the shift, he begins to worry that they are laboring under an illusion, that the towers will suddenly snap back in from the dimension into which they have been nudged and everyone will be crushed.

The Blue Lady is nearly empty that night when they arrive. Hookers in the back, Alicia in her customary place. The juke box is off, the TV muttering—a blond woman is interviewing a balding man with a graphic beneath his image that identifies him as an anthrax expert. They sit at the bar and stare at the TV, tossing back drinks with dutiful regularity, speaking only when it's necessary. The anthrax expert is soon replaced by a terrorism expert who holds forth on the disruptive potentials of Al Qaeda. Bobby can't relate to the discussion. The political sky with its wheeling black shapes and noble music and secret masteries is not the sky he lives and works beneath, gray and changeless, simple as a coffin lid.

"Al Qaeda," Roman says. "Didn't he useta play second base for the Mets? Puerto Rican guy?"

The joke falls flat, but Roman's in stand-up mode.

"How many Al Qaedas does it take to screw in a light bulb?" he asks. Nobody has an answer.

"Two million," says Roman. "One to hold the camel steady, one to do the work, and the rest to carry their picture through the streets in protest when they get trampled by the camel."

"You made that shit up," Pineo says. "'I know it. Cause it ain't that funny."

"Fuck you guys!" Roman glares at Pineo, then takes himself off along the counter and goes to reading a newspaper, turning the pages with an angry flourish.

Four young couples enter the bar, annoying with their laughter and bright, flushed faces and prosperous good looks. As they mill about, some wrangling two tables together, others embracing, one woman earnestly asking Roman if he has Lillet, Bobby slides away from the suddenly energized center of the place and takes a seat beside Alicia. She cuts her eyes toward him briefly, but says nothing, and Bobby, who has spent much of the day thinking about things he might tell her, is restrained from speaking by her glum demeanor. He adopts her attitude—head down, a hand on his glass—and they sit there like two people weighted down by a shared problem. She crosses her legs, and he sees that she has kicked off a shoe. The sight of her slender ankle and stockinged foot rouses in him a sly Victorian delight.

"This is so very stimulating," she says. "We'll have to do it more often."

"I didn't think you wanted to talk."

"If you're going to sit here, it feels stupid not to."

The things he considered telling her have gone out of his head. "Well, how was your day?" she asks, modulating her voice like a mom inquiring of a sweet child, and when he mumbles that it was about the same as always, she says, "It's like we're married. Like we've passed beyond the need for verbal communion. All we have to do is sit here and vibe at each other."

"It sucked, okay?" he says, angered by her mockery. "It always sucks, but today it was worse than usual."

He begins, then, to unburden himself. He tells her about him and Pineo and Mazurek. How they're like a patrol joined in a purely unofficial unity by means of which they somehow manage to shield one another from forces they either do not understand or are afraid to acknowledge. And now that unity is dissolving. The gravity of the pit is too strong. The death smell, the horrible litter of souls, the hidden terrors. The underground garage with its smashed, unhaunted cars white with concrete dust. Fires smouldering under the earth. It's like going to work in Mordor, the shadow everywhere. Ashes and sorrow. After a while you begin to feel as if the place is turning you into a ghost. You're not real anymore, you're a relic, a fragment of life. When you say this shit to yourself, you laugh at it. It seems like bullshit. But then you stop laughing and you know it's true. Ground Zero's a killing field. Like Cambodia. Hiroshima. They're already talking about what to build there, but they're crazy. It'd make as much sense to put up a Dairy Queen at Dachau. Who'd want to eat there? People talk about doing it quickly so the terrorists will see it didn't fuck us up. But pretending it didn't fuck us up…what's that about? Hey, it fucked us up! They should wait to build. They should wait until you can walk around in it and not feel like it's hurting you to live. Because if they don't, whatever they put there is going to be filled with that feeling. That sounds absurd, maybe. To believe the ground's cursed. That there's some terrible immateriality trapped in it, something that'll seep up into the new halls and offices and cause spiritual affliction, bad karma…whatever. But when you're in the middle of that mess, it's impossible not to believe it.

Bobby doesn't look at Alicia as he tells her all this, speaking in a rushed, anxious delivery. When he's done he knocks back his drink, darts a glance at her to gauge her reaction, and says, "I had this friend in high school got into crystal meth. It fried his brain. He started having delusions. The government was fucking with his mind. They knew he was in contact with beings from a higher plane. Shit like that. He had this whole complex view of reality as conspiracy, and when he told me about it, it was like he was apologizing for telling me. He could sense his own damage, but he had to get it out because he couldn't quite believe he was crazy. That's how I feel. Like I'm missing some piece of myself."

"I know," Alicia says. "I feel that way, too. That's why I come here. To try and figure out what's missing...where I am with all this."

She looks at him inquiringly, and Bobby, unburdened now, finds he has nothing worth saying. But he wants to say something, because he wants her to talk to him, and though he's not sure why he wants this or what more he might want, he's so confused by the things he's confessed and also by the ordinary confusions that attend every consequential exchange between men and women.... Though he's not sure of anything, he wants whatever is happening to move forward.

"Are you all right?" she asks.

"Oh, yeah. Sure. This isn't terminal fucked-uppedness. 'Least I don't think it is."

She appears to be reassessing him. "Why do you put yourself through it?"

"The job? Because I'm qualified. I worked for FEMA the last coupla summers."

Two of the yuppie couples have huddled around the jukebox, and their first selection, "Smells Like Teen Spirit," begins its tense, grinding push. Pineo dances on his barstool, his torso twisting back and forth, fists tight against his chest, a parody—Bobby knows—that's aimed at the couples, meant as an insult. Brooding over his bourbon, Mazurek is a graying, thick-bodied troll turned to stone.

"I'm taking my masters in philosophy," Bobby says. "It's finally beginning to seem relevant."

He intends this as humor, but Alicia doesn't react to it as such. Her eyes are brimming. She swivels on her stool, knee pressing against his hip, and puts a hand on his wrist.

"I'm afraid," she says. "You think that's all this is? Just fear. Just an inability to cope."

He's not certain he understands her, but he says, "Maybe that's all."

It feels so natural when she loops her arms about him and buries her face in the crook of his neck, he doesn't think anything of it. His hand goes to her waist. He wants to turn toward her, to deepen the embrace, but is afraid that will alarm her, and as they cling together, he become insecure with the contact, unclear as to what he should do with it. Her pulse hits against his palm, her breath warms his skin. The articulation of her ribs, the soft swell of a hip, the presence of a breast an inch above the tip of his thumb, all her heated specificity both daunts and tempts him. Doubt concerning their mental well-being creeps in. Is this an instance of healing or a freak scene? Are they two very different people who have connected on a level new to both of them, or are they emotional burn-outs who aren't even talking about the same subject and have misapprehended mild sexual attraction for a moment of truth? Just how much difference is there between those conditions? She pulls him closer. Her legs are still crossed, and her right knee slides into his lap, her shoeless foot pushing against his waist. She whispers something, words he can't make out. An assurance, maybe. Her lips brush his cheek, then she pulls back and offers a smile he takes for an expression of regret.

"I don't get it," she says. "I have this feeling…" She shakes her head as if rejecting an errant notion.

"What?"

She holds a hand up beside her face as she speaks and waggles it, a blitheness of gesture that her expression does not reflect. "I shouldn't be saying this to someone I met in a bar, and I don't mean it the way you might think. But it's…I have a feeling you can help me. Do something for me."

"Talking helps."

"Maybe. I don't know. That doesn't seem right." Thoughtful, she stirs her drink; then a sidelong glance. "There must be something some philosopher said that's pertinent to the moment."

"Predisposition fathers all logics, even those disposed to deny it."

"Who said that?"

"I did...in a paper I wrote on Gorgias. The father of sophistry. He claimed that nothing can be known, and if anything could be known, it wasn't worth knowing."

"Well," says Alicia, "I guess that explains everything."

"I don't know about that. I only got a B on the paper."

One of the couples begins to dance, the man, who is still wearing his overcoat, flapping his elbows, making slow-motion swoops, while the woman stands rooted, her hips undulating in a fishlike rhythm. Pineo's parody was more graceful. Watching them, Bobby imagines the bar a cave, the other patrons with matted hair, dressed in skins. Headlights slice across the window with the suddenness of a meteor flashing past in the primitive night. The song ends, the couple's friends applaud them as they head for the group table. But when the opening riff of the Hendrix version of "All Along The Watchtower" blasts from the speakers, they start dancing again and the other couples join them, drinks in hand. The women toss their hair and shake their breasts; the men hump the air. A clumsy tribe on drugs.

The bar environment no longer works for Bobby. Too much unrelieved confusion. He hunches his shoulders against the noise, the happy jabber, and has a momentary conviction that this is not his true reaction, that a little scrap of black negativity perched between his shoulderblades, its claws buried in his spine, has folded its gargoyle wings, and he has reacted to the movement like a puppet. As he stands Alicia reaches out and squeezes his hand. "See you tomorrow?"

"No doubt," he says, wondering if he will—he believes she'll go home and chastise herself for permitting this partial intimacy, this unprophylactic intrusion into her stainless career-driven life. She'll stop coming to the bar and seek redemption in a night school business course designed to flesh out her resume. One lonely Sunday afternoon a few weeks hence, he'll provide the animating fantasy for a battery-powered orgasm.

He digs in his wallet for a five, a tip for Roman, and catches Pineo looking at him with unalloyed hostility. The kind of look your great enemy might send your way right before pumping a couple of shells into his shotgun. Pineo lets his double-barreled stare linger a few beats, then turns away to a deep consideration of his beer glass, his neck turtled, his head down. It appears that he and Mazurek have been overwhelmed by identical enchantments.

Bobby wakes up a few minutes before he's due at work. He calls the job, warns them he'll be late, then lies back and contemplates the large orange-and-brown water stain that has transformed the ceiling into a terrain map. This thing with Alicia...it's sick, he thinks. They're not going to fuck—that much is clear. And not just because she said so. He can't see himself going to her place, furnishings courtesy of The Sharper Image and Pottery Barn, nor can he picture her in this dump, and neither of them has displayed the urge for immediacy that would send them to a hotel. It's ridiculous, unwieldy. They're screwing around is all. Mind-fucking on some perverted soul level. She's sad because she's drinking to be sad because she's afraid that what she does not feel is actually a feeling. Typical post-modern Manhattan bullshit. Grief as a form of self-involvement. And now he's part of that. What he's doing with her may be even more perverse, but he has no desire to scrutinize his motives—that would only amplify the perversity. Better simply to let it play out and be done. These are strange days in the city. Men and women seeking intricate solace for intricate guilt. Guilt over the fact that they do not embody the magnificent sadness of politicians and the brooding sympathy of anchorpersons, that their grief is a flawed posture, streaked with the banal, with thoughts of sex and football, cable bills and job security. He still has things he needs, for whatever reason, to tell her. Tonight he'll confide in her, and she will do what she must. Their mutual despondency, a wrap in four acts.

He stays forever in the shower; he's in no hurry to get to the pit, and he considers not going in at all. But duty, habit, and doggedness exert a stronger pull than his hatred and fear of the place—though it's not truly hatred and fear he feels, but a syncretic fusion of the two, an alchemical product for which a good brand name has not been coined. Before leaving, he inspects the contents of the top drawer in his dresser. The relics are the thing he most needs to explain to her. Whatever else he has determined them to be, he supposes that they are, to a degree, souvenirs, and thus a cause for shame, a morbid symptom. But when he looks at them he thinks there must be a purpose to the collection he has not yet divined, one that explaining it all to Alicia may illuminate. He selects the half-shoe. It's the only choice, really. The only object potent enough to convey the feelings he has about it.

He stuffs it into his jacket pocket and goes out into the living room where his roommate is watching The Cartoon Network, his head visible above the back of the couch.

"Slept late, huh?" says the roommate.

"Little bit," Bobby says, riveted by the bright colors and goofy voices, wishing he could stay and discover how Scooby Doo and Jackie manage to outwit the swamp beast. "See ya later."

Shortly before his shift ends, he experiences a bout of paranoia during which he believes that if he glances up he'll find the pit walls risen to skyscraper height and all he'll be able to see of the sky is a tiny circle of glowing clouds. Even afterward, walking with Mazurek and Pineo through the chilly, smoking streets, distant car horns sounding in rhythm like an avant garde brass section, he half-persuades himself that it could have happened. The pit might have grown deeper, he might have dwindled. Earlier that evening they began to dig beneath a freshly excavated layer of cement rubble, and he knows his paranoia and the subsequent desire to retreat into irrationality are informed by what they unearthed. But while there is a comprehensible reason for his fear, this does not rule out other possibilities. Unbelievable things can happen of an instant. They all recognize that now.

The three men are silent as they head toward the Blue Lady. It's as if their nightly ventures to the bar no longer serve as a release and have become an extension of the job, prone to its stresses. Pineo goes with hands thrust into his pockets, eyes angled away from the others, and Mazurek looks straight ahead, swinging his thermos, resembling a Trotskyite hero, a noble worker of Factory 39. Bobby walks between them. Their solidity makes him feel unstable, as if pulled at by large opposing magnets—he wants to dart ahead or drop back, but is dragged along by their attraction. He ditches them just inside the entrance and joins Alicia at the end of the bar. Her twenty-five watt smile switches on, and he thinks that though she must wear brighter, toothier smiles for co-workers and relatives, this particular smile measures the true fraction of her joy, all that is left after years of career management and bad love.

To test this theory he asks if she's got a boyfriend, and she says, "Jesus! A boyfriend. That's so quaint. You might as well ask if I have a beau."

"You got a beau?"

"I have a history of beaus," she says. "But no current need for one, thank you."

"Your eye's on the prize, huh?"

"It's not just that. Though right now, it is that. I'm"—a sardonic laugh—"I'm ascending the corporate ladder. Trying to, anyway."

She fades on him, gone to a gloomy distance beyond the bar, where the TV chatters ceaselessly of plague and misery and enduring freedom. "I wanted to have children," she says at last. "I can't stop thinking about it these days. Maybe all this sadness has a biological effect. You know. Repopulate the species."

"You've got time to have children," he says. "The career stuff may lighten up."

"Not with the men I get involved with…not a chance! I wouldn't let any of them take care of my plants."

"So you got a few war stories, do you?"

She puts up a hand, palm outward, as to if to hold a door closed. "You can't imagine!"

"I've got a few myself."

"You're a guy," she says. "What would you know?"

Telling him her stories, she's sarcastic, self-effacing, almost vivacious, as if by sharing these incidents of

421

male duplicity, laughing at her own naivete, she is proving an unassailable store of good cheer and resilience. But when she tells of a man who pursued her for an entire year, sending candy and flowers, cards, until finally she decided that he must really love her and spent the night with him, a good night after which he chose to ignore her completely…when she tells him this, Bobby sees past her blithe veneer into a place of abject bewilderment. He wonders how she'd look without the make-up. Softer, probably. The make-up is a painting of attitude that she daily recreates. A mask of prettified defeat and coldness to hide her fundamental confusion. Nothing has ever been as she hoped it would be—yet while she has forsworn hope, she has not banished it, and thus she is confused. He's simplifying her, he realizes. Desultory upbringing in some midwestern oasis—he hears a flattened A redolent of Detroit or Chicago. Second-rate education leading to a second-rate career. The wreckage of morning afters. This much is plain. But the truth underlying her stories, the light she bore into the world, how it has transmuted her experience…that remains hidden. There's no point in going deeper, though, and probably no time.

The Blue Lady fills with the late crowd. Among them a couple of older middle-age who hold hands and kiss across their table; three young guys in Knicks gear; two black men attired gangsta-style accompanying an overweight blonde in a dyed fur wrap and a sequined cocktail dress (Roman damns them with a glare and makes them wait for service.) Pineo and Mazurek are silently, soddenly drunk, isolated from their surround, but the life of the bar seems to glide around Bobby and Alicia, the juke box rocks with old Santana, Kinks, and Springsteen. Alicia's more relaxed than Bobby's ever seen her. She's kicked off her right shoe again, shed her jacket, and though she nurses her drink, she seems to become increasingly intoxicated, as if disclosing her past were having the effect of a three-martini buzz.

"I don't think all men are assholes," she says. "But New York men…maybe."

"You've dated them all, huh?" he asks.

"Most of the acceptable ones, I have."

"What qualifies as acceptable in your eyes?"

Perhaps he stresses "in your eyes" a bit much, makes the question too personal, because her smile fades and she gives him a startled look. After the last strains of "Glory Days" fade, during the comparative quiet between songs, she lays a hand on his cheek, studies him, and says, less a question than a self-assurance, "You wouldn't treat me like that, would you?" And then, before Bobby can think how he should respond, taken aback by what appears an invitation to step things up, she adds, "It's too bad," and withdraws her hand.

"Why?" he asks. "I mean I kinda figured we weren't going to hook up, and I'm not arguing. I'm just curious why you felt that way."

"I don't know. Last night I wanted to. I guess I didn't want to enough."

"It's pretty unrealistic." He grins. "Given the difference in our ages."

"Bastard!" She throws a mock punch. "Actually, I found the idea of a younger man intriguing."

"Yeah, well. I'm not all that."

"Nobody's 'all that,' not until they're with somebody who thinks they are." She pretends to check him out. "You might clean up pretty nice."

"Excuse me," says a voice behind them. "Can I solicit an opinion?"

A good-looking guy in his thirties wearing a suit

and a loosened tie, his face an exotic sharp-cheekboned mixture of African and Asian heritage. He's very drunk, weaving a little.

"My girlfriend…okay?" He glances back and forth between them. "I was supposed to meet her down…"

"No offense, but we're having a conversation here," Bobby says.

The guy holds his hands up as if to show he means no harm and offers apology, but then launches into a convoluted story about how he and his girlfriend missed connections and then had an argument over the phone and he started drinking and now he's broke, fucked up, puzzled by everything. It sounds like the prelude to a hustle, especially when the guy asks for a cigarette, but when they tell him they don't smoke, he does not—as might be expected—ask for money, but looks at Bobby and says, "The way they treat us, man! What are we? Chopped liver?"

"Maybe so," says Bobby.

At this the guy takes a step back and bugs his eyes. "You got any rye?" he says. "I could use some rye."

"Seriously," Bobby says to him, gesturing at Alicia. "We need to finish our talk."

"Hey," the guy says. "Thanks for listening."

Alone again, the thread of the conversation broken, they sit for a long moment without saying anything, then start to speak at the same time.

"You first," says Bobby.

"I was just thinking…." She trails off. "Never mind. It's not that important."

He knows she was on the verge of suggesting that they should get together, but that once again the urge did not rise to the level of immediacy. Or maybe there's something else, an indefinable barrier separating them, something neither one of them have tumbled to. He thinks this must be the case, because given her history, and his own, it's apparent neither of them have been discriminating in the past. But she's right, he decides—whatever's happening between them is simply not that important, and thus it's not that important to understand.

She smiles, an emblem of apology, and stares down into her drink. "Free Falling" by Tom Petty is playing on the box, and some people behind them begin wailing along with it, nearly drowning out the vocal.

"I brought something for you," Bobby says.

An uneasy look. "From your work?"

"Yeah, but this isn't the same...."

"I told you I didn't want to see that kind of thing."

"They're not just souvenirs," he says. "If I seem messed up to you...and I'm sure I do. I *feel* messed up, anyway. But if I seem messed up, the things I take from the pit, they're kind of an explanation for..." He runs a hand through his hair, frustrated by his inability to speak what's on his mind. "I don't know why I want you to see this. I guess I'm hoping it'll help you understand something."

"About what?" she says, leery.

"About me...or where I work. Or something. I haven't been able to nail that down, y'know. But I do want you to see it."

Alicia's eyes slide away from him; she fits her gaze to the mirror behind the bar, its too perfect reflection of romance, sorrow, and drunken fun. "If that's what you want."

Bobby touches the half-shoe in his jacket pocket. The silk is cool to his fingers. He imagines that he can feel its blueness. "It's not a great thing to look at. I'm not trying to freak you out, though. I think..."

She snaps at him. "Just show it to me!"

He sets the shoe beside her glass and for a second or two it's like she doesn't notice it. Then she makes a sound in her throat. A single note, the human equivalent of an ice cube *plinking* in a glass, bright and clear, and puts a hand out as if to touch it. But she doesn't touch it, not at first, just leaves her hand hovering above the shoe. He can't read her face, except for the fact that she's fixated on the thing. Her fingers trail along the scorched margin of the silk, tracing the ragged line. "Oh, my god!" she says, all but the glottal sound buried beneath a sudden surge in the music. Her hand closes around the shoe, her head droops. It looks as if she's in a trance, channeling a feeling or some trace of memory. Her eyes glisten, and she's so still, Bobby wonders if what he's done has injured her, if she was unstable and now he's pushed her over the edge. A minute passes, and she hasn't moved. The juke box falls silent, the chatter and laughter of the other patrons rise around them.

"Alicia?"

She shakes her head, signaling either that she's been robbed of the power to speak, or is not interested in communicating.

"Are you okay?" he asks.

She says something he can't hear, but he's able to read her lips and knows the word "god" was again involved. A tear escapes the corner of her eye, runs down her cheek, and clings to her upper lip. It may be that the half-shoe impressed her, as it has him, as being the perfect symbol, the absolute explanation of what they have lost and what has survived, and this, its graphic potency, is what has distressed her.

The jukebox kicks in again, an old Stan Getz tune, and Bobby hears Pineo's voice bleating in argument, cursing bitterly; but he doesn't look to see what's wrong. He's captivated by Alicia's face. Whatever pain or loss she's feeling, it has concentrated her meager portion of beauty and suffering, she's shining, the female hound of Wall Street thing she does with her cosmetics radiated out of existence by a porcelain *Song of Bernadette* saintliness, the clean lines of her neck and jaw suddenly pure and Periclean. It's such a startling transformation, he's not sure it's really happening. Drink's to blame, or there's some other problem with his eyes. Life, according to his experience, doesn't provide this type of quintessential change. Thin, half-grown cats do not of an instant gleam and grow sleek in their exotic simplicity like tiny gray tigers. Small, tidy Cape Cod cottages do not because of any shift in weather, no matter how glorious the light, glow resplendent and ornate like minor Asiatic temples. Yet Alicia's golden change is manifest. She's beautiful. Even the red membranous corners of her eyes, irritated by tears and city grit, seem decorative, part of a subtle design, and when she turns to him, the entire new delicacy of her features flowing toward him with the uncanny force of a visage materializing from a beam of light, he feels imperiled by her nearness, uncertain of her purpose. What can she now want of him? As she pulls his face close to hers, lips parting, eyelids half-lowering, he is afraid a kiss may kill him, either overpower him, a wave washing away a tiny scuttler on the sand, or that the taste of her, a fraction of warm saliva resembling a speck of crystal with a flavor of sweet acid, will react with his own common spittle to synthesize a compound microweight of poison, a perfect solution to the predicament of his mortality. But then another transformation, one almost as drastic, and as her mouth finds his, he sees the young woman, vulnerable and soft, giving and wanting, the childlike need and openness of her.

The kiss lasts not long, but long enough to have a history, a progression from contact to immersion, exploration to a mingling of tongues and gushing breath, yet once their intimacy is completely achieved, the temperature dialed high, she breaks from it and puts her mouth to his ear and whispers fiercely, tremulously, "Thank you.... Thank you so much!" Then she's standing, gathering her purse, her briefcase, a regretful smile, and says, "I have to go."

"Wait!' He catches at her, but she fends him off.

"I'm sorry," she says. "But I have to...right now. I'm sorry."

And she goes, walking smartly toward the door, leaving him with no certainty of conclusion, with his half-grown erection and his instantly catalogued memory of the kiss surfacing to be examined and weighed, its tenderness and fragility to be considered, its sexual intensity to be marked upon a scale, its meaning surmised, and by the time he's made these judgments, waking to the truth that she has truly, unequivocally gone and deciding to run after her, she's out the door. By the time he reaches the door, shouldering it open, she's twenty-five, thirty feet down the sidewalk, stepping quickly between the parked cars and the storefronts, passing a shadowed doorway, and he's about to call out her name when she moves into the light spilling from a coffee shop window and he notices that her shoes are blue. Pale blue with a silky sheen, and of a shape that appears identical to that of the half-shoe left on the bar. If, indeed, it was left there. He can't remember now. Did she take it? The question has a strange, frightful value, born of a frightful suspicion that he cannot quite reject, and for a moment he's torn between the impulse to go after her and a desire to turn back into the bar and look for the shoe. That, in the end, is what's important. To discover if she took the shoe, and if she did, then to fathom the act, to decipher it. Was it done because she thought it a gift, or because she wanted it so badly, maybe to satisfy some freaky neurotic demand, that she felt she had to more-or-less steal it, get him confused with a kiss and bolt before he realized it was missing? Or—and this is the notion that's threatening to possess him—was the shoe hers to begin with? Feeling foolish, yet not persuaded he's a fool, he watches her step off the curb at the next corner and cross the street, dwindling and dwindling, becoming indistinct from other pedestrians. A stream of traffic blocks off his view. Still toying with the idea of chasing after her, he stands there for half a minute or so, wondering if he has misinterpreted everything about her. A cold wind coils like a scarf about his neck, and the wet pavement begins soaking into his sock through the hole in his right boot. He squints at the poorly defined distance beyond the cross-street, denies a last twinge of impulse, then yanks open the door of the Blue Lady. A gust of talk and music seems to whirl past him from within, like the ghost of a party leaving the scene, and he goes on inside, even though he knows in his heart that the shoe is gone.

Bobby's immunity to the pit has worn off. In the morning he's sick as last week's salmon plate. A fever that turns his bones to glass and rots his sinuses, a cough that sinks deep into his chest and hollows him with chills. His sweat smells sour and yellow, his spit is thick as curds. For the next forty-eight hours he can think of only two things. Medicine and Alicia. She's threaded through his fever, braided around every thought like a strand of RNA, but he can't even begin to make sense of what he thinks and feels. A couple of nights later the fever breaks. He brings blankets, a pillow, and orange juice into the living room and takes up residence on the sofa. "Feeling better, huh?" say the roommate, and Bobby says, "Yeah, little bit." After a pause the roommate hands him the remote and seeks refuge in his room, where he spends the day playing video games. Quake, mostly. The roars of demons and chattering chain guns issue from behind his closed door.

Bobby channel surfs, settles on CNN, which is alternating between an overhead view of Ground Zero and a studio shot of an attractive brunette sitting at an anchor desk, talking to various men and women about 9/11, the war, the recovery. After listening for almost half an hour, he concludes that if this is all people hear, this gossipy, maudlin chitchat about life and death and healing, they must know nothing. The pit looks like a dingy hole with some yellow machines moving debris—there's no sense transmitted of its profundity, of how—when you're down in it—it seems deep and everlasting, like an ancient broken well. He goes surfing again, finds an old Jack the Ripper movie starring Michael Caine, and turns the sound low, watches detectives in long dark coats hurrying through the dimly lit streets, paperboys shouting news of the latest atrocity. He begins to put together the things Alicia told him. All of them. From "I've just been to a funeral," to "Everybody's ready to go on with their lives, but I'm not ready," to "That's why I come here…to figure out what's missing," to "I have to go." Her transformation…did he really see it? The memory is so unreal, but then all memories are unreal, and at the moment it happened, he knew to his bones who and what she was, and that when she took the shoe, the object that let her understand what had been done to her, she was only reclaiming her property. Of course everything can be explained in other ways, and it's tempting to accept those other explanations, to believe she was just an uptight careerwoman taking a break from corporate sanity, and once she recognized where she was, what she was doing, who she was doing it with, she grabbed a souvenir and beat it back to the email-messaging, network-building, clickety-click world of spread sheets and wheat futures and martinis with some cute guy from advertising who would eventually fuck her brains out and afterward tell the-bitch-was-begging-for-it stories about her at his gym. That's who she was, after all, whatever her condition. An unhappy woman committed to her unhappy path, wanting more yet unable to perceive how she had boxed herself in. But the things that came out of her on their last night at the Blue Lady, the self-revelatory character of her transformation…the temptation of the ordinary is incapable of denying those memories.

It's a full week before Bobby returns to work. He comes in late, after darkness has fallen and the lights have been switched on, halfway inclined to tell his supervisor that he's quitting. He shows his ID and goes down into the pit, looking for Pineo and Mazurek. The great yellow earth movers are still, men are standing around in groups, and from this Bobby recognizes that a body has been recently found, a ceremony just concluded, and they're having a break before getting on with the job. He's hesitant to join the others and pauses next to a wall made of huge concrete slabs, shattered and resting at angles atop one another, holding pockets of shadow and worse in their depths. He's been standing there about a minute when he feels her behind him. It's not like in a horror story. No terrible cold or prickling hairs or windy voices. It's like being with her in the bar. Her warmth, her perfumey scent, her nervous poise. But frailer, weaker, a delicate presence barely in the world. He's afraid if he turns to look at her, it will break their tenuous connection. She's probably not visible, anyway. No Stephen King commercial, no sight of her hovering a few inches off the ground, bearing the horrid wounds that killed her. She's a willed fraction of herself, less tangible than a wisp of smoke, less certain than a whisper. "Alicia," he says, and her effect intensifies. Her scent grows stronger, her warmth more insistent, and he knows why she's here. "I realize you had to go," he says, and then it's like when she embraced him, all her warmth employed to draw him close. He can almost touch her firm waist, the tiered ribs, the softness of a breast, and he wishes they could go out. Just once. Not so they could sweat and make sleepy promises and lose control and then regain control and bitterly go off in opposite directions, but because at most times people were only partly there for one another—which was how he and Alicia were in the Blue Lady, knowing only the superficial about each other, a few basic lines and a hint of detail, like two sketches in the midst of an oil painting, their minds directed elsewhere, not caring enough to know all there was to know—and the way it is between them at this moment, they would try to know everything. They would try to find the things that did not exist like smoke behind their eyes. The ancient grammars of the spirit, the truths behind their old yet newly demolished truths. In the disembodiment of desire, an absolute focus born. They would call to one another, they would forget the cities and the wars…. Then it's not her mouth he feels, but the feeling he had when they were kissing, a curious mixture of bewilderment and carnality, accented this time by a quieter emotion. Satisfaction, he thinks. At having helped her understand. At himself understanding his collection of relics and why he approached her. Fate or coincidence, it's all the same, all clear to him now.

"Yo, Bobby!"

It's Pineo. Smirking, walking toward him with a springy step and not a trace of the hostility he displayed the last time they were together. "Man, you look like shit, y'know."

"I wondered if I did," Bobby says. "I figured you'd tell me."

"It's what I'm here for." Pineo fakes throwing a left hook under Bobby's ribs.

"Where's Carl?"

"Taking a dump. He's worried about your ass."

"Yeah, I bet."

"C'mon! You know he's got that dad thing going with you." Pineo affects an Eastern European accent, makes a fist, scowls Mazurek-style. "'Bobby is like son to me.'"

"I don't think so. All he does is tell me what an asshole I am."

"That's Polish for 'son,' man. That's how those old bruisers treat their kids."

As they begin walking across the pit, Pineo says, "I don't know what you did to Calculator Bitch, man, but she never did come back to the bar. You musta messed with her mind."

Bobby wonders if his hanging out with Alicia was the cause of Pineo's hostility, if Pineo perceived him to be at fault, the one who was screwing up their threefold unity, their trinity of luck and spiritual maintenance. Things could be that simple.

"What'd you say to her?" Pineo asks.

"Nothing. I just told her about the job."

Pineo cocks his head and squints at him. "You're not being straight with me. I got the eye for bullshit, just like my mama. Something going on with you two?"

"Uh-huh. We're gonna get married."

"Don't tell me you're fucking her."

433

"I'm not fucking her!"

Pineo points at him. "There it is! Bullshit!"

"Sicilian ESP.... Wow. How come you people don't rule the world?"

"I can't *believe* you're fucking the Calculator Bitch!" Pineo looks up to heaven and laughs. "Man, were you even sick at all? I bet you spent the whole goddamn week sleep-testing her Certa."

Bobby just shakes his head ruefully.

"So what's it like...yuppie pussy?"

Irritated now, Bobby says, "Fuck off!"

"Seriously. I grew up in Queens, I been deprived. What's she like? She wear thigh boots and a colonel's hat? She carry a riding crop? No, that's too much like her day job. She..."

One of the earth movers starts up, rumbling like T-Rex, vibrating the ground, and Pineo has to raise his voice to be heard.

"She was too sweet, wasn't she? All teach me tonight and sugar, sugar. Like some little girl read all the books but didn't know what she read till you come along and pulled her trigger. Yeah...and once the little girl thing gets over, she goes wild on your ass. She loses control, she be fucking liberated."

Bobby recalls the transformation, not the-glory-that-was-Alicia part, the shining forth of soul rays, but the instant before she kissed him, the dazed wonderment in her face, and realizes that Pineo—unwittingly, of course—has put his grimy, cynical, ignorant, wise-ass finger on something he, Bobby, has heretofore not fully grasped. That she did awaken, and not merely to her posthumous condition, but to him. That at the end she remembered who she wanted to be. Not "who," maybe. But how. How she wanted to feel, how she wanted to live. The vivid, less considered road she hoped her life would travel. Understanding this, he understands what the death of thousands has not taught him. The exact measure of his loss. And ours. The death of one. All men being Christ and God in His glorious fever burning, the light toward which they aspire. Love in the whirlwind.

"Yeah, she was all that," Bobby says.